The
Machalniks

Birth of an Air Force

A NOVEL
By
DICK BERMAN

THE MACHALNIKS, by DICK BERMAN

Published by: PelhamGrp
Delray Beach, FL 33446

www. dickberman.com

© 2017 Dick Berman
First edition: September, 2017
Second edition: February, 2018

For permissions contact:
Publicity@dickberman.com

For information about special discounts available for bulk purchases, sales promotions, fundraising and educational needs for *The Machalniks*, contact: sales@dickberman.com

Cover Picture Designed: by Tauseef Ahmed
Book layout and design by: sarcopress.com

ISBN: 978-0-9987164-2-8

The Machalniks is a work of historical fiction. Apart from the well-known actual people that figure in the narrative, many actions of the fictional characters are a composite of actual events. Some characters, scenes and chronologies have been altered, consolidated or invented for dramatic purpose. Dialogues are entirely products of the author's imagination and are not intended to depict actual events or to change the fictional nature of the work. In all other respects, any resemblance to actual persons, living or dead, events, or locales is entirely coincidental or used fictitiously.

For Michelle, Jill, Eric, Danielle, Joshua, Ariel and Caleb

"Our immortality comes through our children and their children. Through our roots and branches. The family is immortality."

Amy Harmon, From Sand and Ash

Contents

Therefore say, Thus saith the Lord God; "I will even gather you from the people, and assemble you out of the countries where ye have been scattered, and I will give you the land of Israel."

Ezekiel 11:17

CHAPTER 1
December 6, 1947
New York

I F I KNEW what awaited me when I stepped on the train for my trip to New York City that chilly December morning, I probably wouldn't have boarded.

Within weeks, the direction of my life would change in ways I could never have imagined. I would find myself pitted against the F.B.I., the United States Treasury and State Department, risk fines, imprisonment, and even the loss of my citizenship. And that was the easy part. Short months later, I'd be risking my life.

My name is Michael Kaplan, Mike to my friends, and the story begins in the summer of 1946 when my wartime buddy, Harold "Skippy" Shapiro, got in touch with me. He suggested we get together to celebrate our discharge six months earlier from the U.S. Marine Corps. We served together as combat pilots, survived our tour in the Pacific, and were now settled into civilian life.

Skippy had never been to New England, so he volunteered to venture to my hometown of Boston from his apartment in Brooklyn, New York. When he arrived, he wanted to see the famous historic sites he'd read about in school. We spent the weekend visiting places like Bunker Hill, The Old North Church, Concord, Lexington Green, and Plymouth Rock.

We even caught a Boston Red Sox home game against the New York Yankees. Ted Williams, a fellow Marine Corps pilot, was back in the lineup after his discharge. Hitting two home runs and a double, he didn't disappoint the hometown fans. Red Sox 8, Yankees 2. Skippy didn't mind. He was a Brooklyn Dodgers fan. Before he boarded the train Sunday to return home, we agreed to do it again next year.

So here I was, a year later, Saturday morning, December 6, 1947, on my way to New York City. Skippy thought this would be a great time of the year for our second annual get together. "You can't beat the sights and sounds of New York City during the holiday season," he said.

I caught the 8:14 morning express out of South Station and pulled into Grand Central at 1:56 in the afternoon. The air was awash with the din of arriving and departing trains as I gripped my overnight bag and strolled up the platform to the terminal.

Entering the mammoth main hall, I spotted Skippy waving to me just outside the exit ramp. It was Saturday, the beginning of the weekend, yet the throng of people darting around like a colony of ants inside a glass ant farm was bigger than regular weekday commuter traffic back at South Station.

After giving each other a brief hug, we weaved our way through the bustling crowd to the cabstand outside on 42nd Street. We played catch up on what was new in our lives since we'd last seen each other.

Ten minutes later, we arrived at the Roosevelt Hotel at the corner of 45th Street and Madison Avenue. On the ride over, Skippy told me instead of commuting from his apartment in Brooklyn, he was staying there also. He'd already checked in and dropped off his suitcase.

"This was one of those venerable fancy old hotels until Conrad Hilton recently purchased it and modernized it," Skippy said, as we walked in the lobby. "Now, the Roosevelt is the first hotel in the country to have a television set in every guest room."

I was excited. I didn't own a television, and I'd read in the *Boston Globe* sometime last summer there were only forty-four thousand homes in the entire country that did. I remembered standing outside an appliance store with friends in September, watching the first ever broadcast of the World Series on television through the store's window.

After I checked in, and for the rest of the day, Skippy became my tour director as I experienced the wonders of Gotham. I'd fought a war half a world away but had never been to Manhattan. The Empire State Building, the Statue of Liberty, Rockefeller Center, Chinatown, Little Italy. It was a whirlwind day. That night we hit four hotspots, ending the evening at the famous Copacabana nightclub at 10 East 60th Street.

SUNDAY MORNING I awoke with a headache. What a night. We were two young, single guys, and boy had we painted the town. It ended with us trying to pick up two hot chicks at the Copa bar. Our mission was to ply them with alcohol and have them join us back at our hotel rooms. The mission, as it turned out, proved unsuccessful. The only thing I brought back to the room was the makings of the hangover that was pounding inside my skull.

We agreed last night we would sleep in and meet at ten o'clock for breakfast in the Roosevelt Grill, located in the lobby. This would give us a few hours to spend together before I had to catch the 2:00 p.m. train back to Boston.

I dragged myself out of bed and rummaged through my shaving kit for aspirin. I downed three and hobbled into the shower. After lathering and rinsing with hot water, I stayed a few minutes longer; holding my head under a cold spray, hoping it would help the vexing ache in my skull. It didn't.

I dressed, packed my overnight bag, and took the elevator downstairs to check out. As I approached the front desk, I laughed to myself. Here I was, so excited to have a room with a television set … and I never even turned it on.

"Your account has already been paid," the cashier informed me.

I said, "There must be some mistake."

"No," he politely replied, "there is no mistake, the bill is settled."

I asked by who, and he said he did not know. Of course it had to be Skippy, I thought, but why would he do that?

Well, easy to find out. I checked my bag with the bellhop and walked to the entrance of the restaurant. It was two minutes after ten. About to ask the maître d' if Skippy already arrived, I saw him wave to me from a table near the rear of the room. He wasn't alone. There were two men sitting with him who seem to follow my every step with unusual interest as I weaved my way between tables.

At first I thought they might be two of the pilots we'd served with and Skippy arranged for them to show up as a surprise. As I moved closer and got a better look, I didn't recognize either of them. I wondered who they were.

The two men rose and stood next to my friend when I reached the table.

Skippy made immediate introductions. "This is Mike Kaplan," he said, gesturing in my direction. "Mike. Let me introduce Paul Shatz and Noah Meir."

We shook hands and I settled into my seat, Shatz to my right, Skippy to my left, and Meir across from me. When Meir said hello, I picked up on an accent but couldn't place it. It would be hard to describe him other than trim, oval-shaped face, dark hair, and a straight nose. Someone who just blends into the crowd. Shatz, on the other hand, had a muscular build, long nose, square chin, with dark slicked-back hair. What made him most noticeable were his eyes. They looked onyx in color and seemed to bore into me.

The waiter arrived seconds later, followed immediately by a busboy who brought a basket of sweet rolls. I ordered a Bloody Mary. The aspirins were beginning to take effect on my headache, but I figured a little bit of the hair of the dog wouldn't hurt either. The others ordered coffee to start and asked the waiter to give us a few minutes before we ordered our breakfast.

After the waiter and busboy left, I turned to Skippy. "Why did you pay my hotel bill?"

"I didn't. Paul did."

My eyes narrowed, and I turned to Shatz. "Why would you do that?"

"Because I want your help. Call it a sign of good faith."

"My help? You want my help with what?"

"Before I get to that, I'd like to ask you something. Skippy tells me you fly for an air freight company."

"Yes, for Boston Airfreight, out of Logan Airport. What has that got to do with you paying my bill?"

"What kind of plane do you fly?"

"A surplus C-46 transport. Why?"

"But you were a fighter pilot, like Skippy. How do you know how to fly a C-46'?"

I was getting inpatient and a little pissed with this guy. He was asking me questions but wasn't answering any of my mine.

"A childhood friend was a pilot for the Air Transport Service and landed a job with Boston Airfreight after his discharge. He got me my job there. Seems I have a knack for flying and can pretty much fly anything with about an hour or so of instruction. He taught me to fly a C-46. Look, I don't want to be rude to a friend of Skippy, but enough questions. Answer mine. Why did you pay my bill?"

Shatz leaned back a little in his chair and seemed to relax a bit, like I'd just passed some sort of test.

"Please, indulge me for one more question," Shatz said, leaning forward again in his seat.

"Shoot," I said.

"What kind of a Jew are you?" he asked.

"What?" I replied, shocked by his question. I pulled the linen napkin from my lap, threw it on the table, and pushed out of my chair. "Where the hell do you come off asking me a question like that?" I turned to my friend. "Skippy, what the —"

Before I could finish the sentence, Shatz touched my arm, and I spun back to him, my hands clenched into fists.

He looked up at me, holding up his hands, palms out. "Please," he said, interrupting me in a calm voice. "I'm not looking to pick a fight. It was a serious question. Take a minute and think about it. Are you a religious Jew? Are you a secular Jew? Do you even think about yourself *as* a Jew? That's what I was asking you. What kind of a Jew *are* you?"

I looked back at Skippy. "What the hell is going on?"

"Mike, there's nothing bad here," he said reassuringly. "Talk to the man. Answer his question. Trust me. You'll understand soon. I promise. "

I had no reason not to trust Skippy, so I sat back in my seat. I looked down at the table, picked up my spoon, and began to tap it lightly on the tablecloth, both to calm down and give myself a chance to think about his question and how to respond. A half a minute passed before I put the spoon down, methodically lining it up next to the knife. I took a deep breath and turned to face Shatz.

"I'm not that religious, so I guess that makes me more of a secular Jew," I said. "I was born and raised a Jew. It's who I am. To tell you the truth, I don't think too much about it. Unless, of course I have a run-in with some anti-Semite asshole who has a problem with me because I'm Jewish. Then I'm forced to think about it, because that occasionally involves some thrown punches." I paused a heartbeat. "Did that answer your question?"

"It did."

"Good," I said, gritting my teeth, "because now I have one for you. Why did you ask me, and what fucking business is it of yours anyway?"

"Fair enough. But before I answer, one more quick question. Did you hear about the United Nations vote a couple of weeks ago on the partitioning of Palestine, where they're going to create a Jewish State and a Palestinian State?"

"Sure. It was in the *Boston Globe.*"

"What do you think about it?"

The waiter appeared with my Bloody Mary. The conversation paused while he served coffee to the others. I took a healthy sip, trying to figure out where this conversation was going.

When the waiter left, I said, "To tell the truth, I didn't think that much about it." I shrugged. "I mean, it's a good thing that the Jews from Europe have a place to go, but that's about it."

"Well, what if I told you that might not happen? That all those Jewish holocaust survivors might end up not having a place to go."

"What are you talking about? We just said the U.N. voted for it. It's a done deal."

"Actually, it's very far from a done deal. When the British pack up and leave next May 15th, the Zionist will formally declare the existence of a Jewish State. And the next day the leaders of five surrounding Arab countries, with over sixty million people, have publically stated they intend to attack the new country and drive the six hundred thousand Jews living there into the Mediterranean Sea."

"What? How can that be? Where's the United Nations?"

"No one is going to help us," Meir said, speaking for the first time.

"'Us'? Who exactly are 'us'?" I asked, turning to the man across the table.

"I'm from the Jewish Agency of Palestine. I'm the assistant to the Haganah Chief of Station in the United States."

"Haganah? What the hell is the Haganah?"

"Among other things, we're the ones that try to breach the British blockade and land the Jewish survivors in Palestine. And soon, we will be the only fighting force standing between the Arab attack and the slaughter of over six hundred thousand Jews. The next Holocaust."

I pushed back in my chair. *This is getting crazy*, I told myself. *I don't understand any of this.*

Meir continued. "For thousands of years on Passover, Jews all over the world say, 'Next year in Jerusalem.' We've held a faith that we will have our homeland once again. The new State of Israel is our homeland. A place that will protect Jews from their enemies. A place where Jews can live in peace. But, the Arab nations that surround it don't intend to let us have it."

"Mr. Shatz, I'm confused," I said. "I don't know why I'm here or what you and Mr. Meir want with me."

"Call me, Paul, please," Shatz said. He glanced briefly at Meir. "What Meir just told you was for context. Now, let me get to the point and answer your question. The Arabs are going to attack. That's a fact, and they've publicly said so. But, there's an arms embargo for the Middle East, and the Jews in Palestine, the Haganah, have virtually no weapons to defend themselves. I plan to help. I've got planes, mostly C-46's. I'm going to fill them with the weapons they desperately need and fly them to Palestine. I'm going to break the embargo, and I need pilots. I want you to be one of them. What do you say?"

Stunned and at a loss for words, I sat in my chair shaking my head. *This man is crazy*, I thought. "Ahh, I don't know what to say, except ... wow."

"That's why I asked what kind of a Jew are you. Are you Jewish enough to want to help us? Are you willing to be your brother's keeper?" Shatz asked. "You're here because Skippy already volunteered to be one of my pilots and said you might be willing to join us."

"You can't possibly expect me to give you a decision now."

"I don't. Take a few days, then let me know. I hope you'll join us. If you don't, I'll be disappointed... but understand. All I ask is, either way, you don't say a word to anyone about this conversation."

I chuckled. "Oh... you can be sure I won't. I have a feeling if I told anyone, they'd think it was the craziest idea they'd ever heard. And I can't say they'd be wrong."

I looked at my watch. Damn, it was already 1:30. I had to get out of there, or I'd miss the 2:00 o'clock train.

I stood. "Gentlemen, I've got to run. Skippy, I had a great time yesterday. And, as far as this morning... it sure as hell has been interesting... to say the least."

"Will you consider it?" Shatz asked.

"Against my better judgment, I will."

I shook everyone's hand, but when I came to Shatz, he held mine a little tighter and leaned in to me. In a voice just above a whisper, he said into my ear, "To be fair, I've got to tell you one more thing while you're deciding whether to join us. If you do, you could be risking fines, imprisonment, loss of your U.S. citizenship, and possibly your life."

He paused for a heartbeat, then with a half grin said, "Have a safe journey back to Boston."

CHAPTER 2
December 7, 1947
Train to Boston

I HAD GOTTEN STUCK in traffic and sprinted into the terminal. The clock over the departure board showed 1:59. I breathed a small sigh of relief when the board showed the 2:00 o'clock express to Boston was delayed until 2:06. I raced through the terminal, bounded down the platform, and hopped on the steps of the last car just as the conductor stuck his head out from between cars halfway down the train and yelled, "All aboard!"

Breathing hard as I walked between cars, I found an empty seat two cars later. After hoisting my suitcase into the overhead rack, I flopped into the seat. I pulled out a handkerchief, wiped perspiration from my forehead, leaned my head against the cool window, and closed my eyes. My headache was back. I didn't know if it was from the tension of rushing and almost missing my train or the conversation that took place earlier.

With my eyes closed, the monotonous rhythmic clacking of the wheels over the rails had a hypnotic effect. The more I listened, the less I thought about my headache and soon fell asleep.

My eyes flew open as I was jolted awake, my body thrust forward by the train's lurching stop. I heard the conductor shout, "Stamford, Connecticut!" from the front of the car. I looked at my watch. I'd slept for about thirty-five minutes. My headache was gone.

Studying the faces of passengers streaming across the station's platform toward the stairs leading down to the parking lot, not one looked Jewish. I'd heard stories that Stamford, Connecticut, was a bastion of anti- Semitism. Stereotyping maybe, but if the W.A.S.P. looking faces parading by me were any indication, the stories were probably true.

With a gentle bump, the locomotive began to pull the train out of the station. As it picked up speed and the Connecticut landscape flickered by, I thought about today's conversation. Was I willing to face the dangers and the consequences Shatz said could lay ahead if I joined his harebrained scheme? I guess it boiled down to how I'd answer his question.... What kind of Jew am I?

Leaning my head against the window, I thought back to when I was twelve years old and told my father I didn't want to be Jewish anymore. He made me go to Hebrew school each weekday afternoon from 4:00 to 6:00, right after public school let out at 3:30. He said it was to learn about Judaism, but most importantly, to learn Hebrew for my Bar Mitzvah.

I began Hebrew school at age ten, and then, two years later, I wanted to stop. "It's like having to go to jail for two hours each day, just because I'm Jewish," I pleaded with my father.

My father and mother were immigrants from a small village in Ukraine, about seventy miles from Kiev. They fled to the United States in 1909 to escape the anti-Jewish pogroms. Between themselves, they spoke some Russian but mostly Yiddish. To me, my parents spoke some Yiddish, but mostly their broken English, because they wanted me to assimilate.

"You must go," he said.

"Why?" I whined.

"Because we have traditions," he said. "One you have no choice. You only eight days old when you have *bris*. Circumcising is covenant made between God and Abraham and take place from then until now.

"Second is becoming a bar mitzvah. You become man in eyes of Jewish people and accountable for your actions. These two traditions celebrated for the last five thousand years and you not going to break them."

"But..."

"No buts," my father interrupted in a firm tone. "No more discussion. I was a bar mitzvah, my papa, his papa, and his papa, forever. And you be a bar mitzvah, and your sons, and their sons, until there no more world or no more Jews."

"Then I don't want to be Jewish anymore," I said. I felt tears trickle down my cheeks.

My father's eyes became cold as he glared at me. His face flushed, and I could tell he was mad, angrier than I'd ever seen him before. He opened his mouth to say something, but didn't. He just turned and left the room.

Our conversation took place on Saturday afternoon, giving me the rest of the weekend to think about it. I came to understand how strong Jewish tradition was to my father and what a disappointment I was to him when I uttered the words, "I don't want to be Jewish anymore." On Monday, I went to Hebrew school as usual and never again complained about it. The next year, at the traditional age of thirteen, I had my bar mitzvah.

IN THE DORCHESTER section of Boston where I lived, the Jewish area made up just a small part of its total population. The majority of its residents were Irish Catholic. During my early teen years, my parents, relatives, and neighbors spoke about the latest anti-Semitic incidence.

I was old enough to know that virtually all of the anti-Semitism came from the Irish community.

More than half of Boston's Jews lived in sections of Dorchester, Roxbury, and Mattapan, mostly clustered close to Blue Hill Avenue, a four mile main street and shopping center that ran through all three sections. Gangs of Irish kids would invade Blue Hill Avenue at night, what they called Jew Hill Avenue, attacking Jewish kids who walked alone or in small groups. They also vandalized stores owned by Jewish merchants.

When I was fourteen, during the Yom Kippur service, the most sacred of all Jewish holidays and the only one I actually observed, the Rabbi in his sermon tried to explain it. Their anti-Semitism, he said, was driven by bitterness and frustration, their attempt to compensate for the ills of the Irish ghetto—alcoholism, social, and economic immobility. I shook my head and stared at him in disbelief. Did he think trying to explain why they did it somehow excused it? Who gave a damn why? They were anti-Semitic, and we were their targets.

I lived in a Jewish cocoon and didn't have my first actual anti-Semitic experience until the day after I graduated junior high school. Prior to the start of summer vacation, all incoming tenth grade students were required to report to Dorchester High School for a two-hour orientation. That morning, before orientation began in the auditorium, I needed to use the bathroom. Approaching the urinals, on the walls above them, written in chalk, I saw the words "Kill the Jews," "Down with the Jews," and "Fuck the Jews."

I felt the hairs rise on my neck and arms. The stories my parents told about anti-Semitic attacks flashed in my mind as I quickly whirled around to see if anyone was coming at me. I fled the bathroom, seeking to immerse myself in the anonymity of the crowded auditorium. My stomach was in knots as I counted the minutes until orientation was over and I could get to the safety of my house.

When my father arrived home from work that night, I told him what I saw. He didn't say anything for a few minutes; he just stared at the back of his hands, deep in thought. Finally, he looked at me. "I call your mother's cousin, Harry Slotnick. I want you to spend summer with him."

I knew Harry. He'd been a highly ranked amateur boxer, and at age twenty-one, turned professional. He did well in his first six fights, but after getting knocked out in the next two, he decided to retire. Harry now worked where I played basketball with my friends, as a youth counselor at the Hecht House, the Jewish Community Center in Dorchester.

Harry was somewhat of a hero to the Jewish community. One night, a bunch of Irish thugs were looking for Jewish kids to beat up, but instead of going to Blue Hill Avenue, they decided to go to the Hecht House with the same intention. They arrived too late. Everyone had gone for the night except Harry, who was left to lock up the building. As he headed to the bus stop, the gang of hoodlums attacked him. The next day, newspapers reported five Irish youths were found in the area of the Hecht House badly beaten, needing hospitalization. Everyone in the community knew it was Harry when he came to work the next day with bruised knuckles.

I spent the next eight weeks with Harry as my tutor. Lifting weights, skipping rope, working the speed bag and heavy bag. Sit-ups and push-ups until I was exhausted, and my muscles ached beyond description. Harry was unsympathetic. In a makeshift ring, he taught me the fine art of boxing. By the first day of high school, I'd added twenty pounds of solid muscle. More importantly, I developed complete confidence in my ability to protect myself.

I signed up to play football. On the second day of practice, Joe Burke, a senior and star fullback on the team, approached me from the rear as I sat on the bench in front of my locker.

"Hey, kike," he said, "what the fuck do you think you're doing? This team isn't for sissy Jew boys. Get the hell out of here before you get the shit kicked out of you!"

Dressed only in football pants and a tee-shirt, my helmet, cleats, and other equipment already in my locker, I tried to ignore Burke. But he wouldn't let it go. Jabbing me in the back with his finger, he taunted me again. "Did you hear me, Jew boy? I said turn in your equipment and get the fuck off the team."

I rose and faced Burke. He stood about five feet, ten inches tall with a broad muscular build that made him a terrific fullback. He could bulldoze his way through defensive lines like a wrecking ball through the side of a brick building. I had about three inches in height on him, and we both weighed in at about 190 lbs.

I put up my palms. "Joe, I don't want any trouble. I just want to play football."

Over Burke's shoulder I saw a bunch of guys from the team standing in the locker room, watching. I was the only Jewish kid on the team, so I knew no one was going to step in if I needed help.

"I don't give a shit what you want, Christ killer," he said as he pushed me back against the lockers.

Something clicked inside me. I decided if I was ever going to make a stand against a bully anti-Semite, this might as well be it.

"How can I be Christ's killer? I didn't even know the man."

Probably wasn't the smartest reply to make, because Burke's face grew red with rage. "You fucking Jew bastard. You're dead meat."

He lunged at me, and I saw his right arm move in an arc as he swung at my face. Harry's training kicked in, and I reacted instinctively. I blocked his roundhouse swing with my left forearm and threw a right hook. Harry taught me to use my legs and propel my whole body behind a punch. I caught Burke on the side of his jaw, and he fell like a ton of bricks. I immediately spun toward the rest of the team, fists clenched, expecting a bunch of them to charge at me. No one did.

I could see it on their faces... shock at what had just happened. Burke, a senior, star fullback, and team captain, was the toughest guy on the squad. And there he was, on the floor, put there by a sophomore... and a Jew.

That was the end of my football career at Dorchester High School. The next day, when Coach Callahan found out his star fullback was in the hospital with a broken jaw and out for the season, he summoned me to his office and kicked me off the team.

As a result of the locker room fight, the so called tough guys gave me a wide berth in school. I never got hassled, and no one ever called me an anti-Semitic name to my face again. I wish I could say the same for some of the other Jewish kids in school.

Five weeks after my run in with Burke, my good friends Jacob Hodas and Harvey Blaustein were walking home from school when a gang of Irish kids beat the shit out of them. Someone called the cops. When they arrived, rather than arrest the gang members, the police released them and arrested Jacob and Harvey for protesting the cops' decision to let the Irish kids go.

They were held overnight at Police Station 11 where they were called "yellow Jews" and beaten with rubber hoses by the cops. To make matters worse, an Irish Catholic judge found Jacob and Harvey guilty of participation in an "affray," as he called it, and fined them ten dollars each. The Jewish community, including me, was mad as hell, but the authorities turned a blind eye. Not surprising since there were a hell of a lot more Irish voters than Jewish voters in Boston.

After my run in with Burke, I didn't experience any more personal anti-Semitic issues until a minor exchange I had when I went to the recruiting office to join the Marine Corps after graduating college in 1942. There was a war on, and I wanted to do my part. After filling out the paperwork, I was called into an office where a sergeant sat behind a desk. He told me to sit. After he finished reading my file, he squared it up on his desk and said, in a deep southern accent, "Says here you're a Hebrew. That right, boy?"

"That's right," I said, staring him straight in the eyes.

"Y'all know the Marine Corps is a real tough outfit, don't cha? Our basic training is the hardest of all those other pussy branches."

I snapped back, "I'm not worried about it, Sergeant. If someone like you could make it through, it'll be a breeze for me."

A couple of seconds passed before a slight grin creased the sergeant's mouth. "Ahh bet it will, boy, ahh bet it will. Y'all got balls. Welcome to the Marines."

"SOUTH STATION NEXT! South Station next!" the conductor called out, snapping me back from my memories. I looked out the window and saw the Gillette razor blade factory in South Boston, putting us about five minutes away from the terminal.

By the time the train pulled into the station, I had my answer to Shatz's question. It really didn't matter *what* kind of Jew I am. The fact is, I *am* a Jew, plain and simple. I made my decision. If there were Jews willing to fight for a homeland after thousands of years in exile, I was going to be part of Shatz's crazy scheme and help them.

CHAPTER 3
December 7, 1947
Hawaii/New York City

SEVEN TIME ZONES to the West, Melvin "Mel" Pinter crouched behind a Quonset hut with his cousin, Ray Hirsh, three buildings from his target, the Ordnance Depot at Schofield Barracks, a few miles outside of Honolulu.

"Is he gone?" Pinter whispered.

"Not yet. Give it another minute."

PINTER LEANED THE back of his head against the metal building, the events in his life that led him to this place flashi through his mind.

He wasn't particularly religious growing up, even though he came from a family with a deep Jewish identity, including a paternal grandfather who was a cantor in a synagogue. Yet, here he was, about to steal armaments for the Jews in Palestine.

After receiving his law degree in 1941, he'd spent four years as a combat pilot flying a Mustang P-51 in Europe. One month after Germany surrendered, the Army Air Forces transferred him from England to a temporary station at Lindsey Air Base, in Germany.

He'd heard stories from soldiers assigned to Lindsey about the Nazi concentration camps. Some of the G.I.s were part of the liberation forces that entered the camps and spoke of the atrocities that had taken place, especially to the Jews. Pinter found it hard to believe it could be as bad as they described. He had plenty of free time waiting for his discharge papers, so he decided to see for himself.

The town of Dachau, located a half hour drive from the center of Munich, in the American Occupation Zone, was the site of one of the camps. There he witnessed firsthand the vestiges of the Holocaust. The stories the soldiers told didn't begin to describe the depravity. He walked through the concentration camp, stopping at the ovens, the barracks, and mass graves.

Fueled by the horror and revulsion at what he saw, he had to exercise maximum self-control to prevent the contents of his stomach from spewing to the ground at his feet. *Once again*, he thought, *another of the countless attempts throughout history to exterminate Jews.* Inflamed by rage, the experience rekindled his reverence for his Jewish identity and heritage.

After the war, he practiced law in Brooklyn but found it unfulfilling. He always wanted to be a writer and found part-time employment with *The Villager*, a small Brooklyn newspaper, as a contributing editorial writer.

One of his legal clients, who knew about his part-time job, told Pinter that a friend of his was the owner of the *Las Vegas Sun*. "I know he's looking for newspaper reporters. Would you be interested?" he asked Pinter one day.

"I'd be willing to talk to the man," Pinter replied.

Three weeks later, Pinter's client told him that he'd sent copies of his editorials to the owner of the *Sun*, and the man wanted to meet with him.

Pinter flew to Las Vegas, liked the man he'd be working for, and took the job—for two reasons. The first was the owner made him a great offer. He would write editorials, work as a roving reporter, and would be the sole writer of a monthly entertainment magazine, *Life in Las Vegas,* to be inserted into the *Sun* newspaper. The second reason was because he fell in love with the town, which seemed to be a perfect paradise of majestic mountains, infinite skies, and balmy air that looked and felt like warm, breathable crystal.

On November 1, 1946, Pinter was in his office working on the *Life in Las Vegas* insert for the following month when a good looking man, about five feet, ten inches tall, impeccably dressed, walked in. Pinter thought he looked familiar.

"Are you Pinter?" he asked.

"Yes."

The man put out his hand. "I'm Benjamin Siegel."

The name and face suddenly clicked in Pinter's head. *Bugsy Siegel.*

"I'd like to offer you a job," Siegel said."I've been reading your stuff in *Life in Las Vegas* and like your style. As you know, I'm opening the Flamingo Hotel next month. I'd like you to be the publicist for it. "

"I'm flattered," Pinter said, "but I can't leave my job here. I've got a contract, and besides, I love what I do here."

"The contract here is no problem. I've already spoken to the owner. They're willing to take double what your contract is worth to buy you out of it. And, I'll give you a contract with me paying you four times what you're making here."

Wow! "Why? I mean, why do you want me that bad."

"I like your writing, and I think you'll be good for the hotel. I also checked you out. I like to surround myself with smart Jewish guys. You're from Brooklyn, and I like that. And, you're a lawyer." Siegel smiled. "So I'm gonna pay you one dollar as a retainer. That way, you're my attorney. Anything you might hear that could be of interest to anyone is covered by lawyer-client privilege, and you can't reveal it."

Working for Siegel, Pinter told his close associates, was at times rewarding... and at times, more terrifying than being in combat. Rewarding because Siegel treated him like a kid brother. Perhaps because they were both from New York and Jewish. Siegel instructed the staff at the Flamingo that for Pinter, drinks, food, and access to the headline shows were always on the house.

The scary part of working for Siegel was when he requested, maybe demanded would be a better word, that Pinter join him whenever he entertained gangsters from back east at the hotel. Meyer Lansky, a boyhood friend of Siegel and of Charles "Lucky" Luciano, the most powerful underworld boss in the country, was a frequent visitor.

Pinter would also often find himself sitting with reputed Jewish members of what the press called Murder, Inc., a team of killers for hire, formed by Siegel and Meyer Lansky. Italian assassins Albert Anastasia and Jack Parisi, also members of Murder, Inc., were frequent visitors. Many Las Vegas hoodlums attended the dinners, and because he had the confidence of Siegel, they came to accept Pinter as part of their circle.

Pinter quit his job as publicist for the Flamingo after Siegel was murdered in Beverly Hills in June, 1947. Five months later, in early November, he took a trip back to Brooklyn. During the visit, his cousin Ray Hirsh introduced him to Noah Meir of the Haganah.

"We're the underground army fighting to establish a new Jewish State in Palestine," Meir told him.

Pinter asked how he could help. The Haganah agent replied, "We need munitions. Guns, bullets, anything will help."

Pinter spoke to his mobster connections to find out where he could get the needed armaments. The consensus was Schofield Barracks in Hawaii because of the vast number of weapons turned in and stored there from the fighting in the Pacific. Pinter tried to get the mobsters to steal the munitions for him, but they weren't interested in getting involved. They didn't want to run afoul of the U.S. Government.

Pinter was going to have to do this without their help. He knew his cousin Ray, a petty burglar in Brooklyn who had the skills for breaking and entering, would help. After all, Ray was the one who made the introduction to Meir of the Haganah. Hirsh would get them in, and Pinter, although he'd been a pilot, knew weaponry from his time in the service. He'd know what to look for.

A MONTH LATER, here he was, about to steal weapons from a U.S. Army depot in Hawaii. *How ironic*, he thought, *that today is the first day of Hanukkah*. What a great Hanukkah present this will be for the Haganah.

"Okay, the guard's gone. Let's move," Hirsh said.

The men made their way between the buildings until they reached the rear door of the armory. *It's make or break time.* Pinter gave the knob a twist and the door opened. He grinned. The one thing his Las Vegas connections were willing to help out with was to bribe a G.I. Pinter met with the soldier yesterday, explained what was needed, and gave him the money. *The guy just earned every penny he was paid.* They quickly slid inside.

Pinter pulled out a flashlight and spread his fingers over the lens to filter some of the light. He looked at his watch. 11:00 p.m. The G.I. told him he had to get out of the building before 5:00 a.m., when the ordnance sergeant started his day.

They scrambled up and down aisles, inspecting the stenciled crates, until they came to the ones they were looking for. M3A1 submachine guns, commonly known as 'grease guns,' and crates of .45 caliber cartridges for them. Across the aisle, MK II hand grenades.

Pinter and Hirsh hustled. The weight of each case required both men to carry it. They had to lug them over three hundred yards to the gate the G.I. left open for them, stack them in a stolen truck hidden in a grove of palm trees, all without being spotted by sentries. By 3:00 a.m. they'd loaded 63 crates of submachine guns, 100 cases of cartridges, and 22 cases of grenades.

"That's it," Pinter huffed, unbuttoning his shirt and flapping it to circulate air around his dripping torso. "I don't want to push our luck, and I'm too damn hot and tired to carry any more. I'm going back to lock the door. When you see me come back through the gate, start the truck, and get us the hell out of here."

Pinter fixed his shirt and darted back to the ordnance building. As he reached around the door to turn the inside lock, he heard voices close by. He quickly slipped into the building, pulled the door tight behind him, and engaged the lock. He moved to the side of the door and flattened his back against the wall. His heartbeat surged.

A voice, coming from just outside of the thin metal wall near his head, said, "I didn't see anything." Pinter's body stiffened.

A second voice replied, "I'm not sure I did either, but let's check it out anyway."

Sweat trickled down Pinter's neck and back. When the doorknob rattled, he twitched and pressed his back tighter against the wall, his heart hammering. He was trapped in a building filled with weapons, could get shot, and didn't have a gun in his hand to defend himself.

"This is locked. Let's check the next building."

Pinter did not move from his spot for five minutes. Finally, he took a deep breath to relax, edged himself to the door, and inched it open. If the guards were still close by, he was a dead man. He peeked outside. The area was empty. He set the door lock and hot footed it through the gate to the waiting truck. The engine was running, and Hirsh pulled away before Pinter had his door completely closed.

Two days later, the weapons, in a sealed shipping container, were put on a freighter in Honolulu Harbor bound for Los Angeles. Pinter and Hirsh boarded a plane and arrived on the mainland to await the shipment.

On the day the freighter arrived, the front page of the *Los Angeles Times* had an article about the State Department cracking down on shipments of weapons to Palestine and how they were increasing their search of ships to look for them.

Hirsh finished reading the article out loud to Pinter and slammed the paper on the table. "After all that work and the chances we took, we're going to lose the weapons."

"No, we won't," Pinter said.

"How do you figure that?"

"I don't know yet, but I'll come up with something."

Five hours later, Pinter had a plan in motion.

After a few phone calls, his Las Vegas mobster connections reached out to their friends in Los Angeles. This resulted in a security guard at the dock being paid off to let Hirsh and Pinter board the freighter. The Los Angeles mobsters also bribed two longshoremen to have the container with the contraband placed on the deck of the freighter for easy access. Their fee included helping unload the merchandise.

At ten minutes after midnight, Pinter and Hirsh pulled alongside the freighter in a forty-foot, seagoing yacht they'd stolen from the Marina Del Rey Yacht Club earlier that evening. Tying it off tight against the side of the ship, they lowered the dingy and rowed to the dock. After a few words with the security guard, they boarded the freighter. Meeting up with the two longshoremen, they began off-loading the weapons, lowering the cases over the side by rope onto the stolen yacht.

Four hours later, with Pinter at the helm of the yacht, the munitions were out of Los Angeles Harbor, out of the reach of the State Department, on the way to Ensenada, Mexico.

After speaking with Meir earlier and laying out the plan, the Haganah agent told Pinter they would arrange to have the weapons moved from Ensenada to Mexico's east coast and onto a ship bound for Greece. From there, the goods would be loaded onto fishing vessels plying the Eastern Mediterranean where they would be delivered to Haganah fighters waiting on a beach somewhere south of Haifa. Pinter went back to Las Vegas, and Hirsh went back to Brooklyn.

CHAPTER 4
January 4, 1948
The State Department
Washington, D.C.

On December 18, 1947, Clark Clifford, presidential aide and domestic advisor to President Harry Truman prepared a draft public statement for Truman. The President would announce his intention to recognize the Jewish state when it formed this coming May 14. The White House sent a copy of the draft to the State Department for review.

Secretary of State George Marshall and others in the State Department had done everything in their power to prevent, thwart, or delay the President's Palestine policy in 1947. Now that the U.N. granted partition, Marshall urged Truman not to grant diplomatic recognition to the Jewish state. Instead, he wanted Truman to side with the rapidly growing sentiment in the United Nations in favor of a trusteeship, succeeding the British Mandate when they withdrew from Palestine on May 14.

Truman was aware of Marshall's strong feelings against recognition, and the State Department knew the President was sympathetic to it. Truman asked Marshall to a meeting to see if they could reach any common ground. Marshall asked Under Secretary of State Robert Lovett to accompany him.

LATER THAT AFTERNOON, after the White House meeting, Cordell Tipton, administrative assistant to Frank Cunningham, Director of Near Eastern and African Affairs, asked his boss, "How did the meeting go this morning?"

Cunningham recounted what his boss, Robert Lovett, had told him. "It wasn't pretty. Marshall lost his temper and all but threatened to resign if Truman recognized the new Jewish State after the British leave. Lovett told me his gut tells him Truman's going to go against Marshall and do it."

Tipton was livid."Those fucking Jew lovers are going to gum up our entire Mid-East policy. Can't they understand that not giving recognition is the smartest thing to do? It's the numbers. There are fifty million Arabs on one side and about six hundred thousand Jews on the other. They don't have a chance of survival. Why don't Truman and his Jew-loving friends face up to reality?"

"I agree," Cunningham said. "Marshall believes Palestine should just handle the influx of Jewish refugees. He's convinced if we side with the Jews on the partition, we'll make enemies of the Arabs who will cut off our oil and access to the Suez Canal. He also thinks if the Jews have a country they'll become cozy with the Soviets, who would love to have a base of operation in the Middle-East. Truman apparently doesn't share the same concerns."

"Well for me, those damn Jews are just too pushy," Tipton said. "We have to keep pressing Truman and his ilk not to declare recognition of a Jewish State."

"We will," Cunningham replied. "On a different subject, how are we doing on enforcing the United Nations Mid-East arms embargo?"

"Nothing specific has happened since we stopped those two ships from New York trying to smuggle guns to Palestine last week, "Tipton said. "By the way, how we got the U.N. to pass the embargo was brilliant."

Cunningham chuckled. "You're right. They actually bought the bullshit that it was meant to limit the scope of violence, when all it really does is penalize the Jews. The British are still going to provide weapons to Arab countries, and a lot of those will leak into Palestine. When the Arabs invade after the British leave, the Jews will have next to nothing to meet the onslaught; no tanks, no air force, and only a meager number of weapons. The Arabs said they were going to finish what Hitler didn't, and I say good riddance."

"Amen to that," Tipton replied.

"Back to the embargo," Cunningham said. "What did you mean nothing specific has happened? Is there anything *not* specific that happened?"

"There is something I'm keeping my eye on," Tipton said. "As you know, the F.B.I. has the Jewish Agency headquarters in New York under surveillance, since it's no secret the Agency is staffed by the Haganah. I got a report today that a man named Paul Shatz has met three times over the last two weeks with Noah Meir, Assistant to the Haganah Chief of Station."

"And the significance of that is...?"Cunningham asked, cocking his head.

"I'm not sure. According to the F.B.I., Shatz is a flight engineer with TWA. What got my interest is that he recently bought one war surplus Constellation and four surplus C-46s."

"They're very expensive. How can he afford them on a flight engineer's salary, and what's he doing with them?"Cunningham asked.

"Affording them is not as big of a deal as you may think. It's true that each of the planes cost $150,000 to build. But, as war surplus, all you have to do is go to the Reconstruction Finance Corporation, RFC, show them your discharge papers proving you're a veteran, and you can buy them for $5,000 each. They're just sitting in storage out in the desert. It's more profitable to try to sell them than to turn them into scrap metal."

"What's he doing with them?"

"He told the RFC he set up a business called Shatz Aviation. He's going to prepare the aircraft to meet civil aviation requirements. Claims a war buddy, a Harold Shapiro, has the licenses to operate a commercial airline company called Jersey Airlines and that Jersey will lease those planes from him."

"So far, I don't see anything suspicious. It looks like two more Jews going into business for themselves, trying to make money. Isn't that what those people do?" Cunningham said.

"On the face of it, yes. But, like you asked before, how can he afford them on a flight engineer's salary? What if he can't? What if the money is coming from the Jewish Agency, and that's why he's been meeting with Meir?"

Cunningham sat back and stroked his chin. "Interesting. Why do you think the agency would fund buying planes? What good would they do them here in the United States? They can't get them to Palestine because we'd consider that a violation of the embargo and impound them."

"I don't know that they *did* fund the purchases. But if they did, it might be worthwhile keeping a close eye on Shatz to see what they are up to."

"I agree. Do it."

CHAPTER 5
January 6, 1948
New York City

S IX DAYS INTO the New Year, Hirsh called Pinter.

"Can you come to New York?" Hirsh asked. "I want you to meet a guy."

"Who?"

"His name is Paul Shatz."

"When?"

"This week."

"Why?"

"Not on the phone. But it's important."

"Okay. I'll come in Friday for the weekend."

Pinter arrived at LaGuardia Airport, formally called New York Municipal Airport until six months ago, and called Hirsh.

"Meet me at the Copacabana tonight, around nine," Hirsh said. "The reservation will be in my name."

"I'll be there."

He arrived at the Copa at exactly 9:00 p.m. and asked for Hirsh's table. The maître de escorted him to a curved black leather booth on a raised dais, close to the stage floor. Ten feet away, couples danced, swaying to the band playing the newest hit song, *Dance, Ballerina, Dance*. He liked that song.

His cousin Hirsh sat at one end of the curved booth with three men. He recognized Noah Meir of the Haganah sitting at the opposite end. He didn't know the two sandwiched in the middle but presumed one must be the guy Hirsh wanted him to meet.

Pinter shook hands with his cousin, who slid toward the middle of the booth next to the two strangers, making room for him on the end seat.

"Good to see you again Noah," Pinter said.

"You too, Mel. And thank you for that shipment you arranged from Mexico. It was much appreciated."

"My pleasure. Took a little—"

Pinter stopped when he felt a hand on his shoulder. He turned and saw Meyer Lansky. He wasn't too surprised to see Lansky at the Copa. The real owner of the nightclub was Frank Costello, boss of the Luciano New York crime family, and Lansky was a senior member of the New York crime syndicate.

"Mel. How are you?"

"Fine, Meyer. And you?

"Can't complain. I got some people waiting for me," he said, nodding toward a table in a far secluded corner. "Saw you when I walked in. Just wanted to say hi. Didn't mean to interrupt your conversation. You take care," Lansky said, patting Pinter's shoulder.

"Yeah, you too, Meyer."

A waiter approached, and Pinter ordered a Dewar's on the rocks. He'd developed a taste for scotch whisky while stationed in England during the war. When the waiter left, he turned back to Meir. "As I was saying, took a little time and effort, but happy to be of help."

Pinter's gaze shifted, and he addressed the two strangers. "Which one of you is Paul Shatz?"

"I am," said the man with a muscular build, dark hair, and onyx-colored eyes.

Pinter addressed the other man. "And you are?"

"Mike Kaplan. I work with Shatz."

"So tell me," Pinter asked, returning his attention to Shatz, "why did I just fly across the country to meet you?"

"I'm looking to raise money and need it fast. Noah and Ray thought you might be able to help."

"What do you need the dough for?"

"To refurbish some planes I bought."

"For what?"

"I'm going to use them to fly weapons into Palestine, over the British blockade, for the Haganah. Mike is one of my pilots."

Pinter raised an eyebrow. He looked at Meir. "Explain."

Meir hesitated until the waiter, who'd reappeared to put Pinter's scotch on the table, left.

"We got word last week that Czechoslovakia is willing to sell us weapons. The problem is getting them to Palestine. Shatz tells me it's about fifteen hundred miles flying distance from Czechoslovakia. The planes need refurbishing to be able to make it."

Pinter turned to Shatz. "I was just a fighter pilot, but that seems a long way. Can they fly that far straight through?"

"No. We'll have to make stops. But before that, we have to get the planes to Czechoslovakia. That means crossing the Atlantic. We'll also have to make stops along the way to do that, but it can be done. I need money to fix them up so they can make the trips, and Meir doesn't have that much."

"Fix them up how?"

"Strip them of all unnecessary weight. Install basic navigation systems that were removed from them when the planes were decommissioned. Add rubber bladder fuel tanks inside the planes to add flying range. Things like that."

"How much do you need?"

"I'm sure $30,000 will do it."

"When?"

Shatz grimaced and shrugged. "Yesterday."

Pinter pondered the request. *I can kick in a few thousand. Who else can I get to help?* As he thought about it a bit more, it came to him.

"I'll be back in a couple of minutes," he said, sliding out of the booth.

He strolled in the direction Lansky had gone. As he drew near his table, he saw Albert Anastasia and Jack Parisi. He'd met them a couple of times at the Flamingo. Both were stone cold killers, charter members of the notorious Murder, Inc.. Anastasia was speaking to Lansky but stopped when he saw Pinter drawing close to their table.

"Albert, Jack," Pinter said.

"Mel," both responded, nodding in recognition.

"Meyer, can I have a minute?"

"Sure. Sit down."

"Private?"

Lansky rose, and they walked toward the men's room. In the empty hallway, Pinter related the conversation he had minutes before with Shatz and Meir.

"Can you help me raise some of it?" Pinter asked.

"You'll have it all tomorrow."

"All of it? Meyer, I wasn't asking you for all of it, just some help raising it."

"I know you didn't ask. I offered. I may be a lousy Jew, but I'm still a Jew. Where does it get delivered?"

"The agency's office, upstairs in Hotel Fourteen."

"Done," Lansky said. He grasped Pinter's elbow. "Let's go. I've got to get back to my table."

"Thank you," Pinter said, shaking the man's hand.

Pinter returned to his booth, sat, and said nothing for a few seconds, sipping his scotch. He was trying to wrap his head around Lansky's offer. *The whole $30,000.*

"Where did you go?" Meir asked, breaking the silence, a quizzical look on his face.

"I just spoke to Meyer Lansky. He'll have the money for you tomorrow."

"How much?" Hirsh asked.

"All of it."

"All of it?" Shatz and Kaplan exclaimed in unison.

Pinter nodded his head. "That's what the man just told me."

THE NEXT DAY, at 5:00 in the afternoon, Pinter received a call from Meir.

"Thank you. I just got the money," Meir said.

"When?"

"Five minutes ago. You know that singer headlining downstairs at the Copa, Frank Sinatra?"

"Yeah."

"He just walked into my office with a suitcase. Said an acquaintance of his stopped by his dressing room and asked him to bring it upstairs to me. I asked him what was in it. He said he didn't know and didn't want to know. He just laid the suitcase on my desk and walked out. Of course, the minute he left, I opened it. It was all there as promised, $30,000 in cash. And, by the way, no note."

"Okay. Let me know if I can be of any more help."

"You've done enough. Thanks."

CHAPTER 6
January 20, 1948
State Department
Washington, D.C.

BEFORE LEAVING YESTERDAY, Tipton had given his secretary a list of briefing materials for his meeting at 10:30 this morning. He'd told her he planned to arrive at the office at 8:00 and needed the information on his desk by then.

Although the meeting was an off the record conversation, with no entry in the official visitor's log book, Tipton never met anyone from a foreign country or interest without thorough preparation. He was familiar with the organization the visitor represented but wanted additional in-depth background material.

The morning traffic had been heavier than normal. As a result, Tipton didn't get to his office until 8:30. He hadn't seen his secretary, Marsha, when he walked by her cubicle, but she was obviously somewhere in the building. In the middle of his desk she'd set a carafe of coffee, cup and saucer, spoon, a small pitcher of milk, and sugar bowl. Neatly stacked at the upper left-hand corner of the desk she'd placed two briefing folders. *Efficient as always.*

Taking off his suit jacket and hanging it on the back of his chair, he poured a cup of coffee, added a splash of milk and two spoonfuls of sugar. He savored the first sip. The coffee was piping hot. Marsha must have put the carafe on his desk only minutes before he arrived.

He reached for the folders and slid them close. He settled first on the one labeled Grand Mufti, putting the other to the side. Holding the coffee cup in one hand, he took another sip and began to read the summary.

In 1921 the British High Commissioner appointed Amin el-Husseini, Grand Mufti of Jerusalem, the highest official of religious law. In 1937, evading an arrest warrant for inciting the Arab populace to rise up against British rule, he fled Palestine and took refuge first in Fascist Italy and then in Nazi Germany.

During the war, he'd collaborated with both Italy and Germany, making daily Arabic language propaganda radio broadcasts from Berlin, continually urging his listeners, among other things, to exterminate the Jews living in Palestine.

At the war's end, Husseini came under French detention and protection. He faced charges as a war criminal by Britain and the United States. The Mufti successfully persuaded the French government that he could advance their interests in the region, and the French authorities facilitated his escape.

In May 1946, the Mufti arrived in Cairo but remained in hiding for weeks due to the war crimes charges. Although at the time he was not allowed to set foot in Palestine, the Arab League enthroned him as the new leader, the Grand Mufti of all the Palestinian Arabs, not just those in Jerusalem.

After his elevation as Grand Mufti, he proclaimed, "The Arab battle with world Jewry is a question of life and death, a battle between two conflicting faiths, each of which can exist only on the ruins of the other." He went on to say, "Arabs must together attack the Jews and destroy them as soon as the British forces withdraw."

Tipton closed the folder and leaned back in his chair. *My thoughts exactly.*

He took a sip of coffee. It had grown cold. He topped off his cup with more hot coffee from the carafe.

He moved the Grand Mufti folder to the side and grabbed the folder with material on the Muslim Brotherhood. His 10:30 appointment was with Ammon Hazem, a representative of the Muslim Brotherhood, working out of the Egyptian consulate in Washington, D.C. The Muslim Brotherhood was currently the largest and strongest political organization in Egypt, with one and a half million members.

Tipton perused the file. Since the Mufti's detention in France, the Brotherhood had tirelessly defended and extolled him and issued threats against his enemies. Responding to rumor that the Zionists had sentenced the Mufti to death, the Brotherhood stated, "One hair of the Mufti's head is worth more than the Jews of the whole world, and should one hair of the Mufti's be touched, every Jew in the world will be killed without mercy."

Tipton had never met Hazem. According to the file, he had visited the State Department a year and a half ago, in June, 1946, representing the Brotherhood, and brought an ominous warning. He proclaimed that the United States and Britain would suffer dire consequences if either government tried to pursue prosecution of the Grand Mufti, now living in Cairo, as a war criminal. Hazem stated that the Brotherhood was ready to sacrifice themselves whenever and however necessary in order protect the Mufti.

At that time, the pro-Mufti campaigns and the potential for disorder and riots on the part of the Muslim Brotherhood played a crucial role in the decision of the Egypt-dominated Arab League to appoint Amin el-Husseini as the Grand Mufti of the Palestinians. The Brotherhood was a force to be reckoned with.

When Frank Cunningham, Director of Near Eastern and African Affairs, received the formal request from the Egyptian Embassy to set up the meeting with Hazem, he had no choice but to accept. He made it clear Hazem was not a recognized part of the Egyptian delegation, and the meeting would have to be strictly unofficial. As such, Cunningham's position dictated he could not meet with a member of the Muslim Brotherhood. Tipton was selected for the assignment.

Tipton scanned a report sent by the U.S. Embassy regarding the Arab League's meeting in Cairo a month ago. The Brotherhood had brought a parade of one hundred thousand demonstrators into the streets. According to the Embassy report, the Prime Ministers of the Arab states stood on the terrace of the Savoy Hotel acknowledging salutes from the passing parade.

The Arab League's response to the demonstration was to express its consent to train volunteers for jihad in Palestine. The training was organized partly by Egyptian officers and partly by Brotherhood members. The report concluded that it looked like a reluctant Egypt was going to begin active participation in the fighting in Palestine which was sure to come.

TIPTON STOPPED READING when he heard the soft knock on the door.

"Come in."

The door opened slightly, and Marsha poked her head in. "Good morning, Mr. Tipton. Mr. Hazem, your 10:30 appointment is here ... a little early. "

Tipton glanced at the clock on the wall. 10:10. *Where did the morning go*, he wondered?

"Thank you, Marsha. And thank you for coming in so early, for the hot coffee, and as usual, for the excellent work on the briefing papers."

Tipton thought he saw a small blush cross her cheeks. She really didn't handle compliments well.

"Show Mr. Hazem in." Tipton rose and put on his jacket.

His secretary closed the door only to re-open it a few seconds later. She stood to the side, holding the doorknob as the Brotherhood representative walked past her.

Tipton's eyes followed Hazem as he walked toward his desk. He was about 5 feet, 8 inches tall, dark hair with a neatly trimmed full beard and mustache to match. He wore an ill-fitting dark blue suit, white shirt, with an emerald green tie, sprinkled with small yellow dots. It looked like an outfit one would get off the rack from a department store's bargain basement. *Clearly, the man is not trying to impress me with his sense of style.*

"May I freshen up your coffee and bring Mr. Hazem a cup?" his secretary asked.

"I'm fine," Hazem replied.

"I am too, Marsha. Thank you. Please close the door."

Tipton pointing to one of the two arm chairs in front of his desk. "Have a seat," he said to Hazem.

Tipton observed Hazem's gaze wander about the office, lingering when it came to the pictures perched on his credenza on the far wall.

"Something wrong?" Tipton asked. It wasn't the first time a visitor was thrown by his choice of pictures.

"No, not really. Just an interesting choice on your credenza. Most men have pictures of their wife, children, family, even their prize car or boat. You have pictures of Charles Lindbergh and Henry Ford. I find it an unusual selection, that's all," Hazem said, speaking with a British accent.

"Not so unusual. I'm not married, so no wife or children. I was an only child, both my parents are dead, so no family. I get seasick easily, so no boat, and I view my car as strictly a means to get me from point A to point B."

"And the pictures of Lindbergh and Ford?"

"Both men I greatly admire. I share some of their beliefs, as I believe you do."

"And what may those be?"

"A discussion for later. I'm curious. How did you acquire a British upper class accent?"

Hazem smiled. "Ah, yes. My accent. I suppose it does seem out of place, coming from an Egyptian."

"It does, and particularly from a highly placed member of the Muslim Brotherhood, which has no current affection for the British."

"The short version. My father was, and still is, Deputy Director of the Ministry of Tourism in the king's government. We were among the privileged. From age four, I attended private schools run by the British for the children of British Diplomats, British Army Officers, senior Egyptian Army Officers, and Government Officials. The teachers were all from England, and all classes were conducted in English, so naturally I acquired their accent. Obviously, I wasn't a member of the Brotherhood back then."

"So how did you end up in the Brotherhood?"

"King Farouk is a corrupt and ineffectual leader. He allows us to be de facto ruled by the British, who continue to occupy Egypt under the ruse of protecting the Suez Canal. I joined the Brotherhood which, among other things, wants the British... and the king, gone."

"But, your father. You said he still worked—"

Hazem interrupted. "My father and I have different points of view. He's made his choice of loyalty, and I made mine."

You're a cold bastard. Glad you're not my son.

Opening the folder he'd been reading before Hazem arrived, Tipton glanced down and tapped his finger on a sheet of paper. "According to these reports from our embassy, you are one of the leaders of the paramilitary wing of the Brotherhood, the Special Apparatus, who are attacking British and Jewish interests in the country. The report also states the king is being pressured to declare the Brotherhood a danger to the country and dissolve it," Tipton said, his tone matter-of-fact.

"I categorically deny—"

Tipton held up his palm. "Stop. Don't deny. You and I both know it's true. But it's not an issue, at least for now. Let's move on. Tell me why you wanted this meeting."

Tipton was pretty sure he knew why. Probably to again threaten the U.S. Government about having the Grand Mufti stand trial as a war criminal.

Hazem shifted in his seat. "Before I get to that, you were going to tell me about the pictures of Lindbergh and Ford."

"Fine," Tipton said. *Let's see if you are who I think you are.* "Years ago, back in September, 1941, I attended an America First Committee rally in Iowa where Lindbergh was the featured speaker. Lindbergh said, 'I believe the United States should not get involved in the war in Europe, and we have to limit the amount of the Jewish influence that is pushing us in that direction.' He went on to say, 'Whenever the Jewish percentage of the total population becomes too high, bad reactions seem to invariably occur.'"

A conspiratorial grin creased Tipton's mouth, his head tilted slightly and his eyebrows rose. "Can I take it, based on your attacks on Jewish interests in Egypt, you share Lindbergh's feelings on the Jews?"

"Tell me about Ford." Hazem said.

Tipton shrugged. "A cautious man, I see." *Probably thinks my question is a trap. Doesn't want to commit a blunder,*

Tipton rose from his desk, moved to the credenza, and picked up the thick leather-bound book, about the size of a tabloid newspaper, that lay flat between the pictures. He moved back to his desk, putting the voluminous tome down in the middle.

"In the early 1920s, Ernest Liebold, Henry Ford's closest aide and private secretary, purchased a weekly newspaper for him. It was called The Dearborn Independent. Ford required every franchise nationwide to carry the paper and distribute it to its customers. As a result, it reached over seven hundred thousand readers."

Settling back in his chair, he continued. "Liebold was the editor, but Ford made it his personal newspaper. Every week, for 91 issues, it chronicled what he considered, as he termed it, the 'Jewish menace,' in a headline. One of the first articles to appear was by Ford himself, in which he wrote, 'If fans wish to know the trouble with American baseball they have it in three words—too much Jew.'"

Tipton tapped the book with his index finger. "In 1927 a libel lawsuit was brought against the paper, and Ford personally. It was initiated by a San Francisco lawyer named Aaron Sapiro. At the same time, Jews at the Anti-Defamation League organized a boycott of Ford products. Ford yielded to the pressure and bad publicity. He closed the paper and issued a public statement apologizing to Sapiro and Jews the paper offended. Shortly after it closed, the most popular and aggressive stories were chosen to be reprinted into this, four volumes called *The International Jew.*"

He pushed the chronicle toward Hazem. "Go ahead. Take a look." The Egyptian pulled the book closer and began thumbing through the pages.

"I share many of Ford's and Lindbergh's feelings about Jews and Jewish influence, and I believe you do also. They are mostly responsible for the Partition vote in the United Nations last November." Tipton paused. "And I think I know why you requested this meeting."

Hazem's head snapped up from the book. "What do you mean?"

Tipton's mouth curved in a grin."You want to warn the United States, as you did last year, to leave the Grand Mufti alone. No prosecution as a war criminal. Am I right?"

Hazem sat straight up, his posture stiff, his jaw tight. "That's correct. I'm here to remind you of our commitment, that there will be attacks in the United States if any harm comes to the Grand Mufti. That thousands of Americans will die. "

Tipton slammed his hand on the desk. His expression hardened "You foolish, foolish man. Do you really think the United States is afraid of you and your threats or will be cowed by them?"

He tapped the file in front of him. "This folder contains a full dossier of the Brotherhood... and you. All it will take is for our Ambassador in Cairo to contact his counterpart at the British Embassy," he said, his voice cold as ice. "A phone call will be made to the Egyptian government, you will be recalled to Egypt, met by the police, arrested, thrown in prison without charges, and never be heard from again." Tipton's eyes bored into the Brotherhood agent sitting across from him.

Hazem's face blanched as he sagged in the chair and tugged at his shirt collar.

Tipton gave Hazem a few seconds to absorb the impact of his words before continuing. "But your threat is unnecessary," Tipton said, adopting a warmer tone. "Our goals here at the State Department are the same as yours. When partition takes place and the Jews of Palestine declare an independent country, do you think we don't know the surrounding countries will attack and destroy them? We know all about the cache of weapons hidden in Palestine, supplied to the Brotherhood by the Nazis during the war. Why do you think we pushed through the arms embargo? It was to prevent the Jews from arming themselves against you. They'll be like lambs led to the slaughter."

He'd thrown Hazem off his game. The man sat in stunned silence, mouth agape.

"We don't care what happens to the Jews and we don't want the Grand Mufti tried. We want him to take charge in Palestine. And most importantly, we want the Brotherhood, Egypt, and the other Arab countries to remember who your friends are. The United States Department of State supports your cause and is on your side."

"I don't know what to say," Hazem said, haltingly. "I wasn't expecting this. Thank you. How do we—how do I—repay you? "

"I may need to call on you, unofficially. There's a man buying surplus airplanes. He may or may not be connected with the Haganah in the United States. I'm not sure at this point. The F.B.I. is watching him. If it turns out he's going to be a problem, for both of us, and I can't stop him through the F.B.I., I'll need other help to stop him."

Hazem straightened up in his chair. "It's yours. Whatever you need."

CHAPTER 7
February 10, 1948
Burbank, California

I MOVED TO CALIFORNIA a month ago. Shatz found me a room at a small hotel in Van Nuys, twenty minutes from our base of operations at the Burbank Airport. My parents were not happy, so to placate them, I said, "I'll only be out there for a few months." That part was true since I would soon be in either Czechoslovakia, Palestine, or flying between the two.

I loved the wintertime weather in California. I read in the *Los Angeles Times* that six inches of snow dropped on Boston yesterday, with another thirteen inches due to be dumped today. The paper said they would have blizzard condition winds and temperatures not expected to climb above ten degrees. Here, a brilliant sun sat in a cloudless sky, temperature a comfortable sixty-two degrees, with a light wind at five miles per hour.

Glad I'm here and not in Boston, I thought, as I pulled up to the closed gate at the airfield. Before I could get out of my car to open it, the same black Hudson that had been parked along the fence for the last two weeks whipped around me, blocking the entrance. I knew who the occupants were. I took a deep breath.

Two men wearing dark suits approached, one on each side of the car. The one on the driver's side tapped on my window. I rolled it down, and he thrust his F.B.I. credentials in my face. "Michael Kaplan?"

"Yes."

"My name is Special Agent Sullivan. I'd like to talk with you."

I'd been expecting the encounter. "Talk to me about what?"

"Would you mind stepping out of the vehicle?" Sullivan asked.

"No problem," I said.

I leaned against the driver's door, folded my arms across my chest, and furrowed my eyebrows. "What's this about?" No sense in giving them any reason to confirm what I expect they already thought they knew.

"We understand you work for Shatz Aviation. That true?"

"Yes. Why?"

"Mind telling us what you do there?"

"Sure. A war buddy of Mr. Shatz, a guy named Harold Shapiro, has licenses to operate a commercial airline. He's calling it Jersey Air, and he's going to lease his planes from Shatz. I'm a pilot. When the mechanics finish getting the planes ready to pass the civilian air inspection, my job will be to train the pilots who'll fly them."

The secret to keeping a lie believable is to be consistent. This was the same story Shatz told the Reconstruction Finance Corporation, RFC, when he purchased the planes.

"And that's what they're going to be used for? Nothing else?"

"As far as I know. Why? Do you know something I don't?"

"We have reason to believe the planes may be destined to Palestine. If they are, we're here to remind you and Shatz that there's an arms embargo, and it's illegal to help any country in the Middle East. If we catch you or anyone else connected to these planes trying to break the embargo, you're facing severe penalties."

I smiled and shook my head. "I don't know what gave you that crazy idea, but you guys are way off base. These planes are going to Jersey Air."

"Really? Then you wouldn't mind telling me about your meeting last month at the Copacabana where you and Shatz met with Mel Pinter, his cousin Ray Hirsh, and Noah Meir of the Haganah."

My mind raced. I needed to come up with something. Stay close to the truth, I reminded myself. "Not at all. Shatz bought the planes but needed money to fix them up. He'd met Meir before and contacted him to see if he could put him in touch with any wealthy Jews who might be willing to invest in his business. Meir contacted Hirsh, who in turn contacted his cousin Pinter. Pinter has money and the connections that Meir doesn't. That's all there is to it. Are you telling me that because I was at the meeting, I'm being watched because you think I'm trying to break this arms embargo?" I snickered.

"Maybe," the agent said. He seemed to be scrutinizing my face to see if I was lying. "Or maybe you're gonna use the planes for something completely different but no less illegal."

"Wait a minute," I said, throwing my hand up."Are you actually telling me if your crazy theory that I'm using the planes to break a Mid-East arms embargo isn't right, you've got a fall- back theory? Are you kidding me?" I laughed in his face. A good defense is a strong offense. "Go on, I'd love to hear that one."

"Tell us about Shatz's connection to Meyer Lansky."

"I don't know what you mean."

"It's a simple question. What's his connection to Lansky?"

"I don't think he has one."

The agent's mouth curved into a smile. "You're lying," he said.

"No, I'm not."

"Really? And he didn't meet with him at the Copacabana last month?"

I quickly decided the best thing was to tell him the truth or at least a partial one. "Neither Shatz or I had ever seen Lansky before he stopped by the table that night. If you know about that night, then you know he wasn't at the table for more than maybe thirty seconds before he left."

"True. But Pinter has history with Lansky and other well known criminals. They greeted each other at your table, and later Pinter had a private conversation with Lansky outside the men's room."

"Look, as you said, they had a private conversation. Since neither Shatz or I were part of it, how would we know what they said to each other?" I wanted to get away from these guys. "If you have no other questions, I'd like to get to the hanger."

The agent stared at me for a couple of seconds. "No, no more questions. But remember, we're watching you and Shatz... closely."

As the other agent pulled their car out of the way, Sullivan swung the gate open and stepped to the side. I slipped back in my car and drove very slowly through the gate. As I passed by, Sullivan said through my open window, "Looks like you got the money to fix the planes. From where?"

I pretended I didn't hear him and kept driving.

THE SIGN ABOVE the wide open hanger door said Shatz Aviation, Burbank, California. Two C-46's and a Constellation sat outside, the bright sun reflecting off their metal surface. Inside, three mechanics were working on two of the C-46's Shatz bought from the war surplus depot at CalAreo Field in Chino, some sixty miles west of Burbank.

After Shatz bought the planes, he rented the hanger, and I flew them in from Chino. He bought spare parts with the money Lansky gave us, also using some of it to hire the Jewish mechanics working in the hanger. He knew them from his time in the Air Corps, and they were happy to join the cause.

"Mike," Shatz yelled to me, waving me over to him when I walked inside. He sat at his make-shift office desk, an eight-by-four foot piece of plywood perched on top of three saw horses placed along the right side of the hanger. "The F.B.I. still outside?"

"Yeah. They finally got around to stopping me. As expected, they grilled me on what we're doing. Oh, I did learn something. They know about our meeting with Meir at the Copa last month. That's why they're watching us. They're convinced we're working with the Haganah to try and evade the blockade. I laughed at them and told them they were crazy."

Shatz frowned. "Not so funny. They're causing problems. They've been here for two weeks, and every day the mechanics come to work an agent takes pictures of them and their license plates. A couple of times when the mechanics have left, an agent has stopped them and asked what they're working on. The men are getting nervous."

I shrugged. "Shouldn't be a problem as long as they tell the truth. They're not doing anything wrong. They're getting planes ready to meet civilian aviation requirements for a commercial airline. Nothing illegal about that."

"That's what they tell them," Shatz said, "but the Feds aren't buying it. The agents keep reminding them about arms embargo and the fines, imprisonment, and loss of their citizenship if they help break it in any way. They stress that just working on a plane used to break the embargo is a crime."

Shatz let out a sigh, the corners of his eyes crinkling. "It's pure intimidation but it's working. I'm having a hard time getting more mechanics. There are a lot that would like to help, but word gets around, and they're scared to work here. And now that the F.B.I. knows we're working with the Haganah, it could get tougher to get more men."

"They don't know we're definitely working with the Haganah," I said. "They think we might be, but they're not sure, because they also saw us with Meyer Lansky. The agent today spent a few minutes grilling me about your connection to Lansky. The impression I got is they think we also might be in some kind of criminal conspiracy, even though I told them neither of us had ever seen Lansky before he stopped by the table that night. I don't think they believed me."

"But that's the truth."

"Yeah, well we know that, but they don't. Seems because Pinter has a history with Lansky, and we spent time at the table with Pinter, to the F.B.I. that spells a possible criminal conspiracy."

I leaned against the wall and grinned. "But that's good news. I don't think they're sure if we're working with the Haganah or involved in something with the New York mafia. It will keep them off balance for awhile, and awhile is all we need."

CHAPTER 8
February 21, 1948
Burbank

S HATZ AND I bought five more C-46's and two more Constellations in ten days since the F.B. I. stopped me at the gate, bringing the total fleet to twelve planes. The new purchases remained at the war surplus depot at Cal-Areo Field in Chino waiting for us to pick them up.

Finding more pilots for the mission became the next priority, so Shatz started a concerted recruiting effort. He contacted some of the Jewish friends he'd made around the world while serving in the Air Corps. Those friends put him in touch with others. He also reached out to Noah Meir to see if he could help.

Through friends of friends, we hit pay dirt with two contacts. One held a headquarters position with the California Air National Guard, and the other had a similar position in New York. They each told us there were lists with the names of all personnel who served in the Air Corps during the War, including their specialty. But neither one had access to them.

We knew the lists would be a great source for potential pilots, but how could we get our hands on them? The two contacts couldn't help, and we didn't know anyone else high enough at either guard unit to get them for us. We racked our brains until finally Shatz said, "If we can't get them legally, we'll have to get them illegally. There is only one person we know who can help us do that."

He contacted Mel Pinter in Las Vegas, explained the situation, and asked if he could help. Pinter said he'd get back to us.

Two days later, a stranger arrived at the hanger and handed a cardboard box to Shatz. "Compliments of Mel Pinter," he said and drove away. I looked on as Shatz opened the box. Packed inside was the California Air National Guard list. "Want to bet Pinter got his syndicate friends in California to break into the Guard headquarters and steal it?" Shatz asked, grinning."And you know what? I don't give a damn how he did it."

The same day we got our list, Noah Meir called Shatz from New York City telling him the list for the New York Air Guard was delivered to his office that morning. He said Skippy Shapiro was already working with it. *Thank you, Pinter.*

I spent the day scanning the California list, checking off Jewish sounding names that had 'pilot' written next to them. The next morning I began placing phone calls. I knew I couldn't just come out and ask if they would be interested in illegally flying arms to Palestine. Who knew if they would be a potential candidate or someone that would turn us in to the authorities? So I came up with a plausible explanation for my call, one that would let me feel them out.

The first three calls I made were a bust. In two cases, the person was at work, not expected home till early evening. The third had moved out of state three months ago. At 10:30, I made my fourth call. The name was Saul Lapin. When he answered, I introduced myself as Mike Kaplan from the membership committee of the Jewish American War Veterans and asked if he was interested in joining.

"Sure," he said. I told him I had a few background questions for the membership form. "No problem. Ask away," he replied. I got him to confirm his address, asked about his current employment, whether or not he was a member of a synagogue and other broad questions, trying to ferret out the measure of the man.

I liked his answers so I decided to move to the close. "As American Jews, the JAWV plans to raise money to help the Jews in Palestine. Are you okay with that?"

"Absolutely. I'm happy to do anything I can to help them."

Great reply.

"I have one more question, which granted, is a little off subject about joining the JAWV. Do you think the Arabs will attack the Jews in Palestine when they declare their independence?"

"Unfortunately, yes," he replied. It was a two word answer, but the palpable anger I heard in his voice convinced me it would be safe to tell him why I had really called.

"Saul," I said, "My name really is Mike Kaplan, but I'm not from the Jewish American War Veterans. I'm calling for a completely different reason, and please, hear me out and don't hang up. The short of it is, we're gonna break the Mid-East arms embargo by flying weapons to the Jews in Palestine to defend themselves when they're attacked. I've got twelve planes to do it. What I need is pilots to fly them, and I know you were a pilot in the war. Will you help?"

"When and where do you want me?" Lapin replied, catching me off guard. I wasn't expecting such a quick positive response.

"Wait a minute. Before I answer that, there's something you need to know. If you get caught helping us in any way, you're risking fines, imprisonment, and potential loss of your citizenship. We're already being watched by the F.B.I.."

"Okay. I understand. Now, as I said, when and where do you want me?"

This guy didn't hesitate for a second. Just like that, he was in. I could feel my eyes start to well and fought hard to keep my emotions in check. Shit, even I had needed time to think it over when I was asked. Sure, maybe it was just a few hours on the train heading home to Boston, but at least I thought about it. Not this guy. *God, please let me find more like him.*

"Let me call you back tomorrow afternoon," I replied. "In the meantime, here's my phone

number. Listen, this is a very big step. Think it over. I want you to be absolutely sure. If you

have any questions, you call me. Okay?"

"Okay," he said, and we disconnected.

At three o'clock that afternoon I walked over to Shatz sitting at his makeshift desk.

"How's it going with the recruiting?" he said, lifting his head from the stack of papers he was poring over.

I grabbed a chair from next to the filing cabinet and slid it to face the desk. Tilting backward, leaning against the wall, I shook my head. "It's been one hell of a crazy day. To start with, the fourth person I called and the first one I actually spoke with this morning, was a guy named Saul Lapin. He shocked the hell out of me when he immediately agreed to help. No questions.

"That was at 10:30. I thought, this was going to be great. I'll have all the pilots I need before noon. For the next two and a half hours... nothing. I made at least fifteen calls. I either got a busy signal, no answer, the person wasn't home, or it just didn't feel right."

I pitched the chair upright. Leaning over to the ice chest against the wall, I fished around the cold water and chunks of ice, grabbing a bottle of Coke. I popped the cap on the chest's built-in bottle opener and took a sip. It felt soothing flowing down my parched throat.

"I was getting frustrated and a little dejected. Then, about 1:30, my phone rang. The guy introduced himself as Daniel Prager. He said he was a friend of Saul Lapin, who'd called him and said I was looking for pilots to break the arms embargo. He told me he flew B-25 bombers in the Pacific and wanted to volunteer. He's currently an art student at UCLA. Then he said he has a buddy, Owen Landau, who was also a B-25 pilot, and he wants to volunteer. Landau is also an art student at UCLA with Prager."

I took a sip of Coke. "I asked Prager why. He said because he's a Jew, and he and Landau want to help the Jews in Palestine. And also, as artists, they want to visually record the birth of the new state. In fact, their only condition in volunteering is to be able to bring cameras and art supplies with them. I agreed to it."

"That's great," Shatz said."Now we have three pilots, plus you."

"Four, plus me."

"Four?"

"Yes, four. Like I told you, it's been a crazy day. An hour after I spoke to Prager, I got another call. From Mel Pinter. He told me he'd just got off the phone with Skippy Shapiro who's been on the phone all day, going through the New York Guard list. Skippy's got seven definite volunteers and three possibles. In one day."

"But you said four plus you out here. Who's the fourth?"

"Pinter."

Shatz's eyes widened. "Pinter?"

"Yup,"

Shatz straightened up in his chair, shock written on his face. "Why?"

I shook my head. "I asked him the same question. I said you've got a great life in Vegas. You're a lawyer, you've got a great job at the newspaper. Why do you want to risk all that?"

I took another sip of Coke. "He said, 'You forgot something. I'm also a Jew. They can always take away my law license. They can always take away my job. No one can ever take away me being a Jew. I'll be out there tomorrow. Oh, and one more thing. I was a fighter pilot. Someone's going to have to show me how to fly a C-46.'"

CHAPTER 9
Burbank, California
Miami, Florida

Shatz knew the F.B.I. would remain parked outside the airport fence watching us, so he devised a plan to get them off of our backs. He called Skippy Shapiro and told him to rent a hanger at the Millville, New Jersey, airport for Jersey Airlines. Through Noah Meir's contacts with Jewish organizations around the United States, hangers were also rented for Jersey Airlines at small private airports in St. Louis, Cleveland, Miami, and San Francisco.

"Why?" I asked when he told me.

"Simple," he said. "If they're going to watch us, I don't want to make it easy for them. They'll have to have agents cover all those places, but they won't know what we are doing." He laughed. "We're going to fly one or two planes to each location, leave them for a day, and then take off for another location. When they think we're at one place, will be at another. And when they see us there, will be someplace else."

The man is either a genius or completely crazy, I thought. *Or maybe a little bit of both.*

Prager, Landau, and Pinter arrived on February 24, and for the next couple of days I trained them to fly the C-46 and the Constellation. Prager and Landau were pretty easy to train. Our planes and instruments had a lot in common with the bombers they flew in the war. Pinter and Skippy Shapiro, who arrived on February 25, took a little more time. Flying a fighter was nothing like flying a C-46 transport. I gave them both a crash course, and two days later, we all went to Chino to pick up the C-46s and Constellations we bought and flew them back to the hanger in Burbank.

Shatz decided it was time to get moving on his plan for the F.B.I., so we all took off from Burbank on February 28. It didn't matter that some of the planes would not pass civilian air inspection at this point. We could still fly them, just not for commercial purposes yet.

Shapiro and Pinter headed to Millville, Lapin to San Francisco, Landau to St. Louis, and Prager to Cleveland. Lapin, Landau, and Prager would stay at the airport hangers for two days, giving the F.B.I. enough time to set up surveillance teams. Then they would take off and head cross country to Millville which will be our real base on the East Coast.

I headed to Miami. Shatz, who always sat in the rear of the cockpit in the flight engineer's seat during the war, now occupied the right hand copilot seat. The flight would take us close to eight hours, even with a moderate tailwind. We made small talk during the first few hours and also took some quiet time.

After flying for five hours, I was getting bored. I remembered Shatz telling me he'd never flown a C-46, so to break up the monotony, I decided I'd teach him how to fly one. We were in the air, a half hour east of Austin, Texas, where I'd stopped to refuel, when I asked him, "Would you like to take the controls?"

"Are you serious?" he asked. "I told you, I've flown other planes, but not this one."

"Don't worry," I chuckled. "Just follow my instructions. I'm not going to let you do anything that will get *me* killed."

I began his lesson by pointing out the location of the basic instruments needed to fly the plane. "As you know from other planes, there are really only these six you have to be concerned with," I said, tapping the altimeter, airspeed indicator, turn and bank indicator, vertical speed indicator, the directional gyro/heading indicator, and the artificial horizon. Shatz followed my finger as I pointed. "I'll watch the other gauges."

Shatz tapped each gauge I'd pointed out and repeated what I said it was for.

"Ready to try it?" I asked.

"Sure, let's give it a whirl."

I gave him the heading, height, and airspeed I wanted him to maintain and said, "The plane is yours." I took my hands off the yoke.

As time passed, I gave him new headings, which he executed perfectly. I had him make some slight altitude and air speed adjustments, again executed flawlessly. However, after two hours of flying, I could tell the excitement and novelty of actually flying the plane was starting to wear off. We'd left land and were flying over the waters of the Gulf of Mexico. His eyes began to wander, first looking at the sky, then scanning the endless body of water stretching to the horizon, spending less time watching the instrument panel.

"Getting bored?" I asked.

He smiled. "You can tell, huh?"

"Sort of. Sitting cramped in the seat for hours on end gets boring if the weather is fine and all you're doing is making slight corrections to keep yourself headed to where you want to go. That's why I chose to be a fighter pilot. When you went up, there was always danger. You felt alive, more alive than you ever felt on the ground. The adrenaline was constantly pumping. You knew any minute you could run across an enemy pilot that might be just a little better than you. If that happened, you'd be dead."

I glanced over at Shatz. He nodded his head as if he understood what I was saying. But I knew he didn't. Not really. You had to have been there. When I was in a dogfight with a Japanese Zero, the feelings coursing through my body were indescribable. Not that I couldn't put words to the feelings; it was that the words would be inadequate, not able to really convey what flowed through me.

"Okay, I'm taking back control of the aircraft." As I grasped the yoke in front of me, he released his hands. "So tell me. How come you came with me to Miami, instead of heading to the Millville base?"

"We're going there to do more than just create another place to make the F.B.I set up surveillance teams," he replied."Yesterday afternoon, while you guys went to get the planes, I set up some meetings."

"Okay for me to ask with who?"

"Yes," he said, smiling.

When he didn't say anything for thirty seconds, I got it. He was being cute with me. I decided to play his game. "Okay, I'll bite. With who?" I said, trying to sound exasperated.

He laughed. "Since you insist. My first meeting is with a guy named Harvey Hecht. I never met him, but he knows Noah Meir well. Seems Hecht has a lot of Jewish friends who told him they're concerned about the Arabs attacking the Jews in Palestine when the British leave. His friend put him in touch with Meir because he wants to help. That itself is pretty interesting, since Hecht isn't Jewish."

"So why are you meeting him?"

"Meir told me about him last year when I was in New York. When Hecht went into the produce export business after the war, he bought seven decommissioned B-17 bombers that he uses to transport fruits and vegetables. He offered Meir two of them, and he's not asking a dime for them. I'm stopping by to thank him and make arrangements to take the planes."

"That's unbelievable. And Hecht never told Meir why he wants to help? It can't be just because he has Jewish friends, can it?"

Shatz shrugged. "I have no idea. All I know is what Meir told me."

"Speaking of Meir, what do you know about him?" I asked.

"Not much. What I do know I got from Pinter's cousin, Ray Hirsh. Right after the War, there were groups of Jews that began making trouble for the British in Palestine, hoping it would make them withdraw their occupation forces. The most prominent were the Haganah, the Irgun, and the Stern gang. While they all wanted the same thing, getting the British out, each used different tactics to accomplish their goal.

The Irgun and the Stern Gang were militants who specifically targeted and killed British soldiers and policemen. The Haganah carried out attacks but did not intentionally target soldiers or the police with the sole purpose of killing them. Rather, they liberated interned immigrants, bombed the country's railroad network, and conducted sabotage raids on radar installations and bases. They also continued to organize illegal immigration."

Shatz stopped his commentary when we suddenly hit a pocket of turbulent air, violently shaking the aircraft. Within a minute we cleared the problem and Shatz continued.

"Much of the Haganah work relied on gaining intelligence. That brings me to Meir. He's a master spy for the Haganah who began his career spying on the British in Palestine. He made his mark with his ability to recruit people who provided valuable information. Hirsh told me I'd be surprised where he has people spying for him here in the United States."

I was impressed. I'd figured Meir for a shrewd man. Shatz just confirmed it.

Just as I was about to ask Shatz about the other meeting he set up, I was contacted by Miami approach. I was thirty miles from the airport. The flight controller gave me weather conditions and my landing vectors to runway L65. I began making landing preparations.

We still had about fifteen minutes to touchdown when I got around to asking Shatz about the second meeting. When he finished telling me, I shook my head in amazement. I knew I was right about him. He's either one of the most brilliant men I've ever met... or he's certifiably crazy.

CHAPTER 10
March 5, 1948
Miami Beach, Florida

WE GOT INTO Miami the night before at 7:45. By the time we finished with the paperwork and got out of the airport, it was close to 10:00. We were both bushed, so we headed straight to the Versailles Hotel on Collins Avenue in Miami Beach.

Our first appointment was at 2:30 that afternoon with Harvey Hecht at his office in his warehouse adjacent to the Miami airport. We took a cab out to see him. Hecht couldn't have been more cordial or a more gracious host. He took us in his car to the company's private hanger located on the outer perimeter of the airport to see the planes he was donating. While Shatz spoke with him outside, I climbed into the cockpit of one of them and checked it out. Everything looked like it was a well maintained aircraft.

When we were ready to leave, Hecht insisted we take his car back to the Versailles, saying he would arrange to have it picked up at the hotel after we left Miami. We got back to the hotel around 5:00. We had two hours to kill before our seven o'clock meeting, so we headed to the bar and talked about the plan for tonight. Just before we landed in Miami the night before, Shatz told me about that evening's appointment.

He'd realized for some time that he had to do something about the planes. We couldn't fly them to Palestine because the British were still there and would confiscate them. They also couldn't remain in the United States too much longer because the U.S. government might do the same.

While the current Mid-East arms embargo banned only military-type aircraft from leaving the United States, that rule was going to change shortly. Meir, the master spy, got word through a source in the State Department that they planned to place a new embargo in effect. It would put a limit on the weight of any aircraft leaving the country, effectively stopping our C-46's and the Constellations.

Shatz had figured a way to get the planes out of the country, and that night's meeting was crucial to its execution. The plan was complicated and would require some finesse, but if it worked, Shatz would pull off the feat of the century, a maneuver that would outfox the United States State Department and their Mid-East arms embargo.

We had dinner reservations at Joe's Stone Crab, the renowned restaurant in South Miami Beach, with a retired Air Corp Major named Marty Flynn. He was married to the niece of the President of Panama, Enrique Adolfo Jiménez. Lansky arranged the meeting through Miami Jewish gangster boss Sammie Kaye, who had connections with corrupt officials in Cuba and Panama, including Jiménez.

We were five minutes late arriving at the restaurant. Flynn and his wife were already there, each holding a half-filled martini glass. After the introductions, I took stock of the couple. Flynn looked to be about thirty years old. He had a shock of red hair, light complexion, and green eyes. I guessed his wife to be about the same age. She was a knockout. Shoulder length, jet black hair complemented high sharp cheekbones, brown bedroom eyes, a dainty straight nose, all surrounded by flawless, smooth, copper skin.

I was mesmerized, but thankfully the appearance of a waiter to take our drink order prevented me from making a fool of myself by staring at her too long. Flynn made small talk, asking about our flight and how we enjoyed the warm Miami weather. Mrs. Flynn didn't speak.

The waiter returned with our drinks. After he left, Shatz said, "Mr. Flynn, Mrs. Flynn," nodding to each in turn. "I hope you don't mind but I'd like to get right to the purpose of this meeting. As you are undoubtedly aware, Panama is one of very few Central or South American countries that does not have their own national airline. I'd like to have you set up an introduction for me with President Jiménez. I have a proposition I believe he will find most attractive which will remedy that situation."

"And your plan is what?" Flynn asked.

"It's pretty straightforward. I will offer President Jiménez a ready-made National Airline. I already have a fleet of C-46's and Constellations which I will sell to the government of Panama for the token sum of one United States dollar each and provide the pilots to fly them. In return, my proposal is that we will run the airline and receive half of its profits."

"That's it?" Flynn asked.

"That's it. Hardly a deal President Jiménez should turn down. His government needs to make no investment in airplanes, the government gets half the profits... and gets a National Airline."

"And what is in it for us?" Mrs. Flynn asked, speaking for the first time.

So much for us needing to use finesse. Meir warned Shatz to expect the probability of Flynn looking to be paid for the introduction, but it was expected to come from him, not his wife. Oh, well. I guess she proved the truth of the expression beauty is only skin deep.

"Ten thousand dollars. That's a non-negotiable figure to be paid after the introduction," Shatz said, giving Mrs. Flynn a hard stare.

"Give us a number to contact you," Mrs. Flynn replied, in a matter-of-fact businesslike tone.

Shatz removed a fountain pen from his jacket pocket and wrote a number on a napkin. He folded the napkin in half with the number on the inside and handed it to Mrs. Flynn. She put it in her purse without looking at it and slid out of the booth. As her husband was sliding out to join her, she said," It was a pleasure meeting you. Enjoy your dinner. You'll find the stone crabs and the mustard sauce delicious. We'll be in touch."

As I watched them walk away, Shatz said, "Lansky told Meir the Flynns would expect to be paid, that their going rate was $10,000, and we should make it clear it would not be a penny more. He said that's how they make their living, providing access to her uncle, who is even more corrupt than them."

"How do you know that?" I asked.

"Meir said the meeting with President Jiménez is just a formality. The deal is already done. After we have our meeting with Jiménez, Sammie Kaye, who has been bribing Jiménez for years, is going to pay him $100,000 to lock in the deal."

"Where's the $100,000 coming from? We know Meir doesn't have that kind of money."

"Lansky and Kaye are putting it up. As to why, my guess is for the same reason Lansky gave us the $30,000 to outfit the planes. As he said to Pinter when we met in New York, they may be lousy Jews, but they're still Jews and want to help.

"But why bribe Jiménez? The deal we're offing is a good one for Panama on its own."

Shatz shrugged. "Meir asked Lansky the same question. Lansky said because that's the way things are done down there. That's why I won't feel one bit bad later when we fuck Jiménez."

I WAS IN the hanger in Millville a week later when Shatz quick-stepped out of his office, grabbed me by the arm, and pulled me to a secluded spot fifteen feet from where I had been standing.

"I just got a call from Flynn... the husband," he said. "He told me I have a meeting with President Jiménez two days from now at the Presidential Palace in Panama City, Panama."

"That's great," I said. "When are you leaving?"

"You're coming with me. We'll leave tomorrow morning. We're flying Moses down there." Moses was the name he gave to the first C-46 he bought. The crew in Burbank outfitted it with passenger seats so the new Civil Aeronautics Administration Civil Aviation would buy the ruse that the plane was really being outfitted for commercial use by Jersey Airlines. He'd named the plane Moses because he'd freed the Jews from bondage in ancient Egypt, and Shatz believed our C-46's would do the same for modern day Jews in Palestine.

CHAPTER 11
March 14, 1948
Panama City, Panama

SHATZ AND I left New Jersey for Panama, a flight of close to nineteen hundred nautical miles. With our maximum range of seventeen hundred nautical miles, we couldn't fly straight through and stopped in Jamaica to refuel. We decided to stay overnight in order to arrive fresh the next day for our meeting. We left at 7:30 in the morning for Panama City, arriving three hours later at 10:30.

We taxied to our assigned parking spot. Three police cars pulled up alongside the plane before the engines were shut down. I secured the aircraft while Shatz popped open the door and lowered the steps. He went down first; I followed. My feet had just touched the tarmac when a military jeep, followed by a black Cadillac limousine, pulled up about fifteen feet from us. A police officer hopped out of his car, rushed to the back door of the limousine, opened it, and snapped to attention.

Seconds later, a man emerged. He was a few inches short of six feet tall. Maybe in his late fifties, slicked back grey hair, dark bushy eyebrows, broad nose, and a wide mouth, which broke into a huge smile as he approached us.

"Gentlemen," he said in heavily accented English, "welcome to Panama. I am Enrique Adolfo Jiménez, President of Panama. Welcome to my Country." Shatz and I introduced ourselves. Jiménez stepped closer, grabbing us each in turn by the elbow with one hand and shook our hand vigorously with the other."If you will give me the pleasure to accompany me in my car, we will drive to the Presidential Palace together."

Holy shit, I thought. The president came out to the airport himself to meet us. But, as I pondered this for a few seconds more, I thought, *Why the hell wouldn't he? He's getting $100,000 cash for a meet and greet, and he believes, a Panamanian National Airline to boot.*

With our police escort, it was a short twenty minute ride to the palace. The president played tour guide, pointing out the sights along the way. He said nothing as we passed the ramshackle slums with their tin roofed shanties outside the airport but became quite animated as we grew closer to the capital.

We arrived at the palace, which in reality was nothing more than a large three-story office building with an ornate entrance. In the lobby, there was a special elevator used only to reach the third floor. The sign next to the call button said, in Spanish and English, "Office of the President of Panama." The elevator doors opened at an anteroom where his three secretaries sat. It was at least forty foot by thirty foot with a fourteen-foot-high ceiling.

Two 10-foot solid mahogany doors opened into Jimenez's private office. To say his office was decorated to impress would be an understatement. It had to be at least one hundred feet long by sixty feet wide. An eight-foot-wide red carpet stretched from the entrance doors down the length of the room. It ended at a five-foot-deep by seven-foot-wide mahogany desk with walnut, burl, ebony, and cherry veneers, with intricately carved detailing in the mahogany. Matching credenzas lined both sides of the room. Paintings and tapestries hung on the walls; heavy maroon drapes framed the windows.

Shatz's plan would fuck Jimenez royally when it came to the airline. After seeing the slums, this office, and knowing he was getting a $100,000 bribe, I had no second thoughts or qualms about it.

Maybe Jiménez would even be overthrown as a result. Wouldn't that be sweet and well deserved?

The meeting with the president lasted twenty minutes. He had asked the attorney general to attend. A translator was also present as the attorney general did not speak English. When we were all seated, Jiménez asked Shatz, in English, about his niece in Miami. I was sure it was his way of letting us know he expected her to get the introduction fee. Shatz said she was fine, signaling he understood the message. Shatz then proceeded to lay out the proposal, speaking slower than normal, giving the attorney general a chance to keep up through the translator.

Since it was already a done deal, Jiménez asked a few perfunctory, non-consequential questions and turned to the attorney general. "Do you have any questions?" he asked in Spanish.

"Only one. Who will be drawing up the contracts to assign the planes to the Panamanian Government?" The translator related the question to Shatz.

"Our lawyers will begin the paperwork the minute we get home. We should have it completed in a few weeks. In the meantime, as a sign of good faith, if we can get the Panamanian registration paperwork done while we're here, I'll prepare the planes to fly down."

After the translation, the attorney general said, "*Muy bien.*"

Jiménez instructed the translator to go with us and help us get the registration numbers. We thanked him and departed. As we were leaving the building, the translator, whose name was Miguel, said President Jiménez was giving us a car to use while we were here.

Miguel drove us to a different building to get the registration numbers, and that's where we ran into a problem. He took us to the maritime office. The people there knew how to register ships. They knew how to register radios and other communication devices. But the people had no idea how to register airplanes for a national airline, because there had never been one.

Shatz and I had to put our heads together to try and figure this out. We had to get twelve legal, legitimate registrations before we left the country.

"Okay," I said. "First thing I think we need to do is come up with a name for the airline." I turned to Miguel. "Write down in Spanish how to say Panama National Airline."

He grabbed a piece of paper from the counter and wrote *Lineas Aereas de Panama Sociedad Anonima*. LAPSA.

"All right. Now we have a name." I turned to Manuel. "Get this to the head of this department. I want him to know we are here at the direction of President Jiménez. Tell him, if he wants to keep his job, he will get us twelve airplane registrations for LAPSA immediately. I don't care if he has to take the same paperwork he uses for ships and change the word ship to airplane in it. I'm not leaving this office until I have the twelve legal registrations. Tell him if I don't have them soon, I'll arrange for President Jiménez to make the request."

Miguel moved to a desk and told the clerk what I said. The clerk blanched, rose quickly from his desk, and led Miguel to an office at the back of the room. A minute later, the door opened and Miguel, followed by a man who I guessed was the boss, emerged.

The boss stood in front of Shatz and me, speaking rapidly in Spanish. Miguel jumped in. He must have told him we didn't speak Spanish because the boss began talking to Miguel. I didn't know what was said, but I heard Miguel say Jiménez twice, and each time the boss seemed to recoil. After a back and forth three minute conversation, the boss wheeled about and yelled at three clerks who followed him back to his office.

"They will be a while," Miguel said. "Come, we will have something to eat." He took us to a club called Tierra Feliz for lunch. In English, he said it means Happy Land. While it was also open for lunch, it was really a nightclub.

"Did he give you any idea how long it will be?" I asked Miguel.

"Maybe two hours. Maybe three.

We settled into a booth and let Miguel order for us. He suggested *sancocho*, a chicken stew and *ropa vieja*, made with shredded beef in a spicy tomato sauce served over rice. The food was delicious. We still had plenty of time after we ate, so Miguel suggested we try Panama's most famous drink, *Seco*, a sugar-cane-distilled alcohol served with milk and ice. This too was delicious, but the rum was very strong, so we nursed the drinks.

Two and a half hours later, we returned to the maritime office. The boss was perched on the corner of a desk, apparently waiting for our return. He had a brief conversation with Miguel as he handed him a thick envelope.

Turning to us and handing the envelope to Shatz, Miguel said, "He say you have twelve registrations for airplanes inside. They are documented with the Commerce Department and now, officially planes of *Lineas Aereas de Panama*. He also include official *Lineas Aereas de Panama* identification cards for each pilot. You only need enter the pilot's name and glue his pictures to card."

Miguel drove us back to the airport. As we were leaving the car to board our plane, he said, "Maybe you will have a job for me. I will come to work for you at the airline?"

My stomach dropped. I didn't give a crap about us screwing Jiménez, but Miguel was a nice guy. He had no way of knowing there wouldn't be a LAPSA for very long, that it was just a scam, a means to an end.

CHAPTER 12
March 20, 1948
Millville, New Jersey

CORDELL TIPTON LOOKED through the panes of window glass at the swirling snowflakes falling on the city. *They don't call it a city*, he thought, watching the flakes piling on the outside sill. Officially, they call it the District of Columbia. Everyone who works here says 'in this town,' not 'in this city' or 'in the District.' And sometime today, 'this town' is going to have seven inches of snow.

Later this afternoon or early evening, the plows will start clearing the roads. Already, most of the people at States had left work, and it was only 1:00 in the afternoon. Around town, most of the other civil servants were leaving or already left. But not me. No, not me.

Tipton was upset, thinking he'd have to stay and probably end up sleeping on the couch because the roads would be impassable, all to make sure everything ran smoothly in the Middle East for the fucking United States Government. All because those fucking Jews in Palestine want to muck up things for us with the Arabs. And now, it's not just the Jews in Palestine he might have a problem with, it was with Jews here in this country, too.

Tipton swiveled his high back leather chair away from looking out the window to face his desk. He picked up his phone and dialed the Egyptian Embassy.

When the phone was answered, he asked to speak to Ammon Hazem.

"Ammon Hazem," the man at the other end answered.

"No names. Do you know who this is?" Tipton said.

When the reply came back with a yes, Tipton said, "I hear there are people at the Millville, New Jersey airport, west of Atlantic City working on refurbishing some surplus war airplanes, supposedly to fly for a commercial airline in the United States. I wonder if they might be on a different mission, maybe a deadline to get them ready well before... say May 15. I certainly hope nothing like a fire in the hanger or damaged engines happens to ruin their plans. By the way, did you know that while we're having all this snow in Washington the weather forecast for Millville tonight is only for partly cloudy skies?"

Before Hazem could say anything, Tipton hung up.

NOAH MEIR KNEW the F.B.I. was watching Haganah headquarters in New York City. Ever the master spy, he also kept watch... on the enemies of the Jews in Palestine. That included the Egyptians and particularly the Egyptian Embassy in Washington, D.C., which his intelligence people reported was providing office space to the Muslim Brotherhood.

Gadi Dubinski was one of the Haganah agents stationed in Washington, D.C. His sole responsibility was to keep tabs on the Muslim Brotherhood's leader, Ammon Hazem. Every day he would follow Hazem from his apartment in Alexandria, Virginia, to the embassy, follow him wherever he went if he left the embassy, and follow him back to his apartment at night. At that point, another agent would take over surveillance until the next morning when he was relieved by Dubinski, who would start the process over again. It was Dubinski who told Meir of Hazem's trip to the State Department.

Each morning, Dubinski would park his car in a lot diagonally across from the State Department. The location gave him a clear view of the building's front entrance as well as the entrance ramp to the parking garage beneath. The owner of the lot was Jewish. He let Dubinski stay in his car for as long as he wished and to enter or leave the lot anytime as needed.

Today, the snow was falling at a rapid rate. Dubinski turned the engine on for ten minutes to heat the car and run the wipers to clear the snow before shutting it down to save fuel. He always carried three jerry cans of gasoline in the trunk so he didn't have to break off surveillance to stop at a gas station.

Where the hell is he? Everyone's getting out of town early. Why isn't he?

At 4:30 Dubinski saw Hazem's car pull out of the underground garage. He wasn't alone. There was one man in the passenger seat and one in the back. Dubinski pulled out of the lot and followed the car down 21st Street to Constitution Avenue.

Instead of making a right turn onto Constitution and crossing the Arlington Memorial Bridge to Alexandria, Virginia, Hazem made a left onto Constitution. *Shit. He's not headed home. Where's he going in this fucking storm?*

Dubinski followed the car through the driving snow as it made a left onto 17th Street before making a right onto Rhode Island Avenue, which is also U.S. Highway 1. After passing Brentwood, he knew Hazem was heading out of town. Staying as far behind as he dared without losing sight of the car, Dubinski cautiously tailed them.

FOUR INCHES OF snow had already fallen when Hazem and his two companions left Washington to drive to New Jersey. He hadn't seen any evidence that plows had even begun to clear the roads, and coming from Cairo, a place that never had snow, he found the driving treacherous. He gripped the steering wheel tightly, his knuckles white. Strong winds buffeted the car, and snow packed streets caused the car to slip and slide. Three times in the last half hour he'd almost run off the road and twice nearly missed sliding into cars he tried to pass.

Driving north on Route 1, when Hazem reached College Park, Maryland, the snow and winds grew less intense, and by the time he reached the outskirts of Baltimore, the snow was down to flurries, and the winds had died down considerably. He left Route 1 north of Baltimore, switching to U.S. Highway 40. At New Castle, Delaware, and took the fifteen minute ferry ride to Pennsville, New Jersey, and continued on U.S. Highway 40 before heading south to Millville. Consulting the map he'd used at the embassy to locate the airfield, Hazem and his two companions arrived at the target mile marker at the side of the road, a half mile from the Millville Airport at 11:12 at night.

It was bitterly cold outside, evidenced by the thick clouds of exhaust from the tailpipe billowing past the passenger window. The men donned dark watch caps and fur lined gloves. Before leaving the embassy, they attired themselves with thick soled leather boots, woolen socks, winter pants, and long sleeve plaid shirts. They slipped on heavy winter parkas, which they had taken off while driving, and pulled the watch caps down over their ears.

Leaving the car, Hazem saw the vapor formed by their breath when they exhaled. Moving to the trunk, his men removed two jerry cans filled with gasoline. Hazem grabbed a small canvas bag. Inside were six bombs made of four sticks of dynamite taped together with a timer attached to the detonator cap.

Taking a flashlight from the trunk, Hazem illuminated a compass to get his bearings. Turning to get a heading, he pointed at a spot in the woods and began to walk. The other two followed close behind.

W<small>HEN</small> H<small>AZEM</small> <small>HAD</small> stopped at a diner in Rosedale, north of Baltimore, Dubinski pulled to a dark secluded spot at the rear of the parking lot. He grabbed two jerry cans from the trunk, emptying one and using most of the second to top off his gas tank. After replacing the cans in the trunk, he relieved himself beside the car and got back in to keep watch. He still had some leftover coffee in a thermos and an apple. The coffee was cold but he drank it anyway. He was munching on the apple when Hazem and the two men walked out of the diner and resumed their trip.

When they took the road to New Castle, Delaware, Dubinski was puzzled. This wasn't the way to New York City, which is where he thought they were headed. When they pulled up to the ferry dock in New Castle for Pennsville, New Jersey, he figured it out.

They're going to Millville. The planes.

He had ten minutes before the ferry was due to leave. From a phone booth near the ticket office, he called Noah Meir and told him where he was and where he was pretty sure Hazem was headed. Meir said he would call Millville and alert Shapiro and that he should keep following them but at a safe distance. Dubinski was the eleventh car to board the ferry, seven behind Hazem. On the New Jersey side, he followed them on U.S. Highway 40 before they turned off, heading south.

D<small>URING</small> <small>THE</small> <small>WAR</small>, the Millville Army Airbase had been used for fighter pilot gunnery training with over fifteen hundred pilots passing through the base in three years. All pilots were of officer rank and a two-story, sixty-room officers housing unit had been built for the four weeks of each training class. After the war the base was decommissioned, and the housing complex was sold to a real estate developer who turned it into a motel. Kaplan, who'd arrived in Millville the day before from Panama, and the other pilots and mechanics, were housed at the motel.

I was sound asleep when the telephone woke me at 10:00. It was Meir.

"You better get down to the hanger with some men. One of my agents just called and said he thinks three guys from the Muslim Brotherhood are headed your way. If they are, you can bet it isn't a social call."

"Got it," I said.

In less than five minutes, four pilots were assembled around me. We bounded down the stairs to the parking lot, piling into Baron's car. Ten minutes later we were at the hanger.

After we arrived, Shapiro and another pilot pulled the only weapons we had from a locker. Two handguns and a box of ammunition. The weapons had been bought by one of the mechanics two weeks before as a precaution and stored away.

HAZEM AND HIS men trudged through the frozen, shin-deep snow covered woods. More than once, each had stumbled when a foot landed on a fallen branch hidden beneath the crust-covered, white blanket. The bitter cold made what should have been a ten minute trip turn into a half hour odyssey before they arrived at the edge of the woods and the open expanse of the airfield.

When the three-quarter moon broke through the clouds, Hazem spotted a cluster of C-46's and a Constellation sitting in the open around a hanger. What he had not taken into account was the hanger would be six football fields away from where he stood. There was no cover of any kind. They would have to traverse the distance in the open. The large hanger doors were closed, but a light was shining through the window in the small entrance door, a car parked a few feet away. *Probably a night watchman sitting inside, staying warm.*

He turned his eyes to the sky. A large mass of clouds was slowly moving toward the now visible moon. "When those clouds block out the moon," he whispered, pointing skyward, "we're going to make a dash in the dark to the planes. Mostafa, you take the jerry cans, and head to the side of the hanger. Wait ten minutes, splash the gasoline on the walls, set it off, and run like hell back here."

Reaching into the canvas sack, he removed three bombs. "Here," he said, handing them to Gayar. "I'll take the Constellation first. Get them planted in the cockpit, and get out fast. If you have trouble getting inside a plane, put it on a wing near an engine. Set the timer for twenty minutes. When you're done, meet back here. If anyone one is around, they'll be too busy fighting the fire to check out the planes."

The three men stood watching the sky. When the first cloud passed in front of the moon, turning the night dark, they raced across the airfield to the planes and hanger.

"Ain't anyone coming out here to try something tonight," Bruce Baron said, sitting in the hanger, basking in the warmth of a space heater after just finishing a circuit around the hanger and the planes. "They'd have to have the IQ of a tree stump in Georgia. It's colder than a witch's tit out there."

"I hope you're right," I said, "but when Meir called me, he was pretty certain about it."

"Well, maybe whoever he thought was coming realized they'd freeze their balls off, got smart, and are gone home to sleep in a nice warm bed," Baron said, smiling. "If'n I had my druthers, that's where we should be." Everyone laughed.

A few minutes passed in silence when Baron began wrinkling his nose. *Sniff. Sniff.* "Y'all smell that?"

"What?" I asked.

Sniff. Sniff. "That. Y'all don't smell it? It smells like gasoline."

Sniff, Sniff. "Yeah, I think I smell something, too," one of the other pilots said.

"Me too," said another.

The five of us prowled the hanger, sniffing as we went, trying to pinpoint the location of the smell.

"Guys," I said, standing next to the hanger wall. "Over here. Smells like it's coming from here."

Baron moved next to me. *Sniff. Sniff.* "That all is gasoline, and it's coming from outside."

"Shit," I yelled, rushing to the entrance door. "They're trying to burn down the hanger."

I burst through the door with two of the pilots on my heels, racing to the side of the hanger. As I rounded the corner, I saw a man holding a large can, walking sideways in the opposite direction, splashing its contents on the wall. *Son of a bitch.* Sprinting, I closed the distance between us. The man with the can must have heard me because he stopped splashing the gasoline and began to turn.

I propelled myself at the man, becoming airborne for a milli-second. At that same time, the man defensively threw his arms out to ward off the attack. The can of gasoline hit me on the side of my head, knocking me down. The man raced by me, yelling out something in a foreign language. As I lie dazed on the cold ground, one of the other pilots yelled, "They're going after the planes."

I struggled to my feet, holding on to the side of the hanger for support. On wobbly legs, I made my way to the front of the hanger, able to see three men running into the woods. I caught a fleeting glimpse of the face of one of them."Y'all better check out the planes," Baron yelled to the others.

Ten minutes later, we gathered around the space heater inside the hanger. Lying on the floor were four disarmed bombs we took from the cockpits; the timer wires removed from the detonating caps.

"How's your head?" Baron asked me.

"I'll probably have a headache for a few days, but I'll be fine."

"Who the hell were those guys, and why did they try to blow up the panes and burn down the hanger?" Baron asked.

"Don't know, but the guy with the gas can yelled out to his pals in something that sure as hell wasn't English. And what the hell?" I said, pointing to Baron's waist. "You've got one of the pistols tucked in your belt. Why didn't you shoot at them?"

"They were running faster than a 'possum being chased by a pack of hunting dogs. I wouldn't get close enough to shoot at them. But that wasn't the big reason."

Baron shook his head, pulled the pistol from his waistband and a box of bullets from his jacket pocket. "The main reason I didn't shoot at them," he said, "is this." He held the pistol in his left hand. "This is a .38 caliber pistol, and these," he said, holding up the box of bullets in his other hand, "are .45 caliber rounds. The damn bullets don't fit."

CHAPTER 13
March 23
Tulsa, Oklahoma

WHEN SHATZ HEARD about the attack in Millville, he immediately set up security measures, with around the clock guards at the facility in New Jersey. He contacted Pinter in California who did the same.

When I entered the hanger at 9:30 that morning, three days after the attack, I found Shatz walking in circles around his desk, rubbing his chin between his thumb and forefinger, deep in thought. I didn't want to disturb him when he was in one of his thoughtful moods, so I grabbed a chair and sat, waiting for him to acknowledge my presence.

After sitting in silence for five minutes, I said, "Shatz, is everything all right?"

He stopped walking and turned to me. "When did you get here?"

"About five minutes ago. You were so deep in thought I didn't want to disturb you. What's got you so pensive? Have we had any security issues out in California?"

He walked to his desk chair and plopped down. "Nah. This is a different thing. Back in January, I bought a surplus B-17. It's at Tinker

Air Force Base, outside Oklahoma City. I called there this morning to make arrangements to pick it up at the end of the week. Even though they took my money, they said they're denying me access to it. They said a man named Tipton from the State Department called and told them I was going to use the plane to break the Mid-East arms embargo and requested they deny me access to it."

Shatz got out of his seat and sat on the edge of his desk in front of my chair. "When you came in, I was thinking how to get my hands on it. I spoke with Meir about it yesterday. He said he knew a mechanic who worked on the base and would help if the money was right. I was thinking about how I could use him."

"Come up with anything?"

"Not until I just saw you. Now I do. You and I are going to steal it."

Shatz and I flew commercial, landing in Oklahoma City at 5:27 in the afternoon. After picking up the one suitcase packed with both our belongings, he slid into a phone booth and made a call. Tinker Air Force Base and Shatz's B-17 were located thirty miles east of the airport.

Leaving the car rental lot, I decided we better grab something to eat. Who knew when we'd get another chance, and it was going to be a long night. I stopped at a diner a mile outside the airport where we both ordered cheeseburgers, french fries, and cokes.

"Who did you call before?" I asked, before popping a fry in my mouth.

"Meir's contact. He's going to meet us at the plane tonight at nine to get his payment."

"How much?"

"Five hundred bucks."

"That's a lot of moola. What's he doing for it?"

"He's towed the plane to the end of a runway that's not used much anymore and had the fuel tanks filled. We're giving him the keys to the rental. He'll return it to the airport for us."

"Okay, he's earning his pay."

It was dark when we left the restaurant at 7:30, the three-quarter moon peeking in and out of clouds. Following our contact's instructions, we drove to an access road near the base, reaching it at 8:45. Knowing the base was an active facility, we'd packed our Army Air Corp leather flight jackets with captain's bars on the epaulets to blend in. We discussed what we would say when challenged at the gate for ID's but had no idea if it would work. We didn't have a plan B.

"You drive," I said to Shatz as I slid into the passenger side. "You've got the kind of face people seem to trust."

We drove down the access road, swung onto the main boulevard leading to the front gate, and stopped at the guard booth. Shatz rolled down his window. Before he had a chance to begin the spiel he'd concocted about losing his ID, the guard spoke first. "You here for Major Jeffries surprise party, sir?"

"Yup," Shatz said, not missing a beat.

"Don't know if you heard the location changed. More people than expected are coming, so they moved it from the officer's mess to hanger seven. Go straight down this road to the third stop sign and make a left. You'll see the cars parked outside. You can't miss it."

"Thank you, airman," Shatz said as he rolled up his window and put the car in gear.

"This will work out great as long as the guard doesn't watch out taillights. Our contact told me to go to the fourth stop sign and make a right until I come to the end of the road. If he sees me going right, instead of left, we're in trouble."

Before reaching the fourth stop sign, Shatz slowed down until we were traveling at fifteen miles an hour. When we reached the stop sign, he turned off the headlights, which turned off the taillights. At that speed, as he made the turn, he didn't need to step on the brake, so, if the guard was looking up the dark road, he wouldn't see brake lights turning right in the distance. Twenty feet onto the new road, the moon broke through the clouds, and we could make out the silhouette of the B-17 ahead of us.

We pulled up next to the open hatch door located low on the fuselage, just in front of the left wing. Our contact, Shatz only knew him by the name Joel, was leaning against the landing gear, the ladder hanging from the open hatch partially obscuring him. Shatz walked over, handed him his five hundred dollars in an envelope and the keys to the car.

"You're gassed and ready to go," Joel said.

"Thanks," Shatz replied. "Keep the car's lights off when you pull it away."

I led the way up the ladder into the belly of the plane. Once Shatz got in, pulled up the ladder, swung the door up, and locked it, we pulled out flashlights. From this point on, we couldn't risk exposure, and we'd need to do everything that had to be done to get the plane ready to fly using only flashlights.

When Shatz first spoke to Joel, he told him I had flown C-46's but never a B-17. Joel said he'd leave me instructions. Shatz made his way to the copilot's seat and me to the pilot's. There was an envelope laying on it. Settling myself, I held my flashlight well below window level so it couldn't be seen from outside and removed a sheet of paper. It was a diagram showing the location of the basic controls needed to fly the plane, with a notation next to it labeling what it was. That was it, as barebones as you could get.

I spent five minutes familiarizing myself with each control depicted on the diagram and its location. "Here," I said to Shatz, handing him the diagram. "When I tell you, I want you to randomly call out each instrument on this. I'm going to close my eyes and see if I can find them."

"Throttle. Flaps control. Flaps lock. Ignition switch. Landing gear switch," Shatz called out, peppering me, as he ran down the list of controls. The first time I had more hits than misses, but that wasn't good enough. I took the diagram back, studied it before handing it back to Shatz to begin the eyes closed test again. It took me four more tries and twenty minutes until I was confident I had them down pat.

"Okay," I said. "Ready to get this baby off the ground?"

Shatz snickered. "More important, are you?"

"Let's do it."

We donned headsets we assumed were linked to the control tower. I had Shatz use the manual control to prime the engines. Turning the ignition switch for the number one engine, I heard the starter whine just before the motor caught and the propeller began to turn. An initial puff of thick white smoke blew from the sides of the engine before disappearing into the dark night and the engine settled into a smooth idle. I repeated the process for the other three engines.

"Before we turn on any lights, we're going to use the flashlights to do the pre-flight and engine checks here," I said. "Once we start toward the taxiway and runway, I have to turn on the headlights, and someone in the control tower is going to see us." We did the checks. I didn't understand what all the gauges measured, but as best I could tell, nothing looked wrong.

I looked at my watch. It was 9:22. "Okay, let's do this."

I pre-set the flaps then eased the throttle forward. Waiting until the last possible second, I turned on the lights and found the taxiway. I'd seen a sock flying from a pole as we approached the plane, so I knew the wind direction. I didn't know the speed, so I'd have to wing that. When we got on the taxiway, I headed toward the end of the runway that would have us taking off into the wind. It was then that we heard the voice from the control tower over the headsets.

"Aircraft on taxiway. Please identify yourself."

We ignored the request.

"Aircraft on taxiway. Please identify yourself."

Again, we ignored the request and reached the end of the runway. As I turned the plane onto the runway, we heard the frantic voice from the control tower. "Unidentified aircraft, you are not clear for takeoff. Hold at current position."

Ignoring the command, I pressed hard on the brake pedal, and with a firm hand, pushed the throttles forward. The engines roared. When they reached full throttle, I released the brake, and the B-17 lurched forward. Using my feet to control the rudder pedals, I kept the plane centered on the white stripe down the middle of the runway. Ground speed increased as the mighty engines roared, propelling the rumbling aircraft faster and faster. Three quarters of the way down the runway, I gently eased back on the yoke, and we lifted into the air. Retracting the landing gear, we climbed into the deep dark sky.

Shatz knew once we took the plane, the authorities would suspect he had something to do with it. He figured we had some time, maybe ten hours, before they'd put it all together. He couldn't bring the plane to Millville. That would be the first place they'd look, so the day we left for Oklahoma, he arranged for us to land at a private airport outside of Trenton, New Jersey. We had a forty-five mile an hour tailwind and arrived in Trenton a little past 2:00 in the morning. Skippy Shapiro met us and drove us back to headquarters in Millville.

Shatz and I were sleeping on cots, exhausted from the long day and flight back to New Jersey, when two F.B.I. agents woke us up, barging into the hanger, yelling, "We're here for Paul Shatz."

"I'm Paul Shatz," he said, in a thick voice. I swung off my cot. We both stood, Shatz and I dressed in skivvies and sleeveless undershirts. "What's this about?"

"Where's the plane you stole?" one of the agents shouted.

Shatz figured it would take them about ten hours to conclude he'd been responsible for stealing the plane. I looked at the clock on the wall. It was 8:30. I grinned. It took them an hour and a half longer.

"First of all, stop shouting," Shatz said in a soft, calm voice. "You just woke me out of a sound sleep. Second of all, I have no idea what plane you're talking about."

"The one you stole from Oklahoma last night."

"Again, I have no idea what you're talking about."

"The B-17 you stole from Tinker Air Force Base last night."

"I still don't know what you're talking about." Shatz shook his head, leaned down and peered under his cot. "If you're missing a B-17, they're kind of hard to hide. It's not under my cot. Did you see one outside?"

"The answer's no, and stop being a smartass."

"Then I guess I didn't take it. Now, will you please get the hell out of here, and let me see if I can go back to sleep."

The agent glowered at Shatz and let out a loud huff before turning and leaving the hanger.

Shatz twisted to me. "We're not going to fool them for very long. We've got to get that plane out of the country, and fast. Think you and Shapiro can fly it to Czechoslovakia?"

"I'm game if he is."

CHAPTER 14
March 24
Halifax, Nova Scotia
The Azores
New York City

THE F.B.I. WATCHED us at the airfield, the hanger, and sometimes at the motel. I figured we'd have a better chance of making a break for the airport in Trenton after work. After we finished the day at the hanger, the entire team of pilots and mechanics went to dinner, then to the movie theater downtown Millville to see *The Treasure of the Sierra Madre*, starring Humphrey Bogart. It was a great movie, but I only got to see half of it before Skippy, one of the mechanics, and I slipped out a back exit door and drove to Trenton.

During the afternoon, Shatz sent one of the mechanics up to Trenton to pay the ground crew to fill up the plane, including the auxiliary tanks. When they finished fueling, the mechanic stowed two navigation charts in the cockpit. One was for the great circle route to the Azores and on to Czechoslovakia. The second was the great circle route to the Azores and on to the Mediterranean area, in case the need came for us to divert to Palestine. He also stashed food for the long flight, tools, ammunition, and bomb shackles on the floor above the bomb bay doors.

Two of our mechanics had worked on B-17's during the war and drew me a diagram of the gauges in the cockpit with notations on what they measured. I'd paid no attention to them when we took off from Tinker Air Force Base the night before. Our contact, Joel, didn't explain them, and I didn't have the time to figure them out. The mechanics also looked over the diagram Joel had left me depicting the basic controls needed to fly the plane. They added a few additional controls and explained their functions. When I moved to sit in the pilot's seat, the diagrams were laying there.

Shapiro took the copilot's seat. I handed him the diagrams the mechanics made. "Better go over these." I settled down to go over the navigation chart to the Azores and on to Czechoslovakia, setting aside the one for the Mediterranean area. Thirty minutes later, I taxied to the runway, and we lifted off into the nighttime sky at 10:35. The weather was great for flying, partly cloudy skies with a light wind out of the west.

We flew north of New York City, bisecting Long Island Sound, passing between Martha's Vineyard and Nantucket Islands before heading out into the Atlantic to the Azores, still some twenty-four hundred miles away. We started to pick up some light rain over Nantucket, and the winds increased and shifted, now coming at us from the northeast. When we were two hundred miles out from Nantucket, the rain turned to sleet, and the winds grew strong enough to begin buffeting the plane. I was trying to keep the plane steady, holding the yoke firmly with both hands

"In case we need it, where is the closest landfall?" I asked Shapiro.

He picked up the navigation chart, studied it for a half a minute. "Looks like Halifax, Nova Scotia. Why?"

"I don't know what the weather is like ahead of us, but this doesn't look good. Except for last night and now, I have no experience flying this thing. On top of that, the navigation equipment isn't in the best of conditions. Wouldn't be a problem in good weather, but this...." I said, shaking my head. "I'm giving it another fifteen minutes. If it doesn't get better by then, or gets worse before that, we're heading to Halifax."

It didn't take me more than eight minutes to make my decision. The winds were bouncing us around more violently than bumper cars at an amusement park. The sleet had turned to quarter sized hailstones and hitting the windshield hard, with the staccato of a fifty caliber machine gun. I turned and headed to Halifax. When I got close enough, I sent out a radio call declaring an emergency. It was answered by the Royal Canadian Air Force which routed me to their base on the outskirts of Halifax.

When I landed, the tower directed me to park in an area more than six football fields in length away from any other structure. "Why do you think they're making us park out here?" Shapiro asked.

"I don't know, but I don't like it. When they ask, we don't give them our real names," I cautioned.

We were boarded by Royal Canadian Air Force Police. Shapiro and I gave them false names. They told us there were sending the information to the capital in Ottawa, who would pass it on to the U.S. Government. We were told we had to stay on the plane until they heard back from Ottawa.

Two hours later, a Canadian air commodore boarded. He told us that a Mr. Tipton of the U.S. State Department informed Ottawa he suspected we were trying to bring the plane to Palestine, breaking the Mid-East embargo. The air commodore said this had now become a problem for the Canadian government because they were also enforcing the embargo.

I denied the U.S. government claim, but it didn't do me much good when forty-five minutes later Canadian Customs and the U.S. Consulate boarded and did a thorough inspection of the aircraft. When they discovered the navigation chart of the Mediterranean area, enough food for a long flight, as well as the tools, ammunition, and bomb shackles, I knew we were up the creek.

The customs and consulate people left the plane. A half hour later, the Canadian air commodore boarded again. "Our American friends gave us your real names, Mr. Kaplan and Mr. Shapiro, and that you left from someplace in New Jersey. Our Government has made a decision. We're going to release you and the plane later this afternoon on one condition. You must return to New Jersey. To ensure that you do so, we're going to reduce the fuel in your tanks, leaving you with just enough to get you there. Oh, one more thing. Your State Department has arranged for your F.B.I. to send a plane here to escort back."

WHILE WE WERE on the ground, the Canadian Air Force provided me with the weather for the flight back to New Jersey. The only sign left of the storm that forced us to land in Halifax was a layer of heavy clouds covering the skies from Halifax down through Southern New England. That gave me an idea, and I managed to delay the trip back till nightfall.

At 8:00 in the evening, we took off, the F.B.I. escort plane following one minute behind. I was at heart a fighter pilot and had used the dark night sky and heavy cloud cover in combat to elude enemy aircraft. I did the same now. Heading into a thick cloud formation, I nosed the B-17 down, plummeting toward the ocean before pulling up into another thick bank of clouds. As planned, the maneuver lost the F.B.I. escort.

What the Canadians were not aware of is that I was carrying fuel in my auxiliary tanks, and I decided to make a try for the Azores anyway. But it wasn't to be. In the air somewhere over the Atlantic between Nova Scotia and Massachusetts, one engine cowling flew completely off the plane and plunged into the ocean. Fifteen minutes later, two others tore loose. I had no choice but to head back to New Jersey.

I landed at the Trenton Airport, called Shatz and filled him on what happened. He and three mechanics snuck away from the Millville operation and drove up to Trenton. It took the mechanics working most of the night and through the next day, but they got the two loose cowlings repaired. We didn't have a replacement cowling cover for the number four engine.

That night, Shapiro and I tried it again. I took off, headed east, and flew low to avoid radar. We were seven hundred miles out over the Atlantic when Shapiro tapped me on the shoulder and pointed to one of the gauges, then showed it to me on the drawing the mechanics gave us. It was the temperature gauge for the number four engine. Without a cowling cover, it was heating up into the danger zone. If I didn't want a fire, I'd have to shut it down immediately.

I turned to Shapiro. "Decision time. We've got almost seventeen hundred miles to go with three engines. I've never flown this plane before, so I can't guarantee you we'll make it. We can push on, or I can head back to New Jersey. What do you want to do?"

"What do you want to do?" he answered back.

"I don't want to die, and I'm no hero, but I'm willing to give it a try."

"Let's do it then," he said.

We continued in silence. As the hours passed, I watched the fuel gauge indicator drop lower, and I couldn't be sure our navigation was working that well. I began to worry more and more that I'd made the wrong choice. I didn't tell Shapiro that. I didn't need to. Every time I glanced over at him, I could see the worry lines etched on his face growing deeper and deeper. Finally, I breathed a sigh of relief when, in the early hours of the morning, I spotted land. Thirty minutes later, I touched down at the Santa Maria airport in the Azores.

WE LEFT THE plane at the airport to be refueled for our flight to Czechoslovakia and took a taxi into the small town of Vila do Porto. We were bone weary when we woke the proprietor to check into the only hotel on the small island at 5:30 in the morning. He was grumpy, but his mood changed quickly when we paid in advance with American dollars. I gave him an extra three dollars to be assured he'd get us up at 1:00 in the afternoon.

I was dead to the world when I was awakened by heavy pounding on the door and someone shouting in Portuguese. I looked at my watch. It was one o'clock. *Our wakeup.* I groaned, cursed, and shouted back, "Okay. We're up, we're up." I was sure whoever was pounding on the door didn't speak English, but got the message from the tone of my voice. The pounding and shouting stopped. We forced ourselves out of bed, showered, shaved, and got down to the dining room in a half an hour.

We each had a bowl of a traditional Portuguese soup, *caldo verde,* and for dessert, *arroz doce,* rice pudding sprinkled with cinnamon. Over dessert, Shapiro said, "Mike, don't let your head get swelled, but I've got to tell you, you are one hell of a pilot. You might never have flown a B-17 before, but getting us here, on only three engines, was nothing short of fantastic flying."

I don't handle compliments well so all I said back was, "Thanks," and scooped another spoonful of *arroz doce* into my mouth. When we finished the dessert, the kitchen gave us a selection of fresh cheeses wrapped in a cloth napkin to take on the plane. We were both rested, feeling great, and looking forward to getting to Czechoslovakia

Our jubilation was short-lived.

When our taxi pulled up to the B-17, it was surrounded by two black sedans and three police cars. "Oh, shit," I said to Shapiro.

A man about thirty years old, dressed in a brown suit, stepped out of one of the sedans and walked toward the taxi. I paid the driver, and we slid out.

"I presume you are Mr. Kaplan and Mr. Shapiro?"

"Who's asking?" I answered, trying to keep my voice calm and matter-of-fact.

"My name is Barry Ingram, and I am the United States Consul in the Azores. When you disappeared on your escorted flight from Canada, Cordell Tipton of the State Department sent out a teletype to all embassies in Europe and the Mid-East to be on the lookout for you two and a B-17 bomber. Imagine my surprise when the airport notified me of your arrival early this morning."

"So what? I haven't broken any laws flying here."

"Well, Mr. Tipton believes you're headed to Palestine with this plane and that is in violation of the arms embargo."

"Mr. Tipton can think anything he wants. As far as I know, the Azores is Europe, not the Middle East," I said, smugly. "Therefore, no embargo has been broken, and I haven't broken any law."

"Ahh, but you have, Mr. Kaplan," Ingram retorted. "You stole this plane off of a United States Air Force base."

"But the plane is ours. We paid for it."

"That's for the courts to decide. Right now, this plane is now the confiscated property of the United States State Department, and you two are under arrest for stealing it. There's a flight back to New York in two hours. You two will be on it, or you will be in jail awaiting extradition. The choice is yours."

"Can I have a minute to discuss it with my friend?"

"Of course."

I pulled Shapiro to the side. "What do you want to do?" I asked. "We can get on the plane or see if we can make some kind of bail and try to steal our plane back."

"Are you nuts?" he replied. "They'll have this guarded tighter than Fort Knox. Let's cut our losses and take the commercial flight home."

I walked over to Ingram. "Okay, we'll get on the flight to New York."

"Smart choice," he said. "Oh, one more thing. The tickets are $237 each, and you're going to have to pay for them yourselves."

WE EACH HAD over $500 dollars which was going to be used to pay for the fuel, bribes, or other incidentals, so we had the money to pay for the tickets. We were greeted at the airport in New York by F.B.I. agents who took us to the federal courthouse in Lower Manhattan. I put a call into Noah Meir and told him our situation. He said he would have a lawyer down to the courthouse in fifteen minutes.

The F.B.I. put us through the booking process, and thirty minutes after, we were brought to appear before a federal judge. A man named Barry Sanders was waiting in the courtroom and introduced himself as a lawyer, sent by Meir. A few minutes later, the judge entered. The federal prosecutor read the charge against us, "The illegal export of an airplane."

Sanders asked for a sidebar with the prosecutor and the judge. The conversation was animated. From where I sat, the prosecutor kept jabbing his finger at Sanders and shaking his head no. The sidebar lasted about four minutes.

The prosecutor stomped back to his table while Sanders walked slowly to ours, a small grin creasing his mouth. As he got closer, he discreetly placed his forefinger across his lips, signaling us to keep quiet.

"Your honor," Sanders said, "the ownership of the plane is not in question. The United States government acknowledges it sold the plane to a Mr. Shatz, an acquaintance of the defendants. At the request of the State Department, the Air Force prevented Mr. Shatz from taking possession of his plane. The defendants assert they were flying the plane to Czechoslovakia, which is not in the Mid-East and not in violation of any arms embargo. The charge of the illegal export of an airplane is absurd."

"But your honor," the prosecutor said, "they stole the plane from an Air Force base."

"Mr. Kaplan, Mr. Shapiro," the judge said, "since the United States government acknowledges it sold the plane to Mr. Shatz, and the State Department prevented him taking possession of it, we can hold a trial to sort out ownership, possession, and if taking the plane constitutes a theft."

The judge leaned forward, placed his arms on the bench, and gazed at me, a half smile across his mouth. "Mr. Kaplan, I read the file on your recent adventure in Canada. You and I know that at some point that B-17 was going to end up in Palestine. So here's what I'm prepared to do. You did have ammunition and bomb shackles on the plane. Plead guilty to the charge of the trying to break the arms embargo. I'll fine you $100 and impose a one-year suspended sentence. We can end this matter right now and all go home."

Skippy and I looked at Sanders for guidance. He smiled and nodded.

"Your honor, I plead guilty to the charge," I said, with a firm voice. Shapiro did the same.

Ten minutes later, after Sanders paid our fines, compliments of Meir, Shapiro and I walked down the long marble steps outside the courthouse. Shatz told me when I first signed on to his harebrained scheme there was a chance I could be fined, imprisoned, and maybe lose my citizenship. Well, I'd been fined but I was not in prison, and I still had my citizenship. Only one out of three. That was just spiffy with me.

CHAPTER 15
April 12
New Jersey
Panama

"IT'S TOO DANGEROUS. I'm not sure you'll even be able to get the planes off the ground," the mechanic said to Shatz. "They're overloaded way beyond the manufacturer's specifications."

"I understand. If it makes you feel any better, I got a call from California this afternoon. Pinter said the same thing."

It was 8:30 at night. We were meeting in the hanger with the pilots and the mechanics. Shatz was perched on the edge of his desk, his feet dangling inches off the floor. I was sitting in a nearby folding chair.

"But we don't have a choice. We're going to have to ignore the specs," Shatz said."We need to cram every spare part we can in the planes. Once we leave, there won't be any place to get more."

"But —" one of the pilots said.

"No buts. We've been pretty lucky so far. We've dodged some serious shit. Think of the damage that attack on the planes and hanger four weeks ago would have done. Then, look what happened the next week to our intrepid hero, Mike," he said, pointing to me.

All heads turned. Some smiled at me, some snickered, and some laughed.

"It's funny now, but he got himself arrested and fined. Luckily, he stayed out of jail this time, but what if he hadn't? That could have been just the excuse this guy Tipton at the State Department would grab to shut us down completely. I don't know why, but this guy Tipton seems to have it in for us, and he's going to try to hurt us any way he can. We all know how he went after Kaplan and the plane in Canada and the Azores."

The room grew quiet.

"And now we've got a major problem coming up. In three days, the State Department's rule on requiring their approval for exporting aircraft and parts anywhere in the world goes into effect. I'm willing to bet Tipton will try to use that to stop us from leaving the country."

Shatz's eyes roamed the faces of the men in the room. "Look, I know you're not happy with the weight situation. Neither am I. But the calendar isn't our friend. That's why I had the planes fueled this morning and lined up in front of the hanger. My gut tells me we need to be ready to get out of here at a moment's notice."

At 11:00 the next morning, Shatz and I were in the hanger when Baron burst through the entrance door. "Y'all better come quick," he hollered from across the hanger.

"What's going on," I yelled back, rushing with Shatz to the door.

"There's ah T-man outside. He's sayin' he's here to confiscate the planes."

We charged outside, followed by the rest of the pilots. Four strangers are standing next to the first plane in line, one arguing with a mechanic. Shatz and I hustled over.

"What's going on?" Shatz asks the man engaged with the mechanic.

"I'm impounding these planes," the man replied.

"Who the hell are you?"

"Paul Walker," he said, pulling an identification wallet from his jacket and flashing it toward Shatz. "I'm with the Treasury Department. These other men are from the Civil Aviation Administration."

"Under what authority are you impounding them?"

"Treasury received a call from the State Department requesting us to impound them. They said these planes won't meet the weight restrictions under the arms embargo, and they believe it's your intention to fly them to the Mid-East."

"You can't impound them. The weight restriction rule doesn't go into effect for another two days. And besides, how can they know what our intentions are? Are they fortune tellers?"

"Listen, I don't know anything about any rule in two days. When the State Department asks Treasury to impound them today, we impound them today."

"It doesn't make any difference what the State Department said," Shatz replied."These planes are registered to LAPSA. That's short for *Leanas Aereas de Panama Sociedad Anonima*, the Panamanian Government National Airline. Do you get it? They belong to the government of Panama. The State Department has no jurisdiction over them, unless of course, they want to start an international incident."

"I don't believe you. Where's the airline's name? I don't see LAPSA or that other name anywhere."

"Wait right here," Shatz said, wheeling around and marching back to the hanger. Three minutes later, he emerged with a folder in his hand, followed closely by one of our mechanics carrying a ladder. The mechanic laid the ladder on the ground next to the lead plane and hustled back into the hanger.

Shatz put his hand on Walker's shoulder, and maneuvered him toward the nose of the plane, until they were standing near the front landing wheel. The rest of the pilots formed a small circle around them, I stood off to the side.

Shatz pulled a sheet of paper from the folder. "Here's the Panamanian registration for this plane." Waving the folder at Walker, he said, "And the registration certificates for the rest of them are in here."

"This doesn't mean anything," the T-man replied. "How does it prove that this plane belongs to LAPSA?"

While the T-man was trying to put Shatz on the defensive, movement near the wing caught my attention. When I saw what was happening I had to fight hard not to burst out laughing.

The mechanic had set the ladder against the wing, climbed onto it with a can of blue paint and was just finishing painting the letters LAPSA on the fuselage. Thin rivulets of paint trickled from the bottom of each letter. He'd already painted the LAPSA registration number RX-135 on the tail. Five other mechanics are doing the same to the other planes.

I whistled to Shatz. When he looked over, I motioned for him to come to me. The T-man followed. I pointed up to the side of the plane.

"There you go," Shatz said sternly to the T-man. "Proof positive this plane belongs to LAPSA."

The T-man's face grew red. "This doesn't mean anything," he sputtered. "I'm still confiscating these planes."

Shatz stood silent, his brow creased in thought.

"No, you're not,"he said to Walker a few seconds later. Turning to the pilots, he said calmly, "Mount up. We're leaving. Right now."

"You can't do that," Walker shouted. "I just told you. These planes are confiscated property. They now belong to the United States Treasury Department." The T-man turned to the people with him. "Get your cars. Block the runway." Walker's men hopped in their cars and pulled them across the runway, about halfway down.

Shatz glared at Walker. "These planes are the property of the Panamanian National Airline. We're leaving right now. If you don't move the cars, we're going to run them over. And once we get airborne, if you still have a problem, then I guess you'll just have to shoot us down."

IN THE LEAD plane on the taxi strip, Shatz beside me in the copilot's seat, I watched the Feds pull their cars to the far end of the runway. Swinging the C-46 onto the runway, I pushed the throttles full open. Praying I'd be able to gain enough speed to lift the overloaded plane off the ground in time, I kept my eyes glued to the ground speed indicator as we lumbered down the runway.

Silently urging the bird to move faster, I glanced out the windshield. The end of the runway was approaching fast, but my airspeed wasn't quite where it needed to be for takeoff. Mere seconds later, I had no choice. It was now or crash. I yanked back as hard as I could on the yoke and felt the plane struggle to become airborne. A heartbeat later, I felt the lightness as the wheels lost contact with the ground. If I were a betting man, I'd bet the landing gear was not more than ten feet over the Feds' cars as I passed over them.

With a sigh of relief, I banked forty-five degrees to the left before turning ninety degrees to the right. When I reached five thousand feet, I began a slow circling pattern to allow the others to join up. Less than fifteen minutes after Shatz warned Walker we were taking off, all the planes were in formation, headed to Panama. That included the three minutes it took Shatz to call Pinter in California, tell him what happened, and instruct him to take off for Panama immediately.

Our flight plan took us to Kingston, Jamaica, to refuel and then on to Panama. We had clear skies and light winds the entire way. Thirty minutes out, Shatz radioed the tower in Panama City, letting them know the planes belonging to their new national airline, LAPSA, would land shortly.

I was the first to touch down. I couldn't believe the size of the crowd in front of the terminal building as I taxied to it. I saw a small band playing but couldn't hear them over the noise of the engines.

There had to be five hundred people, most holding up signs that read *'Viva LAPSA.' How did they get them done so fast?* I contacted the other six planes, told them we had a welcoming committee, and we'd wait in the cockpit until they all got to the terminal.

When the last of our group pulled up, Shatz and I deplaned. President Jiménez stood next to his presidential limousine, arms wide open in greeting, a big politician's smile plastered across his face. We were not here to offend, so Shatz and I walked over and gave him a hug, much to the delight of the crowd, who roared their approval. Each of our pilots followed our lead and did the same.

"Why did you not give me more time to prepare a proper welcome?" Jiménez asks.

We couldn't very well tell him the truth, that we got out of the States by the skin of our teeth. "The planes were ready, so we saw no need to wait any longer," Shatz replied."We also wanted to get ourselves settled here before we began operations. I was planning to let you know tomorrow or the day after."

"But, my friend," Jiménez said, "this is a momentous occasion for Panama. You left us so little time to prepare, but come, we have a small something inside."

The terminal was packed with people. A quartet playing guitar, violin, bongo drum, and clarinet strolled though the crowd. A podium had been set up. President Jiménez stepped to it and gave a speech lasting five minutes. It was in Spanish. I didn't understand what he said, but it obviously pleased the crowd because they broke out in applause at least ten times by my count.

After the speech, Jiménez brought us to a large private room. An entourage, of what I presumed were government officials, followed behind. I spotted two tables against a wall laden with platters of meats, cheeses, bread, and fruit. Pitchers of lemonade, bottles of Coke, glasses, and a bucket of ice sat on another. My stomach grumbled, reminding me it hadn't been fed all day.

"Where are the rest of your planes?" Jiménez asked.

"They're coming in from California," I replied. "Should be here within the hour."

"Good. Good. Please stay here until they arrive. Eat. Drink. I must go back to my office, but this room is for you and your people for as long as you wish. You give us a national airline. It brings pride to Panama and its people. My country is in your debt." Jiménez circled the room shaking hands with each of our pilots and left.

THE GOVERNMENT OFFICIALS stayed, enjoying the food and drink. They didn't mingle with us. I didn't think they were being rude; I just figured they didn't speak English and couldn't communicate with us. We didn't speak much Spanish, so we stayed in our own small group.

Forty-five minutes later, a man entered the room and told us in heavily accented English that our four planes just called in to the tower and were twenty minutes out. *Four? There are supposed to be five.*

We heard the sound of their engines as they approached the airfield and rushed to the gate. By now, the crowds were gone. I looked out the window and counted the planes as they touched down. There were only four. *Where's the fifth?*

They taxied to where our aircraft were parked at the terminal. Pinter got out of the first one to pull up, followed by Lapin, Prager, and Landau. *Where is Gerson?*

We all rushed outside. "Where is Gerson," Shatz asked.

"He didn't make it," Pinter said, through clenched teeth.

"What do you mean, he didn't make it?"

"He's dead. He crashed taking off from Mexico City. You want to know why he crashed? Because you had us overload the damn planes. With all that extra weight, the plane was too damn heavy. He lost an engine during takeoff and crashed. Hell, the rest of us just barely made it off the ground."

"Are you sure he's dead? Could he have survived?"

Pinter glared at Shatz. I could see the fire in his eyes. "He was fourth for takeoff. I was on the tarmac behind him, engines idling, waiting to follow. Like the guys before him, because of the extra weight, he needed to use the entire runway to get airborne. I saw him lower his flaps at the last minute to try to get some extra lift.

"It worked, and he got about a hundred feet off the ground when he lost an engine. His wing dipped, and he crashed into an empty field at the end of the runway. His fuel tanks were full. The fireball from the explosion shot fifty feet in the air. I raced my plane to the end of the runway and tried to taxi as close as I could to get to him, but there was a fence. I hopped out of my plane and started to climb the fence. Through the fence I saw flames had engulfed the entire front half of the plane. It was about a quarter of a mile away, and I could feel the heat from where I was. There was nothing I could do. So am I sure he's dead? Yeah, I'm sure."

He opened his mouth to say something else but seemed to catch himself. He turned and walked into the terminal. The other California pilots looked at Shatz the same way Pinter had. I could see the anger on their faces. They followed Pinter into the terminal, with the crew from New Jersey close behind, leaving only Shatz and me outside.

"I can't believe Gerson's dead. Good God," I said, banging my fist against my thigh. I felt nauseated. "I'm the one who recruited him. If I hadn't, he'd still be alive."

"Look, I feel as bad about it as you do, but you can't blame yourself. It's not your fault," Shatz said. "Gerson and all these guys volunteered. Every one of them knows each time they get in the cockpit of a plane, there's always a chance something can go wrong."

"Yeah, well thanks for saying that, but it doesn't make me feel much better or change the fact that he's dead. And what makes it worse, Pinter and the guys from California blame you, and I think the guys from New Jersey might feel the same. And that's not good because the last thing we need is for the mission to come down on our heads. They're pissed, and you've got to do something. And fast, before it festers."

"I'll do something right now," he said, as he shoved open the door and stormed into the terminal. I followed on his heels. Shatz opened and closed his fists as he marched down the hallway.

He entered the private room and swept a pointed finger at the Panamanians. "*Sali! Sali!*" Shatz shouted. He clapped his hands and jerked his thumb toward the door. I jumped out of the way to avoid getting run over as they hustled by me. When the last one was gone, Shatz pointed at me. "Close the door."

Shatz walked up to Pinter, his face tight. "Okay. Let's have it out right here. Are you blaming me for Gerson's death?"

"You bet your ass I am. If you didn't have us overload the planes, he would have made it off the runway and still be alive."

Shatz covered his eyes with a hand for a brief second. When he pulled it away, I saw his downturned facial features, the slack eyes. "I didn't know Gerson well, certainly not as well as you guys in Burbank. But I knew him, and I'm as sick about him getting killed as you are."

Then he refocused on Pinter. Shatz's eyes narrow and his face harden. "But let's say you're right. Let's say overloading the planes did play a part in the crash. But, it played only a part. Every one of you took off overloaded from either Burbank or Millville, Mexico City, or Kingston, and you didn't crash. If his engine hadn't failed, he'd have made it, too. "

Shatz puts his hands on his hips. "As far as flying an overloaded plane, I took the same risk as all of you. I'd never ask Gerson, you, or any other pilot in this room to fly in a plane I wasn't willing to fly in myself."

Pinter said, "But —"

"No, no buts," Shatz growled. His voice became cold. "While you're bitching about Gerson getting killed, he's just one man. There are hundreds of Jews in Palestine being killed every week. They're counting on us to get to Czechoslovakia and bring them the weapons they need to survive. This is bigger than Gerson... or even me. So all of you, make up your minds. Do you want to go back to the States and mourn for Gerson, or do you want to continue what you signed up for and help the people counting on us?"

The room grew silent. Shatz's head swiveled slowly about the room, eyes locked firmly on each man's face as he came to it. After he stared down the last man, he said, "Anyone who wants to leave, go now. Find some people on the tarmac to help you unload the spare parts and pile them on the ground next to the terminal. Without you to fly the plane you brought down, it won't do me any damn good down here. For all I care, you can take it back to the States and sell it. But for the rest of you who want to continue with the mission, as far as I'm concerned, this matter is closed. And it better be for you, too."

No one left.

CHAPTER 16
April 12
Washington, D.C.

"WHAT DO YOU mean, they took off with the planes?" Tipton yelled into the phone.

"Just what I said," replied Treasury Agent Paul Walker. "They're gone."

"How could you let that happen? You had orders to confiscate the planes. They were breaking the law."

"Well, about that," Walker replied, "they weren't actually breaking the law. It doesn't go into effect for another two days. And besides, you and I don't have any authority over the planes."

"What are you talking about?"

"Those planes belong to the Panamanian government."

"What? What do mean they belong to the Panamanian government?"

"That's what I said. He showed me paperwork, registration certificates. The planes are legally owned by the Panamanian National Airline. It's called LAPSA."

"I never heard of it," Tipton said. "It's got to be some kind of trick."

"Look, I won't say you're wrong. I questioned them about it. There were no markings on the planes. Then this guy Shatz had his people paint the names and registration numbers on the planes while I was standing there. But, the paperwork he showed me appeared legal, and the registration numbers on them matched the numbers they put on the planes."

"You still shouldn't have let them leave until I had a chance to verify it."

"Look, Mr. Tipton, I tried. I had three cars block the runway. This guy Shatz told me outright he was leaving and if I didn't move the cars, he'd run them over. I had no choice."

"You screwed up. You shouldn't have let them take off."

"Hold on there a minute, Tipton," Walker said, raising his voice. "Let's get some things straight. First of all, I don't work for you. Second, Shatz was technically right. The law doesn't go into effect for two more days, so he wasn't breaking it. And last, if those planes really do belong to the Panamanian government, I would have been blamed for causing an international incident, and no thank you, I wasn't about to do that."

"Yeah, but—"

"No, sir. You're the State Department. I suggest if you have a problem with this, get in touch with the government of Panama, and see if it's true."

"But," Tipton said, but stopped when he heard the dial tone. Walker had hung up on him.

"EMBASSY OF EGYPT," the operator answered.

"May I speak to Ammon Hazem?"

"One moment."

"Ammon Hazem," the man at the other end answered.

"No names. Do you know who this is?" Tipton said.

"Of course."

"Meet me in my office this afternoon at 3:00"

"Why?"

"Just be here."

Hazem was ushered into Tipton's office at precisely 3:00 and took a seat in front of Tipton's desk.

As soon as his secretary left, Tipton said, "I need you to go to Panama."

"Panama? Why?"

Tipton told Hazen about the conversation he had with Walker that day. "I've got a gut feeling something is up. I don't believe those planes belong to the Panamanian government. I need you to get down there and find out what's really going on."

"Why not have your embassy in Panama find out?"

"Because I can't involve the State Department. Not now, anyway. Besides, if I'm right and these planes are somehow headed to Palestine, you've got as much at stake as we do."

"Okay. I'll get down there in a couple of days and check it out."

"No, you're leaving tomorrow morning. I've already booked your flight. Here's your ticket."

CHAPTER 17
April 13
Panama

THE MEN WERE not in a good mood. Although they seemed to have accepted Shatz's admonishment that the mission had to go on, and to set aside blaming him for the plane going down, I could tell Gerson's crash still weighed heavy on them.

President Jiménez's office made arrangements for us to stay at a hotel in Panama City, located in the Casco Viejo section, known as the old city, near the entertainment district. Shatz and I thought a night out on the town might help get the men in a better frame of mind. The only place we knew to take them was Tierra Feliz, the restaurant and nightclub we'd visited with our translator, Miguel, a month ago. It was three blocks from the hotel.

I was at a table with Pinter, Lapin and Prager. Pinter was working on his fourth beer, me on my third. "I lost some good friends in the war, but that was war, and we knew the danger," Pinter said to me. "But this, this is different. We're not at war, at least not yet. I felt Gerson died unnecessarily and I know I probably over-reacted with Shatz. But even though Gerson joined us six weeks ago, and I didn't really know him that well, he was still one of us. And it sucks."

"How do you think I feel?" I said. "I'm the reason he joined us. If I never contacted him, he'd still be alive."

"You can't think of it like that. You explained what the mission was. He wanted to help. It was his choice to be part of it."

"Yeah, I know you're right, but..."

"No. There's no but. I understand now that Shatz was right. He needed us to pack the planes the way we did with the spare parts. It was just a bad break, a freak accident that one of Gerson's engines died on him. It could have happened to any one of us, including you and Shatz."

We sat quietly for about a half a minute. Then Pinter stood, held up his beer bottle and said, "Gentlemen. To Gerson."

We all rose and held up our beer bottles and glasses. "To Gerson," we said, in unison,

The toast seemed to lighten the mood. Or maybe it was the amount of alcohol we'd consumed. For whatever the reason, it worked. Any tensions that lingered with the men seemed to evaporate. Some of the guys even began to crack jokes.

I was surprised a half hour later when our translator, Miguel, walked in.

"Hola, my friend," he shouted as he walked to my table.

"Miguel. What are you doing here?" I asked. I stood and when he reached me and put out his hand for a shake, I grasped it and pulled him close for a hug. I really liked this guy and felt guilty about what we were going to do to him, and his pride about finally having a national airline.

"I find out my new friends are here. How can I not come to see them," he said, throwing his arms out wide, a big smile on his face.

He'd told us on our last visit to the nightclub, in English, the name Tierra Feliz meant Happy Land. It proved to be the case tonight. Miguel translated and helped us order food. When it came time to leave, we asked Miguel to get the bill for us. He returned empty handed.

"The owner told me he cannot accept money," he said, "from the pilots who bring Panama their own airline."

The owner had no idea there would not be a Panamanian airline. It made me feel guilty. I couldn't do that to the owner, so I pulled $400 from my wallet and insisted Miguel bring it to the owner.

"He will be insulted," Miguel said.

"Tell him I will be insulted if he doesn't take it, and we will never come back again if he refuses."

The owner took the money and my conscience felt better. Well, maybe just a little better.

As we made our way back to the hotel, the guys were in a good mood. I don't know if it was directly related to the substantial quantities of alcohol they consumed, and I didn't care. At least for a few hours that night, they'd put aside their grief. I hoped it would hold into tomorrow.

When the new day began, I woke with a hangover. I made my way down to the dining room for coffee and saw the rest of the guys were already there. They were not faring any better than me. A buffet was set up at one end of the room, but the food was untouched. The men sat with their elbows on the table, heads down, faces resting in cupped hands. When the waiters refilled their coffee mugs, the men would alternate between taking sips and lowering their heads back into their palms. No one spoke.

Shatz came in ten minutes after I got there and said we had taxis waiting outside to bring us back to the airport. The men dragged themselves to their feet and shuffled outside.

When we arrived, Shatz led us to an empty store in the main terminal that had *Leanas Aereas de Panama Sociedad Anonima* stenciled on the glass window with LAPSA above it. He unlocked the door, and we all piled inside.

"Welcome to your new office," he said, sweeping his arm out.

There were six desks and chairs in the middle of the room with ten visitor chairs arranged along the wall. A table under the window, just inside the door, held colorful brochures with the LAPSA logo printed on the front showing a picture of one of our C-46's underneath the logo.

"Where did these come from?" I asked Shatz, picking up one of the brochures.

"They were on our plane. I had them made two weeks ago. I knew we'd have to make the airline look legitimate, so I had a friend design the brochure and get them printed. We have to appear to be a real airline until we can get out of here. Speaking of that, I'm leaving in an hour on a Pan Am flight to Miami. I can't take a chance on going back to New York, so Meir is coming down to meet me there. We have to work out the logistics of getting us from here to Czechoslovakia. While I'm gone, I'm leaving you and Pinter in charge."

AS ARRANGED, MIGUEL came to the office in the early afternoon. I hired him the night before to be our translator. For the next two days, we had light traffic as people passed through the terminal, spotted the window, and came in to find out about LAPSA. We gave them brochures, and as instructed, Miguel told them we would not be operating as a passenger airline for another four weeks.

The men seemed to put Gerson's death behind them. At night, Tierra Feliz became our hangout, and each time, Miguel joined us. The third night we were there, the woman came in with two girlfriends. As she neared my table, I couldn't tear my eyes off of her. She had dark-eyes and long brunette hair that set off her pretty heart-shaped face and sensual mouth. Her light olive skin screamed exotic to a guy like me from Boston. She was about five-and-a-half-feet tall with long legs, a trim figure, and medium-sized breasts. When she walked past me, I saw her ass sway seductively. She wore a pair of wide-legged trousers and a white peasant blouse. I was instantly in lust. She and her two friends sat at a table near to ours. I could not stop looking.

"Miguel, do you know that woman in the white blouse?" I ask, nodding in her direction.

Miguel glanced over. "No. Why?"

"Why? Jeez, Miguel, are you blind? She's gorgeous."

He chuckled.

"I've got to meet her," I said. I got to my feet and walked to her table. I saw her eyes lock on me as I approached.

"Hello. My name is Mike, and I'd like to buy you a drink."

She stared up at me. Her sensual mouth broke into a small smile, showing off ivory white teeth.

"Can I buy you a drink?" I asked again.

She looked up at me with wide eyes. "*No hablo mucho inglés. Por favor, habla despacio.*"

I didn't speak much Spanish, but I knew what that meant. For the last two days when someone spoke to me in Spanish and I didn't understand them, I would say "*No hablo mucho espa*ñol." I don't speak much Spanish

I didn't know what to do. I turned back to my table and saw Miguel looking at me. I waved him over.

"Miguel, please tell her I'd like to buy her a drink."

I listened as he spoke to her. I didn't understand what he said, other than he said a lot more words that needed to be said just to say I'd like to buy her a drink. And, I heard the word LAPSA spoken at least three times. What I did like was each time I heard him say LAPSA, she looked at me and her smile got bigger.

They exchanged a couple more sentences before Miguel turned to me. "Her name is Maylin. It means beautiful jade, and it is a fitting name. Look at her eyes." What I first thought were dark eyes were actually shamrock green in color.

"She told you she doesn't speak much English and asked you to speak slowly," he continued. "I told her you are one of the men who are giving Panama their own national airline. She said she heard about the American pilots doing this and is very pleased to meet you. She said she thinks you are quite handsome and would very much like to have a drink with you."

From an empty table, I pulled two chairs over for Miguel and me. I sat next to Maylin, and Miguel sat between her two friends. He ordered the drinks for all of us, and Maylin and I talked, through Miguel as an interpreter. She was twenty-three, worked in a construction office in downtown Panama City, and the two girls with her were her roommates. I told her about Boston, my time in the war, and the story about us coming down to start LAPSA for Panama. She asked me about our plans for LAPSA. I stuck to the cover story.

I was mesmerized. I couldn't take my eyes off of her. She seemed to feel the same. We'd been talking for fifteen minutes when one of her roommates said something, and she shook her head no. That was followed by a brief conversation and a conspiratorial glance from the roommate.

"What's going on?" I ask Miguel.

He smirked and raised an eyebrow. "Her roommate said they were bored and it was time to leave. She said no. The roommate asked her why. She said she wanted to spend more time with you. Her roommate asked how long, and she said maybe until tomorrow morning."

I looked at Maylin. She smiled at me and toyed with a lock of her hair. My eyes blazed with lust and her eyes sparkled with... what? Desire? I reached across the table and put my hand on hers. She glanced down where we touched, lifted her face, and her mouth curved into a bigger smile.

"Tell her friends they can leave. Maylin will be just fine."

Her roommates said something to Maylin then rose and left the nightclub. Miguel patted me on the back, winked, and went back to join the other pilots. I picked up her hand, turned it, and kissed her palm, lightly licking it. I thought I felt her shudder. I stood, gently pulled her to her feet, and led her out of the nightclub, never casting a glance at my friends as we left.

We walked the three blocks to my hotel in silence. I held her hand and I thought I felt it occasionally tremble. Whether it was from nerves or desire, I had no idea. When I led her into my room and closed the door behind us, I had my answer. She spun around and threw her arms around my neck. Her lips closed on mine with a kiss that can't be described as anything less than carnal. Her tongue slithered into my mouth, darting in and out, like a striking cobra. I pushed my tongue into her mouth, and our tongues danced with each other's.

While we devoured each other's mouths, I moved a hand between our bodies and gently cupped her breast, rubbing my thumb across on her erect nipple. I was already semi-erect. We held the kiss for a couple of minutes before she broke it. She pushed herself away and stepped next to the bed. Swaying her body, as if listening to music only she could hear, she removed her clothes in slow seductive moves.

When I was in college, just before joining the Marines, some friends and I went to the famous, many said infamous, Old Howard Burlesque Theater, in Scollay Square, downtown Boston. The undisputed queen of the strippers was Ann Corio and for good reason. When she removed each article of clothing, she made you feel she was doing it for you alone and unbridled sex would soon follow. Corio was an amateur compared to Maylin.

As each article of her clothes dropped to the floor, my mouth became drier, and I became harder. When she dropped her last piece, she stared into my eyes, and I saw pure animal lust.

Maylin slinked back to me, like a leopard about to pounce on its prey. She pushed me against the door, pulled my shirt out of my pants, and unbuttoned it. She pulled it off my shoulders and dropped it on the floor. Next, she yanked my undershirt over my head, and it landed on my shirt.

Dropping to her knees, she removed my shoes and socks, and looked up at me with smoldering eyes as she unbuckled my belt, unzipped my fly, and slid my pants down to my ankles. She ran her hands softly across the bulge in my shorts before reaching for the waistband and pulling them down.

I couldn't wait anymore. I kicked my pants and shorts loose from my legs, bent down, and scooped her into my arms. I rushed to the bed, threw her on top of the covers and my body on top of her. At this point, neither of us needed any foreplay. She opened her legs wide, grasped me, and guided me to her entrance. I thrust and we became one.

We picked up a rhythm; each time I plunged down, she rose to meet me. I knew I wouldn't last long. When I heard her breathing grow rapid and her moans become louder, I knew it wouldn't be a problem. Minutes later, she let out a wail as her orgasm hit. Her body stiffened, her arms pulled tight, and I felt her nails dig into my back. I followed her seconds later.

We lay in bed panting. I racked my brain, trying to remember Spanish words, to say something to her. I tried, "*Eso fue fantastico.*" I thought it meant, "That was fantastic."

I must have got it right because she purred, snuggled tight against me, and said, "*Sí, lo era*" I didn't know what the words after *sí* were, but the *sí* part was good enough for me.

We went at it two more times during the night. The first was when she woke me up. While I was sleeping she must have done her magic because I woke to find her sitting on top, riding me. What a way to wake up, I thought.

The second time, I woke her. We were sleeping spoon fashion, my front snuggled against her back. In my sleep I must have thrown my arm across her, and my hand held her breast. I don't know what woke me, but I liked the feel of her breast and felt myself harden. I snuggled closer, pressed my lower body against her firm behind and squeezed her erect nipple. She murmured and wiggled her backside against my erection. Minutes later I took her from behind. When it was over, I fell into a deep slumber.

Sunlight streamed into the room through a gap in the shade and woke me the next morning. I looked at the clock on the nightstand. 7:10. I rolled over to Maylin. The bed was empty. I felt the sheets. They were cold. I hopped out of bed and walked to the bathroom. She wasn't there. I looked at the floor by the foot of the bed. Her clothes were gone. She was gone.

I got to the LAPSA office in the terminal at 8:55 a.m. and shot immediately over to Miguel's desk. I grasped him by the elbow. "What's going on?" he asked, as I pulled him outside into the terminal.

"What's Maylin's last name? Where does she work? Where does she live?"

"I don't know. She never tell me her last name, and I have no have idea where she lives. She say she work for construction company in Panama City, but no mention name. Why do you ask me these things? Did she rob you?"

"No. No. Nothing like that. We went back to my room last night and it was... good. But when I woke up this morning, she was gone and I don't know how to find her."

"Did she leave note?"

"No, I looked."

"Well, my friend, maybe she does not want you to find her."

"After last night, I don't think that's the case."

"Then if she wants to see you, my friend, she will find you."

I hated to think Miguel was right. I thought Maylin and I had something more than just a one night stand. But maybe that was all it was to her.

Miguel and I went back into the office, and I moved over to the desk I'd been using. I thought about checking out construction companies in the Panama City phone book or calling information at the telephone company but did neither. I didn't know her last name, so what good would that do? And maybe Miguel was right. If she wanted to see me again, it would be up to her.

"What did you find out?" he asked in English.

"It is as you were told. The planes belong to the Panama National Airline, and the Americans will be the pilots. They have an office at the airport. It is a real thing," she replied, also in English.

"You sure?"

She smiled. "I'm sure."

"Okay. Here's your money," Hazem said, handing over a stack of bills. "As agreed. Two hundred U.S. dollars."

She counted the money and put the envelope in her purse. "Nice doing business with you," Maylin said.

CHAPTER 18
May 3, 1948
Panama
Casablanca

IT HAD BEEN three weeks since Shatz left for Miami and three weeks since my night with Maylin. Each night I went to Tierra Feliz hoping she would be there. Each time I was disappointed, and each night I wallowed in self-pity. The night before, I finally realized all I would ever have of that night was a great memory.

I didn't have much time for self-pity during the daytime. Pinter and I had the pressure of making sure the men followed the training schedule Shatz set for the pilots. They had to take the planes out every day for short flights. Most of them hadn't flown since they were in the war, and they needed to hone up on those skills, as well as navigation. With the extra weight of the spare parts, as we hopscotched our way to Europe and with the loads of armaments we'd eventually be carrying to Palestine, we paid particular attention to practicing takeoffs and landings.

We were getting pressure from President Jiménez. As far as he knew, LAPSA was a legitimate airline, and for the last three weeks he'd kept pushing us, asking what the delay was in starting operations. Pinter and I threw out one excuse after another but always ended the conversation by saying we were very close. I knew we were actually very close, because May 14 was when the British mandate ended, and we'd be gone from Panama before that.

I WAS SITTING at my desk checking the pilot's morning practice schedule, when Baron yelled that Meir was on the phone and wanted to talk to me.

"This is Kaplan."

"It's Meir. Shatz is on a plane back to Panama City. He asked me to call and tell you to have the planes fueled and ready to leave when he gets there."

"Today? Why so fast? I thought Shatz said we were going to play out the LAPSA charade for at least ten days."

"He was, and that was the plan until last night when an old friend of his tracked him down, here in Miami."

"What happened?" I asked.

"I'm going to tell you, but Shatz doesn't want you to repeat this. He wants to tell the men face to face."

"I'm not sure I like the sound of that."

"You won't, but it doesn't change what I'm going to tell you. Shatz has this friend who works for TWA as a pilot based in London. During the war, he was stationed in England where he flew bombers out of a Royal Air Force base. He made a lot of friends with the RAF pilots while he was there. Last week he flew into Cairo, and when he was checking into his hotel with the rest of the crew, one of the RAF pilots he knew from the war spotted him and invited him to have drinks at the RAF officer's club."

"The RAF has an officer's club in Cairo?"

"Yeah. With the tacit agreement of King Farouk, the British still occupy Egypt under the pretense of protecting the Suez Canal. They have military installations and a few air bases scattered throughout the country."

"Is this guy Jewish?"

"Yeah, but I don't think the Brits know that or they would never have invited him to their club."

"So why did this guy track Shatz down?" I asked.

"While he was having drinks with a few of the pilots, he casually mentioned the newspapers back in London were filled with news about the British Army pulling out of Palestine and the founding of the State of Israel. One of the RAF pilots said to him, 'It will never happen. They'll be attacked by all the surrounding Arab countries.'"

"Yeah, but why did he track Shatz down to tell him that? I think everyone in the world already knows that's gonna to happen."

"True. But it's what the RAF pilot said just after that, that made him track Shatz down. He asked the pilot if he thought the Egyptians would attack and the guy replied, 'Of course... and they're going to be using us.'"

"How can they do that?" I asked. "They're British pilots. That would be an outright act of war by the British Government against another country, even if the country is only hours or days old."

"That's what Shatz's friend asked him. The RAF pilot said the plan was for them to resign their commissions, with agreement from the British government it would only be temporary, and they'd become technical advisors to the Egyptian Army, although they would be the ones actually flying the planes in combat."

"Holy shit. It's bad enough the Arab countries are going to attack. Now they're going to be attacked from the air by seasoned combat pilots?"

"And now you know why Shatz's friend thought it was important enough to track him down," Meir said. "His friend heard through the grapevine about Shatz's plan to fly weapons into Palestine and wanted to warn him he might run into British Spitfires flown by RAF pilots. Time is closing in faster than we expected. That's why you have to have the planes ready to pull out and be on your way to Czechoslovakia as fast as possible."

SHATZ ARRIVED AT the Panama City airport at 2:00 in the afternoon. He pulled me outside the office and told me he wanted to have a meeting with all of us after the office closed. Not all the guys were there, so I left to round them up. I took me a few hours to find them all. I got back to the terminal office with the last one at almost 6:00. Miguel had gone by then.

Shatz started the meeting by telling the men the same story Meir told me that morning. "So now you know why we have to leave now. If I thought the calendar was working against us in New Jersey, it's worse now."

Pinter said, "You said you were going to Miami to work out the logistics to get us to Catania, Sicily. Did you?"

"Yes. I contacted the embassies of the countries we need to land in, as a representative of *Lineas Aereas de Panama*, and secured landing rights for LAPSA planes. I told them it was to map their airport before we set up a sales office there."

"Is everything set up in Catania?" Baron asked.

"Yes. Meir spoke to his people in Rome. It's all set. They finally got to the right people to pay off. We can use the airport there as our staging base between Czechoslovakia and Palestine." He paused. "Okay, now we're gonna go outside and start pulling duplicate spare parts out of each plane. We need to lighten the load so we can fill the auxiliary tanks to make it across the Southern Atlantic."

He turned to me. "While you were out, I called Jiménez and told him we were leaving tomorrow morning for a survey run to determine the best routes to Europe for passenger and cargo flights."

By 11:30 we regrouped in the office. The extra spare parts were piled on the tarmac next to the terminal and the auxiliary tanks topped off. "Okay, guys. Let's go get some rest," Shatz said. "Tomorrow is going to be a long day".

WHEN WE GOT to the airport the next morning, I swore under my breath. President Jiménez was there with what looked like half the Panamanian government.

"My friends," he said, "this is a great day for Panama. We came to wish you a safe flight and watch the first flight of our airline." Shatz thanked him, shook his hand, and said we had to leave right away. We headed to our planes.

Once again, I was the first plane to take off, with Shatz sitting in the copilot seat. We flew to Paramaribo, Dutch Guyana, and then on to Natal, Brazil. Because the State Department had forced us to become a Panamanian Airline, it gave us legitimacy, and when we landed in Natal, British South American Airway allowed us to use their facilities to refuel. Baron's plane needed repairs, and he wouldn't be able to leave with us.

Now began the most dangerous part of the flight. We were about to cross the vast open waters of the South Atlantic. It was almost two thousand miles and ten hours of flying time from Natal to our next stop in Dakar, Senegal, on the Africa continent. If the engines didn't perform, the weight was too much, we hit bad weather, or we ran low on fuel, we'd meet a watery grave.

We left Natal and began the journey across the South Atlantic. We landed in Dakar without incident. After we refueled, the plan was to wait until all the planes landed before we'd take off on the next leg of the trip. But not all our planes landed. Goldstein, one of the New Jersey crew didn't show up. After three hours, I knew something was wrong. Even under the worst of circumstances they should have been here by now.

I pulled Shatz a few feet away from the guys gathered in the terminal. "What are we going to do? Do you think he crashed?"

"I don't know. If he did, there's nothing we can do about it, and we can't wait here. We have to go."

Shatz walked back to the other pilots. "I don't want a repeat of how you guys felt about Gerson, but it's decision time. We don't know where Goldstein is. He may have gone down. He may have had engine trouble and turned back to Natal. In either case, staying here won't accomplish anything, and it won't get weapons to Palestine. Show of hands, how many want to keep going?"

Every hand went up.

OUR NEXT STOP was Casablanca, Morocco. It was early evening when we landed. As we taxied toward the terminal, I could see there was some kind of demonstration going on outside. We parked our planes and went to the airport manager's office. I saw the demonstrators marching back and forth in front of the terminal, holding signs and shouting something in Arabic.

"What's going on out there?"Pinter asked the manager.

He replied in heavy accented English, "They demonstrate against the Jews."

"What are they saying?" I asked.

"They say what is on signs. Down with Jews. Kill the Jews. Death to the Jews."

I tried not to react, and I bit the inside of my cheek, hard.

Shatz quickly changed the subject. He said to the manager, "While our planes are being refueled, we'd like to take a quick trip into town for dinner. Do you have anyone we can pay to guard our planes?"

"What about some of those men?" he asked, pointing to the demonstrators marching outside.

"Them? Can we trust them?" Shatz asked.

"Of course, they work here at airport."

"Okay. They're hired," Shatz said, with a straight face. It didn't escape me, and I'm sure the others, that we'd just hired a bunch of anti-Jews to guard the planes that would soon be helping Jews.

WHEN WE GOT back to the airport after dinner in Casablanca, the airport manager handed Shatz a telegram. It said, "*Catania changed, call Re'uven,*" and gave a telephone number in Rome. He asked the manager where he could make a private call to Rome.

"You must make it from post office in Casablanca," the manager said, "but it is closed until morning."

We took taxis back into town and found a hotel. The next morning, Shatz was first in line waiting for the post office to open. He gave a clerk, who spoke some English, the telephone number in Rome and the name of the man he wished to speak with. After he paid in advance for the call, he was ushered into a booth by a different clerk to wait for the call to be put through. Ten minutes later, the phone rang.

"Hello," Shatz said.

"This is Mr. Shatz?" the voice asked.

"Yes, it is."

"I have to make sure you are who you say you are. Who do you know in New York with an office in Hotel Fourteen?"

"You mean Meir?"

"Yes, that is who I mean. You are no longer able to use airport in Catania. The Americans and British suspect we are using it as a staging area and they pressured Italian government to make it off-limits. Your new landing place is Zatec, Czechoslovakia."

"Czechoslovakia?"

"Yes. You can get there?"

"I'll find it."

Shatz hung up. The original plan was to use Catania as our base of operations, fly from there into Czechoslovakia, pick up the munitions, and fly back to Catania before heading to Palestine.

Now we're going to be based in Czechoslovakia. Behind the Iron Curtin.

CHAPTER 19
May, 1948
Zatec, Czechoslovakia

"THANK GOD YOU finally come here," the man said. He hugged me in a tight embrace, my arms trapped to my sides, and lifted me off the ground. I'd just stepped away from my C-46.

When he put me down, I said, "Glad to be here. Who are you?"

It was May 5. I'd just landed, with the rest of our planes at the airfield in Zatec, Czechoslovakia.

"My name is Mordechai Alon. My friends call me Modi, and now, so will you," he said, with a huge smile. "And, what is your name?"

I laughed and shook his hand. "I'm Mike Kaplan. Nice to meet you."

"And who is this?" Modi said, pointing behind me.

I turned and saw Shatz step up behind me. "This is Paul Shatz."

"You are Shatz?" he said. Shatz suffered the same fate as me. Alon pulled him into a tight bear hug and lifted him off the ground. When he put Shatz down, he said, "I know you are the man responsible for getting us these planes. Thank you. We are waiting for them. Munitions are piled, and ready to fly to Palestine."

"Thanks for the enthusiastic greeting, but who exactly are you?" I asked.

"Oh, sorry. I am squadron commander." he said. "Come, we'll go to headquarters."

Alon led our group to what could best be described as a ramshackle hut. "I'm sorry, we put this up just one week ago. The Czechs give us this abandoned airfield. As you see, there is no tower and no hangers. Only two other buildings like this, which we use for equipment."

"How many are you?" I asked.

"There are six of us here now. One and a half weeks ago, the Czech government agreed to sell us twenty-three Messerschmitt Me 109 fighter planes. They also allow us to use part of this airfield as a base for your airlift of weapons and to train us on flying the Messerschmitts."

"Have you ever flown a fighter plane?"

"Yes. I was a pilot for the RAF in 1945. They put me in Cairo for a while then transferred me to fly P-51 Mustangs from Ramat David, outside Haifa. But, with tension between Jews and British occupying Palestine growing, I guess they don't want a Jew flying combat plane there. They wanted to transfer me to England. Palestine is my homeland, so I resigned."

"So you didn't fly combat in the war?" Shatz asked.

"Not in that war, but I fly combat in my war," Alon said, throwing his shoulders back, a satisfied smile on his face.

"What do you mean your war? It hasn't started yet," Shatz said.

"You think no? We have been fighting ever since partition declared last November. The Arabs begin attacking almost the day after, cutting off and attacking settlements. Our air force, the *Sherut Avir*, has only a few light planes like Piper Cubs and a Bonanza. We use them to supply settlements, escort convoys, and sometimes dropping bombs."

Pinter, who'd been listening to the story, jumped in. "How the hell do you drop bombs from a Piper Cub?"

Alon laughed. "You do what you must do. The Bonanza is a six-seat plane. I fly it and have a copilot. When we see the enemy, my copilot becomes what you would call in English 'a bomb chucker.' He goes back in plane where we have twenty-five pound bombs. I fly over the enemy, he opens door, pulls safety pin, and throws bomb out door on them. Sometimes, when I fly alone in Piper Cub, I keep hand grenades on my lap. When I see enemy, I pull pin with my teeth and throw grenade out window."

With guys like this, there's no way the Arabs will win.

A man walked in and said something to Alon in, what I presumed, was Hebrew. They exchanged some words before Alon turned to us. "This is my second in command, Ezer Weizman. Ezer, these are pilots who bring in planes from the United States."

Weizman said in English, "It is nice to meet you. I am sure Modi told you how desperate we are for these planes."

Alon said, "Ezer told me the last of ten Messerschmitts we buy is here at field. Come, we go see them."

We followed Alon and Weizman and walked about three hundred yards behind the building we'd been in to where the Messerschmitts were parked.

"I didn't hear an engine before. How did it get here?" I asked.

"They bring all planes on trucks. Fuselage and wings are separate. They re-assemble them here."

"Anyone fly them yet?" Pinter asked.

"No, "Alon replied."We are waiting for Czech instructors."

Pinter went to one of the planes and walked around it. He'd been in combat against them over Europe. "They don't look as scary on the ground as they did coming at me in the sky with guns blazing," he said.

"Mind if I take one up?"I asked Alon.

"We haven't even run engines yet," he replied.

"No time like the present,"I said.

"I must tell you something about plane before you take it up."

"Tell us what?" Shatz asked.

"This is not same Messerschmitt the Germans used. It is called by Czechs 'the Avia.' They make them for their own air force. The only place to make the Daimler Benz engine here was destroyed, so the Czechs now fit a Junker bomber engine and propeller to Messerschmitt airframe. They warn us paddle-bladed propeller could sometime make control difficult, and with the narrow-track undercarriage, there could be problem with takeoff and landing."

"Well," I said, "why don't I take one of these babies up and see what happens?"

Alon took me back to the shack we'd been in before and outfitted me with flight equipment. Back at the plane, I climbed into the cockpit and looked over the instrument panel until I found what looked like the engine switch. I flipped it on, and the engine came to life. There was something about the sound of the engine that seemed a little strange to me, but I chocked it up to never being in a Messerschmitt before. I taxied to the grass runway.

As I sat at the end, getting ready to take off, the irony hit me. I began to laugh. What the hell was a nice Jewish boy from Boston doing here? I was sitting in a German fighter plane, wearing a German flight jacket with a swastika patch on the front, a German parachute strapped to my back, and I was about to test fly a plane to help Jews these same Germans tried to exterminate.

I reached down and ripped the swastika patch off the jacket, threw it on the floor, then eased the throttle forward. I'd learned during the war that one of the things that made the Messerschmitt such a formable enemy aircraft was it had a powerful Daimler Benz mounted to a lightweight four-thousand-pound body. But, as I pushed the throttle further forward and began to pick up speed, the plane wasn't moving as fast as I thought a Messerschmitt should. Must be the Junker engine I told myself.

When the plane gained what I thought was enough airspeed, I pulled back on the stick. I couldn't have been more than thirty feet in the air when the plane's nose suddenly dipped toward the ground, and at the same time, it pulled to the left. My stomach dropped as I struggled to lift the nose and straighten the plane. I pulled back on the stick as hard as I could, pushed the throttle forward to gain more power, and fought to level out the plane. My heart was hammering.

In what seemed like an eternity, but in reality was just mere seconds, the nose lifted, and the plane leveled out. I took it up to two thousand feet, and as my stomach and heart settled down, I made two passes over the field before bringing it down. I was in my final approach, about to land, when I felt the aircraft pull sharply to the right, the opposite of what happened during takeoff.

I climbed out of the plane and spotted our guys and Alon and Weizman standing near the other Messerschmitts. I marched over. "Messerschmitt? Hell, that thing is more like a piece o'shit," I said to Alon. "How could you buy this piece of crap?"

"And what choice do we have? You see any other country standing in line to sell us fighter planes? Sure, the plane may be, as you say, a piece o'shit, but it is only piece o'shit we have."

That kind of took the wind out of my sails. "You're right. I apologize. We'll learn to make them work for us."

Alon took us to the town of Zatec where he'd secured living quarters for us. "The hotel," he said, "has been renamed. It was called the Kaiserhof when the Germans controlled the country. Now it is called the Hotel Stalingrad, because we are behind the iron curtain and under Russian control. You see how the conquered adapt?"

FOR THE NEXT ten days, the America pilots took turns with the two Jewish pilots practicing on the Messerschmitt piece o'shits. On the eighth day, we found out the engines weren't the only problem with the plane. With Skippy Shapiro in the cockpit, it was the first time we were going to practice a strafing run.

The plane's machine gun was built using World War I technology. It was mounted on the front engine cowl and used a gun synchronizer that allowed the bullets to fire through the propeller. That was great for a Messerschmitt using the Daimler Benz engine and propeller, but these planes used the Junker engine with a wider paddle-blade propeller.

Shapiro came in low over the airfield and began his run, shooting at sand bag targets we'd lined up off to the right of the runway. We heard the sound of his machine gun, and I watched in disbelief as the bullets shredded his propeller, and the plane fell from the sky. I don't know how he did it, but Shapiro was able to control his drop and belly land the plane alongside the runway. He scrambled out of the cockpit and ran like a bat out of hell, expecting the plane to blow up. It didn't.

From that day on, before each practice strafing run, the plane would taxi out to a remote section of the field. We'd set up sandbags, and the pilot would test fire his guns at the bags while on the ground. No other pilot would shoot himself out of the sky because the gun synchronizer wasn't working properly.

Two days before Israel would declare its independence, and before the pilots from Palestine had a chance to take their first gunnery practice, Alon and the rest of the pilots flew home. They knew that after the declaration, the new country would come under immediate attack from the ground and in the air, and they had to be there to fight back.

Before Alon left, he and Shatz established what they called the Air Transport Command, ATC, of the soon to be Israeli Air Force, made up of the planes we brought in from the United States. For the time being, it was decided for diplomatic consideration to Czechoslovakia to leave the LAPSA name and registration numbers on the planes and not paint the Star of David on them.

CHAPTER 20
May 14, 1948
Israel

W E COULDN'T WAIT any longer. It was May 14, and we knew the Jews in Palestine would be attacked on all sides and be low on guns and ammunition. They would also get hit from the air, and Alon and his Piper Cubs were no match for the Royal Egyptian Air Force Spitfires, especially if they had those British RAF pilots flying them.

We had to get the Messerschmitts there, and we had to go now. The problem was, how? A Messerschmitt couldn't fly direct to Israel. It had a range of about five hundred miles, and Israel was over two thousand miles away.

We had pondered the problem weeks before, prior to Alon and the Israeli pilots leaving to go back and fight in Israel, but it was Baron who came up with the solution.

FIVE DAYS BEFORE, Baron had finally arrived in Zatec and told us what happened to him.

He said the engine trouble in Natal took longer than expected to fix. It took three days before he was able to leave. But he ran into a major problem after he left Casablanca. He only knew about our planned original stops along the way and not that the Americans and British pressured Italian government to make Catania off-limits.

When he landed in Catania, the plane was immediately seized by the authorities. They didn't put him in jail. Instead, they told him he was free until the authorities received word from Rome on what they should to do with him.

"Ah went into town and found me a hotel and called Meir in New York," he said. "It was the only number in the United States ah knew where someone might be able to help. Meir told me to sit tight, and he'd contact Rome and have someone there see what they could do."

Baron continued. "The second night in Catania, ah was sitting in a restaurant and noticed this guy staring at me. This wasn't just some peanut farmer, ah mean to tell you. He was big. Maybe three hundred pounds, and ah'd bet most of it was muscle. He looked meaner than a wet panther. He stared at me for fifteen minutes before he sidled over to my table, walking so slow dead flies wouldn't fall of 'im. Ah mean to tell y'all, he sure enough scared the shit outta me. He said something to me. Ah guess it was in Italian, and ah didn't understand a word of it. Ah looked at him and said in English that ah didn't understand.

"'You from the States?' he asked.

"'Ah certainly am,' I replied, as polite as any gentleman from Georgia would.

"'What are you doing here?'

"'It's a long story. Ah sure am positive you're not interested.'

"'Try me.'

"'Why?'

"'You ever hear of Lucky Luciano?'

"'Sure. Hasn't everyone?'

"'I work for him. You a cop?'

"I tried not to laugh in case he'd take it as an insult. 'No, ah am anything but a cop.'

"'Then tell what are you doing here?'"

Baron scratched his nose. "Ah decided to tell him the whole story. Ah figured since he worked for Luciano, ah might as well throw out Pinter's name and his connection with Myer Lansky. It musta been the right thangs to say, because the guy visibly relaxes.

"'Why didn't you say so from the beginning? Is there anything I can do for you?' he asked.

"'Well, since you ask. We're trying to get my plane released. Got any connections? And, as long as you're offerin, got any guns ah can bring with me to Palestine?' Ah laughed, he didn't.

"He called a waiter over, said something to him in Italian, and left. When ah finished my meal and asked for the check, the waiter said the man paid for everything.

"The next morning my phone rang at 9:00. It was a customs official at the airport. He told me my plane had been released, and ah was free to go at any time. Ah scrambled to get dressed and get out of Catania before someone changed their mind. Ah got to the airport twenty-five minutes later. Ah went me to the customs office where an official hands me papers releasing the plane. What was more amazing, he spends the next five minutes apologizing for the misunderstanding.

"Ah thought the day couldn't be more surprising, until ah got on board the plane and saw a large wooden crate that wasn't there when ah left the airport two days ago. When ah opened it, it was filled with brand new Thompson sub-machine guns and ammunition. A note inside said, 'Compliments of Lucky.'"

Baron threw up his hands. "And that my friends is my tale of how ah got here."

Now FIVE DAYS later, Baron said, "Seems to me, how to get the Messerschmitt there is pretty simple."

"Simple, huh?" Shapiro asked.

"Sure. Didn't y'all tell me that the planes were delivered here in pieces by truck?"

"Yeah." Shapiro said.

"So why do we bother putting them together? Just take the pieces off the truck, put the wings in one cargo plane, the rest of it in another, fly them to Palestine, and assemble them there?"

I looked at Shatz. He smiled. "That's a great idea. Let's see if we can do it."

And we did. With a lot of help from the Czechs, we figured out how to fit the wings into one C-46 and the fuselage in another. We had to take the motor and propeller off the fuselage, but it worked.

CHAPTER 21
May 14
Ekron, Israel

O N THE MORNING of May 14, the day before Israel would declare itself a country, we took off from Zatec in two planes. We packed each with half a Messerschmitt, and in every available nook and cranny, we loaded crates of rifles and ammunition. I flew one, Baron the other. Shatz and Shapiro were on board my plane as passengers, lying on the wings of the Messerschmitt.

Timing was critical in the operation. Our plan was to arrive in Israel just after midnight, on May 15, when the mandate officially ended and Israel became a sovereign country. The REAF still controlled the skies, and if we tried to land during daylight, the chance of being spotted and shot down was very high.

The Italian government had made Catania off-limits, but the Haganah found us a substitute refueling field at Ajaccio, Corsica. We arrived just before noon. It was a twenty-six hundred mile flight from Ajaccio to Ekron. We estimated it would take us eleven and a half hours to reach Ekron, so with some time to kill, we went to lunch. I didn't know what would happen if the authorities decided to search our planes and found crates of munitions and a dismantled Messerschmitt onboard.

At just after 1:00 in the afternoon we took off. The flight took us eleven hours and fifteen minutes, and without a stopover, we were beginning to run low on fuel. As I approached what I thought was the coast of Israel at 12:15 at night, my stomach started to do flip flops. I could make out only brief glimpses of a coastline through a layer of thick clouds that hovered over the land.

The people on the ground wouldn't turn on landing lights until they heard our engines. They couldn't give the REAF a target, in case they had planes out on patrol. Of course, that meant I didn't have a target either. The only reason they would turn on landing lights for us that night is because they knew the approximate time we'd arrive and would take the chance it was us and not the REAF.

We'd bought radio communications from the Czechs but only tested them plane to plane, not plane to ground. Even if they worked with a ground station, we didn't know if the Ekron field had one or what radio frequency to use if they did. I called Baron and told him to do a holding pattern over the Mediterranean where it was clear while I flew lower to see if I could find the airstrip. The big problem with my plan was I didn't know where I was going. I'd never been to Israel, never mind flown a plane into it.

The only thing I knew about the Ekron field was that it was supposed to be about a mile or two in from the coast. I flew south over the Mediterranean, following the bits and pieces of coastline I could see through breaks in the clouds, before turning inland and heading north.

I dropped down to two thousand feet. The clouds were so thick, I couldn't see a thing. I flew about ten miles north but saw no sign of the airfield. I turned out to sea, looped around, and began a new run to the south. I dropped down to one thousand feet. The clouds were not as thick as before but still thick at this altitude.

Four miles into my journey south, I thought I saw lights flickering below me through a break in the clouds, but the break was fleeting, and the lights disappeared. *Could they have heard me when I made my pass north and turned on the lights?* I wondered. There was only one way to find out. I turned the plane and headed north once again, this time dropping my altitude to five hundred feet.

I talked out loud to myself. "Dumbbell. You have no idea where you are, and no idea of the terrain. What if there's a mountain or a hill ahead of you bigger than five hundred feet?"

Suddenly, there they were. I saw lights. They were small flickers through the clouds, but I could see what looked like two lines of lights marking a landing strip. I looped around, keeping my eyes locked on the lights, and dropped down to two hundred feet. The clouds were gone at this altitude. I lined myself up and brought the plane in for a landing.

A Jeep pulled in front of me when I came to a stop; a man stood up waving a flashlight, beckoning me to follow him. I followed him twenty feet off the runway when he waved me to stop. Trucks pulled up next to the plane. I heard the cargo door open, and as I made my way out of the cockpit, people were already unloading the crates of rifles and ammunition.

I climbed out of the plane and stood next to Shatz and Shapiro who'd already deplaned, staying out of the way of the unloading activity. Two minutes later, a Jeep pulled up, and a man wearing what looked like an officer's uniform hopped out. "*Shalom*," he said. "I am Captain Biton, base commander."

"*Shalom*," Shatz said.

"Is there not supposed to be another plane?" he asked.

"Yes," I replied. "And you have to stop these people from unloading this one. He's circling out at sea, and I have to get back up there and show him how to get to the field."

"I can't let you do that. We need the munitions. And besides, you have a Messerschmitt inside. We need it."

"With all due respect, sir, you're an idiot. There's only half a Messerschmitt in there. The other plane is out there with the other half, and he's running very low on fuel. If he goes down, you can't fly half a Messerschmitt or get the munitions he has on board. I'll give you five more minutes to unload, then I'm going up to get him.

"I can't let you do that," the captain said.

Shatz turned to the captain. "Don't you try to stop him. If you do, you'll have to explain to Prime Minister Ben-Gurion why no more flights will be landing with munitions and the other Messerschmitts."

The Captain glared at us, turned, and yelled out something in Hebrew. The unloading process stopped, and the trucks, both loaded and empty, pulled away from the plane.

"Get me some fuel," I yelled.

A few minutes later, a truck pulled up alongside the plane. Cans of fuel were handed from one person to the next, until they reached the plane, and poured into the gas tank.

I climbed back into the cockpit, pulled to the end of the runway, and took off. Once I climbed into the clouds, I knew finding the airfield again would be dicey. I watched my compass headings and airspeed closely, locking them into my mind so I'd have the approximate location of the airfield when I returned with Baron.

I called Baron on the radio as I flew through the clouds, headed out to sea. He said he didn't know where he was, other than he was flying north and south routes about a mile off the coast. I told him I had a flare gun I'd use to mark my position and to watch for it. A blast of air hit me when I opened the side window, extended my hand out, and shot the flare straight up.

"Ah see it," Baron called to me over the radio. "Ah'm headed your way."

It took him five minutes to pull alongside of me. "Stay close," I told him over the radio.. "There's almost no visibility until you're down below two hundred feet. Stay tight and on my right."

Baron was a great pilot, but I have to admit, he made me nervous. When I said to stay close and tight, he stayed way too close and too tight for me. Just one small gust, or him losing sight of my plane for just a second or two, and we'd hit each other.

I chose not to look at him and to concentrate only on my compass heading and airspeed as I tried to reverse my flight back to the base at Ekron. I guess I was a good pilot, too, because when I dropped to just below two hundred feet, there was the airfield a half a mile away. I looked to my right. Baron wasn't there. I looked to my left. No Baron.

Then I looked up. I don't know how it happened, but he was about twenty feet above me and dropping for his landing approach. My heart nearly exploded in my chest. I jammed the stick forward to bring my nose down, pushing the throttle full open. I held my breath. The tail of Baron's plane passed overhead, mere feet from my cockpit.

I leveled out my C-46 and followed Baron's plane down.

"What the hell happened up there?" I yelled at Baron after we'd been directed to the trucks again, and I climbed out of my cockpit.

"Ah lost you above two hundred feet. Ah didn't know you were below me. When ah broke through the clouds, ah thought you already landed."

After the planes were emptied and refueled, Shatz and Shapiro took off for the return trip to Zatec. Baron and I were taken to a nearby barracks to grab some shut eye.

At dawn, I was awakened violently by the screeching wail of an air raid siren. Baron and I scrambled out of bed, dressed, then dashed outside. A female soldier yelled at us in Hebrew, which we didn't understand, but her frantic waving arm and pointing to sandbags surrounding what looked like an underground bunker, didn't need translation. We ran like hell and leaped down the stairs. It turned out to be a false alarm. Twenty minutes later, the other occupants began to move out of the bunker, and we followed close behind.

The base commander, Captain Biton, approached as we headed back to the barrack. "How did you like your morning wake-up call?"

"Could have lived without it. Get a lot of them like that?"

"No. But I wish I could say the same for Tel Aviv," the commander said, grimly.

"What do you mean?"

"This morning, the Egyptians hit Tel Aviv. There's no air opposition to stop them. They bombed the central bus station. Thirty-seven dead, so far."

"I'm sorry," I said. It was inadequate, but what else could I say?

"Instead of sorry, get those Messerschmitts in the air," Biton said.

"That's a problem. The Haganah had to hire Czech mechanics to reassemble the planes. They won't get here for at least a week."

The Captain's shoulders droop. "A week?" Maybe some of our mechanics can do it?"

"Have any of your men every worked on a Messerschmitt?"

"No. But—"

"Captain, I've got to fly those planes. Let the Czech mechanics do their job."

CHAPTER 22
May 17-20
Washington, D.C.
Rome

"EMBASSY OF EGYPT," the operator answered.

"Ammon Hazem, please?"

"One moment."

"Ammon Hazem," the man answered.

"No names. You know who this is?" Tipton said.

"Of course."

"Meet me at the bar at the Manger Hay Adams Hotel."

"Why?"

"Do you know where it is?"

"Yes. At Sixteenth and H."

"Then just be there. Four o'clock."

Hazem arrived five minutes early. Tipton was already there, seated on a stool at the end of the long oak bar. Hazem seated himself on the empty stool next to Tipton.

"I'm going to make this quick," Tipton said. "I need you to go to Rome right away."

"Rome? Why?"

"The Brotherhood has an operation working out of Rome, so you know the Haganah's headquarters in Europe is also based there. Seems we've issued a bunch of passports lately to Jews who were pilots in the war, and I got a telex from our embassy in Rome yesterday telling me a lot of those pilots have been spotted going in and out of the Haganah's headquarters."

"So, what do you think is going on?" Hazem asked.

"I don't know but I've got a feeling something is up. At the beginning of the year, all U.S. passports were stamped with the warning, *'Not valid for travel to or in any foreign state for the purpose of entering or serving in the armed forces of such a state.'* Maybe they're using Rome as a staging place, trying to get around us finding out they're really headed to Palestine and to prevent us from stopping them."

"Do you really think that's what they're doing?"

"I don't know. But if it is, I told you before, you've got as much at stake as we do in making sure none of those damn Jews get there to help. I want you in Rome and using your Brotherhood resources to find out if my gut is right. If it is, stop them." Tipton slid off his stool, threw a twenty dollar bill on the bar, and reached into his jacket pocket. "Here's your ticket. You leave tomorrow morning."

I'd been sent from Ekron to Haganah headquarters in Rome yesterday, to meet up with a group of pilots. Most were from the States, with a few from Canada and England. My job was to bring them to Zatec in two days for training on the Messerschmitts. After I introduced myself, I told them they were free to explore the city, to have a good time. I also admonished them not to get in any trouble. "If you end up in jail, we'll get you out. I just don't know how long it will take, and if you miss the trip to Zatec in two days, it may be a while before we can get you to there."

One of the pilots, David Chernoff, was from Rhode Island. He and I went to lunch so I could play some catch-up, like how the Red Sox were doing early in the season, and other news about Boston and the rest of New England.

We were in Il Melino, a mid-priced restaurant. Chernoff was in the middle of telling me about Ted Williams' latest accomplishments when he suddenly stopped talking and looked over my right shoulder. I turned to look. Two men were being led to a table.

"I met one of those guys this morning, right?" I said, turning back to Chernoff.

"Yeah. Lennie Cohen. I just met him yesterday. We flew over together from New York. Interesting guy. His parents moved to Palestine in 1924. He was an RAF fighter pilot during the war. He's a pilot for British Overseas Airline and heard about Shatz's plans through the grapevine, so he flew to the States to sign up."

"Who's the guy he's with?

"You don't know who that is? That's Buzz Beurling."

"And I'm supposed to know who he is?"

"You never heard of the 'Falcon of Malta'?"

I looked at Beurling, then back to Chernoff. "No. What's a 'Falcon of Malta'?"

"There was a story about him in the *Boston Globe*. You never read it?"

"I guess not. What's so special about him?"

"He's a war hero. In one fourteen day period on Malta, he shot down twenty-seven enemy planes. That's how he picked up the moniker the 'Falcon of Malta.' He has a total confirmed thirty-one kills."

Thirty-one kills. I was impressed. This time, I took a good look at him. He was a tall, good looking guy with a shock of unruly blond hair, dressed in an RAF uniform. He had a careless personal appearance;

there was nothing spit and polish about him. He didn't look much like a war hero.

I walked over to Cohen and Beurling's table. "Why don't you join Chernoff and me at our table? It'll give us a chance to get better acquainted."

"Sounds swell. By the way, meet Buzz Beurling."

We shook hands and made our way back to my table. "They tell me you're not Jewish. I've got to ask," I said to Beurling, "why are you fighting for us?"

"I was brought up in strict observance of my Christian faith in a sect that believes more in the Old Testament than in the new one. I believe the Jews deserve a state of their own after wandering around homeless for thousands of years. I just wanted to offer my help."

"Okay. Got another question. I was a fighter pilot in the Pacific. I had four confirmed kills in three years. They tell me you shot down twenty-seven enemy planes in fourteen days. How the hell were you able to do that and still live to tell the story?"

"Practice and tactics."

"What do you mean?"

"When I was a kid, I read every book about the World War I aces I could get my hands on and learned combat flying techniques from them."

I was fascinated. "Like what?"

"Were you a pilot during the war?"

"Yes. In the Pacific."

"Good. So you know what I'm talking about when I tell you about deflection shooting."

"Yeah. It's shooting ahead of a moving target so that the target and your bullets meet where you think the plane is going to be, not where it was when you took the shot. We called it leading the target. It offered the best chance to knock a plane out of the sky because you're shooting at the whole side of the plane."

"Correct. So, how close would you fly at an enemy plane to take a deflection shot before you broke away?"

"I don't know, maybe six hundred or seven hundred yards."

"But at that distance, it would be very hard to hit a deflection shot."

"You're right. That's why we always came up behind their plane, so we had a straight on shot."

"That's why you only had four kills, and I had thirty-one kills. I'd only engage enemy aircraft at 250 yards or less."

"Two hundred fifty yards or less? Are you crazy?"

Beurling chuckled. "That's what a lot of the other pilots called me. I'm not always perfect. Although, I've obviously survived, I've been shot down five times."

I shook my head. "Crazy or not, I'm glad you're joining us."

When we finished and were walking out of the restaurant, Beurling said to me, "You ever fly a Norseman?"

"No. Why?"

"I'm taking one up tomorrow morning. Would you like to join me?"

"Yeah, sure. What time?"

"Meet me at Urbe airfield. Around 10:00?"

"I'll be there," I said.

HAZEM CALLED TIPTON. "You're right. I think there is something going on. I saw some of the men from the passport pictures you gave me going in and out of Haganah headquarters today. And you know those pictures you showed me a month ago, the ones the F.B.I. took of the pilots in California and New Jersey? I spotted one of them coming out of headquarters this morning with another man and followed them to a restaurant. A few minutes later, two other men came in and had lunch with them. I recognized one of the second two. He'd been in the papers. He's a war hero from Canada named Buzz Beurling. I think he's part of their group."

Tipton took a deep breath. *Buzz Beurling. Flying with those Jews? What a fucking public relations nightmare that'll be.*

"Listen to me very closely," Tipton said. "I don't care how you do it. Take any means possible, but do not let Buzz Beurling fly with those Jews."

"Any means?" Hazem asked.

"Any means," Tipton responded.

THAT NIGHT, CHERNOFF, Cohen, and I did the town. We asked Beurling to join us, but he declined. Rome was a great city to be in if you were American and had U.S. dollars. We hit a bunch of night spots. We all got lucky. I met a lovely Italian girl who invited me back to her apartment where I spent the night.

I woke up the next morning at 8:00 to meet Beurling at 10:00. But my lovely new sweetheart wanted me to stay a little longer and used some pretty convincing persuasion. At 9:30, I called Beurling. "I won't be able to make it."

"No problem. Lennie Cohen is here. He'll go up with me."

"HAZEM. THIS DAIKI. That man you told us to watch? Beurling? He just showed up at the airport and asked the manager to get his Norseman fueled and ready to leave in half an hour."

"Can you get on the airfield without being noticed?" Hazem asked.

"I think so. Why?"

"Get to Beurling's plane. If he goes up in it, I don't want the plane to come back down in one piece."

I LEFT THE girl's apartment at 2:30 in the afternoon and went to Haganah headquarters to finalize the plans for leaving for Zatec. It was May 20, and I had to have all the *Machalnik* pilots ready to leave tomorrow. I sensed something was wrong. Everyone was usually quiet, busy doing their work, but this afternoon the mood was stoic.

I made my way to Asher Gittelson's office, the Haganah agent I'd been working with to make the travel arrangements to Zatec.

"What's going on?" I asked. "Everyone seems so somber"

"Beurling and Cohen are dead."

"What ...what happened?" I stammered in disbelief.

"I don't have all the details. He and Cohen took off from Urbe his morning to test-fly a Norseman. Soon after take-off, witnesses reported seeing flames coming from the Norseman's engine before it crashed. Their bodies were burned beyond recognition. It's only because people saw Beurling and Cohen get on the plane and taxi to the runway that we know it was them."

I grabbed a chair and slumped into it. I shuddered when I thought how they died, burned beyond recognition. My hands were clammy, so I tucked them into my armpits. I would have been on that plane instead of Cohen if I hadn't met that girl, and she didn't want to play around this morning,

"HAZEN? IT'S DAIKI. That situation we discussed this morning? Beurling won't be flying for the Jews. I took care of it.

CHAPTER 23
May 29
Ekron

S HATZ AND PRAGER flew in the night before. Most of the rest of our crew, as well as some of the Israeli pilots, a couple of Canadians, and a South African named Eddie Cohen, were already billeted at Ekron. The afternoon before we dodged a bullet. Two Royal Egyptian Air Force Spitfires attacked the airfield. They did a bomb run, dropping what I figured to be a couple of 150 pounders, destroying one of the two hangers on the field. Fortunately, it was the empty hanger. If they hit the other one, all four of the recently assembled Messerschmitts would have been destroyed. The last of the four to be assembled was completed the night before.

We were gathered together in the mess hall. Alon called the meeting. He was the commander of our group, personally appointed to the position by Prime Minister Ben-Gurion. Most of us Americans thought twenty-five years old was pretty young to be a squadron commander. But they'd never had a formal military before, so everyone was young.

"We should come up with a name for the squadron," Alon said

Baron asked. "Y'all got a suggestion?"

"The 101 Squadron," Alon replied.

"Why 101?" Baron asked.

Alon laughed. "Because if the enemy ever finds out about us, let them think there are at least a hundred more just like us."

Shatz laughed. "Sounds good to me."

"Me, too," came mummers from the others.

"I'd like to make a suggestion on a different subject," I said to Alon.

"Sure, go ahead," he replied.

"This is tactical. The Japs clobbered us at Pearl Harbor, and one of the main reasons was because they bombed and strafed the hell out of Hickam Air Base. They hit our planes on the ground and eliminated any kind of air opposition. The Egyptians are attacking us from their air base at El Arish. Why don't we make the first mission of the 101st to attack the base, and knock out as many planes as we can? It might help even the odds a little."

"Y'all mean a sneak attack, like the Japs did?" Baron asked.

"We didn't know we were at war with the Japs until they attacked and caught us by surprise. That was a sneak attack. The Egyptians are already at war with Israel, so it won't be a sneak attack like the Japs. It'll just be an unexpected one."

"I like it," Alon said. "Let's get the mechanics to hang some bombs, and tomorrow we'll practice flying with them."

"Ahh ... I don't think so," I said. "We haven't even test-flown the four pieces o'shit yet. I don't want the first time up in them to be with one hundred and fifty pound bombs strapped to their wings." I turned my palms up. "You know, just in case something goes wrong."

"You're right," Alon said. "Let's take them out for a test flight tomorrow. I'll have the mechanics get the bomb racks and the bombs ready today. If everything is good tomorrow, we'll hit El Arish the next day."

"Good idea," I said.

Alon looked at me. His lips broke into a small grin. "I have another good idea. I may be the squadron commander, but I don't have any combat experience. So, on the ground, I'm the boss. In the air, you are."

"What?" I sputtered.

"Look, you're a great pilot. Everyone knows that. You've flown combat missions in the Pacific. You've got experience I can't come close to. So when we're in the air, you lead; we'll follow."

I didn't know what to say, so I said the only thing I could. "Okay."

I went to sleep that night feeling good. We were going to fight. We had a battle plan: test the planes tomorrow and attack El Arish the next day.

THE NEXT MORNING, Alon, Ezer Weizman, Eddie Cohen, and I were outside the hanger doing preflight checks on the Messerschmitts. Alon said I was boss in the air, so I selected the pilots. I picked Alon because he was the squadron commander. I picked Weizman because, from what I'd seen back in Zatec, he was a good pilot, and for the sake of moral, the attack on El Arish should be half Israeli. I picked South African Eddie Cohen because I'd also seen him fly in Zatec, and pound for pound, he was one of the best pilots in a fighter plane I'd ever seen, even on this 'piece o'shit.'

After doing our ground checks, I walked over to Alon. "You want to go up first? If not, no problem if you want me to go first."

"No, I'll go first. I'd like to—"

Before he could finish, a Jeep came barreling toward us and screeched to a stop. I didn't understand the Israeli uniform markings, but it was definitely an officer who jumped out. He spoke rapidly to Alon in Hebrew. Alon turned to me. "This is Colonel Perez, sent by General Avraham. They need us to get these planes up now. The Egyptian Army is only fifteen miles from Tel Aviv. The Haganah held them up for two weeks by blowing up the Ad Halom Bridge over the

Lakhish River, but it's been repaired, and the Egyptians are on the move."

"Tell the colonel we can't. We haven't tested the engines on these planes. We don't know if they'll even get off the ground. Tell him our plan to test the planes today, and if it goes well, attack El Arish tomorrow."

"Sir," the colonel said to me in English, "I'm aware you're an American, and you came here to help Israel fight. But you have to understand, if you don't stop the Egyptian Army now, they'll be in Tel Aviv tomorrow morning, and the war is over. There will be no Israel."

So much for hitting the Egyptian planes on the ground. I remembered the Yiddish expression my mother used to say: Man plans, God laughs.

CHAPTER 24
May 29
Skies over Israel

THE CZECH MECHANICS immediately began attaching the bomb racks underneath the Messerschmitts. Every available mechanic pitched in, aided by the Israeli mechanics they were training.

They did the installation in record time. Within an hour, the planes were ready, each armed with two 150 lbs bombs attached to its racks. I climbed into my aircraft and started the engine, which sounded fine. Taxing to the runway, Alon was close by on my right. I readied myself for the plane to pull to the left as I took off, but it lifted straight into the air. I glanced over toward Alon. His plane was also doing fine.

I was the lead plane in the formation. The colonel said the Egyptians were ten miles to the south of us, near Ashdod, but I didn't know exactly where that was. I hadn't been off the base since my arrival, except for the hotel to eat and sleep, and didn't know Israeli geography. Headed west toward the Mediterranean, I glanced over at Alon. He waggled his wings and gestured wildly with his arm, indicating he wanted me to go in the direction he pointed. He knew Israel better than me, so I banked, pulled up on his wing, and followed.

Six minutes later, we'd covered a lot of terrain, and there they were two miles ahead. It looked like the entire Egyptian Army. For as far as I could see, stretched out in a single column, were troop carriers, armored cars, and tanks moving north toward Tel Aviv. The colonel estimated there were five thousand Egyptians. I wouldn't argue the number.

I'm not a religious person. I don't believe in God, at least not the all powerful benevolent deity the Jewish religion prays to. I'd like to believe; I just don't. I'm not sure whether that makes me an atheist or an agnostic. I stopped believing long before I saw the Nazi death camps. They only reinforced the feeling. No all powerful benevolent deity would allow something like that to happen.

But a Marine Gunnery Sergeant once told to me there are no atheists in a foxhole. I suppose there's a grain of truth to that. When you're facing the sure prospect of death, you'd like to believe in something more powerful than yourself. So hedging my bet in case there was a God, I said a quick *Sh'ma*. It's our oldest prayer, the bedrock on which the Jewish religion stands. "*Sh'ma Yisra'eil Adonai Eloheinu Adonai Echa.,* Hear, O Israel, the Lord is our God, the Lord is One."

With that said, I moved passed Alon into the lead and checked the skies in all directions. The column below had no air cover. I nosed my plane over into a steep dive and took aim at the tank in front, leading the column. I let loose my bomb, pulled up, and headed west before making a looping turn to come back for another run with my last bomb. I'd made a direct hit on the tank. A billow of smoke rose in the sky from it, like an eerie black finger. The others had also done well. Smoke poured from two other tanks and an armored car.

I decided to try for a target further down the column on my next run. It might stop or slow them down for a little longer if they had to maneuver around damaged vehicles in the middle, not just at the front. I took aim at what looked like a tanker truck. Seconds after I dropped the bomb, my plane vibrated from a thunderous explosion, and a fireball shot forty feet in the air.

Again I turned west, climbed to 3000 feet, and made a 180 degree turn. I came in from the east, the sun at my back and in their eyes. I made a quick 90 degree turn, positioning myself to fly right down the middle of the convoy. It also made me a smaller target to hit. I dropped to three hundred feet and began a strafing run.

I flew over the first thirty vehicles and opened up with my machine gun. The bullets ripped into half a dozen troop carriers before the Egyptians began to scatter out of their single column. As they pulled off the road and into the desert, puffs of antiaircraft shells exploded on my left. I swept out again to the west and looked back. The other three planes were strafing the Egyptians.

I decided to try to throw the enemy off stride and hit them from a different direction. This time, I climbed to eight thousand feet, did another half circle turn, and flew east, high over the scattering vehicles. A mile past the enemy, I swung around and came at them from the west instead of the east and further to the south.

I swooped down to three hundred feet, lined myself on another tanker truck, and pushed my thumb on the trigger. Nothing. I pushed again. Nothing. I knew I still had plenty of ammunition. I pushed again. Still nothing. Bile rose in my throat. The gun was jammed. At the same time, my plane began to bounce about from the concussive explosions of antiaircraft shells.

Swooping high and to the west, I was able to follow the flight of the rest of my team as they started their strafing run. There was no machine gun fire coming from either Alon or Weizman. *Bet their guns jammed, too.*

Eddie Cohen didn't have the same problem. He strafed the hell out of them. His bullets tore up one armored car after another. "Go get them, Eddie!" I yelled in my cockpit. Alon, Weizman, and I were no more use in the sky, so I began heading north to the base. Minutes later, they caught up with me.

I glanced back to see if Cohen's plane was catching up. My stomach muscles clenched. I gasped, screaming, "No!" He'd been hit by flak. Dark black smoke billowed from his engine, and it looked like part of his right wing was missing. He was headed west, toward the Mediterranean. I turned to follow, Alon and Weizman right behind.

We got a half mile out over the water. "Turn!" I yelled. "Turn north." Of course, he couldn't hear me. We didn't have radios in the planes. The rest of his right wing ripped from the plane, and the aircraft began a spiral descent, twisting its way toward the sea. Cohen hit the water. The three of us circled the crash area for fifteen minutes. There was no sign of Cohen, and what pieces of the plane that were left began to sink into the sea. There was nothing we could do. I signaled Alon and Weizman to follow me home.

I landed first. Weizman followed. I'd just turned toward the hanger and spotted Alon's plane. He'd made his final approach and was less than a quarter mile from the end of the runway. *Oh, shit.* Only his left landing gear had lowered, and I didn't think he knew it. There was no way to let him know. My neck muscles tightened. All I could do is to sit in my idling plane, squeeze the control stick in a death grip, and watch.

It didn't help that not only had the right landing gear not gone down; the piece o'shit Alon was flying had a tendency to pull to the right when it landed. His left wheel hit the ground. A second later, the plane buckled and collapsed onto its right side. The tip of the wing dug into the ground and snapped off, causing the plane to spin like a top for three revolutions before it came to a stop in the dirt, ten feet off the runway. Alon leaped from the cockpit and scrambled away in case the plane burst into flames. It didn't.

It wasn't until Weizman and I pulled our planes to the hanger and dismounted that I became aware that my mine was damaged. A burst of flak had nicked an oil line. A swath of oil stretched from the engine, down the length of the fuselage, to the rear stabilizer.

The three of us made our way back to the ready room, the one we used for meetings. The rest of our pilots were already there. Alon told them what happened to Cohen. To the group from the States, it felt like losing Gerson all over again. But this time it wasn't Shatz they blamed. It was war. It didn't change the feeling of loss we had, but at least this was something we could understand. We'd lived with it, either in the Pacific or over Europe.

Being the boss in the sky, I had to say something. "I don't know what good we did out there today, but we suffered a tremendous loss—Eddie Cohen. And although it doesn't come close to being the same, we suffered more than that. I'm not taking anything away from anyone in this room, but for all practical purposes, today the entire Israeli Air Force went into battle, and we lost one-quarter of our pilots. To add salt to the wound, three-quarters of our entire fleet of fighter planes were either destroyed or knocked out of service."

AN HOUR LATER, we were all still in the ready room. I'd just taken a sip from my second glass of whiskey when the door opened and Colonel Perez walked in. He marched over to Alon, threw him a salute, and against any military etiquette I'd ever seen, pulled him into a hug.

He turned to the rest of us. "General Avraham asked me to personally deliver the news. Tonight, our intelligence people picked up a message from the Commanding General of the Egyptian Army column you attacked this morning. It was sent to army headquarters in Cairo."

He reached into his shirt pocket and pulled out a slip of paper. "We broke their code weeks ago. The message reads, and I quote, 'We have been heavily attacked by enemy aircraft. We are dispersing.'"

Perez looked from me to Alon then moved to the front of the room and faced the pilots. "You did it. You stopped the Egyptians from overrunning Tel Aviv. This war is far from over, but it almost was. If not for what you did today, there would never be an Israel."

He stiffened to attention and snapped his hand up in a salute.

CHAPTER 25
May 30, 1948
Treviso, northern Italy

SHATZ WAS STANDING next to his C-46 in Zatec, LAPSA still painted on the fuselage, when two men walked over to him. "You Shatz?" one of them asked.

"Yup," he replied.

"Hi. My name is Aaron Finkel, but most people call me 'Red,'" he said, grinning and pointing to an unruly head of carrot colored hair. "This here is Syd Antyn. We're from the States. We just finished training on the Messerschmitts and need a ride to Israel. They said you were headed there, and we could grab a lift. That okay?"

"If you don't mind sitting on crates of munitions for seven or eight hours, you're more than welcome," Shatz replied.

The men stood by the plane for the next fifteen minutes as the ground crew finished loading crates of machine guns and ammunition inside.

"How did you end up here?" Shatz asked Finkel, as the final crate was loaded into the plane.

"I was working as a salesman, sharing an apartment in Brooklyn with a friend of mine. We'd been pilots in the same squadron, flying P-47s over the hump in China. One night, maybe four weeks ago, I'm sleeping, when all of a sudden I'm being woken up by a guy sitting on the edge of my bed, shaking my shoulder. I pop up, fist clenched, ready to pop the guy, when he holds up his hands and says, 'Take it easy.' I don't know who the hell he is but figure my roommate must have let him in.

"I calm down slightly, push myself a foot or two away from him, still clenching my fists, and ask, 'Who the hell are you?'"

"I'm from the Haganah," he says. "I know you're a pilot, and I want you to fly for the Jews in Palestine. What will it take for you to do it?"

"So, I'm sitting on my bed, in the middle of the night, trying to clear my head, trying to process what he just said. And I'm thinking, any Jews willing to stand up and fight for their lives, deserve all the help I can give them. Sliding off the bed, I tell the guy, 'Give me a bottle of rye whiskey, supply me with cigarettes for as long as I'm over there, pay me $30 a month, and I'll do it.' So, here I am."

Shatz laughed. "You're just the kind of crazy we need."

They took off for Israel from Zatec with a planned stopover in Ajaccio, Corsica. But early in the flight, the engine began to run rough, and Shatz made an emergency landing in Treviso, Italy. He thought back to the story Hal Auerbach told him about when he was forced to land at the Treviso base two weeks ago, so he wasn't worried.

"I WAS FLYING the C-46, with the disassembled Messerschmitt inside, over the snowcapped Alps at around fourteen thousand feet when I entered Italian airspace," Auerbach said to Shatz. "And waiting for me up there was an Italian Air Force fighter plane. He moved into position off my left wing and signaled with his hand and by lowering his landing gear that he wanted me to follow him and land. The sky was clear, I had no place to hide, and he had four machine guns tucked under his wings, so I graciously accepted his invitation and followed him. We landed at the Italian Air Base at Treviso, north of Venice.

"When I got out of the plane with my crew, we were greeted by the Commandante, who told us we were under arrest. He suspected we were smuggling arms to the communists in Italy trying to overthrow the government. He questioned us for hours. He spoke pretty good English. But it was with a southern accent, which with his Italian accent, sounded funny. I had to fight hard not to break out laughing.

"He was also suspicious when I asked to phone the Israeli Embassy in Rome. I guess I couldn't blame him. Here I was, flying a Panamanian registered plane with the Panamanian Air Line logo LAPSA painted on the side, supposedly headed to Casablanca, asking to call the Israeli Embassy in Rome.

"He finally let me call Rome, and a couple of hours later he said his superiors called him, told him we were on innocent passage to Israel. We weren't smugglers helping the communists, and we should be permitted to leave.

"At that point the Commandante became friendly. He put us up in a hotel and picked us up the next morning. I asked him if we could go to a wholesale food market, and he drove us there himself. I bought so much food, he had to arrange to have a truck come from the base to pick it up and bring it to our plane. He had our plane refueled, and to show my appreciation, I gave him ten cartons of American cigarettes.

"Before we left, I asked the Commandante where he learned English and why it sounded like he had a Southern accent. He said during the war he'd been a POW in a camp in Mississippi for two years and learned English listening to the local radio broadcasts. Go figure."

PULLING OFF THE end of the runway in Treviso, Shatz was guided to a parking area where he deplaned. The same base commander who had previously proven friendly to Auerbach was there to greet him. The

Commandante did not bother searching the plane for contraband, taking Shatz's word that he was flying civilian cargo to the Americas.

Shatz checked the engine and found it was an iced-up carburetor that caused the engine problem. He knew it would only take an hour for it to defrost, and they could be on their way.

But when the base commander left the area, an Italian soldier decided to peek inside the plane where he saw Finkel, Antyn and some crates. The soldier pointed his gun at Finkel and demanded he open the box he was sitting on. Finkel refused and said not until the base commander returned. The soldier backed off, and Finkel and Antyn used the time to collect and destroy potentially incriminating documents in the cockpit.

When the Commandante returned, he was with regional chief of police. They insisted Finkel open a crate. Shatz tried to convince them the crates carried surveying equipment. But anybody who has ever seen an ammunition box knows what the hell is in it. The machine guns were in much longer boxes, and they were in two layers.

Even though Shatz told them it was surveying equipment, the Commandante insisted on opening up one of the longer boxes. Finkel took the cover off. The top layer had the tripod for the machine gun. But the guts of the machine gun were not in the top layer. When they saw the tripod, Shatz said to the Commandante, "See, that's for the surveying equipment."

Then the regional chief of police said, "Open up the rest of it." And there it was, the air-cooled barrel of a machine gun. It was obvious what it was, and you couldn't call it surveying equipment. .

The Italians took Shatz, Finkel, and Antyn into custody. They thought Shatz was running guns for communists somewhere in Italy. Shatz asked to make a phone call which they allowed. He called Danny Agronsky, publicly the local LAPA official, but secretly in charge of the Haganah's European air operations.

As the group was hustled toward the base's jail. Shatz shouted indignantly that they were Americans and could not be treated in this fashion. The base commander asked if he wanted to see the U.S.

consul. Shatz declined. The U.S. arms embargo was in place, and all three of them could lose their citizenship if the State Department got involved.

Agronsky secured their release, and they caught a flight to Haifa on a Jewish-owned South African airline... but not before they spent three nights in jail

CHAPTER 26
May 30
Skies over Northern Israel

I'D CONSUMED SIX whiskeys before hitting the sack the night before at 11:00, but they didn't help. I tossed and turned for hours. I'm sure one reason was that I probably still had some residual adrenaline in my system from the day's mission. Probably the main reason was because every time I closed my eyes, I kept seeing Eddie Cohen's plane plummeting into the sea.

"Kaplan, get up," I heard someone say. He was gently shaking my shoulder. I moaned and rolled onto my back. The room was dark. I blinked my eyes a few times, trying to make out the face of the man standing next to my bed.

"Weizman?"

"Yes"

"What's the matter?"

"Get up. We've got a mission."

I stretched my arms and glanced out the window. It was dark outside. "What time is it?"

"Four-thirty. Come on. Get up. We've got to go."

Four-thirty. I guess I finally fell asleep.

"Go where? What mission?"

"There's a report of an Iraqi light armor column heading toward Kfar Yonah. We've been told to stop them."

"What do you mean we? We lost two planes yesterday, and mine's damaged. You've got the only flyable one left."

"The mechanics worked on yours all day yesterday. They've got it fixed."

My mouth felt as dry as the Negev Desert, and my head hurt from the whiskey.

"Come on, Kaplan. We've got to go. Now," Weizman said.

I got dressed in record time and hustled behind Weizman as he set a fast pace to the hanger. When we entered, Weizman went right to his plane to begin his preflight check. I moved over to mine. Three mechanics were attaching two-one hundred and fifty pound bombs to it, and two more were loading ammunition for the machine guns. I spotted Mojmir, one of the two senior Czech mechanics. All the American pilots called him Mo.

"Mo," I called out, "are you sure this is ready to fly?"

Mo nodded. "Yes. We fix. Just cut in oil line. We fix. It good." He lifted his hand and touched the tip of his finger to the tip of his thumb, the universal sign for okay. I'd seen what Mo had done to get the planes ready to fly, so if he said it was good to go, it was good to go.

I was halfway through my preflight check when Weizman called me over to a large table with a map of Palestine lying on top.

"Where did you get the map?" I asked.

"From the British. I had to do an after-action report on yesterday's mission. Alon told me, and I told General Avraham, that when we took off yesterday, you didn't know where you were going, and Alon needed to show you. So the General sent this map, left behind by the British."

"Great. So show me. Where are we going?"

"We're here, in Ekron," he said, pointing to the spot on the map. He drew his finger in a straight line northeast and stopped at a place called Tulkarm. "The Iraqi armored column was headed here about two hours ago. The kibbutz was abandoned three days ago. Everyone moved over here," he said, tapping his finger on a place called Kfar Yonah. "We think this is their objective."

"How far is it from here to Tulkarm?"

"About 138 kilometers. For you, about 85 miles."

I glanced out the window. It was still dark outside "This map is great, but if I can't see what's below me, it doesn't do me much good." I looked at my watch. It was 5:15.

"When's sunrise?" I asked.

Weizman checked his watch. "In about fifteen minutes. Tulkarm is slightly east, so it will get lighter there a little sooner."

"Did they give you any plan of action? Do they want us to hit anything special or just attack the column?"

"There's a railroad station they want us to take out in Tulkarm so it can't be used by the Iraqis or Syrians, but the key objective is to hit the column hard. The Iraqis are the largest of the Arab armies attacking us. Headquarters believes if we can stall them, the others might hesitate."

Before taking off, Weizman and I decided we would attack the column by coming in from the east, putting the rising sun at our back and in their eyes.

I told Weizman to leave the map in the hanger because it wouldn't do me much good. I had a general idea of the direction we were going but didn't know the names of towns, roads, or rivers below. Weizman would take the lead. I'd stay on his right wing until we spotted the Iraqi column. At that point, I'd take the lead.

We took off at 5:30. The sky was just beginning to go from ink black to a mixture of yellow and orange. As we gained altitude, I saw the bright yellow top of the sun peek over the horizon. I'd decided against flying at maximum speed, which was around 304 knots. While it would get us over the target in fifteen to seventeen minutes, it would also use valuable fuel, which was in short supply. At 175 knots, we would arrive at Tulkarm in twenty-five minutes.

Twenty minutes later, Weizman waggled his wings. He waved his arm in a circle and pointed to his left. The Iraqi column was four miles away. They had advanced about a mile past Tulkarm, headed west toward Kfar Yonah.

I took the lead. We were at fifteen thousand feet and not likely to be spotted by the enemy below. I took us out east until I spotted the village of Nur A-Shams that I'd seen on the map. It was three miles from Tulkarm. I turned west, dropped down to two thousand feet, and began my run at Tulkarm first, and the column next. Weizman followed on my tail.

The battle plan was for both of us to drop one bomb each on the railroad station, fly low over the column, and drop our remaining bomb on the front end of the advancing column. Then, we would swoop around and strafe the column from the rear to the front, keeping the rising sun in their eyes.

We executed the plan perfectly. We'd taken out a couple of tanks and trucks near the head of the column, and as we passed back over Tulkarm, circling for another strafing run, billows of smoke rose from the destroyed train station.

I turned, dropped down to one thousand feet again, and began my run, with Weizman three hundred yards behind. I was halfway down the column, machine guns blazing, when I saw the black smoke from exploding antiaircraft shells straight ahead. I immediately pulled back on the stick to gain altitude, thrust the throttle forward to gain speed, and peeled off to my left... but not fast enough.

Bang. My plane bounced violently up and to the side. Thick, black smoke spewed from my engine. *Shit.* I headed due west and climbed to ten thousand feet. The needle on my oil gauge had already dropped past the three-quarters line and continued to creep toward empty. *I'll never make it back to Ekron.*

I had to keep going west, toward the Mediterranean, away from Arab held territory. My mind flashed back to Weizman's map. I racked my brain, trying to recall some details of what airfields, or a friendly kibbutz or town, were in the direction I was headed. I knew I was north of Netanya, but there was no airfield near it. Kfar Vitkin, I remembered. It was a kibbutz about six or seven miles north of Netanya on a straight line with my heading. I nursed my plane that way.

The smoke from the engine was getting thicker. The oil gauge was almost down to empty, and I was losing altitude. I saw the Mediterranean about two miles away. Looking through the black smoke at the ground below, I didn't see any place for me to land safely. I'd have to bail out over water. The plane had already dropped to twenty-five thousand feet, and I was fighting the stick to keep it from dropping faster.

All my training taught me that I needed a lot more altitude to bailout, but I had no choice. It was either bailout or drop the plane into the sea and hope it didn't bust up and kill me then, or drown me after. I popped the canopy, unclipped my seat belt, and prepared to bail.

When I thought I was far enough out to sea, with my altimeter showing fifteen thousand feet, I bailed out. Seconds later, I pulled the ripcord. When the chute fully opened, I couldn't have been more than four hundred feet over the water. A gust of wind pushed me sideways, just before I hit the water... hard. I felt a sharp pain in my right side.

I hit the quick release on my parachute before it filled with water and dragged me under. I treaded water, trying to get my bearings. I saw the shoreline. It had to be three miles away. Fighting the throbbing fire in my side and shoulder, I kicked off my flight boots and began to swim with one arm. It was long and painful, each stroke sending searing pain shooting through my right side.

I swam for almost an hour. I wasn't going to make it. The pain was too great, and I was exhausted. Accepting my fate, I stopped swimming and let my lower body drift down toward the bottom of the sea. *What the hell?* My toes touched bottom. When I straightened my legs, I was standing waist high in the water. I'd been swimming for about an hour in water I could have stood up in at any time. I didn't realize it because I was so far out. *Son of a bitch.* Holding my right arm with my left hand, I waded painfully to the shore.

When I reached the sandy beach, I dropped to my knees to catch my breath, but each inhale brought a sharp pain like a knife jab to my side. I gently pressed my hand to my right ribcage, causing a repeat of the pain. My shoulder was on fire. *Must have broken some ribs.*

The sound of a gunshot snapped my head up. A crowd of men had crested a sand dune and were coming at me. One was holding a rifle, the rest brandishing what looked like pitchforks, shovels, and clubs. They were yelling and screaming. *Oh, shit. They must think I'm an Egyptian pilot. I bet they don't even know that Israel has an air force with fighter planes.*

I stood up and raised my left arm over my head in surrender. I couldn't lift my right arm. The mob was shouting at me in Hebrew. I didn't speak or understand it and had no idea what they were saying. My mind raced. I had to say something, to let them know I was Jewish, not an Arab.

I reached back in my mind to what I had been taught. Jews all over the world celebrated the same holidays, especially Yom Kippur, the most sacred, and Pesach, the exodus from Egypt.

"Yom Kippur! Pesach! Gefilte fish! Matzo! Pesach! Gefilte fish! Matzo!" I shouted, over and over.

It seemed to work. They slowed down their menacing approach, moving slowly and cautiously toward me. I kept repeating the mantra until they were only a few feet away. I had one more trick up my sleeve. I put my hand on my chest and said the *Sh'ma.* That did it. They lowered their weapons and helped me back to Kfar Vitkin.

They had a doctor at the *kibbutz* who spoke some English. He examined me in the common room used for eating and meetings. It looked like half the *kibbutz* stood around watching. He said I had a dislocated shoulder and thought I had a couple of bruised ribs but didn't have X-ray equipment to be sure. When he popped my shoulder back into place, I swear my scream could be heard back in Tel Aviv.

While taping my ribs, he asked me where I came from. I told

him I was an American *Machal*, based in Ekron. I told him about the planes and the mission I'd been on. When he translated it to the kibbutzim, and they heard Israel had an air force and was fighting back, a loud cheer went up.

CHAPTER 27
May 30-June 3
Israel

THE PEOPLE FROM Kfar Vitkin got me to a hospital in Netanya that afternoon. Alon and Weizman drove up from Ekron and met me there.

"What happened to you?" Weizman asked.

When I told them the story, both men roared with laughter when I got to the end about using Yiddish. It even sounded funny to me, and I laughed with them, even though it hurt me when I did.

"What happened to you?" I asked Weizman. "I saw you begin your strafing run then pull up fast and fly off."

"I'd just started my run when something hit my windshield and smashed it, splattering me with glass. I couldn't see anything so I had to return to base. When I landed, they found bird feathers and blood next to the opening. A damn bird strike took me out. They also found I took a few bullet strikes to the wings, but they'll get those repaired."

A doctor came into the room as I was putting on my shirt, and said I was free to go. "Your shoulder is fine and the X-ray shows no broken ribs, but I'm sure they're badly bruised. Keep the tape wrapping on for a few more days, and you'll be fine. I wouldn't recommend flying for at least a week."

Alon said to me, "You won't have a problem with that prescription. The only operational plane we have left is Weizman's. Three were delivered to us today and seven more to the airfield in Herzliya. The Czech mechanics and the Israelis they're training started assembling them right away at both locations, but we won't have anything that can fly for a few days."

We left the hospital and drove back to Ekron. Approaching the base, I saw smoke. Weizman sped onto the base and headed the car toward the source of the smoke. He screeched to a stop next to a bunch of men hosing down a half assembled Messerschmitt.

"What happened?" Alon asked.

"A couple of Egyptian Spitfires strafed us a half hour ago," one of the ground crew told Alon. "Good thing they didn't go for the hanger, or we would have lost Weizman's plane and the other two we're working on." Weizman translated the Hebrew for me.

Alon said, "Headquarters thinks we're too close to the Egyptian base at El Arish. I think we should move the 101st squadron up to Herzliya. What do you think?"

Weizman and I agreed. Alon said he'd send a request to headquarters.

We were bivouacked in Tel Aviv at the Golan Hotel. Located next to the beach, it had a large indoor bar and patio that stretched to within feet of the beach. That night, pilots decided to celebrate my safe return by having a party.

Everyone had a great time, particularly at my expense as the story of my yelling in Yiddish was retold over and over, sometimes even embellished. I didn't mind. All the pilots, but Modi Alon, got pretty wasted.

The next morning, Weizman missed the Jeep transport to Ekron. Borrowing Alon's motorcycle, he hit a crater caused by a mortar, flew over the handlebars, breaking a bone in his left hand. He was taken back to Tel Aviv. Unaware of what happened to Weizman, Alon had sent all the other pilots to Herzliya that morning. That left him the lone pilot in Ekron who could fly.

IT WAS MID-AFTERNOON, three days later, on June 3. Work on the two remaining piece o'shits proceeded smoothly at Ekron, and they were almost operational. Weizman and I were not. The doctor told us both we had to wait at least another week before he'd clear us for combat.

We were in the hanger when a soldier burst through the door, gesturing and yelling. "What's going on?" I asked Weizman.

"He's telling Alon two Egyptian C-47 Dakota bombers, with two Spitfire escorts, were spotted headed to Tel Aviv."

"Dakotas aren't bombers," I replied.

"These are. The Egyptians converted them into bombers. They've been attacking Tel Aviv daily. They fly over the city, and a crew in the back throws bombs out the cargo door. Like we do with the Piper Cubs. But these are bigger planes, with more and bigger bombs. The other difference is, we go after only military targets. With them, the whole city is their target, so almost every casualty is civilian. General Avraham wants us to stop them."

"With what? We've got only one plane and one pilot who can fly."

"That's right," Alon said. "And I'm going up now."

He turned to one of the Israeli mechanics and spoke rapidly in Hebrew. In less than ten minutes, the crew had made sure the plane's fuel tank was topped off, and there was a full load of ammo for the machine guns. Minutes later, Alon was in the cockpit, engine running, and pulling out of the hanger. Weizman and I moved outside and watched him take off.

HOURS LATER, WEIZMAN and I were sitting outside the hanger, scanning the skies for Alon's plane. "There," Weizman shouted, pointing to a speck off in the distance to our right, about two o'clock on a watch. Alon touched down a few minutes later, taxied to the hanger, and climbed out of the plane.

Alon smiled. "I got the Dakotas."

I let out a yell and grabbed him in a bear hug. "Tell me."

"I thought I might intercept them before they got to Tel Aviv, so I headed there first, thinking I'd work out from the city. But when I got there, the Dakotas were already circling above with their Spitfire escort

"I flew west, out over the Mediterranean, so I could approach with the sun behind me to mask my attack. Then I turned around at high speed and approached from underneath. I waited until the last second then shot up behind the first Dakota and opened up with a long burst. I didn't need to look back at it. I knew it was a goner.

"I didn't want to mess around with the Spitfires at this point, so I zoomed past them, made a tight turn, and came back, head-on, at the second Dakota. The pilot tried to get away. The plane slogged into a turn, trying to escape over the sea. But at my speed, it couldn't. The way I came in, the two Spitfires couldn't position themselves to defend it. I lined up and fired. It staggered out over the sea before crashing.

"I wanted to go after the Spitfires next, but when I turned to engage them, they were headed back to Egypt. I think they must have been shocked that we had a fighter plane and that Jews had actually been able to defend themselves in the air... and attack them."

"Alon," Weizman said. "Do you realize what you just did? You scored the first Israeli Air Force air-to-air victory."

CHAPTER 28
June 9-11
Herzliya

AIR FORCE COMMAND agreed with Alon's recommendation to move our fighter base out of Ekron after the Egyptian raid on it a week before We pulled the unit back from the frontlines, north to Herzliya. It had a sixty-five thousand foot unpaved runway, aligned north/south, bulldozed inside orange groves. Alon thought the unpaved strip would handle the finicky Messerschmitts better than concrete. The base had a water tower we used as the control tower, and we sheltered the planes between orange trees, beneath camouflage netting.

Most of the ferry service of munitions and Messerschmitts, as well as flight training on the piece o'shits, was turned over to *Machalnik* pilots who'd arrived in Zatec from the United States, Canada, England, and South Africa. That allowed Shapiro, Pinter, Lapin, and Landau to come to Herzliya the day before and fly combat missions with the 101st fighter squadron. Along with the other pilots already on station, for the first time we had all the pilots from LAPSA together in Israel.

It was early afternoon. Alon went to Tel Aviv for a meeting and left me in charge. I was in his small office, my feet up on the desk, reading a two week old copy of the *New York Times*.

Ring. Ring. I picked up the receiver. Before I had a chance to say hello, someone began speaking very fast, in Hebrew.

"Stop! Stop!" I shouted, as loud as I could, trying to get the person to hear me over his excited talking. "Speak English! Speak English!" I kept yelling, until my words finally got through to the person on the other end of the line.

"Who is this?" the voice asked, in English

"Kaplan,"

"Where's Alon?"

"Went to a meeting in Tel Aviv."

"Who's in charge up there?"

"I am."

There was a split second pause. "This is Captain Rosenthal from General Avraham's staff. Four Spitfires were just spotted heading north, about four miles west of Sderot. That puts them seventy miles south of Tel Aviv. We're sure that's where they're headed. You've got to try to stop them. "

"Will do," I said. I hung up and rushed from the office to the ready room.

"Pinter. You're up. Let's go."

"Where?"

"We're stopping some Spitfires from hitting Tel Aviv."

Pinter bolted out of his seat and followed me as I sprinted out the door to the hanger.

In the five days since Alon knocked the two Egyptian Dakotas out of the air, the Czech and Israeli mechanics had been busy. They finished repairs on the two Messerschmitts that had been in the hangers in Ekron. In addition, they had almost completed putting together the two Messerschmitts that had been flown into Herzliya three days ago in the C-46s.

I yelled to Mo to move the two planes outside. The crews dropped what they were doing and pushed them toward the hanger door, as a mechanic hopped up on each plane and checked the magazines, making sure they were fully loaded. Seconds later, each turned to me and gave a thumbs-up.

While the planes were put in position outside, I pulled Pinter to the map table. Since I got shot down, I'd studied the map, familiarizing myself with the geography and topography of Israel.

"Here's where they were sighted twelve minutes ago," I said, pointing to where the planes were seen.

"This is us," I said, tapping Herzliya on the map, "and here's Tel Aviv, ten miles south of us."

Running my finger southeast in a straight line, I continued, "We'll pick them up here," indicating Rishon LeZion, five miles south of Tel Aviv.

"You fly high cover on my right, and follow me to the intercept point. Once we spot them, you're free to engage."

We made our way to the planes. My rigger strapped me into my parachute and safety harness. I did a quick check of my fuel and oil gauges, giving the ground crew a quick salute, letting them know I was all set. They pulled away the wheel chocks. Pinter followed me, engines roaring, to the end of the runway. Pushing the throttle full open, I took off, Pinter on my tail.

It was hot and hazy as we headed toward Tel Aviv, and the intercept point. We still didn't have radios, but a resourceful Israeli mechanic acquired some walkie-talkies which we used to communicate. The trouble with them is we had to be fairly close to each other, and it was hard to hear over the loud Junker engines.

I flew at ten thousand feet, Pinter two thousand feet above me. We'd been in the air about ten minutes, and my flying suit was already soaked from the heat in the cockpit. About five miles in front of me,

I saw a large swath of cumulus clouds. I was about four thousand feet above them, putting their tops close to six thousand feet in the sky. Maybe I should fly into them for a few minutes and let the cockpit cool down, I thought.

Wiping perspiration from my brow and sweat from my eyes, I looked down to see four Spitfires breaking out of the cloud bank. They were two thousand feet below me, five miles away, and headed straight for Tel Aviv.

I grabbed the walkie talkie from the holder next to my knee. "Pinter, come in." No response. "Pinter, come in." Still no response.

"These things are useless," I yelled in frustration, slamming the unit back into the holder.

I climbed up beside Pinter and waggled my wings to get his attention. When he looked over, I waved my hand in a circular motion and pointed down, toward the enemy aircraft. Pinter looked where I was pointing, nodded, and gave me a thumbs-up.

It was clear the Spits hadn't seen us because they took no evasive action. They probably weren't even looking for enemy planes. I flipped up the guard on my firing button, took a deep breath, and rolled over into a dive.

Coming up behind the rear Spitfire, I opened up with a two second burst from my machine gun. The plane rolled, dove down, breaking to his left. Within seconds, traveling at 325 knots, I flashed by him. Before I could turn into the other Spits, they broke formation and scattered in different directions. Making sure none were on my tail, I went after the one I'd fired on. He headed into the clouds. *Shit.*

I tried to follow as he weaved in and out of the clouds. This was a repeat of the dogfights that took place during the war in Europe. A German Messerschmitt against a British Spitfire. Only this time, it was a Jew flying the German plane, and an Egyptian in the British one.

I'd pick up the Spit, get ready to fire, then lose him again as he found shelter in another bank of clouds. *Where are you?* My heart was thumping in my chest, my hands and feet felt cold and clammy. I was having an adrenaline rush.

Then the pilot made a fatal mistake. Instead of staying hidden in the clouds until I gave up, or he could turn the tables and attack me, I spotted him making a break for the sea, leaving himself out in the open with no place to hide. I opened up with a two second burst and saw parts of his plane fly off. He dove and rolled, trying to get me off his back. I followed.

I remembered the lesson Buzz Beurling gave me about deflection shooting. I came at the Spit from the side and closed to within two hundred yards. Leading the plane, I opened up with a three second burst to where I thought he'd be, not where he was. I watched the plane burst into flames and begin to break apart as it plunged into the sea just off the coast. I broke off my pursuit. He was done.

I immediately scanned the skies for the other Spitfires. I didn't see any. I looked for Pinter. He was nowhere in sight. I headed back to Herzliya, hoping he was okay. When I landed, Pinter was standing next to his plane. I didn't see any damage to it.

"You all right?" I asked.

"Yeah, I'm okay," he replied, with a nod.

"What happened to you?"

"I got on the tail of one of the Spitfires but lost him in the clouds. When I broke out of the clouds, I couldn't find any of them. I checked the area and realized I didn't know where I was. I was lost, and my fuel was low, so I headed north, in the direction of the base. It took me a while before I got my bearings and found the field. Sorry I wasn't more help."

"Don't sweat it," I replied.

When we entered the ready room, the rest of the pilots stood and applauded. I didn't understand, but before I could ask, Weizman came up to me and shook my hand.

"Congratulations," he said.

"For what?"

"You have the honor of being the first pilot in the Israeli Air Force to shoot down an enemy fighter plane in combat."

I felt a sense of pride, but it was short-lived. Minutes later a report came in. The other three Spitfires had regrouped and bombed Tel Aviv.

A COUPLE OF days later, the morning of June 11, Alon and I were having breakfast on the patio at our hotel in Tel Aviv. The sky was blue with just a few wispy clouds. Strong winds pushed six-foot high waves in from the Mediterranean. I watched them curl before they broke, and then the calm water gently lapped the shoreline before ebbing back out to sea.

"Alon," I said, "even though we intercepted the Spitfires two days ago, they still ended up bombing Tel Aviv. We've got to stop them beforehand, and I don't think it should be just in dogfights."

I took a sip of my orange juice. "Remember the day we hit the Egyptian column coming at Tel Aviv three weeks ago? We had a different plan. We were going to hit El Arish and take out the Spits on the ground. I think we should do that now. It's the only way we can hurt them and slow down the attacks on Tel Aviv. We have four planes that are combat ready. We can do it."

Alon tapped his fingers on the table as he turned it over in his mind. After a minute, he said, "When do you want to do it?"

"Tonight after dark, or tomorrow morning at daybreak."

"We'll do it tomorrow morning."

But, once again, my mother's words, "Man plans, God laughs," held true.

There would be no attack on El Arish. That afternoon, word was passed down. At six o'clock this evening, a United Nations brokered truce would go into effect.

CHAPTER 29
June 11-July 8
The Truce

THE TRUCE WAS the best thing to happen to me.

Since arriving in Israel, my mind and body had been on a constant high. The adrenaline that flowed from being in actual combat, or prowling the skies looking for enemy aircraft, knowing at any minute I could be in a life or death battle, never seemed to leave my body. My mind and body maintained the razor sharpness of imminent combat. To go from that to inactivity was a relief.

The way we worked the adrenaline out of our system also turned out to be the best time I had since arriving in Israel. We partied. Boy, did we party. Every night we would all congregate at the bar in the hotel.

On the third night of the truce, a bunch of us were sitting at a table in the bar, when Skippy Shapiro said, "Ya know, we should have some kind of an emblem for the 101ˢᵗ."

"What do you mean?" I asked.

"I mean, like a lot of us guys did in the war. A picture to put on our planes. Not necessarily a picture of Betty Grable," he said, laughing, "but something on the sides of our fighters, unique to the 101st."

Alon said, "That's not a bad idea. How about a scorpion?"

"Why a scorpion?" I asked.

"Because I saw one once on a plane in the RAF and thought it was neat."

"I have a better idea," I said. "Who's our main enemy in the air? The Egyptians, right? So, like with the Jewish people thousands of years ago, why not choose something to do with the Angel of Death. After all, it wasn't until God unleashed the Angel of Death that Pharaoh let our people go. And isn't that sort of what we want now? For the Egyptians to let our people go, or at least leave Israel alone?"

"Yeah," Alon said. "I like that."

"Now, all we have to do is figure out what we want it to look like," I said.

"How about something like this," Prager said, holding up a cocktail napkin. While we were discussing the Angel of Death idea, he and Landau, our two UCLA art students, had been sketching and drew a skull wearing a flying helmet surrounded by wings.

The next day, the symbol was painted on the side of every Messerschmitt in the 101st squadron.

One of our pilots had a sister who worked for a company in New York City that made baseball hats. He contacted her, sent a copy of the logo, and asked if she could get us some hats with the death head logo and the 101st on them. A short time later, a box arrived from New York with twelve dozen red baseball hats with the logo and the 101st embroidered on them. Everyone in the squadron wore them, even when off duty. Bartenders and patrons at all our watering holes soon began calling us "the red hats."

ONE OF THE guys in the 101ˢᵗ, Irv Paris, was quite the ladies man. He was a good looking guy, but there had to be more than that for him to be able to pick up as many girls as he did. It seemed every night he'd leave the bar headed to his room with a different girl. I didn't know how he did it.

Six days into the truce, I found myself sitting at the end of the bar next to him. "Irv, you've got to tell me. What's your secret? How do you always get so many pretty girls to leave with you?"

He laughed. "You jealous?"

"Damn right I am. How do you do it?"

He looked around to see if anyone was listening. No one was anywhere near us. Nevertheless, he leaned in close, and in a soft voice said, "The number one secret to getting girls is to listen to them. Most guys start off by talking about themselves. Let the girl talk; listen to what they say. Compliment them on how they look or how insightful they are. If you do that, you'll be ninety percent ahead of every other guy they meet. And if they're not talkative, be funny, make them laugh, or flatter them."

During the third week of the truce, I walked into the bar and spotted Pinter, Prager, Landau, and a few of the other guys from the 101ˢᵗ sitting at a table on the outdoor patio drinking, smoking, laughing, having a great time. Next to them was a table of six young Israeli women, some dressed in khaki shorts and white blouses, some in dresses.

I joined my friends, but my attention was drawn to a gal who was sitting at the next table near my right shoulder. I guessed her to be in her early twenties, dirty blonde hair, slate blue eyes, gentle nose, high cheekbones, and lips that curved naturally into an easy smile. She was willowy, looked to be medium height, and wore a yellow summer dress. The scent of jasmine wafted from her.

Ten minutes after I arrived, she left the table, drink in hand, and strolled to the four-foot-high rail that separated the patio from the beach that ended at the shore of the Mediterranean Sea. She stood with her back to me, gazing out at the sea and the clear starlit night.

I walked over to her. "Hi, there. I'm Mike."

She turned her head and shoulders. "Hello, Mike. I'm Rachael. You're obviously one of the American pilots."

"How did you know?"

She grinned and pointed at my head. "The red hats give you away."

My hand flew up to my head. I smiled. "Kind of does, doesn't it?" I took a sip of my drink. "Your English is very good. Where did you learn to speak it?"

"We have four families from America living in our *kibbutz*. They teach me English, and I teach them Hebrew. And where are you from in America, Mike?" she asked.

I was about to respond when I remembered Irv's advise. Nope, I wasn't going to talk about myself. I was going to let her talk and listen to what she had to say.

"Actually, since I'm a stranger in your country, tell me about you. Where do you come from? What do you do?"

"I come from here. I'm a *sabra*."

"What's a *sabra*?" I asked.

"It's the Hebrew word for anyone born in Israel."

"You were born here? Boy, that shows how much I don't know. Here I thought every Jew in Palestine came from somewhere else."

She laughed with what I thought was the most wonderful laugh I'd ever heard. "No, my father came to Palestine in 1904 at the age of twelve to avoid the Russian draft."

"What do you mean to avoid the draft? How could he be drafted? You said he was only twelve," I said, laughing.

She smiled. "How little you know about your fellow Jews. Yes, it's true he was only twelve. But in Russia, going all the way back to the middle 1800s, all Jewish boys were required to serve twenty-five years in the Russian army, starting at the age of twelve. The Russians thought that since this was a year before they would be bar mitzvah, it would destroy their Jewish identity."

"And have to serve for twenty-five years? You're kidding, right?"

Rachel shook her head. "No, sadly I'm not."

Wow. "So how did he get to Palestine if he was only twelve?"

"With my grandfather. He'd avoided the draft. Most Jews did or tried to. He wanted my father to have a better life, so they left Russia and came here."

"How did your grandfather avoid the draft?"

"Yes. Those that ended up in the czar's army were usually there because of Cossacks who attacked their village during a *pogrom*. If they found boys of draft age, were they beaten and dragged from the village to serve in the army. My grandfather hid."

"And what about your mother?" I asked. "Is she Russian?"

"Yes. In 1914, more than five hundred thousand Jews were ordered to leave their homes in Russia. My mother and her family were given less than 24 hours notice that they had to leave. They had to pack what they could carry and get out. They'd heard stories of what happened in other villages when the people stayed too long. Some were put in prison, but in most cases, they were slaughtered by Cossacks. Most of my mother's village headed to Europe or America. Her family came to Palestine."

I wasn't much of a Jew in the United States, and I felt even less of one listening to Rachel. Sure, I'd seen the Dachau concentration camp and knew what the Germans did to the Jews. But now, hearing Rachael's family history, I realized how Jews were treated in Russia and who knew how many other places.

"And what do you do here in Israel?" I asked.

"I was a farmer in my *kibbutz*. I drove a tractor. Now, I'm a soldier."

"A soldier?

"Yes. I'm from Yad Mordechai. You heard of it?"

"No, sorry. I haven't."

"It's a small *kibbutz* sixty kilometers south of Tel Aviv on a hill along the Mediterranean, overlooking the main road from Gaza to Tel Aviv. It was also in the path of the Egyptian Army coming up the coastline on May 16th, the day after we declared independence. From what our scouts could see, they had about five thousand soldiers, armor, and artillery. We had 130 people to defend ourselves.

That was the column we hit in May.

"We got word to Tel Aviv, and they sent a small armored column to get the 92 children, with some chaperones, out safely. We were left with 110 defenders, twenty of us women. Just after dawn on May 19th, with artillery support, Egyptian infantry and an armored column attacked the *kibbutz*."

Rachel took a sip of her drink and seemed to stare right through me. I could see her eyes darting about, as if seeing the battle once again.

"They made it through a small hole in the surrounding barbed wire fence. We fought back with everything we had. The battle went on for hours. Finally, the Egyptians pulled back, but we knew they'd return. We'd killed dozens of them, but we lost five and had ten wounded. The next day, they attacked again. This time we lost twelve, with twenty-five wounded, including me."

"You were wounded?" I said, seeing Rachel in a whole new light. She was not only a beautiful, desirable woman, but also brave, beyond any female I'd ever met.

"Yes."

"May I ask where?"

The corner of her mouth lifted in a half smile. "Someday, maybe, I'll show you the scar."

I think I blushed. "So what happened? Obviously you made it out."

"The Egyptians spent the next two days shelling the *kibbutz*. They destroyed every building. We huddled in the tunnels and bunkers we'd built months before. We held them off for three days but knew we couldn't do it for much longer. We had too many wounded, were running low on ammunition, and we were just worn out by the fighting. Finally, having no choice, during the night, we slipped out of the *kibbutz* and made our way to a convoy of Haganah vehicles that brought us to Tel Aviv."

Rachel was quiet for a few seconds and then laughed.

"What's funny?" I asked.

"There were Haganah scouting parties in the area the day after we left. They told us the morning after we slipped out of the *kibbutz*, the Egyptians opened up with an artillery attack on the *kibbutz* that lasted for six hours. Those idiots wasted all that firepower on an empty *kibbutz*. That's why we're going to win this war."

RACHAEL AND I became lovers three nights later, and I got to see her scar. She was everything I could want in a woman. Beautiful, funny, intelligent, and tough as nails. It became easy to forget about the war.

We were sitting at a table for two, in an out-of-the-way corner of the patio at the hotel. The night was clear, the sky a canopy of flickering stars, with a three-quarter-full, bright moon reflecting in the shimmering waters of the Mediterranean. We were sipping wine, running our fingertips over the back of each other's free hand resting on the table.

"After this war is over and we finally have our own country, how long will it take you to take care of things in America and move here?" Rachael asked.

My fingers stopped caressing the back of her hand. I felt my breathing stop for a split second. *Move here?*

"Uh, what do you mean, move here? I want you to come to America with me."

"How can you say that? Don't you want to see Israel grow? Be a part of it?"

"Yes, of course I want to see Israel grow. But I'm an American. That's my country; that's my home."

"But you're a Jew," she said.

"Yes, but I'm also an American. I can be both, can't I?"

Seconds ago we'd been staring into each other's eyes. Now, Rachael broke eye contact, her shoulders slumped, and she snatched her hand from mine. "But... but, I thought," she stammered, "I thought you had the same love for Israel I do."

"I do. I want Israel to survive and grow as a homeland for all Jews. Why do you think I'm here? I'm fighting and risking my life every day to make sure that happens. I want it to be a homeland for any Jew that wants it to be their homeland. But I'm an American. I fought in World War II to ensure its survival, like you're fighting here to ensure your country's survival."

Tears filled Rachael's eyes.

"Rachael, I think I'm in love with you. But I can't turn my back on my country. I can't move here." I reached out to hold her hand, but she snatched it away, pushed herself from the chair, and walked briskly away. She never turned to look at me. I never saw her again.

The next day, one day before the official end of the truce, the Egyptians broke it in a surprise attack of two *kibbutzes* in the Negev. I was summoned back to Herzliya.

.

CHAPTER 30
July 9
The Battle of Lydda and Ramle

A S PART OF the twenty-eight day truce, it was agreed that neither side would use the time to improve their positions. An arms embargo was declared, but we paid no attention to it and knew the Arabs wouldn't either. We continued to fly in munitions and Messerschmitts from Czechoslovakia.

High command had made a decision for when the truce ended on July 9. We were going to attack the Egyptian base at El Arish, hitting their planes while they were still on the ground. It was the same plan I'd devised with Alon when we were diverted to stop the Egyptian advance on Tel Aviv back on May 15.

"Kaplan," Weizman said, bursting through the door of the ready room. I was eating lunch. "HQ just called. The Egyptians just broke the truce. They attacked two settlements in the south about an hour ago. HQ wants us to hit El Arish now."

"They couldn't wait one more day until the truce was supposed to end? Those sneaky bastards," I said, pushing myself from the chair. "Just like the damn Japs at Pearl Harbor."

We only had four aircraft combat ready. Alon was flying in on a C-46 today from Czechoslovakia, and I needed Weizman to be here on the base.

"Prager, Landau, Shapiro, you're with me," I yelled, bolting to the door.

We scrambled to our planes, and I lifted off seven minutes later into a clear afternoon sky. Shapiro followed. I was making my turn to wait for the others to form up on me when I saw Landau's damn piece o'shit do its worst. He was about midway down the runway when the plane ground looped, pulled to the right, and tilted sideways. The right landing gear collapsed, and a shower of sparks flew as his propeller struck the ground.

I held my breath. Landau was carrying two bombs. If the plane caught fire, they could explode. I spotted Landau leaping from the cockpit, running like hell.

Prager sat on the runway for twenty minutes while the ground crew cleared the wreckage. Shapiro and I circled the field waiting for him.

We headed south, flying five miles off the coast toward El Arish. A half hour later, I glanced at my fuel gauge. *Damn.* While we were circling, waiting for the ground crew to clear Landau's plane and for Prager to join us, we'd used up too much fuel. There was no way we could reach El Arish, bomb, strafe the field, and return safely.

I signaled the other two planes to follow me as I turned and headed back to base. Then, off in the distance, I spotted a ship at a dock in the port of Gaza. It looked like a freighter with a lot of activity on the dock. I signaled my number two and three to follow me.

As I drew closer, I saw they were unloading troops and supplies.

I wasn't going to take perfectly good bombs back to the airfield. I turned toward the port and dove at the ship. I released my first bomb, pulled up, and headed out to sea. Looking back over my right shoulder through the canopy, I saw I'd missed the ship. The bomb exploded on the dock. It may have taken out supplies and some troops, but I wanted the ship. If we sunk it where it was, it would take the Arabs a long time to clear the wreckage, making the port useless for resupplying purposes.

When I turned to make my second bomb run, I saw that either Shapiro or Prager, or both, had done a better job. Smoke and flames were pouring from the ship's bow. I climbed to eight thousand feet and dove straight down at the ship, released my bomb, and pulled away. My plane shuddered from concussion waves. Thick black smoke poured from the ship's stern. *Yes! Hit the fuel storage.* I headed back to base with a big smile on my face.

I landed, taxied off the strip, and waited for the other two. Shapiro touched down a minute later and pulled up behind me. We sat in our idling planes waiting for Prager. Minutes passed as I scanned the skies. *Where are you?* Images of what-could-be flashed through my mind. My stomach began to roll. *Nah, he must have gone to Ekron*, I thought. Yup, that's it. He made a mistake and went there.

I don't know how much time passed before I finally pushed the throttle forward and taxied to the parking area. I climbed from my plane and stood beside it, leaning against the wing. Shapiro walked over to me.

"What do you think?" he asked.

"He must have gone to Ekron," I said.

Shapiro tilted his head down, looked at the ground and said in a soft voice, "Yeah, that's what must have happened."

I knew he didn't believe it. I felt my eyes well with tears. I didn't believe it either.

OVER THE NEXT two days, reports from towns up and down the coast reported seeing a plane fall into the sea. But the places were so far apart, they all couldn't be true. And no one said they found the wreckage of his plane or his body. We never found out what happened to Prager.

But war goes on relentlessly and leaves little time to mourn. During the truce, Israel had built up its army with refugees, immigrants, and volunteers like us. The C-46 pilots had ignored the truce and flew in more than twenty thousand rifles, hundreds of machine guns, and tens of millions of rounds of ammunition.

During the truce, Ben-Gurion and his cabinet had made a decision. When the truce ended, Israel would go on the offensive, and for the first time, coordinated air and ground operations.

THREE DAYS AFTER we lost Prager, Weizman and Alon called a meeting of all the pilots.

"Gentlemen," Weizman said, "today the Israeli Army is going on the offensive. It's called Operation Dani. We're flying air support. The operation's first objectives are to take the towns of Lydda and Ramle."

Weizman nodded at two soldiers. They unfurled a large map and tacked it to a wall. Weizman moved to one side of it, Alon to the other.

"Here they are," he said, pointing to the two towns on the map. "As you can see, they're roughly twenty-two kilometers from Tel Aviv and forty-five kilometers from Jerusalem. For my American friends, that's thirteen and twenty-eight miles respectively.

"What makes them important is they sit here," he said, tapping the map with his finger, "at the intersection of Israel's main north–south, and east–west roads. The country's main railway junction and airport are in Lydda, and the main source of Jerusalem's water supply is less than fifteen kilometers away."

Alon took over. "Intelligence says there are over two thousand militia, about three hundred professionals from the Arab Legion, and a few hundred Bedouin volunteers. From what we can tell, they're very well armed.

"The 101st squadron has two main objectives. Our job, starting tonight, is to bomb both towns. It's going to be dark, but try not to hit obvious civilian structures. We hope once we start bombing, they'll evacuate, so when our soldiers attack, civilian casualties will be kept to a minimum. Objective number two... try not to damage the runway at the airport. We'd like to be able to use it as a base of operation."

We took off that night, bombing and strafing armored vehicles and clusters of tents. The next morning at dawn, Israeli troops attacked both towns. We heard that the civilians of Ramle were trying to leave, headed east toward the Arab strongholds. Our troops detained military aged men but allowed the elderly, women, and children to go.

That same morning, Israeli troops took control of the airport at Lydda but encountered stiff opposition and were not able to enter and occupy the town itself. Most of the civilians did not leave. That night, Dave Chernoff flew a C-46 over Lydda dropping leaflets, telling the residents to surrender.

Two days later, I flew into the Lydda airport to meet with the commander on the ground to determine what more we could do to help him with air support. While I was waiting in the terminal, I met a reporter from the *New York Times*.

"I heard you speaking English," the reporter said, as he walked up to me. He offered up his hand. "Hi, I'm Art Keffer, *New York Times*."

"Hi. I'm Abe Cohen," I lied, throwing out the most Jewish sounding name I could quickly think of. I was breaking the law fighting for Israel, and he was a reporter. If I used my real name and he put it in the paper, I'd be in serious trouble. For all I knew, I might already be in trouble, but I didn't need to have my name in print.

"Where you from, Cohen?" Keffer asked.

I had a slight New England accent, which I figured he'd pick up on, so again I lied. "New Hampshire."

"You fly that plane in?" he asked.

Too many questions. "Yes, I did. What are you doing here?" I asked, trying to change the conversation.

"I just covered the battle for Lydda and Ramle. One of the worst I've seen, and I covered a lot of them in Europe during the War."

"Why do you say that?"

"Was it you that dropped the leaflets the other night asking the people in Lydda to surrender?"

"No, that was someone else."

"Well, it seemed to work. I was with the first few hundred soldiers who entered the town after their leaders got together and sent word they would surrender. The soldiers used loudspeakers, telling the people to leave their weapons on their doorsteps so they could be collected, and then to come out with their hands raised. Minutes later, people began gathering in the street, waving white flags and willingly entered detention compounds set up in the mosques and churches. In fact, the compounds filled up so quickly, the soldiers sent the women and children home."

"Well, that doesn't sound as bad as you made it sound," I said.

"If it ended at that, you're right. Unfortunately, it didn't."

"What do you mean?"

"Even though the civilians surrendered, a small force from the Arab Legion didn't. They holed up in the police station built by the British. It was more like a small fort than a police station. The mayor and a few other leaders walked to the police station and yelled to the men inside that the town had surrendered, and it was time for them to surrender also."

"Okay, sounds reasonable," I said.

"The Arab legionnaires refused to surrender and opened fire. They killed the mayor and wounded a couple of others."

"No shit?"

"Yeah, they did. But the Israeli soldiers accepted the surrender anyway. They figured they had the town and the station was isolated. They'd just wait out the Arabs inside the station."

"Seems like a good plan," I responded.

"It was... until later that afternoon. A couple of Arab Legion armored cars came into the city and opened fire on Israeli soldiers combing the city for the weapons people were supposed to leave on their doorsteps. Apparently, most of the residents didn't.

"The Israeli soldiers must have thought this was a counterattack. And, it seemed, so did the local militia who hadn't surrendered yet and legionnaires in the police station. All of a sudden, the Israelis were being shot at. Not just from the armored cars, but also from a withering hailstorm of bullets coming from hundreds of windows and rooftops.

"The Israelis didn't know how big the attacking force was. They only knew the truce was broken, and they were taking heavy fire from all sides. Orders were sent out to shoot at any clear target. They threw hand grenades into houses they thought sniper fire was coming from. If anyone ran from the building, they were shot. Anyone outside was considered a threat and shot."

"Where were you?" I asked.

"I thought I was in a safe place with the soldiers guarding the mosques and the unarmed men inside."

"What do you mean you thought you were safe?"

"I don't know how they did it, but apparently some armed militia got inside one of the mosques and opened fire on the soldiers outside."

"What happened?'

"The Israelis were so enraged that they would use a mosque as cover to fire at them, someone fired an anti-tank missile at the mosque. Then the soldiers stormed it, firing at anything that moved. When the shooting was over, I made my way inside the rubble. There looked to be at least thirty to forty dead."

"You make it sound like it was a one-sided fight."

"Oh, no. Don't get me wrong. Your side lost soldiers and had a lot wounded. It's just a shame so many died."

"What happened to the legionnaires inside the police station?"

Keffer snickered. "Oh, you mean those tough guys that wouldn't surrender? They snuck out of the police station and headed out of town when they saw the battle was going against them."

Just then, an Israeli officer came up to me and said, "Come with me."

"Sorry, I gotta go," I said, shaking Keffer's hand.

We went outside, hopped in a Jeep, and drove into Lydda. The officer took me to meet the commander of the Israeli forces that had taken both towns. He was a tall, thin man with a hawkish nose, but what set him apart was the black patch he wore over his left eye.

"Hello," he said holding out his hand. "I'm Colonel Moishe Dyan."

We spent the next forty-five minutes discussing what we did to give him air support, what he felt we could have done better, and how we might help in the future.

Afterward, a driver took me back to the airport, but he made a wrong turn, one that I wish he hadn't. I saw bodies strewn in the streets, alleys, and even some hanging half out of windows. They were almost all men, but I saw a few women and children.

I felt bile rise in my throat. I'd fought in war and undoubtedly killed many. But my war was always from thousands of feet in the air. I'd never seen the death I caused up front and personal. I was seeing it now, and I didn't like what I saw. I hoped the damn Arabs would quit trying to exterminate us and leave is in peace. I knew I was wishing for a miracle, that it wouldn't happen anytime soon... but I could still wish.

CHAPTER 31
June 14/July 15
United States/Zatec/Cairo

S HATZ RECOGNIZED EARLY on Israel's need for planes to fly in much needed supplies of guns and ammunition and for fighter planes and pilots. He also understood Israel would need to bring the war to the Arab countries attacking them, and the best way to do that was to bomb them, inflicting the same damage to them as they did to a helpless Israel.

Months before, he made plans to get B-17 bombers from Miami to Israel. To put that part of his plan into action, he had to get back to the United States. While he was still in Zatec, and on two trips to Rome, he'd been in touch with Noah Meir, requesting the Haganah office in New York recruit crews for Harvey Hecht's B-17s.

Shatz left Zatec on June 2, flying to Spain, then to Mexico City, and from there, by car into the States. He had to hopscotch his way back to the United States because the F.B.I. had issued a warrant for his arrest for arms smuggling. Entering the country in Texas, he was met by two of Sammie Kaye's men, Myer Lansky's friend, who drove him to Miami.

When he arrived in Miami, his first order of business was to call Meir. Convinced the F.B.I. wiretapped the Haganah's phones, it was agreed Shatz would use the name Mr. Apollo.

"Mr. Meir? This is Mr. Apollo. I'm calling to see if you were able to secure the items I requested."

"Yes, I was able to get all you need. They were sent to your distributor's warehouse three days ago, Meir said.

Shatz understood the code. It meant the crews are at Hecht's place in Miami.

"It's a pleasure doing business with you," Shatz said. "Payment will be forthcoming very soon, as I plan to deliver the goods within a couple of weeks."

Shatz was letting Meir know that within weeks the planes would be used to bomb Cairo.

"I FILED A flight plan with the CAA stating the aircraft are going to conduct an aerial survey of the Azores," Hecht told Shatz. They were in the cocktail lounge at the airport in San Juan, Puerto Rico, having flown in the day before with three B-17s and a crew to man each plane. "The planes are legally registered to my company, commercially modified and airworthy. They can fly from Puerto Rico to Israel if they have to."

"We'll stick with the plan and fly from here to the Azores and from the Azores to Zatec."

"I'm going back to Miami," Hecht said. "It's your war from here on out. By the way, I had the crew do a check on the plane. The bomb bay doors are still working, and the bomb control power, wiring controls, and fittings are all in tiptop order."

EACH BOMBER HAD two pilots for the long trip. Shatz met with the crew for his plane. A former B-17 pilot named David Goldberg had been recruited. Goldberg took the pilot's seat and Shatz served as co-pilot. They left San Juan in the morning for the Azores, Goldberg estimating the flight would take twenty-one hours. They carried twenty-four hours of fuel on board.

Airborne for three hours, Shatz went to the hammock they'd installed behind the cockpit and grabbed a nap. Six hours later, Shatz took control of the plane while Goldberg napped. The weather was fine and the flight was smooth as the plane slid over the vast emptiness of the Atlantic Ocean.

They were into the twelfth hour when Goldberg came back and Shatz slid into the co-pilot seat. Shatz was munching on a banana a few minutes after Goldberg took control of the plane, when he cocked his head. He heard something. A sound he couldn't identify, but instinct told him was out of place. *The engines?* He concentrated his hearing, listened intensely. *No, it's not them. But something's off.*

"Do you hear anything strange?' Shatz asked Goldberg.

"No. Why? What do you hear?"

"I don't know. I'm hearing something, like a whistling noise. But I can't place it. I don't know. Maybe I'm nuts."

"That's what I've heard about you," Goldberg said, smiling as he chuckled. "Seriously, I'm a believer in instinct. Go check out the rest of the plane."

"Good idea. I'll take a quick look around," Shatz said. He worked his way aft, opening the door leading into the bomb bay. He didn't see anything out of place, but he could hear it, whatever *it* was. It sounded like the whistling noise the winter wind would make, pushing itself through small gaps in his bedroom window.

He moved ahead, stopping every couple of feet, cocking his head from side to side, straining, and concentrating his hearing. He walked to the bomb bay doors and tilted his head down. They were shut tight. *Not coming from there.* But still he heard it, like a whoosh of air rushing in some place. He walked all the way to the back of the plane. The further back he went, the sound got dimmer and dimmer.

"The sound is coming from somewhere here, near the front," Shatz said to Goldberg as he re-entered the cockpit. "You still don't hear it?"

"Nope."

Shatz checked the windows in the cockpit. They were shut tight. He lifted the door that led to the navigator/bombardier compartment. Now he heard it more distinctly. He grunted as he pulled up the hatch completely, got down on his hands and knees, and stuck his head through the small entrance to where the navigator/bombardier sits.

"Oh, shit."

He saw the navigator, Eli Cohen, was hanging halfway out of the bombardier's turret.

When the B-17s were purchased from the Reconstruction Finance Corporation, the bowl-like Plexiglas turret the bombardier used to judge how well he'd hit his targets had been removed and covered over by sheets of plywood.

Cohen must have stepped on the plywood, and it broke under his weight. He had his arms spread out across what was left of the plywood, his hands and fingertips pressed tight against the wood, holding on for dear life. His lower body was hanging outside the plane, being rocked and whipped around by the rushing wind.

"Goldberg," Shatz screamed, pulling his head from the entrance. "Slow the plane down. Cohen fell through the plywood. He's hanging on by his fingertips. I'm going down. Get some of the guys to help me."

Shatz lowered himself through the hatch and crawled to Cohen. He knew he had to be careful not put any weight on the plywood, or he and Cohen would both plummet to the ocean below.

Cohen's arms and fingers were moving, inch by inch, inward as the wind outside tugged on his body, drawing him closer to being sucked from the plane. Shatz felt the plane decrease in speed but guessed they were still traveling close to 170 knots, 6,000 feet above the Atlantic.

Cohen's face was ashen. His voice cracked with fear: "Shatz, help me. Don't let me die! Don't let me die!" he screamed over the sound of the howling wind coming through the gap in the plywood.

Shatz lay flat on his stomach, keeping as much of his body off the plywood as he could, reached out and grabbed Cohen's jacket at the shoulders. This would have to do until more help arrived. He could get a better hold on him if he could reach down and grab Cohen's belt. But that would put too much pressure on the plywood which seemed to be cracking around Cohen.

Shatz's arms were getting tired from the strain of holding the man. He felt Cohen's body slip a little bit more. *Where the hell are the other guys?*

Just then, the flight engineer stuck his head down into the compartment from the cockpit. "Holy shit," he yelled. "Hold on Shatz. We're coming."

"Hear that, Cohen?" Shatz shouted. "Helps coming. Hang on."

Two of the crew burst through the opening, slid on their bellies to either side of Cohen, each grabbing him by an arm. "At the count of three," Shatz said, "we'll all pull up and back."

Shatz counted off, and they all pulled. Within ten seconds, they had Cohen safe on the floor and sat with him as he rolled into a fetal ball. His body shook uncontrollably. The wind roared louder through the open gap in the plywood.

Shatz left the two others to stay with Cohen and climbed back into the cockpit. "How is he?" Goldberg asked.

"I think he shit his pants."

Goldberg gave Shatz a half smile.

"No. Literally. I think he shit his pants."

Goldberg's smile disappeared.

"Right now, he's curled up in a ball, shaking like a leaf. The other two are sitting with him."

Shatz turned from Goldberg and looked out the window. "Where are the other planes?"

"When I slowed down, we dropped out of formation and fell well behind them. They'll get there a little ahead of us. No big deal."

It turned out to be a big deal. The other two planes landed a half hour before they finally made it to Santa Maria in the Azores. In that short time span the airport became socked in with heavy fog, and it was night.

"Should we try for Lagen? They may not have any fog," Goldberg asked.

"No, It's a British base. They'll confiscate the plane and ship us home for breaking the embargo."

"Okay, we'll try for Santa Maria," Goldberg said.

Goldberg is one hell of a pilot, Shatz thought. Somehow, on the third pass, he got them into Santa Maria. When they were on the ground, fueling the plane, Shatz heard some mechanic say that an Air France plane had just crashed into the hills. *Funny, we made it. They didn't. Was it supposed to be that way?*

Since the America Embassy in the Azores had already confiscated one B-17 from Kaplan and Shapiro back in March, Shatz knew they could be close on their heels again. But, even if the Embassy found out right now that the plane had landed, Shatz bet the Embassy wouldn't send anyone out until the morning, figuring they'd all be tucked in for the night in a hotel.

So, at 3:00 in the early morning hours, less than four hours after they landed in Santa Maria, they took off again. To throw the authorities off, Shatz filed a flight plan for Ajaccio, Corsica, even though they intended to fly straight through to Zatec, Czechoslovakia.

The rest of the flight across Europe went smoothly. The only minor hiccup happened when they were flying over Germany. They must have been picked up on radar at a U.S. Air Force base because a couple of fighters were scrambled to check them out. They looked the plane over, saw it was an American B-17, and flew away. They probably figured it was a bomber from a squadron stationed at another base

After landing the B-17s in Czechoslovakia, the aircraft mechanics got busy with the task of preparing the bombers for their missions.

The planes needed a lot of work. There was no oxygen system, the bomb racks were pulled out, and of course, the U.S. Air Force had removed the expensive Norden bombsight.

No original equipment was available, so the mechanics had to improvise. They jury-rigged bomb racks and a very crude oxygen system. In place of the most accurate bombsight in the world, the American Norden sight, they installed a Czech designed one instead.

The chief mechanic told Shatz it would take about four weeks to get the three planes combat ready.

"We need them sooner," Shatz replied, two days after they arrived at Zatec.

"Not really," the chief mechanic said. "The twenty-eight-day truce starts today. I'll have your planes ready by the time it ends.

ALL SIDES AGREED not to use the truce to rearm and resupply their troops. Each side openly disregarded the agreement. Shatz and all available pilots shuffled between Zatec and Israel, flying C-46s loaded with arms and supplies to Israel.

The truce was supposed to end on July 9, but it was broken by the Egyptians on July 8 in a surprise attack. Using Sudanese and Saudi troops to avoid having to take the blame, they took two *kibbutzim*, dislodging the surprised Negev Brigade.

Fierce fighting by both sides continued after the truce was broken, until the United Nations got both sides to agree to a second truce. It was to take place on July 18, ten days after the first truce should have ended. But, before the new second truce was to start, the Israeli Air Force had a surprise for the Egyptians

Two DAYS BEFORE the second truce would go into effect, Shatz and the all the crews of the B-17s sat in a large room at the Stalingrad Hotel in Zatec, listening to Captain Hochberg, an Israeli liaison officer.

"Men," the tall, thin officer said, "as you know, before the first truce, the Arabs sent their planes to bomb our cities practically without opposition and continued to do it after the first truce was broken. We had no antiaircraft fire to throw at them. There was little fighter opposition, because we had none, or very little. But now, we're going to carry the war into the laps of the Egyptians. We're going to do it tomorrow." He paused, waiting for the excitement to die down.

"Just before the last truce, we sent Dakotas over Damascus to chuck bombs. It created such a huge panic, every foreigner in the city left the next day. We think we can cause the same terror in Cairo. Headquarters believes we'll have the element of surprise and catch them totally off guard."

He turned to an easel on a stand next to him and lifted a cloth cover. It revealed a map of Egypt.

"We thought about sending all three B-17s to Cairo. But because we don't know the strength of Cairo's antiaircraft defenses, it was decided sending all three to one location is an unacceptable risk. So you're being assigned three separate targets." He tapped the map with a finger, calling out each name as he touched it. "Cairo, Gaza, and El Arish Airfield.

"We planned your departure time so the plane going to Cairo will arrive about thirty minutes before a scheduled TWA flight is supposed to be there. If you're challenged by the control tower, you'll pretend to be them.

"Sunset is at 6:58, so each of you will all arrive at your targets well after dark. You'll fly over the Mediterranean echelon starboard formation, each plane flying behind and to the right of the one in front. That should destroy the clarity of any enemy radar readings. When you get within a half hour of Cairo, the planes headed to Gaza and El Arish will break off. When you complete the bombing run, head back to Ekron."

SHATZ'S MIND WANDERED back to a conversation that took place back on May 18. The Egyptians had bombed Tel Aviv with impunity after Ben Gurion declared the State of Israel.

Boom, Boom. Shatz was hunkered down inside a shelter in the basement of the Golan Hotel, the floor beneath his feet vibrating with each blast. The relentless explosions went on for more than fifteen minutes.

When the all clear siren blared, he left the shelter. Standing on the sidewalk outside the hotel, he scanned the surrounding area, looking for bomb damage. He didn't see anything from this vantage point, so he walked down Ben Yehuda Street to Mapu Street. Shatz was about to turn the corner when an elderly man with gray hair and a grey beard, grabbed him by the sleeve.

"You are one of the pilots who brought the planes from America?"

"Yes, I am," Shatz replied.

"Why do you not bomb the Egyptians? Why do you let them bomb us and do nothing to them in return?"

"The planes we brought are not bombers," I explained.

"So," the man replied, turning his palms up, "then get us bombers."

The shuffling of chairs as the crews left the briefing room drew Shatz back to the present. *They're coming old man. They're coming.*

CHAPTER 32
July 14
Prague/Cairo

SHATZ AND THE rest of the B-17 crews joined the thirty-seven ATC pilots and mechanics stationed in Zatec headed into Prague for a night of fun. Mostly Americans, with a few Canadians and Brits thrown in, they piled into a bus for the half hour ride.

On the drive into Prague, Shatz found himself sitting next to a pilot he'd never seen before. "You new?" he asked the pilot.

"Got here three and a half weeks ago. My name is Hans Lehman."

"I'm Paul Shatz. Lehman? Is that Jewish?" he asked.

Lehman laughed. "No, I'm not Jewish. Does that mean I'll have to get off the bus?"

Shatz laughed back. "Sorry. Didn't mean that as an insult. It's just that you're not Jewish, so why are you helping Israel?"

"I'm Swiss. I was on active service with the Swiss Air Force when I heard the Israeli Air Transport Command was looking for help, so I deserted to volunteer. I believe in your cause. I'm well aware of what happened to Jews in Germany. My aunt sheltered many of them escaping from the Nazis when they made it over the Swiss border. The

Jewish people deserve Palestine as their homeland. As a matter of fact, I even have an Israeli passport."

"Really? If I got an Israeli passport, I'd lose my citizenship. Did you lose yours?"

"I hope not. I didn't give up my Swiss passport. The reason I asked for an Israeli passport is if I ever had to make a forced landing someplace, and was carrying my Swiss passport, I'd be delivered to the Swiss Consul. They'd send me back as a deserter. I'll only carry the Israeli one when I fly. When this is over, I'll go back to Switzerland, if I can. If not, I'll live in Israel."

"To do that, first we'll have to win this war. In any event, welcome aboard. We can use all the help we can get," Shatz said.

"Can I ask you a question?" Lehman said.

"Sure."

"You're one of the pilots who brought in the B-17s"?

"I am."

"I noticed the B-17 crews had a meeting today. Does that mean you're leaving for Israel soon?"

"Yes and no," Shatz replied, his lips forming a small grin.

"Is this an American expression, yes and no?" Lehman said.

"It means just that. Yes, we are going to fly them to Israel. No, we are going someplace else first."

"I see. No, I don't see. I'm confused. What does this mean?"

"It means, before we get to Israel, we're making a stop. We're first flying to Cairo to give them a taste of the bombing the Egyptian Air Force has been giving Tel Aviv."

Lehman's head snapped around. "You're not kidding? You're really doing this?"

"Tomorrow night," Shatz said.

Lehman leaned back into the thin padding on the back of his seat. "Wow."

"Yes, wow," Shatz responded with a chuckle.

Shatz looked past Lehman, out the window. While he'd been talking, they'd already entered the city. The bus slowed down then lurched to a stop as the driver hit the brakes a little too hard. Men began getting out of their seats

"I hope to see you in Israel," Shatz said, rising from his aisle seat and sticking out his hand to shake Lehman's.

"Me, too. Knock 'em dead in Cairo," Lehman said, returning the handshake.

Shatz got off the bus and caught up with some of the B-17 crew. He turned toward the bus door and saw Lehman getting off. He was about to call out to the Swiss pilot and invite him to join the B-17 guys when Lehman turned toward the rear of the bus. A man had suddenly appeared out of the dark, and the two shook hands. Lehman and the man didn't linger. They moved quickly back into the dark behind the bus. Shatz shrugged and joined the rest of the men heading out for drinks.

IT WAS EARLY in the evening, the summer sun had not yet set in the sky, and the temperature was balmy. The bus had left them off at the outskirts of the Old Town Square. This was Shatz's first time in Prague, and he asked one of the men, a mechanic named Goldzweig, who'd been to Prague before, if he would take him sightseeing.

"Any specific place you want to see?" Goldzweig asked.

"No, I'll leave that up to you."

"Well, on my first trip here, someone took me to the Jewish Quarter. It's the section of Prague they call Josefov. Want to go there first? There's a museum you might like to see. It's only a ten minute walk from here."

"Sure."

They had been walking along Dusni for about five minutes when Goldzweig said, "There it is," pointing to a building about two hundred yards away.

When they got to the building, Shatz said, "This looks like a synagogue, not a museum."

"It was," Goldzweig said. "It was built in the mid-1800. In 1935, they attached a big wing to the synagogue to serve as a hospital for the Jewish community. They had extra room, so the Jewish leaders of the community decided to take a small part of the building and convert it into a museum to document the history and customs of the Jewish population of Czechoslovakia, as well as preserve artifacts from Prague synagogues demolished at the beginning of the 20th century."

"How did it survive the Nazis? There's no way they would let a museum like that survive."

Goldzweig shook his head. "That's the crazy part. Adolph Hitler himself decided to preserve the whole Jewish Quarter here in Prague as a *Museum of an Extinct Race*. He had artifacts from other occupied countries transported here to be part of the museum."

The museum was open. Inside, Shatz was astounded by the amount and quality of the works of art hanging on the walls.

"How do they still have all these pieces? The war has been over for three years."

"One of the guides told me that around eighty thousand Czech and Moravian Jews were slaughtered during the war. There is almost nobody left to claim the confiscated property. Since the Communists staged the coup d'état back in February and took over the Czech government, no one knows what will happen to all this."

Shatz stayed in the museum for about an hour and a half before heading outside. They walked around the adjoining streets. There was a kosher butcher shop and two Jewish bakeries, but the area didn't have many other outward signs of Jews living in the area. *I wonder if most of the survivors migrated to Israel.*

On the way back from the Jewish Quarter, dusk had given way to the dark of night as they approached the Old Town Square. Goldzweig told him the square dated back to the 12th century, starting life as the central market.

"You'll see a big statue in the square," Goldzweig said. "It's of Jan

Hus, put up to mark the 500th anniversary of his death. He became a symbol of dissidence against oppressive regimes. He opposed church control by the Vatican. His statue was placed in the square facing the large catholic church, standing in defiance of it. When Czechoslovakia came under Communist rule last February, people began sitting at the feet of his statue as a way of quietly expressing opposition against the Communist rule."

Shatz spotted four of the B-17 crew members sitting at one of the patio tables set up between a bar and the sidewalk. He and Goldzweig sat with the men for a half an hour before Shatz excused himself, telling them he was going to go see if he could find a few of the other pilots.

Rounding the statue, Shatz scanned the tables lined along the sidewalk outside of bars and restaurants, looking for his B-17 crew. Loud laughing and boisterous voices speaking English at the far end of the square drew his attention. He saw a lighted sign above the tables. Grand Hotel Praha.

As he neared the tables, he heard a voice yell out, "Shatz, over here!"

He glanced over to see David Goldberg waving to him. Shatz would be copilot to Goldberg on the B-17 that would hit Cairo. Goldberg grabbed an unoccupied chair from the table next to him and motioned for Shatz to sit on it.

"What are you drinking?" asked Harry Bauer, the bombardier on their plane.

"Before you order, hold off for a minute and watch that," Goldberg said, placing his hand on Shatz's arm, then pointing upward to the building across the street.

Shatz followed Goldberg's finger.

"What am I looking at?" he asked.

"That's one of the oldest astronomic clocks in the world. It was built over five hundred years ago." Goldberg glanced at his watch. "In about thirty seconds it's going to be nine o'clock. Watch the two windows above the clock face. They'll open up, and a parade of the

Twelve Apostles will show up, one each in a window. And see that skeleton just to the right of the clock face? His hand will pull down, ringing the bell for each hour."

Sure enough, precisely on the hours, the clock performed exactly as Goldberg indicated.

"Impressive," Shatz said. "Now, order me a beer and tell me where I can find a bathroom."

"Inside the hotel," Bauer said. "Through the entrance, past the inside bar, and to the left."

After finishing in the bathroom, Shatz decided to check out the hotel. Everything from the furnishings to the decorative carvings on all the wood surfaces reeked of upscale and expensive.

Passing the inside cocktail lounge, he decided to check it out. He had taken two steps inside the entrance when he spotted Lehman, the pilot he met on the bus, at a table tucked toward the back. He wasn't alone, but he wasn't with any of the men from the base either. He was in an animated conversation with a woman and a man wearing a suit.

The man had a coppery complexion, Arab looking. The woman was white and attractive in a hard sort of way.

Shatz was about to move to the table to say hello when he saw Lehman slide an envelope across the table to the dark-skinned man, who put it inside his suit coat pocket. A few seconds later, the woman pulled an envelope from her handbag and handed it to Lehman, who smiled and slipped it into his pants pocket. After he refilled the champagne flutes on the table, the three tapped their glasses in a toast.

The dark-haired man stood, said something to Lehman that Shatz couldn't hear, shook hands and turned to leave. Shatz moved back into the hallway and leaned against the doorframe. The dark-haired man stepped out of the lounge and glanced in the direction of the reception desk. For a brief second, he stared at Shatz.

Shatz couldn't be sure, but in that fleeting second, before the man turned his head away, he thought he saw a small quiver of the man's eyelid, a twitch at the corner of his mouth, as if an expression of recognition. Shatz felt the same. Like he'd seem the man before, maybe only fleetingly, but he's seen him some place. *Do I know him? From where?*

Shatz peered around the corner, back into the lounge. Lehman and the woman had left their seats and were headed to the entrance where he was standing. There was no way he would be able to avoid them, so he turned into the entrance and took a step inside. He lightly bumped into Lehman, whose head had been turned talking to the woman.

In less than a heartbeat, Shatz said, apologetically, "Oh, it's you Lehman. I'm sorry. I wasn't looking where I was going."

Lehman turned to him. "Shatz. What are you doing here?"

"I'm outside on the patio having drinks with my crew. Came in to use the bathroom and was checking out this fantastic hotel."

"Yes, it is, isn't it? Oh, where are my manners?" Lehman said. "Let me introduce you to Freda. She's a friend."

"Nice to meet you, Freda," Shatz said, shaking her hand. "Would you like to join us for drinks outside, Lehman?"

Lehman grinned. "Uh, no thanks. As I said, Freda and I are friends and are going to become even better friends." He winked at Shatz, put his arm around her waist, and began walking toward the reception desk. Lehman put his free hand behind his back and gave Shatz a tiny wave of goodbye with his fingers, as he walked away.

Shatz remained where he was, watching Lehman approached the reception desk. He spoke to the clerk for a few seconds, reached into his pocket, and removed the envelope Freda had passed to him. Shatz saw Lehman open the envelope and pull out a handful of currency. He counted some out and laid it on the counter. It looked to Shatz like it was U. S. dollars. Lehman put the remaining bills back in the envelope, and the desk clerk handed him a room key. Lehman and Freda walked up a spiral staircase near the reception desk to the guest rooms on the floors above.

Curious, Shatz waited a few minutes and walked to the front desk. The clerk was a man in his mid-fifties, dark hair, a handlebar mustache, about five and a half feet tall, wearing a dark pin-striped suit. "Excuse me, do you speak English?" Shatz asked.

"Not so well, but maybe good enough," the clerk responded.

"I thought I just saw one of my friends go upstairs a few minutes ago."

"Yes, that would be Pan Lehman."

"Pan?"

"I beg your pardon. Pan means Mr. in Czech."

"You know him?" Shatz asked.

"Quite well. He is here sometimes three, sometimes four nights a week."

"Three or four times? Overnight?"

"Yes. He has a taxi take him in the morning to wherever it is he goes during the day."

"Have you ever seen him with the woman he was with just now?" Shatz asked.

"Many times," the clerk said, with a small grin and a wink.

"Why the grin?" Shatz asked.

"She is a *prostituovat*."

Shatz didn't think that needed a translation, but to be sure, he said, "A prostitute?"

"Yes. One that costs much money. She only has the richest people in Prague as her clients."

He thanked the clerk, handed him ten dollars in American money, and asked him not to mention to his friend Lehman that he saw him with the *prostituovat*. "I don't want to embarrass him," he told the clerk.

Shatz was totally confused as he walked out of the hotel. Something just wasn't right. Who was that dark-skinned guy he thought he might know, and who'd given the impression he knew him? What was in the envelope Lehman gave him? How could Lehman afford to stay in a hotel like this for three or four nights a week? If the woman

Lehman introduce as Freda was a high priced prostitute as the desk clerk said, why did she slip Lehman an envelope with money in it? Wasn't Lehman supposed to be paying her?

CHAPTER 33
July 15
Zatec/Cairo

S HATZ WAS STANDING outside the ready room next to the weather-beaten bus that would take the B-17 crews to the flight line and the bombers. He was talking with David Goldberg, for who he'd copilot today, Norm Jefferies, and Al Steinberg, the lead pilots on other two planes.

"Shatz!" the voice yelled.

He turned to see Zvi Sokolnik, the security officer at the Zatec base, moving swiftly toward him. *This can't be good.*

Earlier that morning, Shatz checked around the base, inquiring about Lehman. No one had seen him, and no one professed to know him, other than to say a quick hello or nod as they'd pass.

The events of last night weighed on Shatz's mind. He couldn't shake a gnawing feeling he'd seen the man who'd been at the table with Lehman before. His gut was telling him it wasn't in a good way. He was pretty sure he didn't know him from here in Czechoslovakia. And what was with the prostitute giving *Lehman* an envelope with money in it, instead of him paying her?

Maybe he had it all wrong, but there were just too many things that bothered him, that didn't feel right, so he took his concerns to the security officer that morning. And now, here was Sokolnik, marching toward him and calling out his name for all to hear. Where was the man's discretion? *What if I had this all wrong about Lehman? Sure, go ahead and embarrass me.*

"Excuse me," Sokolnik said to Goldberg and the others as he grasped Shatz's elbow. "I need a couple of minutes with Shatz."

Shatz saw the raised eyebrows and quizzical looks on the airmen's faces as Sokolnik grasped his elbow and pulled him toward the back end of the bus. Sokolnik turned his back to the pilots and crew, ensuring they could not hear what he said.

"I did some checking on the matter you brought to my attention earlier this morning."

"Was there anything to any of it?" Shatz asked.

"Before I answer, I have a couple of things for you. I understand you were sitting with him on the bus last night going into Prague."

"Yes"

"What did you talk about?"

"Mostly about him. He told me about being Swiss, why he was fighting for Israel, getting an Israeli passport. Things like that."

"Nothing about you?" Sokolnik asked.

"I think I might have told him about myself. I don't remember. Why?"

"Did you mention today's mission?"

Shatz shuddered. Goosebumps popped out on his arms, a sinking feeling formed in the pit of his stomach.

"Yes," Shatz replied, tentatively. "Why?"

"We're pretty sure he's a spy," Sokolnik said. "We've had him under surveillance for a while."

"Oh, shit. He's a spy? Damn. I told him about today's mission."

"We guessed as much."

"Why? What happened?"

"We have two security men living in Prague. They've been keeping tabs on him for a while now. After you spoke to me, I called one of my men there and told him to see if Lehman was still in the hotel. Fortunately, he was still there when my man arrived. He waited in the lobby until Lehman came downstairs and checked out and then followed him to the Egyptian Embassy."

Shatz's legs felt rubbery. He fought back the urge to vomit.

"Egyptian Embassy? What have I done? We have to call off the mission. They'll be waiting for us."

"Maybe. Maybe not."

"What do you mean?"

"First of all, we know that prostitute he was with, Freda, is a spy for the British. We're pretty sure he's giving her information about us to give the Brits, and she's their go-between, paying him off for them. That's probably where the money you saw her give him is coming from. My guess is the sex is thrown in as part of the deal, with the Brits paying for that, too."

"But what about him going to the Egyptian Embassy this morning? He surely told them about today."

"He probably did. But, as far as we know, he's never made contact with the embassy before today."

"But now he has something of value to sell them," Shatz replied.

"But will they believe him? That's the big question, and I'm betting they won't."

"You're betting he won't?" Shatz said, eyes wide in astonishment, his voice rising in pitch. "Well, isn't that just terrific? You're betting he won't, but you're betting with my life and the lives of everyone on these B-17s."

"Keep your voice down," Sokolnik said. "You're right, I am betting with your lives. But it's a good bet. We're pretty sure the Brits have fed information about us, supplied by Lehman, to the Egyptians. We know the Egyptian Embassy has three men watching Lehman every time he comes into Prague."

"You just proved my point. He's —"

Sokolnik held up his palm. "Let me finish. We know the man he was with last night. His name is Ammon Hazem. He's a high ranking member of the Egyptian Brotherhood. He's been in the United States recently. We're not sure why he's here now."

Ammon Hazem. Egyptian Brotherhood. Name doesn't mean anything to me. I know I've seen him somewhere, some place. Had to be in the States. But where, when, how? I can't put my finger on it.

"But that not important now," Sokolnik continued, interrupting Shatz thoughts. "What's important is the surveillance team from the Egyptian Embassy has undoubtedly seen him with Lehman. The Brotherhood is against the Egyptian Government. We're sure anything Lehman tells them about the raid on Egypt tonight will be met with skepticism, a plot of some kind hatched by the Brotherhood."

"That's pretty thin to bet our lives on."

Sokolnik turned his palms up. "That's all I've got. I spoke to my bosses in Israel before coming to see you. They couldn't stress enough how important this mission is. The morale booster for our people alone is worth its weight in gold. Any damage you do to the Egyptians, as you American say, will be frosting on the cake."

"Okay."

"Okay what?" Sokolnik asked.

"Okay, the mission is on."

Sokolnik smiled. "Good. Oh, one more thing. You can't say anything to any of the crews or the pilots." With that, he turned and walked away.

"What was that all about?" Goldberg asked when Shatz rejoined the group.

"Something to do with security clearance for some of the ATC guys that came on board after the LAPSA men. No big deal," Shatz lied.

Beep. Beep. The bus horn sounded. "Let's get a move on," the bus driver yelled from inside

The pilots piled in for the ten minute drive to the flight line and the parked bombers. The planes had been fueled and the bombs loaded the night before. The crew climbed aboard as Goldberg and Shatz did their walk around inspection. Satisfied, they boarded the B-17. Goldberg started the engines, and they went through the preflight checks. It took them almost twenty minutes. Satisfied, Goldberg opened his side window and circled his finger to the ground crew. Shatz watched out his window as one of them scurried beneath the plane, appearing seconds later, dragging away the wheel chucks tied to the end of eight foot ropes.

One of the ground crew gave Goldberg the signal, and the B-17 began to crawl toward the end of the runway, the other two close behind.

It was July 15, at 11.00 am, when the three heavily-laden B-17s struggled into the air. They flew south over the Alps, Yugoslavia, Albania, and Greece. When they were well over the Mediterranean, they formed up into the planned echelon starboard formation.

An hour from their ETA in Cairo, the crew worked in the bomb bay, attaching the bombs arming pins by wires to rings on the bulkhead. When the bombs fell out of their racks through the bomb bay doors, the pins would be yanked out by the wire, arming the fuse to go off on contact.

Shatz was conflicted. Sokolnik told him not to tell Goldberg of the potential danger if the Egyptians in Prague might believe Lehman, that they could be flying into a deathtrap, with Egyptian fighters waiting to shoot them out of the sky somewhere between here and Cairo. What good would it do if I did say something? Shatz thought. Goldberg would listen and fly the mission as planned anyway. He was that kind of guy. But did Shatz owe it to him to at least have the facts and then let him decide? In the end, Shatz decided to keep his mouth shut.

When the formation was a half hour out from Cairo, Shatz saw the two other planes waggle their wings, signaling Goldberg they were breaking formation and heading to their targets. Goldberg waggled his wings in acknowledgment.

As the plane drew closer to Cairo, Shatz began to drum his thumb on the throttle. *It always happens this way before battle.* His senses heightened, going into overdrive. The engines sounded louder, every crick and groan the plane made was amplified. He felt his heart beat faster. Perspiration began to form on his forehead; his mouth was getting dry. He tightened his grasp on the yoke.

Ten minutes out, the Cairo control tower called, asking the plane to identify itself.

Using the information Captain Hochberg gave them the night before regarding the TWA flight due to land in Cairo in half an hour, Shatz answered, "Cairo tower, this is TWA 42."

"TWA 42. This is Cairo tower. You are early."

"Cairo tower. TWA 42. Yes. Picked up strong tailwinds. Request you please turn on the runway lights," Shatz said. Seconds later, the lights came on.

"They sure as hell feel safe down there. Let's show them the penalty for being so confident," Shatz said to Goldberg.

Goldberg banked the B-17 away from the airport, which was on the outskirts of the sprawling metropolis, and steered toward the central area. City lights twinkled in the dark night, making for a beautiful scene. The plane was now on a straight-in bomb run. Using the roadmap in the *Baedeker Tourist Guide Book of Egypt* they'd been given in Zatec, Goldberg easily spotted the aiming point, King Farouk's palace, near the city center.

Shatz leaned to the side and pulled a lever. "Bomb bay doors opening," he called into the intercom.

The bombardier took over. "I have the plane," he said, his voice crackling back.

Shatz heard the hum of the bomb bay doors opening and twisted in his seat, looking back. He'd propped the door behind the cockpit wide open, so he could check to see if any bombs were left or hung up. Looking through the opening, Shatz saw the dozen deadly 500-pounders. He looked at his watch. It was 7:46.

Snap. Snap. Snap. The bomb shackles flew open, and each missile left its perch. One by one they fell, the bombardier sending the explosives hurtling through the night sky, screaming as they plummeted at the quarters of the Egyptian Army's High Command and the Royal Palace.

Shatz looked out his window. As the bombs hit their targets, yellow and orange flames shot into the night sky, followed by billowing columns of smoke. Shatz felt the low, but steady, *boom, boom, boom* of the blast waves, bouncing the plane a little with each one.

It was all over in less than thirty seconds. Goldberg began a 180 degree turn out to the Mediterranean, headed for Israel. Below searchlights knifed through the night sky trying to find them. Seconds later, Shatz saw the puff, puff, puff of antiaircraft shells exploding in the darkness.

Whomp, Whomp, Whomp. Shatz heard, and then felt, the concussion waves buffet the plane. He looked at his watch. It was 7:52. From the time they began their run on the target, only six minutes had passed. He'd bet for the people below it was a lifetime of shock.

AFTER TEN HOURS in the air, Goldberg touched down at Ekron. The other two B-17s were already there. They had bombed Gaza and Rafah, instead of El Arish, because they couldn't find it in the dark. None of the bombers encountered any opposition.

The three planes stayed overnight in Ekron. The next morning, before flying to the squadron's new air base at Ramat David, during his preflight check, the mechanics showed Shatz where they temporarily patched up over one hundred holes in the B-17 from antiaircraft fire.

Shatz shook his head. "How the hell did we even make it here?"

CHAPTER 34
August 1948
Washington, D.C.

"**M**R. TIPTON? THERE's a phone call for you," his secretary said, standing in the doorway to his office. "He won't give me his name but said you would take his call."

"Well, if he won't give his name, hang up," Tipton replied, turning his attention back to his desk and the papers he'd been reading.

"Yes, sir. Oh, he also said the most cryptic thing," she said, turning to leave. "He said to tell you he's a fan of Henry Ford and Charles Lindbergh".

Hazem.

"Wait," Tipton said, snapping his head up. "I'll take the call. Put him through."

Tipton saw the quizzical look on her face. "He's a collector of memorabilia. I met him at a show last week, and I mentioned my admiration of Ford and Lindbergh," he lied, pointing to his credenza and the pictures of both men. "When he told me he had some articles about them I might be interested in acquiring, I asked him to call me when he was in Washington again."

His secretary smiled. She was well aware of his fascination with Ford and Lindbergh. "Yes, sir. I'll put the call right through."

Tipton picked up the phone before the first ring finished."What the hell are you doing calling me at my office?" he snarled.

"Because I have some important news for you," Hazem replied.

"What?"

"Did you know the Jews are getting weapons and fighter planes from Czechoslovakia?"

"What? Who said? How do you know?"

"I know because the Jews have a spy in their operation."

"A spy? What do you mean a spy?"

"Just what I said. A spy. He's selling information to the British, and sometimes the British give some of it to the Egyptian government. I got his contact information from my people in Cairo. He's based at an airfield in Zatec, Czechoslovakia. When he's not on duty, he and the other Americans go into Prague. I met him there two weeks ago in a bistro inside a very expensive hotel."

"You're telling me a Jew is betraying Jews?"

"First of all, he's not a Jew. And as far as a Jew betraying another Jew, you're a Christian. You've heard of Judas betraying Jesus haven't you?" Hazem laughed.

"I'm in no mood for jokes. Did you check out his story personally?" Tipton said, raising his voice.

"Yes. They're training on fighters at an airfield in Zatec. And they're loading rifles, ammunition, and other weapons on those C-46s they bought in the United States. I watched them take off. You don't have to be a genius to figure out where they're flying them to."

"What kind of fighters are they flying?"

"German Messerschmitts."

"Messerschmitts? Where the hell are they getting Messerschmitts?"

"From the Czechs. They're copies of what the Germans flew, and they're the same planes the Czech Air Force is using."

"Where are the munitions coming from?"

"From the Czechs. The spy said he's seen them opening up crates and test firing rifles."

"Find out for sure. I need to be sure the spy's information is accurate if I'm going to stop them."

"One more thing. I'm sure you heard about the Jews bombing Cairo two weeks ago?" Hazem asked.

"Yes."

"It could have been prevented. The spy told me about it the night before it happened. I couldn't give the information to the embassy. I'd probably have been arrested if I stepped foot inside. I told the spy to go instead. It was the morning of the raid. I said, 'Tell them, and they'll probably give you a nice reward for the information.'"

"So how did they manage to get away with the attack?" Tipton asked.

"Those bloody fools didn't believe him. They thought it was some kind of trick to extort money from them."

After he hung up with Hazem, Tipton sent a telex message to the American Embassy in Prague asking the Ambassador what he knew about Americans at an air base in Zatec and about the Czechs breaking the arms embargo.

A WEEK AND a half later, Tipton's secretary poked her head in the door.

"Mr. Tipton, John Cunningham is calling from Prague." Tipton glanced at the clock. *3:10 p.m. Cunningham's working late. It's past 9:00 over there.*

"Put him through."

Tipton let the phone ring four times before answering it. *Don't want to let him think I'm anxious.*

"John, how are you, old man?" Tipton said to the United States Ambassador to Czechoslovakia. Cunningham had received his appointment due in no small part to the lobbying of his brother, Frank Cunningham, Tipton's boss.

"I'm fine, Cordell. But this isn't a social call. I had my staff dig into that telex you sent about Americans, planes, and Zatec. I'm embarrassed to say a lot of bad things have been going on under my nose, and I had no idea they were happening."

"Tell me. Give me the short version first, and I'll ask you to flesh it out if I want more details.

"Okay. In a nutshell, planes *are* flying in and out of Zatec, loaded with munitions and parts of aircraft, all headed to Israel. The vast majority of the pilots are Americans."

Tipton squeezed the phone's receiver until his knuckles turned white. He felt his face flush. *Control yourself.* Tipton took a deep breath. "Okay. Now you better lay it out for me, step by step."

"All their air traffic, which by the way, originated from the USA, passes through Zatec. We're still trying to get a tally, but a huge number of cargo flights take off from Zatec after they've been refueled, loaded with airplanes, arms, ammunition, and various other military equipment, bound for Israel. Oh, I learned one other thing. The cargo planes they're using, when they first arrived in Zatec, had the insignia of the Panamanian National Airline, LAPSA, painted on them."

"Those miserable sons-o-bitches. They lied to our people and the Panamanians," Tipton blurted, rubbing his forehead roughly with his fingertips. "How did you find this out?"

"Young men, filled with testosterone, are the same all over the world. It appears their activities didn't pass quietly and unseen. The Americans, when they have free time, drive to Prague to have a good time, hitting the bars and nightclubs. They have lots of American money, and you can buy a lot with that, especially women. The prostitutes of Prague are happy as hell."

Cunningham paused. "Here is where it gets embarrassing for me. It seems the prostitutes augment their income by the selling information, and apparently they've been selling it to the Brits because the Brits knew all about it. Seems the prostitutes didn't think we'd be interested."

"Damn it, John. All this was happening under your nose?"

"Hold on a minute, Cordell. Tell me how you knew about it."

Tipton put his hand over the mouthpiece and took a loud breath. He couldn't tell Cunningham about Hazem. "Someone here in Washington got a tip. I tried to find out from who but couldn't. Besides, what difference does that make now? This is happening on your watch."

"Don't lay this all on me. You're in the States. They deceived and lied to U.S. authorities when they purchased the airplanes from the surplus stocks of the U.S. Air Force. Then they turned Czechoslovakia into a logistic rear echelon, including air bases, flying schools, and a purchasing and smuggling system supplying Israel with war materiel."

Cunningham paused to let his words impact Tipton. "This one is on you now. Czechoslovakia is a member of the United Nations and is expected to obey the embargo decision, instead of disobeying it so blatantly. We and the Brits put the pressure on for the embargo, and now you have to put the pressure on the Czechs to put a stop to them helping the Jews."

"You're right," Tipton said. "Give me a minute. Tipton tilted his head up and stared at the ceiling, his mind racing. Half a minute later, he said, "Okay. Here's what you're going to do. I want you to call in the Czech Foreign Minister. In a face-to-face, with no one else around, tell the minister that Czechoslovakia must immediately stop selling arms and services, close all its military air bases, and chase all Israeli personnel from its territory immediately. If they don't, the United States will report this as a blatant violation of the embargo to the Security Council and recommend that strong economic sanctions immediately be taken against Czechoslovakia."

"You think that will work?" Cunningham asked.

"Of course," Tipton replied. "Czechoslovakia is poor and hungry. It's dependent on the economic help it gets from us and other western countries. It can't allow itself to get punished by economic sanctions. They'll throw those damn Jews out in a heartbeat."

The American ultimatum was passed to the Czechs in mid-August. The Czechs folded. They told the men at Zatec they had three weeks to clear out of the base, and by the third week, all the planes and men were gone from Zatec.

CHAPTER 35
September, 1948
Operation Velvetta

BACK IN EARLY August, before they were thrown out of the country, Czech officials told the Israeli representative in Prague that Czechoslovakia had no more Messerschmitts to sell.

"However, you're welcome to buy some Spitfires," the Czechs said. "They were given to us as a present by Britain after the war. But, we're under a lot of Soviet pressure to *easternize* our military, and the Spitfires don't fit into those plans."

It couldn't have come at a better time for Israel. By mid-July, they had already lost five Messerschmitts and five more were not airworthy. The 101ˢᵗ Squadron was left with 15, and they were diminishing very quickly.

When the Czechs informed the men at Zatec that they had to leave, Israel's Ambassador at Large for the Balkan countries negotiated with the Yugoslav government. Yugoslavia's President Tito agreed to give him an airfield and to allow Israeli planes to fly the route, Czechoslovakia–Yugoslavia–Israel.

President Tito, and his first Prime Minister who was a Jew named

Moshe Pijade, were the first to recognize Israel *de facto* and *de jure*. They made every effort to help the State of Israel in every possible way. There was very strong sentiment to help because Tito's partisans helped the Jews during the war, and some Jews from Palestine had been airdropped into Yugoslavia to work as radio operators for Tito's guerrillas.

Sam Pomerantz, a pilot with the ATC who'd flown with the RAF during the war, was sent to find an appropriate airfield. He looked for a place as close as possible to Yugoslavia's southern border to shorten the flying distance to Israel. He found a suitable airfield near the town of Niksic.

It was a huge green meadow surrounded by hills. A river passed on the west side of the airfield, and the town was on the east side. A railway track passed from north to south just on the outskirt of town. The airstrip could be kept reasonably isolated from civilians.

The Czechs had to throw the *Machal* pilots and planes out of their country due to the pressure from the United States and Britain. But they still needed money, so they agreed to honor the sale of the Spitfires they made in early August.

The newly purchased Spitfires could get to Israel by one of three ways: in a ship, in an air transport, or under their own power.

The Czechs proposed to disassemble the airplanes, pack them in wooden crates, send them to Israel by train and boat, and reassemble them there. But that would take six months, and Israel didn't have that much time. They told the Czechs they wanted to fly them to Israel.

The Czechs were not comfortable with the distance the planes would be required to fly, especially since it included a stretch of 2,250 kilometers (1,400 miles) over the open sea. But once Yugoslavia agreed to allow the Israelis to use the airfield in Niksic for refueling, the Czechs gave their consent.

However, to keep the Americans and the Brits from getting upset, the Czechs required utmost secrecy. The planes had to be painted with Czech insignias, and the crew members were confined to their hotel rooms when not working to prepare for the mission.

The Yugoslavian government also had to be careful. The operation was treated as super-secret because it was opposed by the British and Soviets. The Israelis were allowed to repair and run the base while bringing in the Spitfires and transport planes and modifying them. The Slavs operated several squadrons of Spitfires, so the Israeli flights would not provoke undue suspicion. However, the planes were required to be repainted with Yugoslavian insignias for the flight to Israel so that the shipment would not arouse any scrutiny.

The Czechs continued to insist flying them to Israel was impossible. The plane had an endurance of ninty minutes which was more than enough to operate as a fighter. At cruising-speed, it could fly seven hundred kilometers in ninety minutes. Even if they installed the additional fuel-tank under the belly, which the British design had planned for, it would still only bring its range up to 1,570 kilometers, far short of reaching Israel.

THE CZECHS NEVER took into account Jewish ingenuity and engineering. They had an American volunteer, an aeronautical engineer and a pilot with a commercial pilot license, named Sam Pomerantz. He was sent to Czechoslovakia by Ben-Gurion to check the airworthiness of the airplanes. Determining they were in excellent condition, and after test flying the plane, he figured out how to make them capable of reaching Israel by air.

When the Brits designed the Spitfire, they planned to be able to add a fuel tank under the belly of the plane if ever needed. Pomerantz would not only add the under-belly tank, he'd put two additional fuel-tanks, one under each wing. In addition, he would take parts of the radio out and build a special tank to fit in that space, just behind the cockpit. All the fuel tanks would be connected, boosting the fuel from 85 gallons to 379 gallons, which was enough, he hoped, to take it nonstop from Yugoslavia to Israel.

Carrying such a large and heavy amount of fuel made it impossible to handle the excess weight of the machine guns, ammunition, as well as the radio equipment. The Spitfires would be stripped, and all those items would have to be sent to Israel separately.

The flight from Niksic crossed 2,250 km of open water and would take seven hours to complete. Pomerance estimated each Spitfire would land with a reserve of only 20 minutes worth of fuel.

The Spitfires would be made airworthy by the Czechs in a small aircraft factory and airfield near the town of Kunovice then flown in eight or nine flights, six airplanes in each flight, to Niksic in Yugoslavia. There, they would land, be refueled, and given a last check before taking off again and flying nonstop to Ramat David in Israel.

A South African pilot named Jack Cohen also contributed a brilliant idea. In Israel, the Arabs, mostly the Egyptians, were also flying Spitfires. He suggested putting a red spinner on the propeller, a red stripe down the fuselage, and red and white diagonal stripes on the tail. That way, he reasoned, an Israeli pilot would at least know which Spitfire was friendly, and which wasn't.

A problem arose with the Czechs. The Israelis in Prague, requesting clearance be given to our airplanes to load and fly out the machine guns, ammunition and the various spare parts of the Spits, were refused. The Czechs finally agreed that only Israeli single-engine planes could fly in and out of Czechoslovakia. They were certain small airplanes like that would not be able to carry the necessary cargo.

They obviously knew nothing about the capabilities of the two, single engine Norsemen which would be the ones carrying out the shuttle service.

Each Norseman leaving Kunovice for Niksic could hold the machine guns, ammunition, and vital spare parts for one Spit. The total weight of this cargo was precisely one thousand kilograms, the exact Norseman weight limit. The two planes would carry the contents of two Spits, every day, to Niksic. A C-46 would arrive in Niksic once a week. It would collect the removed cargo for six Spits and fly it to Israel.

On the day a group of six Spits arrived in Niksic, the plan called for a Douglas C-54 Skymaster to fly in from Israel, staffed with two navigators and two wireless-operators, in addition to the pilots. The Skymaster would escort the Spitfire formation, flying ahead and navigating for them, and be their communication channel.

In case a search-and-rescue became necessary, if a Spit had to ditch in the Mediterranean, the Skymaster also had several different dinghies, lifebelts, and a load of different pyrotechnical props. In the event of a problem, the Skymaster would drop a dinghy then continue on to Israel. Two naval vessels would go to sea to cover the route with a third vessel waiting on alert in Haifa harbor. A C-47 loaded with more sea rescue equipment stood ready at Ramat David.

I ARRIVED IN Kunovice on September 18 and trained on one of the Spits for the next six days.

The second day I was there, I ran into Zvi Sokolnik, the security officer at the base in Zatec. He was sitting at a table in the mess hall eating an orange, folders spread in front of him.

"Hey, Sokolnik," I said, moving over to the table.

He looked up, eyes crinkled, brows furrowed. He was trying to place me. When he made the connection, he smiled. "Kaplan, how are you?"

"I'm doing okay." I paused a second. "Got a question. Shatz told me about this Swiss guy he talked to you about. I think his name was Lerner or something like that."

"His name was Lehman."

"Right. Lehman. Shatz said you guys thought he might be a spy. Was he?"

"Yes, he was."

"You arrest him?"

"He's dead. They found him in back of the Grand Hotel Praha in Prague shot in the head. There was also another guy, part of the

Egyptian Brotherhood. He was found lying next to Lehman. Also shot in the head."

"Did they find out who did it?" I asked.

Sokolnik picked up a piece of his orange, slipped into his mouth, and chewed it slowly. He just looked at me as he chewed, not saying anything.

I felt a chill. "Was it us?" I asked.

Sokolnik picked up the last piece of orange, popped it in his mouth, gathered his folders from the table and stood. "Nice seeing you again, Kaplan. Stay safe. I hear you're doing a great job for us." He turned and walked out of the mess hall, never turning to look at me.

ON THE MORNING of September 24, six of us took off in the Spitfires from Kunovice to Niksic, three hundred miles away. With me were Modi Alon, Syd Cohen, and Tuxie Blau, along with Sam Pomerance and Jack Cohen. Pomerance took off first to lead the group. Tuxie Blau took the last spot. Without the built-in radios, we communicated as well as we could, which was poorly, using walkie-talkies. Arriving at Niksic, Blau forgot to lower his landing gear and damaged his plane. He was not hurt, but that left us with only five planes.

We took off for Israel on September 27, led by the Skymaster, what we called the Mothership. Two hours into the flight, I noticed my fuel tanks were not functioning. I had no idea what my fuel situation was, so I used my walkie-talkie, and told the Mothership my problem. We were close to the island of Rhodes, so they suggested I land there. They couldn't jeopardize their fuel, so they all circled until I was down on the Greek island runway, then left for Israel.

I taxied to the control tower and got out. I told an official who came to meet me that I had run low on fuel and needed to buy some. About five minutes later, he came back with some armed soldiers who took me to an office where he began questioning me.

I told him the truth, that I was on a long-range flight to Israel, and

I ran out of fuel. He asked me why my plane had the markings of the Yugoslav Air Force? The Greeks were fighting Communist invaders from Albania and Yugoslavia, and beside the Yugoslavian markings, they found my map with a course line from Yugoslavia to Israel. They also found my American passport, with a Czech visa.

Two nights later, three scary looking guys in dark suits woke me up in the middle of the night, threatening to shoot me. I told them I was not a Communist, but they didn't believe me. They flew me to Athens and put me in an air force prison.

When the four other Spits landed in Ramat David, the Haganah office in Rome was contacted. They got in touch with the Greek authorities, convinced them I wasn't a communist, and paid a $10,000 fine. The Greeks agreed to release me but impounded my Spit. The Haganah office arranged to get me to Rome, and then by boat, back to Israel.

CHAPTER 36
October 15-17
Israel

I was with Rudy Augarten and Syd Cohen drinking coffee in the ready room when Alon walked in. It was 5:30 in the afternoon.

"I need you guys to take up the Spitfires in a half an hour," he said. "We're beginning Operation Yoav. Despite the truce, the Egyptians are stopping our convoys' passage to the Negev, and they're capturing positions beyond the lines put in place when the truce went into effect. Yesterday, they fired on sixteen of our trucks as they passed through their positions. It was a total violation of the truce, and the damn U.N. observes just sat there and watched. They did nothing. So word just came down from the prime minister's office. He said screw them and screw the truce. Starting now, we're fighting back."

"What are we doing?" I asked.

"We have four Spits and two P-51s operational. We can't have the Egyptians launching air attacks on our ground troops, so you're going to hit El Arish. We want you, Augarten, and Cohen to take Spitfires, and take out their planes on the ground. I'm sending up the other Spit and two 51s to escort the B-17s and Beaufighter bombers. They're going to hit Ashkelon and Beersheba tonight, ahead of our ground forces attacking the towns tomorrow."

We took off at 7:30, flew off the coast at twenty thousand feet until we were fifteen miles from the Egyptian forward air base at El Arish. At that point, we dropped down to nine hundred feet, flying echelon right. Augarten was in the lead, followed by me two hundred yards above and to his right, Cohen flying the same spacing with me. At this height and speed, the desert sand dunes seemed to undulate like a slithering snake.

When the air base came into view, we dropped down to four hundred feet. Augarten banked left, heading at a cluster of five Spitfires parked at the far end of the landing strip. I spotted three Spits, each in side by side hangers. Probably being repaired, I thought, as I banked right, heading at them. I had two bombs hanging beneath my wings, and when I got in position, I let them loose. My Spit shook from the shock waves as they exploded.

I pulled up and banked to my left, passing over the end of the runway and the smoking remains of the Spitfires Augarten took out. I climbed to two thousand feet, where I found Augarten and Cohen waiting for me.

As we headed back to base, I glanced down at the Egyptian airstrip. Coming in low, I'd been able to take out all three hangers, destroying the structures completely and the Spits inside. Cohen had placed his two bombs well. He'd blown deep craters forty yards apart in the runway. It would be out of commission for a while, which is what we were looking for, to keep any planes from using the facility while we conducted Operation Yoav.

THE NEXT DAY, Augarten and I were given Spitfires and assigned to provide escort for three Beaufighter bombers headed to help our ground troops in the Negev.

To get more planes operational, our mechanics had worked

feverishly all the day before, and well into the night. They had repaired two of the Messerschmitts, which now sat in front of me at the end of the runway, waiting to take off. Alon and Weizman were the pilots. Their assignment was to go after Egyptian ground forces along the coastal road.

The Messerschmitts took off, and we followed minutes later. Augarten and I met up with the Beaufighters and escorted them to Beersheba. We flew high cover as they dropped their bomb load and escorted them back before returning to our base. It was a milk run; we encountered no enemy aircraft.

I was walking with Augarten to grab a car into Tel Aviv when I looked up to see Alon's and Weizman's planes making their approach to the airstrip. One of the pieces o'shit suddenly pulled up, just as the other plane touched down and pulled off the runway.

"His landing gear didn't come down," I yelled to Augarten, pointing at the plane as it flew past the airstrip.

We watched the plane gain altitude then roll over and begin plummeting to the earth before quickly pulling up, banking to the right, then violently banking left.

"What the hell is he doing?" Augarten yelled.

"I think he's trying to force the landing gear down by pulling high G's and hard turns."

I heard someone running behind us. It was Weizman. *That's Alon up there.*

"What's he doing?" Weizman yelled as he came up beside me. I told him what I thought.

We watched Alon continue the maneuvers for perhaps two minutes.

"Look! It's working. One wheel just dropped down," I shouted.

Seconds later, as the plane headed skyward in an almost vertical climb, the engine sputtered, and a stream of white smoke began to pour from it. The piece o'shit rolled over and began to descend. It looked like Alon was trying to line up with the runway.

"He's going to try for a crash landing," I yelled.

The plane was about a thousand feet off the ground when I heard the engine cut out. I stared in horror as the Messerschmitt began to twist, then spin and spiral toward the ground. The one down wheel was pulling the plane out of its aerodynamics.

"Pull up," I screamed.

It did no good. Split seconds later, the plane slammed into the ground twenty feet off the runway, bursting into flames. We bolted to the burning plane, but the flames and the heat were so intense, we couldn't get closer than thirty feet.

I bent over, hands on my knees, head down, tears trickling down my cheeks. As I gasped for air, my stomach tightened, ripples of nausea rose in my throat. I tasted bile, and began to shake and sweat.

I didn't believe in God. The concentration camps and the slaughter of millions of Jews reinforced that feeling. But standing in this place, at this time, I prayed.

If you're up there, please let him have died instantly on impact, not in the burning wreckage.

Then I let out my anger. *God, if you are up there, you're a son of a bitch. How could you let this happen? This wasn't just my friend you let die. This was Modi Alon. A good man, a national hero. How could you be so cruel?*

THE GROUND CREWS rushed to the burning wreckage. It took them thirty minutes to put out the flames and retrieve what was left of Alon's charred body.

In the Jewish tradition, we buried him the next day. Internment was at a cemetery just outside of Tel Aviv. Sitting next to Alon's pregnant wife on one side was Prime Minister Ben-Gurion. On her other was Weizman. Standing in back of them were members of Ben-Gurion's fledgling cabinet, as well as high ranking military officers.

All the pilots from the 101st that could be spared for the day stood as an honor guard next to the plain wooden coffin. We never had uniforms, so as a substitute, we wore our red baseball hats with the squadron's red and black angel of death logo. It was the best we could do as a sign of honor and respect to our fallen comrade.

As I listened to the rabbi say all the expected words at a funeral, I was more inspired and uplifted by what I saw beyond the grave site. Covering the hillside, a thousand or more people stood in silence, paying their respects to Alon. He'd shot down three enemy aircraft, two of which were about to bomb Tel Aviv when he stopped them. He was the first successful Israeli fighter pilot, their hero.

CHAPTER 37
December 5, 1948
Tel Aviv

I GOT A CALL from Shatz last night. "Can you come to a meeting at the Bristol Hotel tomorrow tonight?"

"I guess so. What's it about?"

"You'll see for yourself. Meet me in the dining room at 6:30." He hung up

It was pouring when I found a parking spot a half a block from the entrance to the hotel. The winter rainy season in Israel arrived in earnest about two weeks before. I ran inside, took off my cap, and shook the water off. I'd just removed my leather jacket, holding it at arm's length to keep my shirt and pants from getting wet, when I spotted Shatz standing at the entrance to the dining room.

"What's going on?" I asked when I walked over.

"There's a lot of dissension with the guys in the Air Transport Command. Since you were part of the group from the beginning and know most of them, I thought your perspective would be helpful. You're not a big part of the operation anymore, so you can look at this more detached than me—or them. What's the old expression? You don't have a dog in the fight."

"What's the dissension about?"

"The Israeli Air Force decided that the ATC should no longer operate as an autonomous civilian operation. They want it to officially be a part of the air force."

"I don't get it. What does that mean?" I asked.

"In simple terms, they want the ATC to become the 106th Air Transport Squadron of the Israeli Air Force, and all pilots flying for it to be commissioned officers in the air force."

"What? The guys are being drafted?"

"That's how some of them are taking it. Let's go inside."

When we walked into the room, there must have been thirty guys sitting around the tables. I immediately spotted many old friends, who got up and came over to me, shaking my hand, and in some cases, giving me a hug. I spotted Shatz talking to a small group of guys off to the side of the room.

Shatz walked up to the front of the room. "Okay. You guys called this meeting. Who wants to get it started?"

Harvey Resnick, one of the volunteers who joined us right after we arrived in Zatec, stood up. "I don't like the way the Israeli government is treating us. I think it sucks, and we should stand up and let them know it."

I was leaning against a side wall. I pushed myself off and said, "Guys, I know a lot of you, and I've flown with a lot of you. But since I moved over to the 101st, I've lost touch. Tell me what's going on." I'd heard Shatz's explanation; now I wanted to hear it from them.

Resnick turned to me. "What's going on? I'll tell you what's going on. First, the government has us now flying converted C-46s, as part of their new airline, *El Al*. We found out they're making a profit on these flights, but they're paying us our wartime pay, not what a pilot would get if he flew as a civilian for a profit-making airline. If they're making a profit, we think we're entitled to receive pay commensurate with a civilian pilot."

Scattered mumbles broke out in the room. "Damn right." "They got some nerve." "They're screwing us."

Resnick held up his hand to quiet the men down. "That's bad. But now they're telling us they've decided to change the Air Transport Command. Seems they don't like the fact we're civilians, and the ATC is a civilian run operation. They've decided, effective January 1st, the ATC will be inducted into the Israeli Defense Force and become the 106ˢᵗ Squadron of the Israeli Air Force. And here's the best part. Everyone who flies the planes will have to be an Israeli officer. In essence, be drafted and become a member of the Israeli Defense Force, or you're out."

I looked at Shatz. "Is this true?"

"Seems so."

"How can they do that?" I asked."The ATC is an all volunteer operation, run and operated by civilians. And, by the way, almost all foreign civilians, not Israelis."

"I understand," Shatz replied.

"So," I said, my voice rising in volume, "now they decide that everything we did for them means nothing? That even though we were the ones who brought them the weapons, munitions, and fighter planes they needed to survive, hell even the damn aircraft they want to make part of this new 106ᵗʰ squadron, now we're dispensable? They don't need us anymore?"

I can't remember the last time I was so pissed off. I could feel the heat rising in my neck. My face must have been a bright shade of red. I was in the 101ˢᵗ fighter squadron, and this didn't even affect me. At least not yet. But I flew with these guys. How could the Israelis be so ungrateful in light of what we'd done for them? If the ATC hadn't flown in the dismantled Messerschmitts that Alon, Weizman, Eddie Cohen, and I used to stop the Egyptian column advancing on Tel Aviv back in May, there wouldn't even be an Israel today.

"Shatz," I said, trying to calm my outrage. "Do you have any explanation of why they're doing this?"

"No," he replied, "but I can take a guess. They probably think the ATC has become so big, and such an integral part of their armed forces, they can't let it continue to be an independent civilian entity. So, they need to make it officially part of the air force. Anyway, that's just my guess."

"And what about drafting us into the air force?" Resnick shot back.

"None of you in this room are Israeli citizens," Shatz replied. "You can't be forced to join the Israeli Army, and they can't draft you. My best guess is that they're going to take over the ATC whether you like it or not. So your choice is, sign up... or don't."

"And what happens if we don't?" a voice yelled out from the middle of the room.

I looked in the direction the question came from. "You want to know what happens?" I said, angrier than before. "I'll tell you what will happen. You're out. You go back home. The U.S.A., Canada, England, South Africa. To wherever you're from. You served your usefulness, and they don't need you anymore."

"I've got another reason why we can't join," Irving Lieberman said, rising and slowly turning his head, looking at every man in the room, before continuing. He'd been with the group for five months. "We're mostly Americans. We can't join a foreign army. It will be bad enough when we go home if the government ever finds out we're over here as volunteers. That might or might not be enough for them to revoke our citizenship. But join a foreign army? They find out, and they'll absolutely revoke our U.S. citizenship. Do what the Israeli's want us to do, and you better accept the fact that you will be, for the rest of your life, an Israeli citizen. Because you won't be an American anymore."

The room got very quiet. I could sense Lieberman's comment struck home... hard. It did for me. We all knew we could lose our citizenship when we agreed to volunteer. But we didn't care at the time.

Resnick broke the silence. "These air force guys really have big balls. Did you notice the timing of this whole thing? They've got Operation Velvetta scheduled for December 18th, and two weeks later, on January 1st, this is supposed to happen. What a coincidence.

Convenient, huh? They want to squeeze one last operation out of us before they dump us."

Resnick was right. Operation Velvetta was the second ATC operation to get Spitfires to Israel. There were 16 Spitfires ready to fly, Czechoslovakia to Yugoslavia to Israel. In early December, promising to pay both countries, they agreed to allow us one last time to use their bases. I was one of the ferry pilots, drawn from 101st Fighter Squadron, scheduled to leave in a few days for Prague and fly the Spitfires out.

"So what are we going to do?" someone yelled out.

"How about we send them a letter?" Lieberman said. "We'll tell them that if they don't forget about this thing happening on January 1st, we all quit. If we all agree to do it and sign it, they have to be smart enough to know they can't run their air force without us."

"Guys," Shatz said, "if you do this before Operation Velvetta, you're putting the operation in jeopardy. Israel needs those Spitfires."

"Good," someone shouted out. "Then they'll realize how important we are and what we do for the country."

The men took a vote and unanimously agreed. A letter was drafted to the chief of staff of the air force. It laid out our position. If the plan to fold the ATC into the air force, and the ultimatum requiring all pilots to join the air force was not withdrawn, all ATC operations would cease on December 9. Also, all those signing the letter would immediately resign from the ATC and request immediate repatriation to their countries of origin.

Shatz didn't like the way the men were handling the situation but agreed to hand deliver the letter the next day.

The next afternoon, Shatz called me and invited me back to the Bristol for another meeting with the ATC guys. When everyone was seated, Shatz moved to a table in the front of the room. He held a single sheet of paper in his hand, stared down at it for a few seconds before he let it drop from his fingers and flutter onto the table. He raised his head, his eyes scanning the room. He took a deep breath.

"I did what I said I would. I brought your letter to the chief of staff of the air force early this morning. He read the letter three times before looking back up at me. His eyes were stone cold. He asked me to wait where I was and left his office.

"I sat in that chair for about a half hour before he returned with this in his hand," Shatz said, reaching down and picking up the piece of paper he'd been looking at.

"It's a statement of retraction. Each of you who signed the ultimatum is required to personally sign a retraction of it. If you don't, you will immediately be repatriated. In a nutshell, sign it or you're gone immediately."

No one said a word. Except for the occasional cough, the scraping legs of a chair legs as someone move to get more comfortable, the room was silent.

"It's a bluff," Lieberman said, breaking the silence. "What are they going to do? Send us all home? They do that, and the ATC is out of commission. There goes their Operation Velvetta."

"It's not a bluff," Shatz said. "He told me point blank. They cannot, and will not, let us get away with issuing an ultimatum to the air force. They need to maintain military discipline, and our ultimatum violates that principle."

"What should we do?" someone yelled out.

"I can't make that decision for you," Shatz said. "It's each man's choice." He picked up the piece of paper and walked out of the room.

WHEN I BOARDED the transport plane two days later with other ferry pilots from the 101st, the pilots of the C-46 were standing next to the cockpit door. I didn't know them but recognized them from the meetings I'd been to with Schatz the last couple of days. When they saw me, they quickly turned their heads, entered the cockpit, and closed the door.

We first flew to Prague then on to the air base in Czechoslovakia where the Spitfires were being made ready for us to fly them to Israel by way of Yugoslavia. Operation Velvetta would get underway in nine days, on December 18.

CHAPTER 38
December 18, 1948
Czechoslovakia/Velvetta II

WHAT THE ISRAELI Air Force planned to do to the ATC nagged at me the entire time I was in Czechoslovakia.

Rationally, I understood why the air force felt they had to have the ATC be an official part of their military. I could almost accept the need to have planes flown by Israeli Air Force officers and not by civilians.

Emotionally, it was another story. Even though I understood their reasons, I felt the air force was wrong in what they were doing and wrong in the way they were going about it.

Shatz called me the night before I left for Czechoslovakia to bring me up to speed. He said that even though the men had agreed to withdraw the ultimatum letter they sent to the air force, the air force would not budge in their demand that each person had to individually sign the retraction statement.

"I think the air force is being vindictive and wants to humiliate the signers," he said.

"What are you going to do?" I asked.

"I haven't decided," he replied. "I'll speak to you when you get back."

Now I understood why the C-46 pilots that flew us to Czechoslovakia never came out of the cockpit, something pilots always did on long flights from Israel. They were still flying, which meant they signed the retraction. That's probably why they hustled into the cockpit when they saw me. They figured I knew and were too embarrassed to face me.

The other thing that bothered me about the ATC situation was it could happen to me. While the 101st Fighter Squadron was officially part of the Israeli Air Force, less than a handful of the pilots were Israelis. Everyone else, including me, was a civilian. We didn't have any officer's rank. and we didn't wear uniforms, other than sometimes our red baseball hats.

Would the air force demand I become an Israeli officer? Would I have to become an Israeli citizen? I suppose I'd have to, because I'd lose my U.S. citizenship if I became an Israeli officer.

"CHECK THE COWLING. I think I saw it vibrating, like a screw or something is loose," I said to the mechanic after I'd taxied to the hanger and climbed out of the cockpit. I'd just finished my third test flight of the Spitfire I'd be flying to Israel by way of Niksic, Yugoslavia. It was three hours after daybreak. I'd cut the flight short because of growing dark clouds drifting in from the southeast. We were scheduled to leave this afternoon. I wasn't sure the weather would cooperate.

Ten disassembled and crated Spitfires had already left by train for a harbor in Yugoslavia, where a ship would transport them to Israel. We desperately needed them, but we didn't have enough pilots to fly them to Israel. It would take weeks for them to arrive. They were relying on us to fly in Spits so they could become immediately operational.

"Anyone know what the weather report is for today?" I asked, walking into the building set aside to operate as our command center, dormitory, and mess hall for Operation Velvetta.

"Not good," Sam Pomerantz said. "There's a blizzard on the way. It's already hit Hungary and Austria, and moving northwest straight for us. Supposed to get here in about three hours. I've got the planes anchored down. We'll just have to sit tight and wait it out. I'll decide what we're going to do after it blows over."

Two hours later, even though it was five minutes past noon, it looked like dusk had settled outside. The dark clouds I'd seen this morning were gone, obliterated by snow falling so fast I couldn't see more than thirty feet out the window. Propelled by fifty mile an hour wind, floodlights mounted on the eaves of the building illuminated the snow blowing horizontally across the field. Drifts were beginning to pile against the wheels of the tied down Spits. Uneven mounds formed by swirling snow were building on the taxiway, and I presumed the runway beyond. I could hear the muted *clank, clank,* of a loose piece of metal being pummeled against the side of the building by the howling wind.

Three and a half hours later, the blizzard was gone. The winds had dropped to ten to fifteen miles an hour, and what snow continued to fall had dropped to just light flurries. I was pretty sure most of it was being blown off the roof of the building, not dropping from the sky.

"I'm going outside to take a look around," Pomerantz said. When he reached the side door, he had to push his shoulder against it to get it to open wide enough to squeeze through. Probably a drift against the door, I thought.

Pomerantz came back inside ten minutes later. "There's about nine inches of snow on the taxiway and the runway, but they also have drifts, some of them three to four feet. We're not going anyplace until it all gets cleared away."

"How we going to do that?" Shapiro asked. "I'm from Brooklyn. When we had snowstorms, the Department of Sanitation hooked plows to the garbage trucks and did the streets. Ain't no DOS here in Czechoslovakia."

"No, but there's something almost as good. The Czechs on the other side of the airport went home early to beat the storm. After they left, I sent one of our mechanics over there. He hotwired a bulldozer they're using to lengthen the runway and parked it behind this building." Pomerantz smiled. "Don't think you're getting off easy. Everyone grab a shovel from the back storeroom. We're going to clear a path to the bulldozer. While they're using it to get the snow off the taxiway and runway, we're going to take our shovels and clean the area around the planes."

A large thermometer hanging on a wall outside the hanger indicted the temperature was minus 11 degrees centigrade. "Does anyone know how much that is in English?" I asked no one in particular, pointing to the thermometer.

"If I did my conversion right, that's about 12 degrees above zero," one of the pilots yelled out.

Even though I'd just left the warmth of the hanger, I shivered when I heard the reply.

We spent four hours outside shoveling around the planes and cleaning the accumulated snow off the wings and the canopies covering each cockpit. We might have been able to get the job done sooner, but because of the bitter cold, we had to take frequent breaks inside the hanger to warm up.

Pomerantz finally called everyone inside. "Everyone try to get some shuteye. I'll see what things look like tomorrow morning in the daylight and then make a decision on what we'll do."

No one argued. We were all bone weary. I felt the cold deep in my bones and waited about ten minutes to try to warm up a little before crawling onto my cot. Despite the sound of loud snoring coming from exhausted pilots, in less than a minute, I joined them, slipping into the arms of Hypnos, the Greek god of sleep.

"EVERYBODY, UP AND at 'em," Sam Pomerantz voice boomed, waking me with a start. All around, I heard groans and expletives as the men woke in various degrees. I lifted my head to see some of them pull covers over their heads and roll over, trying to go back to sleep.

"Come on. Get your asses out of bed. We're going to be wheels up in two hours," Pomerantz yelled. I looked at my watch. It was eight in the morning. The smell of coffee and freshly baked bread wafted into the dorm area from the part of the building set up as the mess hall.

There was a lot of grumbling, but by time 8:45 rolled around, we'd all taken care of our morning bathroom chores, packed up our meager possessions in small handheld duffels, and were woofing down breakfast of bacon, eggs, toast, and coffee in the mess hall section. I had no idea how the Czech cooks we'd hired to staff the mess hall made it in through the snow, and I didn't care. After last night's workout, I was sore, starved, and grateful.

At ten minutes after nine, Pomerantz sent the cooks out to another building so we could have a private meeting.

"I don't like the fact we have to fly out this morning. The weather between here and Niksic is not great," Pomerantz said. "There are snow flurries and heavy cloud cover the whole way. Our people in Niksic say some of the cloud banks might be as high at ten thousand feet. But we've got a Douglas C-54 Skymaster Mothership waiting for us in Niksic to escort us to Israel, and it can't stay on the ground in Yugoslavia too long. So we have to go today."

By ten o'clock, six Spitfires sat on the taxiway, engines running, waiting to take off. Sam Pomerantz would lead group one, with Bill Pomerantz, no relation to Sam, and John McElroy, a non-Jewish pilot from Canada, on his wings. I would lead group two, with Skippy Shapiro and Red Finkel from Brooklyn, the guy that got us our red baseball hats, on my wings. Sam and I had the only airborne radios.

We took off and almost immediately flew into clouds. Pomerantz radioed me, saying he was going to climb above them. At 8,300 feet, they began to break up, and by 9,000 feet I had cleared the cloud cover, with bright sun and blue skies ahead. But the weather didn't hold.

An hour into our six hundred mile trip to Niksic I could see cloud banks ahead. I was flying at ten thousand feet and the tops of the clouds had to be at least three thousand to four thousand feet higher.

Sam and his group were a half mile ahead and about one thousand feet below. "Sam, come in. Sam?" I called into the radio.

"This is Sam."

"Sam I don't like those clouds ahead. They've got to be topping off at fourteen thousand feet or higher. We got mountains in Austria and Yugoslavia that come close to that height."

"Yeah, I saw them," Sam replied. "We'll have to climb above them."

"Are you kidding? We don't have oxygen. If we have to go fifteen thousand feet or higher, we will have a problem. Besides, the heaters in these Spits suck. I'm freezing my ass off at ten thousand feet. It'll be worse if we have to go higher."

"Okay. You take the planes back to base. The Skymaster is waiting, and they don't know what's happening. I'll push on to Niksic and contact you when I get there."

I led my flight down to Pomerantz's group, signaled them through my window to follow me, and banked back toward the base in Kunovice. Pomerantz continued on.

Four hours later, I was in our command center when Shapiro walked over to me. "You hear from Pomerantz?"

"No, not yet."

"He's overdue," Shapiro said.

"I know. I should have heard from him an hour ago. I'll give it another hour. If I haven't heard by then, I'll put a call into Niksic."

Twenty minutes later, the phone on the table next to me rang. It was the pilot of the Skymaster, an Israeli named Ben-Mendel. I listened to him and slowly sank into a chair, clutching the phone. My stomach roiled. I hung up and stared blankly at a far wall.

"Kaplan," Shapiro said, walking toward me, "are you all right? You're as white as a ghost."

"Pomerantz is dead."

"What?"

"Pomerantz is dead. That was the pilot of the Skymaster. The Slavs just called the base in Niksic. They got a report of a plane crashing into a mountain in the northwest. A search party was sent to investigate. They found the wreckage of a Spitfire. The pilot's body was still inside. It was Pomerantz. The best explanation is that he went too high to try to clear the clouds and with no oxygen, he blacked out and crashed"

Shapiro slumped into a chair across the table from me. He rubbed a hand across his face, wiping away a tear at the corner his eye. I wiped my own tears away with my shirt sleeve.

I pushed myself out of my chair. "Okay. Here's what we're gonna do. Tomorrow morning we're flying six Spits out of here to Niksic. Sam wanted Operation Velvetta to be an on time success, and that's what's gonna happen. For Sam."

Shapiro got out of his chair, stood like he was at attention, and said, "For Sam."

THE NEXT MORNING, December 19, we took off for Niksic with me as lead pilot. Clouds still blanketed the terrain. When we reached the coast of Yugoslavia, the weather improved, but for some three hours we had flown in bad weather. We continued along the Adriatic coastline, then turned inland, and all six Spitfires landed at Niksic simultaneously.

Ground crews removed the Yugoslav markings from the Spitfires and painted on Israeli colors. Two Spitfires were judged unable to make the second leg and had to wait to reach Israel inside transports.

Three hours after we landed, four of us were ready to leave for Israel. The Skymaster Mothership headed out first to circle the airfield. Take off for the Spitfires was going to be a tricky proposition.

With the main tank, as well as all auxiliary tanks, filled to capacity with fuel, we were lifting off heavier than we ever had before. Before his death, Sam had addressed this problem. He had a plan. The mechanics would raise the tail wheel of each plane and rest it on the hood of a Jeep. As the Spitfire sped down the runway, the Jeep would drive behind it. This was to help us gain the highest speed possible to lift the weight into the sky.

The four Spits sat at the end of a dry lake, engines idling, as the tail wheels were raised. After getting the signal from the ground, we began to roll down the lakebed, followed by the Jeeps holding up our tail wheels. It was a good thing the lakebed was so large because I needed most of it before I achieved lift off speed. Glancing to my right, I saw the other three Spits front wheels rise from the ground as we headed up to meet the Mothership.

During the flight, to conserve fuel, we flew at an altitude of ten thousand feet. We kept an airspeed of 150 knots, about 180 mph, the cruising speed of the Skymaster. Although I was well dressed, the frigid air was able to penetrate my clothing. We didn't have anything I could use to take a leak in, and after four hours of flying, I thought my bladder was going to burst. I came close to relieving myself on the cockpit floor but knew I'd never hear the end of it if I did.

Finally, we landed at Ekron after five hours and twenty minutes in the air. As happy as I was to be safely on the ground, as soon as we got to the hanger, I leaped from the cockpit and made a beeline to the head. I just made it. When I got back to the planes, one of the ground mechanics told me they had just checked my fuel. There was no more than twenty minutes of fuel left.

As SECOND IN command after Pomerantz, it was my job to break the **news** of his death to his wife, Eleanor. I knew her well. She, Sam, and I had gone out to dinner many times. She was a wonderful woman, full of life, with a great sense of humor. She wasn't born Jewish, and she didn't convert to Judaism, but I felt she was more Jewish than many women I knew who were born Jews. She kept the Jewish traditions alive in their house, celebrating all the holidays.

The next morning, I knocked on her apartment door and waited for her to answer. When she opened it, I took off my red baseball cap. In a microsecond, the smile of seeing a friend faded, and her lower lip began to quiver. She took a half-step back from the doorway, recognition, dawning on her face that I was here to bring bad news.

"No," she said softly, shaking her head, tears shimmering in her eyes. She wrapped her arms around herself and rocked back and forth."No, no, no," she mumbled, still shaking her head.

I stepped quickly into the apartment, wrapping my arms around her shuddering frame, reaching back with my foot to kick the door closed. I held her tight, running my hand up and down her back, whispering, "I'm so sorry. I'm so sorry."

She cried, her tears soaking my shirt. I held her close, trying to comfort her. I don't know how long we stood there.

I felt Eleanor put her hands on my chest and gently push me away. "Please... stay there for a minute," she said and walked into the hallway toward the back of the apartment. She was back in less than three minutes, holding a bunch of tissues. It looked to me like she had gone into the bathroom and washed her face.

"Please," she said, gesturing to a chair. I sat, and she took a seat in a chair directly across from me. "Tell me what happened."

I told her everything, from the blizzard the day before the flight, his decision to fly on without the rest of us, the discovery of his plane and body by the Yugoslavians, and the theory that he passed out from lack of oxygen. She sat stooped shouldered, listening stoically to everything I had to say.

When I finished, we sat quietly. I watched her face, searching for signs of what might be going on in her mind. I had no intentions of breaking the silence. I'd give her as much time as she needed.

It was perhaps five minutes later that she took in a sharp breath and sat upright, straightening her shoulders. She dabbed her eyes with the wad of tissues still clutched in her hand, and said, "He wanted the State of Israel to become a reality. It was something he believed in with all his heart, something worth fighting for. He was doing that when he crashed. If Sam had to go, I'm glad he went this way."

My eyes welled, both for the loss of my friend Sam and at how proud he'd be at the strength and fortitude of this remarkable woman he'd married.

CHAPTER 39
December, 1948
Israel

THE DAY AFTER my meeting with Eleanor Pomerantz, I called Shatz in Tel Aviv. We made plans to meet for lunch at a restaurant we both enjoyed, Mutz Cafe, at the corner of Sheinkin and Melchett Streets. The weather forecast was for clear skies and afternoon temperatures around 15°C, 59° F, just right for enjoying lunch at their outdoor tables.

I was a half a block from the restaurant when I spotted Shatz sitting at a sidewalk table. I watched him lift a spoon of steaming soup to his mouth, blow on it to cool it down, before sipping the contents through his lips.

"Couldn't wait for me?" I asked as I sat in the empty chair set at the table for two.

"Nope. I got here ten minutes ago. I was chilly so I ordered Mutz's famous chicken soup with matzo balls. It's delicious as always."

Just then, a waiter appeared. "I'll have a bowl of the same," I said pointing to Shatz's plate.

After the waiter left, I said, "So, what did you do about the retraction of the ultimatum?"

"I signed the retraction and handed it to General Haman. He took it, smiled, and said he knew I would do the right thing. I told him, 'Yes, I'm doing the right thing.' With that said, I handed him my resignation from the ATC and asked to be repatriated back to the United States."

"You're shitting me. That's a joke, right."

"No, no joke. I think what the guys of the ATC did by issuing the ultimatum was wrong. I knew the Israeli Air Force couldn't, and wouldn't, let it stand. They can't have subordinates issuing demands. I understood that. But forcing each man to individually sign the retraction was chicken shit petty. Worse yet, basically conscripting them into the Israeli Air Force was wrong. They had to know, or should have known, each American would automatically lose their citizenship. If I stayed, it would be like I was condoning what they were doing. That would make me no better than them."

I sat back in my chair, trying to absorb the enormity of what I'd just heard. If it wasn't for Shatz, I wouldn't be here. If it wasn't for Shatz, most of the American pilots in the ATC, as well as the 101st fighter squadron, wouldn't be in Israel.

Hell, if it wasn't for Shatz getting the C-46s from the states, by way of Panama, to Czechoslovakia, and having those planes fly in weapons and Messerschmitts back in May, there probably wouldn't even be an Israel now. And now those assholes put him in such an impossible box, they were forcing him to leave.

"What are they doing about your repatriation?" I asked.

"I'm still part of the ATC. The switch to become officially part of the air force doesn't happen until January 1st. That's less than two weeks from now. I suppose they'll throw me out shortly after that. I'm in no hurry. I'll be ready when they are."

"Do the others know?" I asked.

"I told all the men that were part of the LAPSA group and a few others. I don't want anyone to make a decision based on what I did. Each man should decide for themselves."

I looked down at the tabletop and lightly bit the inside of my lower lip. How did I feel about all this?

"I don't know what to say," I said to Shatz. "It's so stupid. I feel like they used us. Don't get me wrong. I have absolutely no regret about coming here and fighting to have a homeland. But for them to treat us like this... I'm not sure I can give them the benefit of the doubt."

Neither of us said anything for a minute or so. The silence was broken when the waiter appeared with my bowl of soup. Shatz waited until the waiter walked away and said, "Eat your chicken soup. Didn't your mother tell you chicken soup cures all ills?" He looked at me and let out a hearty laugh.

We talked about Operation Velvetta, how many Spitfires were brought into Israel in the last two days, and how the war was going. We both felt that the war was coming to an end, and we would beat the Arabs. It wasn't a case of *if* any more, but more of *when*.

We didn't speak about Shatz leaving or what I might do. We said goodbye after lunch, me heading back to base, Shatz heading to ATC headquarters. I made him promise to call me when he heard about the plans for his repatriation.

FOR THE REST of the month of December, I mostly flew missions in support of our ground troops during Operation Horev, a large scale offensive against the Egyptian Army in the western Negev.

We had moved our base of operations from Herzliya, north of Tel Aviv, to the Hatzor Air Base, south of Tel Aviv near Ashdod, closer to the frontlines. We felt we'd gained air superiority over the Egyptians, enough that we weren't worried about the base being attacked. When the Egyptians sent in their fighters, we were pretty successful in either knocking them out of the sky or having them turn tail and head back to Egypt.

On December 22, I was scheduled to fly an air cover mission for a battalion of the Golani Brigade, which was launching an attack on Egyptian positions along the Gaza-Rafah Road. I was leading the mission. Abbie Goldberg, a *Machalnik* who joined us a few months ago from St. Louis, was my wingman. I took a Messerschmitt since I had experience with it, and I let him take one of the new Spitfires.

I took off, heading west toward the Mediterranean, Goldberg on my left. When we reached two thousand feet, Goldberg pulled alongside me, and we each fired a quick test burst of our machine guns. My piece o'shit gun synchronizer was off, and I watched in shock as my bullets tore into two of my propeller blades. The plane began to shake violently and lose altitude. I banked to my right away from Goldberg and killed the engine before it caused me to spiral out of control. I headed back to land, the piece o'shit now nothing but a glider.

I was dropping like a rock. I pulled back on the yoke trying to maintain altitude. I didn't want to make a water landing if I could avoid it. I spotted the shoreline and a beach coming up fast. The mission was strictly to cover our troops against enemy fighters, so I didn't have to worry about any bombs under my wings. I was going to try to land on the beach if I could reach it.

I knew if I dropped my wheels, they'd dig into the sand, and I'd flip over. It would have to be a belly landing. I figured the worst that would happen is my propeller blades would snap, but what the hell? I'd already shot them to hell.

My first thought was to come into the beach parallel to the water, giving me as much beach sand as I needed to come to a stop. But I was dropping too fast. I wouldn't have the time, or the height, to make the maneuver. As the plane dropped lower and closer to land, I could see a seawall made up of huge boulders protecting a road that ran along the edge of the beach. The wall, maybe ten feet tall, could not have been more than thirty to forty feet from the water's edge.

There was no way the sand would slow me down enough to prevent me from crashing into the wall if I came in straight. The plane was hurtling toward the beach. My altimeter had me at 100 feet, less than a quarter of a mile from shore. I had one shot at pulling this off.

A half a football field from the shoreline, and 15 feet above the water, I pulled back hard on the yoke. The plane bounced when the bottom tip of the tail section made contact with the sea. Using every ounce of my strength, I pulled back on the stick as more and more of the undercarriage came in contact with the water, the friction slowing my speed. I jerked forward against my seatbelt harness when the belly of the plane made contact with the sand. The plane came to rest, ten feet shy of the seawall.

I popped the canopy, hit the harness safety release, and scrambled out of the plane, dropping onto the sand. I heard the roar of the Spitfire and looked up to Goldberg flying toward me up the beach. I raised both arms above my head and with my thumbs pointing up, signaling I was okay. As he passed overhead, he waggled his wings in acknowledgment.

Two hours later, a Jeep brought me back to base. When I arrived, they told me Goldberg had radioed what happened to me, and two other fighters had been sent to fly the mission. The chief mechanic came to me an hour later in the mess hall as I downed my second scotch on the rocks. He apologized for what happened and said when he got the Messerschmitt back they would find out what caused the firing mechanism to go out of sync.

"Suit yourself," I said, polishing off the rest of my scotch. I poured myself another. "But don't expect me to ever fly one of those pieces o'shit again."

CHAPTER 40
December, 1948
Israel

I WASN'T HURT WHEN I ditched the Messerschmitt and the next day was back in the air, but at my insistence, in a Spitfire. I was on a reconnaissance flight and had strafed an enemy position near the Gaza. I was headed back to the base at Hatzor when I spotted what looked like a good-sized enemy column moving toward the Gaza and Egypt. I plunged down and saw armored cars with Egyptian writing on them. As I swooped past the column, some of the armored cars opened fire on me.

I still had some ammunition left, and I couldn't think of a better way to use it up. I flew past the column, turned, and began a strafing run, working my way forward from the rear. I had just opened up for a brief three second burst when I thought my eyes were playing tricks on me. I immediately broke off my run and soared around to have another look. My eyes were not deceiving me. Painted on the hood of a Jeep at the rear of the column, I caught sight of a Star of David.

These were Israelis. They must have captured those vehicles, I thought, and with the war moving so fast, they didn't have time to repaint them. Probably thought I was an Egyptian plane when they fired at me. I flew back to base, told them what happened, and asked them to contact the column to tell them I was sorry. I found out later that afternoon that I knocked out an armored car but thankfully didn't hit any soldiers.

On December 28, I was flying a patrol mission with Chernoff. We were in a couple of Spitfires, each armed with two bombs under our wings. We were in the Gaza area when I spotted a train heading west, toward Egypt. I signaled to Chernoff that I would attack it first. I circled the train, and as I began my dive, black puffs of exploding antiaircraft shells popped up in front of me. They were coming from a sole antiaircraft gun, located on a flatbed car at the rear, two in front of the caboose.

Taking aim at the locomotive, I released my two bombs, pulled sharply up to my right, sweeping back toward the rear of the train. I looked down and saw both my bombs missed the locomotive completely. Hell, they weren't even close. The explosions did nothing but throw a mountain of sand in the air so far from the train I doubted even one grain landed on it. I watched Chernoff make his run. He did no better. Both his bombs missed the locomotive also.

My bomb run had been down the length of the train. I made my strafing run coming in from the side at a slight angle, almost perpendicular to the locomotive at five hundred feet. My plan was to use the same deflection firing maneuver Buzz Beurling taught me. I just wouldn't lead the locomotive by as much as I would an enemy plane flying at three hundred knots.

I opened up with my machine gun, starting about fifty feet in front of the engine. The shells kicked up sand as they marched steadily back toward the approaching train. The locomotive's forward momentum ran it into the hail of bullets, which stitched their way from the front of the engine back to the cab holding the engineer. I came in low over the top of the locomotive and peeled away as Chernoff followed, making his run.

We stayed low to the ground for a mile before pulling up to three thousand feet and circled back to see what damage we'd done. From this height, we could see the locomotive stopped dead in its tracks, steam billowing from the bullet holes in the engine.

I didn't understand why there was no more antiaircraft fire until I spotted a half dozen soldiers running into the desert away from the flatcar holding the gun. Civilians were scrambling out of the passenger cars, crawling underneath them for cover. Women were handing children out the window where they were grabbed by other passengers and shoved underneath the car.

The locomotive was badly damaged. It wasn't going to be used for moving Egyptian troops anywhere. The only soldiers we'd seen were the ones who'd been on the antiaircraft gun, and they were running away. Unlike the Egyptian pilots who bombed civilians indiscriminately when they ruled the skies, we didn't attack the passengers or the passenger cars. Satisfied, we headed back to base and made our report.

The next day, Chernoff brought in a newspaper, laughing as he tossed it on the table in front of me. "What's so funny?" I asked. I knew he didn't read or understand Hebrew.

"This is today's morning's paper from Tel Aviv. One of the Israelis gave me the translation of this story," he said, tapping the Hebrew writing under a headline in bold letters.

"According to the story, you and I destroyed an enemy train carrying a huge cache of weapons and ammunition, and our bombing and strafing caused heavy losses to Egyptian troops moving to reinforce their frontlines. It says as a result of our brave action, we saved the lives of many of our ground troops."

I shook my head in disbelief. I don't know who said it, but I once heard that truth is the first casualty of war. I guess that story showed they were right.

During the rest of the month, there were no dogfights for me. I had been lucky enough to knock out a few Spitfires and Italian made Macchis on the ground at El Arish, but that was all.

On January 2, 1949, I received a message from Shatz to call him at his office at the ATC in Tel Aviv..

"Hi, it's me," I said. "So when are they throwing you out of the county?"

"They're not."

"They're not?" I said, completely thrown off base. "What happened? Did you change your mind and accept their terms?"

"No, and I didn't have to. I was told Ben-Gurion went ballistic when he heard General Haman was throwing me out of the county because I wouldn't accept his conditions. He called Haman and me to a meeting at his office. When we got there, he ripped Haman a new asshole. He screamed at him, saying all his life he worked to bring Jews into the country, not to throw them out. Then he said to Haman, if it wasn't for me, Israel might not even be a country, never mind have an air force for Haman to be the head of. He ordered Haman to apologize, shake my hand, and tell me I was welcome to stay in Israel for as long as I wanted. On top of that, he told Haman he should do everything he could to make me want to stay."

I was dumbfounded. "Was that it?" I asked.

"Almost. Haman looked like he'd swallowed a lemon as he apologized. His face was flushed, and I could tell he was fighting hard to hold his temper in check in front of Ben-Gurion. I thanked him for his apology, and the two of us left the prime minister's office together. When we left the building, I grabbed Haman's arm and stopped him from stomping off. I told him that while I accepted his apology and appreciated the prime minister's gesture, I wanted him to arrange repatriation for me. I told him I was done with him and the air force. I wanted to go back to the States."

"I get it," I said. "They're not throwing you out; you're leaving on your terms."

"Exactly," Shatz replied.

"When?"

"I don't know. Haman sent word that all I had to do is give him forty-eight hours notice, and he'd arrange transportation anywhere I wanted to go." Shatz paused for a second, chuckled, and said, "I think he'd like to have me take him up on it sooner than later."

There was silence for a few seconds. "What are your plans?" Shatz asked, breaking the quiet.

"I haven't decided. But do me a favor. Let me know, well before you speak to General Haman, when you plan to leave. It's possible I might go back with you."

"I will." With that, we disconnected the call.

CHAPTER 41
January, 1949
Israel

ON JANUARY 4, 1949, Egypt contacted the United Nations, agreeing to a cease fire, and an end to the war, if Israel halted all hostilities at 4:00 p.m. the next day. Israel did not receive the offer until late on January 5. They agreed to the terms but set the date of the cease fire for January 7 at 4:00 p.m. Israel was determined to push forward into the Sinai right up to the deadline.

On January 7, on what was to be the last day of the war, Chernoff, Lapin, Shapiro, and I were in Spitfires, escorting twenty Harvard bombers on their way to attack Egyptian positions near the Sinai. About 25 minutes into the flight, some 50 miles south of Fallujah, around the area where the frontlines of our ground forces were located, I spotted a column of smoke. It was eight to ten miles off to my left, rising at least one thousand feet into the air.

"Hey, Shapiro," I called over the radio, "look at that smoke ahead on my left."

"I see it. Want to check it out?" Skippy replied.

"Yeah. Let's do it. Chernoff. You and Lapin stay with the bombers." I peeled off to my left, Shapiro following on my right wing.

As we drew near the smoke, I scanned the sky for enemy planes, didn't see any, and dropped down for a closer look. A truck, two armored cars, and a Jeep were burning, spewing the thick black smoke into the air. There were other armored cars, trucks, and Jeeps, undamaged, all sporting a Star of David on their hood or rooftop.

As I flew over the column of vehicles, at around eight hundred feet, they opened fire on me. I jammed the throttle forward for speed, pulling up and away from the attack below. They must have thought I was an enemy plane coming back to make another pass at them. The firing suddenly stopped. I figured they spotted the Star of David on my Spit.

Twenty seconds after the firing stopped, I got a radio call from a captain in one of the vehicles below, apologizing for shooting at us. He said they thought we were the enemy coming back. He told me to watch out for the planes that attacked them less than ten minutes ago. I called Shapiro and told him to follow me. I climbed to four thousand feet to see if I could spot the planes anywhere near us.

"Kaplan," Shapiro shouted. "Two bogeys, dead ahead and low. They're at about five hundred feet, ready to make another strafing run on the column."

I could see they were Spitfires, and they weren't ours. The reason we'd painted red and white stripes on the tails, and red spinners on the props of our planes, was so we could instantly tell our Spits from the Egyptians. Those planes had neither.

I was about to dive at them when Shapiro yelled, "Kaplan, two Spits at twelve o'clock, about two thousand feet."

They also didn't have our markings, so I pushed my stick forward and dove at them. Shapiro followed, moving to my right. Closing the gap, he opened up at one of them. I was almost on top of the other one, angling for a good shot, when the bogey suddenly pulled up, crossing right in front of me, not more than two hundred feet away.

I squeezed the trigger and blasted him. Pieces of his plane flew off in different direction before it nosed over and plunged into the ground.

In the heat of the moment, when it's either you or the other guy in a dogfight, all you concentrate on is staying alive by killing the other plane. The adrenaline is flowing, and you develop tunnel vision, paying attention to nothing else but your own survival. It wasn't until I followed the plane as it plunged into the ground that the markings on the fuselage registered in my head. It wasn't Egyptian. The plane bore the emblem of the RAF. I'd just shot down a British Royal Air Force Spitfire. *Oh, shit!*

I lost sight of Shapiro and the plane he was after. Whipping my head in all directions, I finally spotted Shapiro, diving toward the two Spitfires about to make a strafing run at the Israeli convoy below.

Before Shapiro reached them to engage, one of the planes must have been hit by ground fire because the engine burst into flames, and I saw the pilot bail out. He couldn't have been more than four hundred feet off the ground when he leaped from the dying plane. The other Spit pulled up and took off to the west. I saw the RAF logo on his plane. Shapiro took off after it.

"Shapiro," I yelled into my microphone, "Stop. Break off. It's not Egyptian. It's a British Spitfire. Let's get back to base."

When we got back to Hatzor, it was 11:30 in the morning. I grabbed Weizman in his office and told him the details leading up to shooting down the British plane.

"I didn't realize it was British until after it happened," I said.

"I know about it," he replied.

"You know? How the hell do you know?"

"I got a call from General Avraham. That plane you saw shot down by the ground troops, the one the pilot bailed out of, they captured him. He was injured. Had a mild concussion and a broken jaw. When they got to him, he identified himself as a lieutenant in the RAF, stationed at their base at the Suez Canal."

"Why were the Brits strafing our convey?" I asked.

"They weren't. The ones that attacked the convoy were Egyptians.

Those four Brits were on patrol over the Sinai, which by the way, they have every right to do because it belongs to Egypt. They spotted the column of smoke, just like you did, and came to investigate. The lieutenant who got shot down wasn't on a strafing run. He was flying low to try to get a good look and identify the convoy."

I slumped in my chair. "I can't believe it," I said. "I shot down a Brit who wasn't even supposed to be in combat."

"Don't beat yourself up. It couldn't be helped. He was in a hot combat zone. He just didn't know how far we'd advanced, and we were in the Sinai. You were defending Israeli soldiers. There was no way you could have known it was other planes that attacked them. You did the right thing, even if we catch hell for it."

I was still in shock and very upset.

"Look," Weizman said, "no one wants to shoot down RAF planes. On the other hand, we know the RAF has been flying reconnaissance missions for the Arabs. Do you know about the British Mosquito spying on us back in October?"

"No."

"Syd Cohen told me the story. All during October, there was this enemy reconnaissance plane. Almost every day it flew over Israel so high we couldn't tell where it came from. The only way we knew it was there was by the vapor trail we saw almost every day. We knew it had to be Arab, photographing our installations. We sent planes up after it, but we didn't have anything that could climb higher than twenty-six thousand feet at the time, and this had to be flying somewhere around thirty-five thousand feet.

"In the afternoon of November 2nd, the intruder was spotted. Based on the vapor trail, it looked like it was headed in the direction of our base at Hatzor where Syd Cohen was the operations officer. Two days before, they got delivery of a P-51 Mustang. It could climb to forty thousand feet. We had a pilot at Hatzor, Ray Peake, who'd flown Mustangs during World War II, so Syd sent him up after the intruder.

"Syd watched from the control tower as the Mustang became a

speck in the sky, chasing after a smaller speck in the sky. The specks seemed to merge, and then one of them headed in the direction of the base. Syd figured it was the Mustang coming home, as the intruder continued its flight. Suddenly, the vapor trail of the reconnaissance plane got thicker, and seconds later, there was a bright flash in the sky. The intruder had exploded and fell into the sea."

"Did you find out where it came from?" I asked.

"Not where it came from but what it was, which is the point of my story. We found the wreckage. It was a British Mosquito. So don't beat yourself up about the British Spit you shot down. They don't have clean hands. They've been spying on us and giving the information to the Arabs for a while. The one you shot down was probably doing the same."

"I guess you're right," I replied.

"The funny thing was when Peake landed, he was ticked off. He bitched that right after he started shooting at the Mosquito, his gun jammed. His gun hadn't jammed." Weizman threw his palms up and shrugged. "He ran out of all the ammunition we had for a Mustang."

BEFORE THE WAR, Yigal Yadin, chief-of-operations of the Israeli Defense Force, was a well-known archaeologist. Two days before, using his knowledge of an old Roman Road built in 70AD which had been completely covered by sand, he was able to send troops to outflank two battalions of the Egyptian Expeditionary Forces in the Sinai. The Israelis mounted an attack from a totally unexpected direction, encircling the Egyptians, who quickly surrendered. Our soldiers were now able to move unchallenged deep into the Egyptian Sinai, toward El Arish,

That day, the British sent word to Ben-Gurion. The Egyptian government was invoking a 1936 Egyptian-British Defense Treaty. Under the terms of the Treaty, if Israel did not immediately withdraw its forces from the Sinai, Britain would be forced to intervene militarily.

Ben-Gurion told his cabinet he suspected the Egyptians invoked the treaty because they panicked at Israel's successful advance. But over the protests of the army, the Prime Minister ordered a troop withdrawal from the Sinai. I was disappointed when I heard about it but could understand why Ben-Gurion caved. Israel couldn't afford to go to war with the British.

ALTHOUGH WE'D AGREED to leave the Sinai, no one trusted the Egyptians not to try a counterattack before the truce went into effect at 4:00 p.m. We knew if they caught our troops anywhere in the Sinai, even though they were heading back to Israel, the Egyptians might attack them, claiming we violated the agreement to withdraw. If for nothing else, they might try it as a face saving gesture for our capture of their two battalions.

At two o'clock in the afternoon, in what could be the last air mission of the war, I was part of a group of fighter pilots sent out to fly air cover for our retreating ground troops. I told Weizman, as an Israeli, he should have the honor of leading it. I would be his wingman. Bringing up the rear was Pinter, with Shapiro as his wingman. We were in Spitfires; Pinter and Shapiro flew Mustangs.

Eighteen miles past the Sinai border, cruising at nine thousand feet, looking for our troops, I spotted the formation of planes. There were two groups, four planes each. I judged them to be ten to fifteen miles away, heading east toward the Israeli border, at about seven thousand feet.

Scanning the barren desert in the direction they were flying, I eyed what looked like a ground cloud of desert sand. It was being kicked up by a column of fast moving vehicles which I gauged to be about twelve miles away. From the direction they were headed, it looked like it was a convoy of our men withdrawing, and the planes were homing in on them.

"Weizman, check your twelve o'clock, two thousand feet low," I yelled into the mic.

"Got 'em," he responded.

"Now, check northeast, twelve miles out. That convoy has to be our men. The planes are headed at them, and they aren't ours. No good reason they should even be here, never mind headed at our troops."

Weizman responded, "Probably Egyptians."

"Yeah. And maybe trying for an easy kill before the truce," I said. "I'm declaring them hostile. Weizman, you're with me. We'll take the four on the right. Pinter, Shapiro, you got the ones on the left."

"Wait a minute, Kaplan," Weizman shouted. "You can't attack them. They haven't done anything hostile. For all we know, they're just monitoring our troops, making sure we're living up to the truce agreement and withdrawing."

"Maybe. Maybe not. But if they're cruising at two hundred knots, they'll be on top of the convoy in about ten minutes. Less if they're going faster. You willing to gamble those soldiers' lives down there that the planes are just monitoring their movement?"

There was no response from Weizman. "That's what I thought. I'm going in. Either be my wingman, or get out of the way."

I climbed to eleven thousand feet to get a better height advantage. When I leveled off, I glance to my left and smiled. Weizman was there beside me. So were the other two. We steadily closed the gap between us and the planes below. They took no evasive action, droning on, unaware of our presence.

"They're British," Pinter bellowed out.

I squinted. I could see the planes clearer now. They weren't Spitfires. They were Tempests. I'd never encountered the Egyptians flying Tempests. Then I saw it. An RAF roundel. They *were* British.

"Kaplan, what do you wanna to do?" Shapiro hollered.

"The Brits said if we didn't immediately withdraw from the Sinai, they would be forced to intervene militarily. Those are our soldiers down there. They're still in the Sinai, and it looks to me like the Brits are planning on intervening militarily. I'm not gonna just sit here and let them hit our men."

"But they're British," Weizman piped in.

"So what? If they attack, a lot of those soldiers are going to get killed. Dead is dead. Doesn't matter who's doing the shooting,"

With a mile and a half distance, and four thousand feet of altitude separating us, I murmured a quick *Sh'ma,* and in what was probably one of the most stupid things I've ever done, banked and dove at the four plane formation on the right.

Am I crazy? These aren't Arabs. They're well trained Brits. God, don't let me die in a damn dogfight with less than an hour before the war ends.

Swooping down behind the rear Tempest, my tracers and bullets stitched a line across the top of the plane. It burst into flames and spun out of control toward the earth. *The shits in the fire now,* I thought, as I lined up to attack another. I opened up with a long burst, streaking past it, never seeing if I hit him. My descent took me below the rest of the Tempests.

Reaching fifteen hundred feet, I pulled back on the stick, climbing and banking to the left. *Shit!* I ran right into a Tempest, hurtling head-on at me, spitting fire. The bullets missed. Before I had a chance to return fire, the plane tore past. I twisted my head back and forth, looking out the canopy for more enemy planes. I checked the rearview mirror for anything behind. Nothing.

Split seconds later, off to my left, I saw Weizman chasing one. *Where are the other two?* I got one in my sight at my one o'clock, and took off after him. I opened up with a two second burst. Missed. Or, if I hit him, I did no real damage.

Suddenly, my plane shook. I felt vibrations. *I've been hit. From where?* Tracers flew across the top of my canopy. I looked in my rear view mirror. A Tempest was on my tail, firing at me. I pulled back on the stick as hard as I could, bringing myself into an almost vertical climb. The Tempest stayed on my tail. Panic set in. I felt a knot in my stomach. I began to sweat.

Think. Think. He's faster than you. You can't outrun him. He's heavier than you. Outmaneuver him.

I quickly pulled out of the vertical climb, leveled off, and began turning in a tight circle. As I went around and around, the Tempest tried to follow, but he was too heavy. As I made tight turns, his arcs became wider than mine. After two minutes, I was able to pull out of my tighter turns and positioned myself behind the Tempest. Now the hunted became the hunter.

"Got ya, you son of a bitch," I yelled, lining him up in my sights. I let loose with a three second burst from my machine guns, followed a second later with another burst. The pulsing vibrations of the guns made my Spitfire quiver with each blast. My bullets ripped through the Tempest. It began to spin to the desert below. I didn't follow. There was at least one more out there, two if Weizman didn't get the one he chased.

My hand was shaking from adrenaline as I reached for the microphone. "Weizman? Weizman, come in," I shouted.

"Kaplan?"

"Who were you expecting? The tooth fairy?"

I don't know why I said that. Nerves? Relief I was still alive? Who knows?

"You okay?" he asked.

"I got hit. Don't think anything vital. I'm still flying and have control. You?"

"I'm fine."

"Did you hear from Pinter and Shapiro?"

"They're on their way back. Pinter and Shapiro got one each."

"Did you get the Tempest you were after?"

"I'm sure I hit it. I chased him west, but he was faster than me and got away."

"Well, maybe we should be heading north and home," I said.

I glance at my watch. It was 4:15. "Hey, Weizman," I said, smiling.

"What?"

"Congratulations. It's past four o'clock. The truce started, and the wars over. You won. You've got yourself a homeland."

There was a brief pause. "You're a Jew, Kaplan. So, so do you."

His words gave me goose bumps. I sat a little taller in my seat and pushed back my shoulders. Then the damndest thing happened. My eyes began to well up.

"I guess you're right," I replied, my voice cracking a little. "I do, don't I?"

.

CHAPTER 42
Post War

"NEXT YEAR IN Jerusalem," is a prayer I recite on the holiest of all holidays, Yom Kippur. The lament, uttered over the millennia, that "next year," every Jew in the world can worship at the site of Holy Temple in Jerusalem. The prayer is now a reality.

The War for Independence is over, and "next year" is now. We did it. For every Jew, no matter where they live in the world, they have their homeland back, that piece of earth they can call their own.

I also have a piece of earth that is mine. America. I'd grown to love Israel, but I am an American. I'd grown to love and respect the Israeli men I fought beside, like Alon and Weizman, but they are from here, and I am from America.

Would I be willing to give up my U.S. citizenship for Israel? Never. But that had been the demand by the Israeli Military to my fellow pilots of ATC. "When the unit is officially folded into the Israeli Air Force on January 1, become an air force officer and accept Israeli citizenship," they insisted.

Every pilot understood doing so meant the loss of their U.S. citizenship. "If you refuse," the Air Force said, "then leave."

To their credit, the majority of the American pilots said no, many using more colorful words than that, and asked to be immediately repatriated home. A handful said yes, willingly giving away their U.S. citizenship. To me, that was a cost too high.

Sixteen of the American ATC pilots chose to stay in Israel, but to become pilots for the newly formed Israeli airline, *El Al*. This was a civilian airline, so they kept their U.S. citizenship.

Prime Minister Ben-Gurion asked Shatz to remain in Israel, as a civilian, to help get the new 106th Air Transport Squadron of the Israeli Air Force, as the ATC was now called, up and running. Shatz agreed.

Ezer Weizman asked me to remain in Israel to help train Israelis as fighter pilots, to fill the vacuum of the departing *Machalniks*. Officially a former pilot of the 101st squadron, I'd be a civilian contractor and would not have to become an Israeli citizen. I agreed, as did Shapiro, Chernoff, and a few others.

I wasn't really looking forward to returning to the United States so fast. The September before, Noah Meir sent word to Shatz that Harvey Hecht had been indicted, charged with two counts of shipping aircraft to Israel without a license, thereby violating the Neutrality and Export Acts. It seems a business competitor learned Hecht gave us the B-17s, the ones we used to bomb Cairo, and turned him in. He was being prosecuted by the U.S. attorney in Miami.

I knew from the time we flew the planes from the U.S. to Panama I risked fines, imprisonment, and the loss of my citizenship. Shatz had warned me from the beginning that I could face the same charges as Hecht when I returned home. I believed I was doing the right thing, as I still do today, and I'm willing to face the consequences. I can't say I relished the idea of being arrested, and that's why I'm not rushing home. But if they catch me and put me on trial, so be it. I'm proud of what I did.

On February 5, Meir called Shatz in Tel Aviv. "Yesterday was Hecht's court date. He pled guilty. Unfortunately, he drew an anti-Semitic judge."

"What makes you say the Judge is anti-Semitic?" Shatz asked.

"I was in the courtroom. The judge, Calhoun is his name, was born and raised in Mississippi. Not exactly a great place to be Jewish. That's part of your country they call the Bible belt, where they really do believe all Jews have horns and a tail. He went to law school there and stayed in the south, moving to Tallahassee, Florida, to practice law."

"But that doesn't make him anti-Semitic."

"True, but I'm not finished. Before the judge pronounced sentence, he told Hecht he didn't understand why an Irishman, born and raised in Irish Catholic Boston, would want to help those troublemaking Hebrews in Palestine. He told Hecht because he broke the law and helped the Jews, he was part of the reason the peace loving Arabs have turned against America."

"You're kidding? He really said peace loving Arabs?" Shatz asked.

"No, not kidding. Then he said that a Mr. Cordell Tipton, of the United States Department of State, contacted him, asking him to hand down the harshest possible sentence against Hecht. Calhoun said Tipton claimed, by aiding the Israelis, Hecht had done irreparable harm to Arab-American relations, jeopardizing our country's reliance on the flow of oil from the Middle East. After repeating Tipton's charge, the judge glared at Hecht and told him he could thank his Jewish friends for the sentence about to be imposed.'"

"That's incredible. He actually said that?"

"Exactly that," Meir said. "Then the judge threw the book at Hecht. Eighteen months in prison and a $5000 fine. We paid the fine for him, but we can't do anything about the prison sentence."

SHATZ AND I were in Tel Aviv, sitting in the lounge of the Golan Hotel, sipping glasses of the weak beer they make in Israel. It was the day after he spoke to Meir about the judge and what happened to Hecht.

"We know the government has warrants out for our arrest. At some point, when we return to the States, like Hecht, we might have to face the law. If that happens," I asked, "out of curiosity, where would you want to be tried?"

"Where would you?" he asked.

"No doubt about it. New York City. It's got a large Jewish population. I have to believe all we need is one Jew on the jury, and we won't get convicted."

"You might be right," Shatz responded, "but I'd rather face it in California."

"Why?"

"Because," he said, laughing, "if they find us guilty and send us to prison like they did Hecht, it's warmer in California than New York."

WORD FILTERED BACK to us that so far, none of the returning *Machalniks* were even questioned about where they had been for so long when they returned to the States, never mind any of them being arrested. Our work was pretty much done, so Shatz, Shapiro, Chernoff, and I decided it was time to go home. On May 5, 1949, we left Tel Aviv for Rome, then to London, and finally to Los Angeles.

I had big concerns that the four of us may not be handled the same as the other returning *Machalniks* when we arrived back in the States. Shatz was the man behind the idea to use planes to break the blockade and fly munitions to Israel. And the government knew it. Shapiro, Chernoff, and I were the part of the first group of American *Machalnik* pilots flying the C-46s to Czechoslovakia and then to Israel loaded with weapons. Later ,we became Israel's first fighter pilots. And the government knew it.

Standing in line behind Shatz, my stomach did flip-flops while waiting for him to clear passport control. When Shatz stepped up to the window and slid his passport under the glass to the agent, I felt sweat form on my forehead. Beads of sweat also trickled down my neck, beneath my shirt collar, into the middle of my back.

Shatz and the agent exchanged a few words. I couldn't hear what they said, but incredibly, the agent stamped his passport, handed it back, and yelled, "Next," as Shatz turned and walked away. I passed through just as easily, as did Shapiro and Chernoff. After grabbing our luggage, we met outside on the sidewalk.

"What the hell just happened in there?" I asked. "How did we not get stopped and arrested? The Haganah office in New York said there are warrants out for the arrest of all of us, didn't they?"

"They did," Shatz said. "All I can think of is, this is a perfect example that in our government, the right hand doesn't know what the left hand is doing. Screw 'em. I'm not going to worry about it."

"Let's go," I said, not feeling as cavalier as Shatz, "before they realize they made a mistake."

We hopped in a cab and rode to the Burbank Airport, pulling up to the hanger area. The sign still hanging above the hanger door. Shatz Aviation, Burbank, California.

"Let's go see what the Feds left us," Shatz said.

In the nearly empty hanger, Shatz's makeshift desk, the four by eight piece of plywood on three sawhorses, was still there, pushed against a wall. So were a couple of small folding tables and some chairs. The filing cabinets were gone. It looked like the Feds cleaned out everything they thought important. Incredibly, the phones were still working. *Who the hell has been paying the bill?*

"What do we do now?" Shapiro asked.

"First, we go find us a place to stay," Shatz said.

"Then what?" Chernoff asked.

"Why don't we go buy a couple of C-46s from surplus and begin an air transport company?" Shatz said.

I looked to see if he was smiling or laughing. He did neither. The man was serious.

SHATZ CONTACTED THE Haganah office in New York and spoke to Noah Meir. He explained his plan to buy two surplus planes, go into the air freight business, and that he needed $10,000 to purchase them. Meir called back two days later. The money would be wired to Shatz the next day, no strings attached. "Consider it a gift from a grateful nation," Meir said.

The money arrived the next morning as promised. That afternoon, Chernoff went to the war surplus depot at Cal-Aero Field in Chino to get us two planes. The supply of aircraft had dwindled significantly. Most had been consigned to the scrap yards. Any suitable ones for our needs were nonexistent. He told us how nervous he was walking around the base, expecting F.B.I. agents to pounce on him at any second.

Two weeks after Shatz received the money, the four of us were in the hanger. Chernoff and Shapiro were on the phone trying to find us someplace other than depot at Cal-Aero Field to buy the two planes and mechanics to work on them.

Shatz was reading the newspaper, feet propped up on his makeshift desk. I was on the telephone with my mother. It was the first time I'd called her since getting back. I wanted her to know I was home and okay.

After promising my mother I'd take care of myself and to call again next week, I hung up. *Click, Click.* Shatz was making the noise. He nodded to me and motioned in the direction of the side door. He got up and strolled to the door. I followed. Outside, Shatz moved to a spot between hangers.

"What's up?" I asked, leaning against the hanger wall.

"This thing with setting up an air freight carrier isn't going to work. When we register with the Civil Aviation Administration, it won't take long for the F.B.I. to get word, and they'll be on us like a hawk swooping down on a rabbit. I'm not going to wait for the Feds to find me. I'm going to turn myself in and get this over with, one way or the other."

I pushed myself off the wall. "Are you crazy?"

"Maybe. But it's my decision. I can't make it for you or the men inside. I want you to get as far away from here as possible before I turn myself in."

"You're right. It's not your decision to make... for me or them. So why don't we go back inside, tell them what you're going to do, and let us decide what we want to do."

It took Shatz two minutes to explain to Chernoff and Shapiro what his plan was and why. It took less than thirty seconds for each of us to tell him we would be standing right next to him when he went to the F.B.I.

Shatz called Meir in New York and told him of the decision to turn ourselves into the F.B.I. He asked Meir if he could get us the name of a good attorney to represent us. Meir said he'd get Barry Sanders, the same lawyer who represented me the year before when we got caught in Canada trying to fly the B-17 to Israel. He was licensed to practice in California as well as New York.

"Hold off until Sanders gets out there," Meir told Shatz, "so he can be with you when you turn yourselves in. One more thing. We'll take of Sanders fee, but you're going to have living expenses while you're waiting for trial. Use the money we sent you to buy the planes."

Sanders arrived in California four days later and met us in Burbank. The next day, the four of us and Sanders walked into the Los Angeles office of the F.B.I. in the new federal courthouse building on Spring Street and turned ourselves in.

We were arrested and held overnight in the Hall of Justice across the street. The next morning, we were brought back to the courthouse and appeared before a federal magistrate for a bail hearing. We were held pending a $5000 bond each, which Sanders posted immediately, and we were released.

Two weeks later, Sanders called Shatz. A trial was set to take place in three months, Tuesday, October 25.

CHAPTER 43
Los Angeles
October, 1949

*Trial of Six Jews Charged with Shipping Planes
to Israel Illegally Opens Today*

TUESDAY, LOS ANGELES (Oct. 25)

*THE TRIAL OF six Los Angeles Jews charged with conspiracy to violate the
Neutrality and Export Acts in the shipment of aircraft to Israel last year
without a license will open in the federal courthouse here today.*

*The defendants—all of whom entered not guilty pleas—will be repre-
sented by former California Supreme Court Judge Isaac Plotnik and
attorney William Levine. Five of the defendants are former U.S. veterans.
The defendants are: Paul Schatz, Michael Kaplan, Harold Shapiro, David
Chernoff, Melvin Pinter, and Raymond Hirsh.*

The story was the headline on the front page of the *Los Angeles
Times*. The *Times* got one of the facts wrong. It wasn't a trial of six Los
Angeles Jews, because none of us were from Los Angeles. We hadn't
even lived in California until some of us came here for a brief time to
Burbank before we left for Panama.

Two major events happened in the three months after we'd turned
ourselves in. The first, our attorney Barry Sanders made the decision

we would be better off having a California based legal team. Meir made inquiries, and when former California Supreme Court Judge Isaac Plotnik heard of the search, he contacted Meir and offered to represent us *pro bono*.

The second event was, since the F.B.I. also had arrest warrants out for Mel Pinter and Ray Hirsh, Judge Plotnik felt it made sense to have us all tried together. Pinter and Hirsh agreed. Although they weren't living in Los Angeles at the time, they agreed to come to California and turned themselves in.

My stomach fluttered in awe when the six of us walked into the courtroom for the first time that Tuesday. The room was huge, particularly compared to the small courtroom we'd been in with the magistrate at the bond hearing. It had to be two hundred feet long, half as much wide, with a ceiling at least twenty-five feet high. A dozen or so spectators were already seated.

It was easy to spot the defendant's table by the eight leather chairs positioned around it. Two for the lawyers, the rest for us. Our attorneys, Judge Plotnik and Levine, were already there waiting for us. Along the side wall, opposite the defendant's table, was the jury box

At the back of the room was the judge's bench, with the witness box next to it on the right. Mounted on the wall high above the judge's bench was the Great Seal of the United States of America, the circular emblem engraved in polished oak.

When I gazed at the seal, it really hit me. The government of the United States of America wanted to put me in jail. This would be another David versus Goliath battle, just like the one I'd just fought in Israel. David won that one, but going against the power and resources of the United States Justice Department, I wasn't so sure about this outcome.

We walked through the swinging doors into the well and shook hands with Judge Plotnik and Levine. Scattered folders and papers, held in place by a few legal books, lay on the table.

"Today we begin *voir dire*," Plotnik said. "That's fancy Latin words for jury selection."

A noise from the front part of the courtroom caught my attention. I turned to see three men walk through the swinging doors and sit at the table across from us.

"Those the guys that want to put me in jail?" I asked Plotnik, nodding at the table.

Plotnik, who'd been looking through some papers, glanced up. "Just the one in the middle. That's Lawrence Wilmet. He's the Assistant United States Attorney for the Central District of California, Criminal Division. The lawyers on either side are his assistants."

Three minutes later, the clerk called out, "All rise," as Federal Judge Franklin Reagan emerged from a door beside the bench and took his seat.

"Be seated," he told the courtroom. Looking down at the court clerk, he said, "The clerk may call the first pool of jurors."

The clerk walked to a door along the back wall, opened it, and glancing down at a sheet of paper in his hand, called out the names of the first twelve prospective jurors. They filed in and took seats in the jury box. The judge made a brief statement explaining what kind of case was to be tried and inquired whether there is any reason the potential jurors could not serve. Two hands went up. The judge asked each why. Satisfied with their answers, he dismissed them.

Next, it was AUSA Wilmet's turn to ask questions. I noticed a few things about the remaining ten potential jurors. For a city as diverse as Los Angeles, there were no Negros, no Mexicans, no Chinese, no women. Only White males.

AUSA Wilmet asked each juror their name and questions as to whether they had any knowledge of the case or had had specific experiences that might cause them to be biased or unfair.

Anyone who had a Jewish sounding name, or in my opinion looked Jewish, the ASUA asked about their feelings about Palestine being a homeland for the Jewish people, how they felt about Arabs, and the recent War of Independence. Each of these jurors were dismissed by the prosecutor "for cause," meaning he believed the juror was prejudiced about the case. After going halfway through the second pool of jurors, it was obvious what the prosecutor was doing.

I tugged on Plotnik's sleeve and whispered, "Wilmet's purposely keeping Jews off the jury. Stop him."

"I can't. If I complain to the judge, I'll have a tough time proving that's his intent. And, the jurors we've already agreed to my have a negative reaction to the complaint. It's not worth it."

The last juror to be seated was a man named Joseph Briscoe. During the *voir dire,* we learned he came to the United States from Ireland in 1938, became an American citizen in 1946, and spoke with a very distinct Irish brogue. During the questioning, he smiled a lot, projecting a kind of light, carefree manner. You could say he charmed the pants off the prosecutor, Plotnik, and even me. When a jury was impaneled, Judge Reagan announced the trial would begin the following Monday morning at 9:00 a.m.

MONDAY MORNING, JUDGE Reagan gaveled the court to order. The AUSA, who had the burden of proof, gave the first opening statement. Wilmet promised that the evidence he would present would prove beyond a reasonable doubt that each of the six defendants violated the Neutrality and Export Acts by shipping aircraft to Israel without a license. He went on to lay out his case. Without naming them, he mentioned the witnesses he'd produce and what they would testify to. He spent over two hours in front of the jury.

It was now the defense's turn. On our attorneys' advice, each of us pled not guilty to the crimes the prosecutor was now claiming we committed. Point of fact is, as a matter of law, we *were* guilty. We did violate the Neutrality and Export Act. Our defense would be based on the proposition that the law we violated was itself unjust.

Plotnik rose from the defense table. "Ladies and gentlemen," he said, addressing the jury, "I will save my opening statement until the government rests its case, and it's the defense's turn to present our side."

For the next four weeks, the AUSA presented witness after witness whose testimony supported the prosecution's case. The clerks who sold us the C-46s, the operator of the Burbank airport where we rented the hangers, the operator of the Millville Airport where we rented the hangers, F.B.I. Agent Sullivan who watched us in Burbank, Barry Ingram, the United States consul in the Azores who caught us with the B-17, and on and on. Slowly, step by step, AUSA Wilmet methodically built his case.

Because our defense was going to be that the law we violated was itself unjust, neither Plotnik nor Levine bothered to cross examine any of Wilmet's witnesses. Each time they said, "No questions, your Honor," when given the opportunity. I saw Wilmet and his two associates' eyes narrow in surprise.

Each evening after court, the six of us, plus Plotnik and Levine, would meet at Nat 'n Al's, a Jewish Deli that opened up three years before in Beverly Hills, a block off of Rodeo Drive. Ira, the manager, always put us at a table way in the back where we had a lot of privacy.

ONE EVENING AT dinner, three weeks into the trial, I said, "I don't know if it's just me, but the jury foreman, Briscoe, is making me nervous. Anyone else feeling that way?"

"What do you mean?" Plotnik asked.

"I can't put my finger on it, just a feeling I have. It's like he's already made up his mind about us. Every once in a while, when a witness is being questioned, it seems he's not even paying attention to the testimony. I see him, almost imperceptibly, move his head and glance at us. If he catches me looking at him, he gives me a fleeting grin, you might even call it a smirk, and quickly turns his head away. I don't know. It's kind of creepy... and scary."

"Why?" Levine asked.

"The other jurors picked him as the foreman. That means they see him as a leader, and that gives him a lot of sway with them. If he's already made up his mind that we're guilty, you think he can't convince them to vote his way?"

"I'll try to keep an eye on him from now on," Plotnik said, "although even if he's already made up his mind, there's nothing I can really do about. If his inattention becomes very obvious, I can say something to the judge. It might get Briscoe, or maybe one of the other jurors, mad at me, but I'll have it on the record if we need to go for an appeal."

From that day on, we all kept an eye on Briscoe. Each night we'd discuss it, and it became apparent that everyone else saw what I did. As testimony was presented by AUSA to build the case against us, Briscoe would look at us, the grin.

Five and half weeks after he began meticulously building his case, witnesses after witness against us, at three o'clock on a Wednesday afternoon, AUSA Wilmet turned to Judge Reagan, and announced, "Your Honor, the government rests."

Judge Reagan said, "It's too late for the defense to begin its case. Court is adjourned until tomorrow morning at 9:00." He banged his gavel, and everyone poured out of the courtroom.

We made our way over to Nat 'n Al's Deli for an early dinner.

After the waiters brought water, rolls and butter, and a big bowl of pickles, Pinter said, "Judge, what's the plan for tomorrow?"

"It's pretty simple. You *are* all guilty of breaking the Neutrality and Export Acts. The AUSA pretty much proved that beyond a reasonable doubt. I'm going for jury nullification, convincing the jury that even if you are technically guilty, they should acquit you anyway, because the law you broke is unjust."

"But can't the judge overrule them or punish them for ignoring the evidence?" I asked.

"No. Criminal courts can't direct a guilty verdict, no matter how strong the evidence is, and jurors can never be punished for the verdict they return. If they nullify, you're free and clear because the

Fifth Amendment's double jeopardy clause prohibits an appeal of an acquittal.

"Oh, one other thing. Hopefully, we'll get an acquittal. But if we don't, the AUSA gave me a strong case for an appeal. You are supposed to be tried by a jury of your peers, but by him purposely keeping Jews from the jury, it was not representative of the community or your peers."

The next morning, Judge Reagan gaveled the courtroom to order. "Is the defense ready?"

Plotnik rose. "Yes, your Honor. The defense calls Cordell Tipton."

Tipton made his way down the side aisle, a broad smile on his face. He pushed his way through the swinging doors and moved to the witness stand. After Tipton was sworn in, Plotnik moved to the lectern in the middle of the courtroom.

"For the record, Mr. Tipton, will you please state your full name and your job title?

"My full name is Cordell Tipton and I am the administrative assistant to Frank Cunningham, Director of Near Eastern and African Affairs at the United States Department of State."

"Thank you, Mr. Tipton. Now if you would for the jury, please describe the Mid-East Arms Embargo and its purpose."

"Certainly. Its purpose was to prevent the shipment of armaments and other materials that might be used for armed conflict. It was a means, if you will, to limit the scope of any potential violence in the Mid-East."

"And the purpose was to limit the weapons that could be used if such violence occurred?"

Tipton sat a little straighter in the witness box. "Exactly," he said, smiling broadly.

"And why did the State Department think there might be violence in the Mid-East?"

"Well, because after the partition of Palestine, we believed the surrounding Arab countries would violently object."

"Did the State Department think the Jewish people living in Palestine might violently object to the partition?"

"What? Of course not. Why would they? They were getting what they wanted."

"So let me get this straight," Plotnik said. "Shortly before the partition vote, there were about six hundred thousand Jews living in Palestine, surrounded by Arab countries with over sixty million people. Did the State Department want to keep armaments out of the hands of those six hundred thousand Jews because they thought they would start a war with sixty million Arabs?"

"No, but—"

"And weren't the British and other countries supplying Egypt and the other surrounding Arab countries weapons and armaments despite supposedly supporting the so called arms embargo?"

"Yes. I mean no. I mean—"

"So when the Arab counties invaded Palestine after the British left, and were going to finish what Hitler didn't, as they publicly said they would," Plotnik pushed on,"the Jews would have next to nothing to meet that onslaught; no tanks, no air force, and only a meager number of weapons. And isn't that just what the State Department wanted?"

"No. No. Why would we?" Tipton pleaded.

"Why? Because if the United States appeared to side with the Jews on the partition, by allowing them to have arms to defend themselves, you were afraid you'd make enemies of the Arabs who'd cut off our oil and access to the Suez Canal. Isn't it true that you and the State Department would rather see six hundred thousand get slaughtered by enforcing the arms embargo as a means to defend themselves, than let that happen? "

"No, you have that all wrong. We just...."

"I have no further questions of this witness. He's excused."

I looked at AUSA Wilmet's face. He looked stunned and did not object. A bedlam of babbling voices filled the courtroom as Tipton slinked out, the smile he'd worn walking in gone as he left.

My eyes shot to Briscoe, sitting in the jury box. He had the same smirk on his face that he'd had for the entire trial. I didn't get it. When the trial seemed to go against us, he had the smirk. When it looked like Plotnik had scored a major point for us, he smirked. Maybe the guy had a mental problem. All I know is he scared the hell out of me. I was more convinced than ever he'd be the one to drive the final nail in our coffin.

"Your Honor, the defense rests." Plotnik gathered his notes from the lectern and walked back to the defense table.

I glanced at Judge Reagan. Even his eyebrows were raised in surprise, but to his credit, he quickly composed himself. Banging the gavel, he said, "Closing arguments will begin at 9:30 tomorrow morning. Court is adjourned."

At 9:30 the next morning, the prosecution was first to present closing arguments. AUSA Wilmet took to the lectern. He summed up the evidence favorable to his side, showing how it proved what he said should prevail in the case, and told the jury they must come back with a verdict of guilty as a matter of law.

Wilmet sat and Plotnik took his place at the lectern. "Ladies and gentlemen of the jury," he said, "this action taken by the government is deeply regrettable, and I am asking you to put what happened in the context of the times. Sixty million Arabs, from five countries surrounding Palestine, decided they were going to prevent the new Jewish State from happening. They publicly said they would finish the slaughter Hitler started and annihilate the Jews in Palestine.

"You heard my examination of Mr. Tipton. Our State Department did what they could to enforce the arms embargo. Why? Because your government was so afraid of making enemies of the Arabs who might cut off our oil and access to the Suez Canal, they would rather see a second Holocaust and let another six hundred thousand Jews get slaughtered. How? By enforcing an arms embargo and taking away their means to defend themselves.

"If you saw a man about to kill your brother, not you, but your brother, and you knew you could get a gun, shoot the man, and prevent your brother's death, what would you do? He's not going to kill you, so you can't claim self-defense if you shoot him. And if you kill him, the law says that's murder. Would you say there are times the law is wrong? That saving your brother's life is more important than any law?

Plotnik turned and pointed to us."These men did what they had to do. Judge them in the light of the situation confronting the Jews in Palestine at the time. That's what these men were faced with. Become their brother's keeper or stand by and watch another slaughter of Jews. Did they break the arms embargo law? Yes, they did. Was the law wrong in this case? Yes, it was."

Plotnik, gathered his notes from the lectern, tapping the edges to square them up. He picked up his water glass and finished what was left in it. "Ladies and gentlemen, I ask you to exercise your right to jury nullification. While it is true my clients did break the law, tell the United States government, and the whole world, their enforcement of the law was, and is, wrong. Thank you."

Plotnik sat next to me. I reached over, tapped the back of his hand, and whispered, "Well done." I glanced at the jury box. Briscoe had that smirk.

THE JURY WAS out for two days. At 11:00 on the morning of the third day, Plotnik got the call that a verdict had been reached. We were to be in the courtroom at 2:00 in the afternoon.

We arrived in the courtroom at 1:45. It was packed. We took our seats at the defense table. I was nervous. Harvey Hecht got 18 months, and all he did was give us planes. If we were found guilty, I didn't want to think of what the judge could give us.

At 2:00 Judge Reagan climbed the bench and ordered the clerk to bring in the jury. "Mr. Foreman, I understand you've reached a verdict?"

Briscoe rose. "Yes, your Lordship, we have."

Judge Reagan smiled. "In this country, I'm referred to as your Honor, not your Lordship."

Low laughter spread through the courtroom.

Briscoe grinned. "Begging your Lord... I'm mean, your Honors' pardon. Yes, we have reached a verdict." Briscoe handed a sheet of paper to the clerk who brought it to Reagan.

Reagan glanced at the paper, then looking at us, he said, "The defendant will rise."

We all stood.

Reagan read from the paper. "In the case of the United States of America versus Paul Schatz, Michael Kaplan, Harold Shapiro, David Chernoff, Melvin Pinter, and Raymond Hirsh, we the jury find the defendants guilty of all twenty counts of violating the Neutrality and Export Acts."

The courtroom erupted. Shouts of, "That's wrong," "Not fair," "Injustice," rang out from the spectators. Judge Reagan banged his gavel until the noise settled down.

When quiet finally took over, Judge Reagan said, "I want to thank the members of the jury for their service. You are excused."

Briscoe popped from his seat. "Begging his Honor's pardon, but wouldn't you be reading the whole of the thing?"

"What do you mean?" Reagan asked.

"If you would be reading the whole of what we wrote, we also said that along with finding these lads guilty, we are recommending absolute leniency in their sentence."

Reagan looked down again at the paper he'd been handed and spent the next few seconds reading. When he was finished, he raised his head and said to Briscoe, "Mr. Foreman, things may be different here than they are in Ireland. In this country, in federal court, only the judge imposes a sentence, not the jury. I am not bound by what the jury wants."

"Well yer Honor, if that's being the case, then I for one am changing me vote to not guilty."

The courtroom once again erupted. When the judge gaveled it to order, Plotnik jumped to his feet. "Your Honor, I request a poll of the jurors to see if any others feel the same."

One by one, each juror stood and said they also would change their vote to not guilty if the judge would not honor their request for absolute leniency.

Reagan, apparently at a loss for what to do, announced there would be a one hour recess. He ordered the jurors back into the jury room to continue deliberation.

"I've been a lawyer and a judge for over forty years, and I've never seen or heard of anything like this," Plotnik said.

Fifty minutes later, Reagan emerged from the side door, just as the jurors were filing back into the courtroom. "Mr. Foreman, I understand the jury has a verdict agreed to by all?"

"That we do, yer Honor," Briscoe said, handing the clerk the verdict form.

Reagan read the form. "The defendant will rise," he said.

We all stood.

"In the case of the United States of America versus Paul Schatz, Michael Kaplan, Harold Shapiro, David Chernoff, Melvin Pinter, and Raymond Hirsh, counts one through nineteen, violation of the Neutrality and Export Acts, we the jury find the defendants not guilty. For count twenty, we find the defendants guilty."

I felt my legs wobble. *I'm going to jail.*

"At this time, I'm prepared to pass sentence," Judge Reagan announced. "Defendants Harold Shapiro, David Chernoff, Michael Kaplan, and Raymond Hirsh. It is the judgment of this court that you each pay a fine of $10,000. Defendants Paul Schatz and Melvin Pinter, it is the judgment of this court that you each pay a fine of $10,000 and you are to lose your United States citizenship. You must surrender your passports within 72 hours." Banging the gavel, he announced, "Courts adjourned".

I slumped into my seat. Of course, I was relieved that none of us were going to jail, but Shatz and Pinter were losing their citizenship.

AT THE DELI that night, the jury foreman, Joseph Briscoe, entered. He made a straight path toward us. Without an invitation, or asking, he grabbed a chair from an adjoining table, swung it around, and sat down at ours.

"How are you lads doing?" he asked.

There was a second or two when none of us said anything. If the others were like me, we were shocked he was even here. Breaking the silence, I asked, "What are you doing here?"

"Just wanted to see how yer all doing. I'd be saying, for a wee bit, t'was pretty much touch and go in the courthouse."

I couldn't contain myself. "Forget that bullshit for now. What happened? I was positive you were the one that was going to get us convicted."

"And why would you have been thinking that?" he replied.

"Why? Because every time I saw you looking at us, you had this smirk on your face. Like you had us guilty from the very first moment."

"What I was trying to let you boyos know is, no matter what the other jurors did, I'd be hanging the jury. There was not a way in the world I'd let them punish you for what you did over there."

"Why? You're Irish Catholic or maybe Irish Protestant. Why do you care about what we did for the Jewish people in Palestine?" I asked.

Briscoe got that sly smirk on his face. "I'd be guessing is that's what that fella Mr. Wilmet thought. But he's a bleeding spanner."

"What's a spanner?" I asked.

"You'd say, 'a fool.'"

"Why?"

"Because I'm Jewish."

My jaw dropped. "What?" I gasped.

"Aye, lad. I'm Jewish. There are only about 3,000 of us in the whole of Ireland, but we make a name for ourselves, we do. That was what all those smirks were about. Just to let yer know, awl was well."

"Well, we didn't know, and you had us worried," I said.

"Sorry about that boyo, but I couldn't be seen talking to you lads, and lettin yeh know, now could I?"

Plotnik was smiling. He said, "No you couldn't. I'd love to let Wilmet know how badly he screwed up with you, but sometimes it's best to let sleeping dogs lay."

Briscoe told us that when Judge Reagan sent the jurors back to the jury room, he'd met with them. Reagan confessed that he thought what the six of us did was the right thing, and the law *was* unjust. But as a judge, he had to uphold the laws on the books, even the unjust ones. Reagan said he couldn't let the defendants go scot-free. They worked out a deal, nineteen not guilty, for one guilty. He'd promised Briscoe and the other jurors we'd get no jail time.

We asked Briscoe to stay for dinner, but he said he'd better leave before anyone saw us together and thought we'd been colluding through the whole trial.

"Here's to the Irish Jews," was the last toast of the night before we headed to the hotel.

CHAPTER 44
After the Trial
1950

THE ISRAELI GOVERNMENT knew in order to maintain the armistice with the Arab countries the Israeli Defense Force would need to remain strong. Ben-Gurion was convinced what had turned the predictions of Israel's all but certain defeat into victory in the War of Independence in 1948 was the ability of the air force to gain air superiority over its enemies. To maintain that tactical advantage, the prime minister instructed the Defense Ministry to build up the inventory of fighter planes.

A young member of Ben-Gurion's Haganah Party, Shimon Peres, was assigned the task of securing the needed planes. On June 21, 1950, Peres called Shatz and asked for his help. "You were able to get C-46s and B-1's for us when we needed them. Do you think you can get us fighter planes from your government's surplus stockpiles?" Shatz promised Peres he'd look into it.

Two weeks later, I walked into Shatz's office just as he was ending a phone call. He was smiling.

"Who was that that made you so happy?"

"A scrap junk dealer in Texas. Those thirty surplus Mustangs I found and was going to buy from the Reconstruction Finance Corporation? Well, I'm buying them from him instead."

"What are you talking about? I thought we had a deal with the RFC for them? Weren't they supposed to give you a price on them today?"

"They were. But when I called this morning, I was told the planes were no longer for sale. When I asked why, the clerk said the sale had been blocked by a man named Cordell Tipton of the State Department."

"That's the same anti-Semite bastard that Judge Plotnik tore apart in court at our trial, isn't it?"

"That's the man. I guess this was him getting payback," Shatz said.

"So what the hell were you smiling at?"

"Actually, that asshole Tipton did us a big favor."

"How do you figure that?"

"Talking with the RFC clerk this morning, he told me the government was going to slice off the plane's wings, cut their fuselage in half, and sell them as scrap to a junk dealer in Texas. He gave me the contact information for the junk dealer. He was the one I was speaking with when you walked in."

Shatz got up and went to the ice chest, one of the few things the feds had left us in the hanger when they cleared out most everything else. He pulled out a bottle of Coke, popped the cap, and took a long swallow.

"Boy, I needed that," he said, walking back to his chair. "Where was I? Oh, yeah. So I asked the junk dealer how much money he would make after he chopped up the planes for scrap metal. When he told me, I offered to pay him back the money he paid the government for the planes, plus five times the profit he said he would have made selling them as scrap."

"Why?" I asked.

"Because if all the government is doing is cutting off the wings and cutting the fuselage in half, I think I can reconstruct them and make them flyable again."

"We can do that?"

"I'm pretty sure we can. I'll fly to Texas to inspect them. If I can do what I think I can, I'll take the planes as is, and he makes five times the profit he would have... for doing nothing. If I can't fix them, he's no worse off than he would have been."

"How much will it cost us?" I asked.

Shatz laughed. "This is the best part. We'll own the Mustangs at fifteen cents on the dollar of what they would have cost if Tipton hadn't blocked the sale to me."

Shatz called Peres and updated him on what was going on.

Three weeks later, Shatz came back from Texas. "I inspected the planes, and I can fix them."

Six months later, our team reconstructed each of the Mustangs, making sure they had all their parts and were operational.

As test pilot, I took up each one and put it through its paces, making sure it was combat ready. After I signed off on each plane, it was disassembled, packed into crates marked, "farm equipment," and shipped to Israel.

While working on the Mustangs, Shatz thought he was onto something. There was no longer an arms embargo. Through a dummy company, he began buying surplus government planes cheaply, fixed them up, and sold them to foreign governments and airlines.

IN THE SPRING of 1951, David Ben-Gurion made his first trip to American as Israel's prime minister. He was on a fundraising tour that took him to Los Angeles. He and Shatz had a good relationship during the war, and he arranged to go to Shatz's base of operations in Burbank.

When Ben-Gurion walked into the hanger, Shatz was out back. He walked over to me. "Mr. Kaplan, I never did get a chance to personally thank you. Your record of accomplishments will stand forever in the annals of the Israeli Air Force. Are you sure we can't entice you to return and take your rightful place as an officer in the IAF?"

"Thank you for the compliment, Mr. Prime Minister. But America is my country. I would no more give up my citizenship than you would give up yours."

Ben-Gurion shrugged. "Can't blame a man for trying," he said with a wide smile.

Just then, Shatz appeared. Without any preamble, the prime minister asked, "So, Shatz, what is it that you are doing here?"

"Yes, it's good to see you too, Mr. Prime Minister," Shatz said, with a wry grin. "I'm renovating these planes from surplus Air Force stock and selling them. Not that much different than when I fixed up the C-46s and brought you a few guns."

"And all you need is just these few pieces of machinery to do this?" Ben-Gurion asked.

"Sure."

"You know, we could use something like this in Israel. Actually, what we could really use is an industry to build us planes, so we don't have to count on anyone else."

"That would be a very smart move. You could buy surplus warplanes, fix them up, and sell them like I am. While you're doing that, you'll be acquiring the skills to build up an aircraft industry," Shatz replied.

"Well, if you think it's such a smart move, why don't you come to Israeli and set it up for us?" the prime minister replied.

"Me? Uh-uh, not me. I wouldn't touch that with a ten-foot pole."

"Why?" the prime minister asked.

"A lot of reasons. Have you forgotten when your air force chief of staff wanted to throw me out of the country a year and a half ago? You think he'd be able to work with me on any project after your intervention to stop him?"

"He'll just have to get over it," Ben-Gurion said, waving his hand dismissively.

"There's still too many hurdles. I don't speak Hebrew. Even if I did, I'm not a politician, and no one could build an aviation industry in the face of the bureaucracies you have in Israel."

"Minor matters. I can handle those for you," the prime minister replied, once again waving a dismissive hand. "Well, maybe except for the Hebrew. You would have to learn some."

"Ahh, I just don't know," Shatz said.

I watched Shatz. I didn't know what he was thinking, but I could tell he was turning something over in his mind. Ben-Gurion held his tongue, apparently content to give Shatz the time to work out whatever he needed to.

"Here's the deal," Shatz said a minute later. "I'll do it under certain conditions. It gets set up as a private corporation, not part of any government entity. I get to hire who I want. I'll try to employ Israelis as much as possible, but I don't get any political hacks or political cronies shoved down my throat for any job."

"Done. Is there anything else?" Ben-Gurion asked.

"Yes. I'll only go if Kaplan agrees to come with me."

I jerked my head around. "What?" I gasped.

"I'll only go if you agree to come with me," Shatz repeated.

"Why?"

"Because I'll need someone to be my right hand man, and it has to be someone I trust implicitly. I trust you more than anyone I know."

"I don't know what to say."

Ben-Gurion put his hands on his hips. "Oh, for God's sake. Say yes already, and let's be done with this conversation."

Epilogue
1968

I MADE THE FIRST of some major changes in my life when I agreed to come back with Shatz in November of 1950. It took us almost three years to get things running, but in 1953, Bedek Aviation Company, with Shatz as co-founder and chief executive officer, began full scale operations. We had seventy employees to start, including me, as its only test pilot. Within five years, the company founded by Shatz, with two Israelis, became the largest private employer in Israel. We were an all-purpose service operation, located in a hanger near Lod, in the central part of the country, just a little west of Tel Aviv.

TWO YEARS EARLIER, I'd made another major change in my life. It was in March of 1951, five months after I arrived in Israel. I tracked down Rachael Zuckerberg. The information I'd received was that she still lived in Yad Mordechai. She'd once described it to me as a small *kibbutz* sixty kilometers south of Tel Aviv on a hill along the Mediterranean overlooking the main road from Gaza to Tel Aviv.

I'd last seen her in July, 1948, almost two and a half years before. I remembered our last time together like it was yesterday. I told her I was in love with her but couldn't stay and turn my back on my country. I couldn't move to Israel. I had reached out to hold her hand, but she snatched it away. She'd left me at the table, never once turning to look back at me. I never saw her again.

As I crested the hill along the Mediterranean in my Jeep, and spotted the Yad Mordechai kibbutz that morning, my mind raced. She had been on my mind and in my heart ever since we broke apart. I was sure I loved her and wanted to spend the rest of my life with her. What if she was married now? Would she even want to see me after all this time?

I pulled into the kibbutz, stopped the first person I saw, and asked her if Rachael Zuckerberg still lived there. The woman jabbed her finger at a building about two hundred yards away.

I pulled up to the building, and through my open car window I heard the sounds of children at play. There was a sign above the screened front door in Hebrew. By the voices coming from inside, I was pretty sure it was a school or children's center of some kind.

I peered through the screen door. About thirty children were scattered in groups, some sitting on the wooden floor playing what looked like a game of jacks, some had pencils and papers and were drawing, and some were reading picture books. All looked to be between the ages of three and eight.

At the front of the room, three women were engaged with a group of six children, standing in front of a blackboard. One of the women had her back to me, writing something in Hebrew on the board with chalk.

I stepped inside and quietly closed the door. Apparently, not quietly enough. The three women turned in my direction.

Rachael was the one at the blackboard. When she recognized me, the piece of chalk she'd been writing with dropped from her hand, breaking on the floor. Her hands flew to her mouth, but not before

I saw her jaw drop open in surprise. I took two hesitant steps toward her, not quite sure how to bridge the space between us.

It wasn't a problem for Rachael. Her hands dropped from her mouth and she rushed at me. When she got two feet away, she launched herself, locking her arms around my neck and her legs around my thighs, almost knocking me off my feet. She rained kisses on my mouth, my cheeks, my nose, my forehead. I returned each and every one of them.

She said something to the other two women in Hebrew. Smiles creased their mouths, and they made shooing motions for us to leave, Rachael grabbed my hand and dragged me out of the building.

I had shown up at the daycare center where she worked at 9:40 in the morning. We spent the rest of the morning under the shade of an awning stretched between two olive trees. Later, she took me to lunch in the communal dining room, where at least sixty pairs of eyes flittered between their plates of food and the two of us. We returned to the shade of the awning, blocking the afternoon sun, and talked some more.

We talked about that last night together and how we both regretted how it ended. When I told her she had been on my mind and in my heart ever since our last night together, she told me she'd felt exactly the same. We talked about our experiences in the war since we'd last seen each other. I told her about the trial in Los Angeles.

Before I left for the night, decisions were made. Rachael and I would be married in three months. We were not going to lose any more time away from each other. She would move to Tel Aviv with me. I would remain in Israel for the next five years, working at Bedek. After that, Rachael would move with me back to Boston for five years. We would then decide which country we would live in. Being young and in love, we felt we could work everything out, never giving a thought to the possibility she would want to go back to Israel and I would want to stay in Boston.

We were married in a traditional Jewish ceremony. On a bright sunlit day in mid-June, with the scent of oranges ripening on trees, Rachael and I became husband and wife. We were wed in the middle of the *kibbutz's* orange groves, under a *hoopa*, canopy, by the *kibbutz's* rabbi. My mother and father had flown in from Boston, Skippy Shapiro from Brooklyn, and Mel Pinter from Las Vegas. Ezer Weizman also attended. Paul Shatz was my best man.

Two years later, on May 31, 1953, my son Aaron was born.

ONE THING HAD led to another, and I didn't leave Israel after the five years Rachael and I agreed to. It was not any pressure from her. It was always my decision, and it always involved work. Bedek had been renamed Israel Aircraft Industries, and we were developing our own aircraft, a V-tailed twinjet trainer of French design. We called it the *Tzukit*, which meant 'swallow' in Hebrew. I was doing all the test piloting on it.

Although we'd won the war in '49 and had signed armistice agreements, the Egyptian mostly, wouldn't let it go. In 1956, we'd invaded the Egyptian Sinai because Egypt blocked the Straits of Tiran to Israeli shipping. U.N. pressure forced us to withdraw, but we won a guarantee that the Straits of Tiran would remain open. While the United Nations Emergency Force was deployed along the border, there was no demilitarization agreement.

In 1967, tensions between us and the Egyptians heightened. In late May, Egyptian President Nasser announced the straits would once again be closed to Israeli vessels. Israel reiterated its position that the closure of the Straits of Tiran to its shipping would be a casus belli, a cause for war. Egypt closed the straights anyway then mobilized its forces along the border with Israel.

My old friend Ezer Weizman had become the IDF's deputy chief of staff in 1966. On June 5, 1967, after Nasser mobilized his forces, Weizman directed my old squadron, the 101st, to launch an early morning surprise air attack against the Egyptian air bases. The raid resulted in totally destroying the Egyptian Air Force in three hours. On the first day of the Six Day War, the Israeli Air Force destroyed a total of 400 enemy planes on the ground, giving Israeli total air superiority.

Simultaneously, the *Tzukit* jets we built at Israel Aircraft Industries were used by the 147th Squadron as close support aircraft for an Israeli ground offensive into the Gaza Strip and the Sinai, which again caught the Egyptians by surprise. After some initial resistance, Egyptian leader Nasser ordered the evacuation of the Sinai. Israeli forces rushed westward in pursuit of the Egyptians, inflicted heavy losses, and conquered the Sinai.

Nasser convinced Syria and Jordan to begin attacks on Israel, claiming Egypt had defeated the Israeli air strike. *Tzukit* jets were deployed against the Jordanian forces on the West Bank to support our ground counterattacks, which resulted in the seizure of East Jerusalem as well as the West Bank from the Jordanians. Our retaliation against Syria resulted in the occupation of the Golan Heights.

When I saw Weizman at my citizenship ceremony that year, he said, "You realize those surprise air attacks taking out the Egyptian planes on the ground was your idea back on the first day of the war in 1948. We were planning to do that before we got diverted to stop the Egyptian column headed for Tel Aviv. But I always remembered what you wanted to do back then. It was a great idea then, and it turned out even better this time."

THAT YEAR I made other major change in my life.

I'd left Israel in 1949 because I refused to give up my U.S. citizenship to become an officer in the Israeli Air Force. I was an American, my passport validated that, and given a choice between the two countries, my allegiance was with America.

I'd been in Israel for eighteen years, and until 1967, according to U.S. law, dual citizenship was illegal. However, in '67 the U.S. Supreme Court ruled that the State Department had violated the Constitution when it refused to issue a new U.S. passport to a U.S.

citizen who had voted in an election in Israel. The decision overturned the law saying, "A person, who is a national of the United States, whether by birth or naturalization, shall lose his nationality by voting in a political election in a foreign state."

With the Supreme Court decision in place, four months before, I applied for Israeli citizenship. My application was expedited because of my service during the War of Independence. Ezer Weizman came to my citizenship ceremony.

"You know, Kaplan, I've never forgotten what we said to each at the end of the last air battle of the war in 1949. Do you remember?" Weizman asked.

"No, I'm sorry. I don't."

"Your words to me were, 'Congratulations, the war is over and you won. You've got yourself a homeland.' Do you remember what I said back to you?"

"Again, no I don't."

"I said, 'You're a Jew, Kaplan. So, so do you.' And now look at you. You're an Israeli, living in the homeland you helped to establish. Mazel Tov."

I found that Weizman had another reason for being at the ceremony. It was serious, but slightly mischievous. "Now that you're an Israeli, like every other citizen, you are subject to serve in the military," Weizman said. "Of course, at your age, it'll have to be the reserves."

Weizman extended his hand to my shoulder. "Michael Kaplan, in my capacity as the IDF's deputy chief of staff, it is my pleasure to welcome you into the Israeli Air Force Reserves, with the rank of lieutenant colonel."

IT'D BEEN EIGHTEEN years since my return to Israel, and I was spending a rainy Friday afternoon in our apartment in Tel Aviv with my son Aaron. At fifteen, he'd passed me in height, measuring a half inch shy of six feet. I enrolled him in a Krav Maga class, the self-defense martial arts taught to the Israeli Special Forces, the Sayeret Matkal. In the six months he'd been going to the class, I'd noticed how much his chest and arm muscles were beginning to fill out.

"Abba, can we go to Masada this weekend?" Aaron asked in English. From the time he began to talk, Rachael and I made sure he learned to speak both Hebrew and English. He was fluent in both. Outside of our home, Hebrew was his language. Inside, he still called me Dad in Hebrew, but English is what we used. After all those years, I spoke some broken Hebrew, and didn't read it very well. I often had to rely on Aaron to be my interpreter.

"Sure," I said, "we can go as long as it's okay with your mother. Is there a special reason why you want to go?"

"We're learning about it in school. You know, how eight hundred Jews held out against ten thousand Roman soldiers for over three years? Sort of a David versus Goliath."

Humph, I thought. What we did back in '48, *that* was David versus Goliath. Six hundred thousand of us against sixty million of them.

"What's going on?" Rachael asked, walking in from the kitchen.

"Can we go to Masada this weekend? Abba said it's okay with him if it's okay with you. Please tell me you don't have other plans."

Rachael laughed. "No, I don't have other plans. Yes, we can go. In fact, let's make a weekend trip out of it. We can drive down to Beersheba tomorrow, stay at a spa for the day, and then leave early Sunday morning for Masada."

Rachael called and made reservations at the spa. The next morning, we drove two hours to Beersheba and checked in. It was late October, and the spa was not busy. We spent the day lounging around the pool filled with mineral water, had dinner, and we were in bed by 10:00.

My alarm went off at 5:00. I nudged Rachael awake before rolling out of bed. I rapped my knuckles on the connecting door to Aaron's room, calling out for him to get up. By 5:30, we had a quick breakfast, filled canteens with water for the climb up Masada, and were on our way. An hour and fifteen minutes later, we arrive at the parking lot on the east slope of the fortress. It was still dark.

I stood at the bottom of the Snake Path, the serpentine trail up the side of the mountain. It was so narrow only three people could walk abreast. That feature is what made it easy for the Jews on the high ground to defend themselves from the Roman army below.

Getting ready to move out, Rachael and Aaron pulled out flashlights to use on the climb. I could see the flickering lights coming from the groups already on the path, winding their way upward.

We began the 450 meter, 1476 foot, trek to the top. Even in the dark, I could feel the heat begin to build as we hiked up the mountain. Stopping twice for water breaks, we reached the summit in little less than an hour. It was worth getting up early for, as we looked out over the Negev Desert from the top of the fortress. The sunrise breaking in the east was spectacular.

We found a table in the visitors' gallery. Aaron and I had backpacks, and we removed the sweet rolls and oranges the spa had put together for us as snacks. We decided to wait until the fortress was fully bathed in sunlight before our exploration.

Boom! Boom! Boom! We'd been exploring Masada with a tour for about an hour when I heard the noise coming from deep in the Negev Desert. "Abba, what's that noise?" Aaron asked.

I knew those sounds all too well. "I'm pretty sure those are bombs. My guess is the air force is doing exercises out in the desert." But as quickly as the sounds came, that's how quickly it stopped.

"Abba! Abba! Look!" my son called out to me ten minutes later, pointing up into the clear blue desert sky.

I saw a pair of jet fighters making a sweeping turn, heading toward us. As they drew nearer, the planes dropped down to about a one thousand feet. Approaching the mountaintop, they began waggling their wings, signaling a friendly hello to the people below.

"Are those yours?" he asked, the excitement clearly ringing in his words.

I knew what he meant. Were those two of the planes we made at our plant in Lod?

As the jets streaked overhead, followed by the loud roar of their mighty engines, my eyes were drawn to the Star of David emblazoned on their wings. My mind flashed back to the first Israeli fighter planes that bore the Star of David, those Messerschmitts, pieces o'shit I'd called them, and the Spitfires.

As the jets pulled away from us, I could see they were not from my old 101st Fighter Squadron. They didn't have the Angel of Death skull with wings emblem. The logo, sketched in a bar on a napkin back in 1948, was still painted on every fighter of the 101st.

I thought back to the birth of the Israeli Air Force. How on that day in May, 1948, when Modi Alon, Ezer Weizman, Eddie Cohen, and I, *were* the entire Israeli Air Force. When we flew the only four fighter planes Israel had, and stopped the Egyptian column headed north, just sixteen miles from Tel Aviv.

I thought of the *Machalniks*, who made up ninety-five percent of the combat pilots during the War of Independence. Men like Shapiro, Pinter, Landau, Chernoff, Lapin and the rest. How the Egyptians bombed Israel with impunity because there was no opposition, until Modi Alon shot down the two bombers over Tel Aviv, and the Egyptian bombing missions all but ended. How, in a matter of just eight months, we went from being virtually nonexistent as fighting force, to achieving air superiority, and dominating the skies.

The birth of the Israeli Air Force happened within days of the birth of the State of Israel. The IAF was not born quietly but kicking and fighting in the heat of battle. And I was there, a midwife for its birth. Maybe I give us more credit than we deserved, but I believe without the *Machalnik* combat pilots, there might not be an Israel today.

"Abba, Abba," Aaron, shouted. He tugged on my sleeve with one hand, pointing to the jets peeling away from the top of Masada. "Are those yours?"

I smiled and patted him on the back. I knew he was asking if I'd built those planes, but I was thinking of the part I played in the birth of the Israeli Air Force.

"Yes, Son," I replied. "I suppose you can say those are mine."

Author's Notes

O NE EVENING AT home, while thinking about what my next novel might be, I was channel surfing. I stopped when I landed on my local PBS station, which was halfway through a documentary called A *Wing and a Prayer*. It is the story of Jewish American airmen, called *Machalniks*, the Hebrew acronym for Volunteers from Abroad, who were instrumental in the creation of the Israeli Air Force during its War of Independence in 1948.

I was so fascinated by what I saw; I bought a disc of the documentary from my local PBS station to watch it again from the beginning. I'd never heard anything about these men, so I began to do some research. I soon found out not knowing their story was not unusual.

Dr. Ralph Lowenstein, retired dean of the University of Florida, College of Journalism and Communications, said in *A Personal Essay* "No one in America knows about us."

He went on to say, "We were and are largely unknown in the United States and Canada. Out of a population of more than 5 million Jews, we numbered only 1,250. It is safe to say that very few North American Jews know about the volunteers. During my own lifetime, no American Jew or Christian who discovered that I had volunteered for Israel in 1948 had ever met another American Jew who did the same. The odds against their knowing someone like me were about 4,000 to 1.

"Immediately after the 1948 war, there was absolutely no publicity about our experience. All American volunteers had violated the terms of their passports, and perhaps other laws then extant, risking at best fines and jail time, and at worst loss of their citizenship. Canadian laws, if applied strictly, could punish volunteers from that country severely. We did not want publicity."

The few books written about these brave men have mostly been historical in nature. This book, *The Machalniks*, is a work of fiction, based on exploits of those Jewish American airmen.

For research in preparing this story, I used scores of books, magazine articles, and websites, far too many to name individually. I would urge readers who would like to know more to start with the following as a first step:

A Wing and a Prayer, a documentary film by Boaz Dvir.

Above and Beyond, a documentary film produced by Nancy Spielberg (sister of legendary producer Steven Spielberg), directed by Roberta Grossman.

I Am My Brother's Keeper: Written by Craig Weiss and Jeffery Weiss

Ups & Downs With No Regrets: The story of George Lichter, Written by Vic Shayne.

Flying Under Two Flags: Written by Gordon Levett.

World Machal website: www.machal.org.il. According to the World *Machal* website, it is dedicated to preserving the history and heritage of *Machal* for future generations.

A Personal Essay: Why the Experiences of North American Volunteers are Largely Unknown, by Dr. Ralph Lowenstein, PhD

The Israeli Air Force Machalniks
—Some Numbers.

THERE WERE 426 *Machalnik* fliers with World War II combat experience, from 16 countries, who served in the Israeli Air Force (IAF), or the Air Transport Command (ATC), from May 15, 1948, through the cease fire and armistice on January 7, 1949. Of the 426—92 were non-Jews.

Ninety-five percent of the 426 were from English speaking countries—182 Americans, 80 South Africans, 53 Canadians, and 50 from the United Kingdom. As a result, English was the official language of the Israeli Air Force until 1950.

Some American *Machalniks*

THIS NOVEL DEALS with mostly the American *Machalniks* who served in the Israeli Air Force during the War of Independence. The names below do not include the brave American *Machalniks* who fought in the other branches of the Israeli Defense Forces.

Space does not afford me the privilege of listing all 182 American *Machalniks* who were in the IAF, fighting in the War of Independence. The ones mentioned below are but a small sampling. To any *Machalniks* currently living, or to the relatives of *Machalniks* no longer with us, my sincerest apologies for those I've omitted.

Al Schwimmer—Called by many the Father of the Israeli Air Force, he used his World War II experience and contacts to smuggle planes and munitions to Israel. His motivation was that he truly believed there would be a second Holocaust and the six hundred thousand Jews in Palestine were going to die. He recruited the pilots and crews, many of who became the nucleus of the Israeli Air Force, to fly the planes to Czechoslovakia and on to Israel.

In 1950, he was convicted of violating the U.S. Neutrality Acts for smuggling the planes into Israel. Schwimmer was stripped of his voting rights and veteran benefits and fined $10,000 but did not receive a prison sentence. He refused to seek a pardon if it required him to say he did something wrong. However, after intense lobbying by the son of another convicted smuggler for Israel, Hank Greenspun, in 2001 President Bill Clinton gave Schwimmer a presidential pardon.

In 1951, at the invitation of David Ben-Gurion, Schwimmer returned to Israel to establish the Israel Aircraft Industries. He led the company for 25 years. It became the major arms manufacturer for the young nation's defense, with tens of thousands of employees and revenue of $1 billion when he left. He died in Israel in June, 2011.

Hank Greenspun—After earning his law degree, Greenspun spent four years in the Army during World War II, working on the camp newspaper and in ordinance, gaining expertise in guns and ammunition. He came to Las Vegas in 1946. He became the publicist for Benjamin "Bugsy" Siegel's Flamingo Hotel. Following the murder of Siegel in Los Angeles in 1947, Greenspun renewed his interest in his Jewish heritage and became a prominent figure in supporting the struggle to establish the State of Israel.

Greenspun took leave from his job at the *Las Vegas Sun* to examine airplane motors, parts, and machine guns in a Hawaii salvage yard. He returned with 42 crates of airplane engines and 16 crates of machine guns and barrels, some of it bought, some of it stolen.

U.S. Customs seized the engine parts, but Greenspun literally hijacked a boat and sailed the machine guns to Mexico, whereupon they were transshipped to Israel. Greenspun continued to smuggle other arms and ammunition to Mexico for delivery to Israel. He was fined $10,000 for violating the Neutrality Act and deprived of his civil rights. He was pardoned in 1961 by President John F. Kennedy. In 1949 he bought the *Las Vegas Sun* newspaper and served as its publisher until his death in 1989.

Lou Lenart—Lenart was born in Hungary, moved to the United States when he was ten, settling in the Pennsylvania coal-mining town of Wilkes-Barre, where he was the target of anti-Jewish taunts. At 17, he enlisted in the U.S. Marines and talked his way into a flight school. He saw action in the Battle for Okinawa and other Pacific engagements.

When Israel declared its independence on May 14, 1948, the Israeli Air Force fighter planes consisted of four Czech versions of the German Messerschmitt. On May 29, a large column of Egyptian forces had advanced to within 16 miles of Tel Aviv. Israel decided to gamble its entire air force fighters in an attack on the Egyptian advance columns.

As the most experienced pilot, Lenart led the attack, along with Israeli, Ezer Weizman (later to become President of Israel), Israeli, Modi Alon, and South African, Eddie Cohen, who died in the mission. The Egyptian troops, who'd been assured the Israelis had no aircraft, stopped their advance and retreated. News reports hailed Lenart as, "The Man Who Saved Tel Aviv."

"It was the most important event in my life," Lenart later told the Israel Air Force Journal. "I survived World War II so I could lead this mission." He died July, 2015, at his home in Ra'anana, Israel.

Milton Rubenfeld—Before WWII began, Rubenfeld, who earned a living teaching airplane acrobatics, signed up with the RAF, where he spent more than two years, participating in the Battle of Britain. Once the U.S. entered the war, Rubenfeld left the RAF and joined the American Air Transport Command as a ferry pilot. He flew pretty much any American aircraft there was..

In early 1948, the Haganah, who knew of his piloting history, asked if he'd fly for the Jews in Palestine. He agreed. In May, 1948, he nursed his damaged plane to Kfar Vitkin, and bailed out over the Mediterranean at only a thousand feet altitude. He hit the water, four or five miles from shore, suffering three broken ribs, a hurt groin, and several cuts.

A tale about the incident goes that Rubenfeld, worried that the locals, unaware that Israel had fighters would assume he was an Arab and possibly inflict harm. Not knowing any Hebrew, he turned to the next best thing—he began shouting in Yiddish. Unfortunately, his Yiddish was almost as limited as his nonexistent Hebrew, consisting of the words, "Shabbos," and, "gefilte fish," which he repeatedly shouted. The locals must have understood, pulled him out of the water, and helped him to safety. Rubenfeld says he doesn't remember what he was yelling.

A side note: Rubenfeld was the father of Paul (Pee Wee Herman) Reuben. He also had a role in the Pee Wee Herman movie, *Big Top Peewee*.

Coleman Goldstein—During WWII, he was a B-17 pilot. After flying in the IAF's 101 Squadron, Goldstein stayed in Israel for 32 years as a pilot for *El Al* Airlines. He died in 2014.

Gideon Lichtman—Is credited with shooting down the first enemy fighter plane in the 1948 war. He grew up in a Zionist household in New Jersey and is the one credited with nicknaming the Messerschmitt Bf 109s, "Messer-shits." He flew some thirty IAF missions

Leon Frankel—A native of St. Paul, Minnesota, Frankel was trained as a torpedo bomber pilot during World War II. Part of the first Navy raid on Tokyo, in a subsequent raid, he was instrumental in sinking a Japanese cruiser and protecting his squadron commander, whose plane was badly damaged. For his actions, he was decorated with the Navy Cross, two Distinguished Flying Crosses, three Air Medals, and two Presidential Citations.

With the Jewish state about to declare its independence in May 1948, Frankel traveled clandestinely to Israel. He joined the country's first fighter squadron and flew 25 missions.

Frankel wrote, "I could not stand idly by, with my experience, while a second Holocaust loomed, with the Arab nations telling the world they were going to destroy the Jewish state."

William Gerson and Glenn King—The two pilots that were killed on April 21, 1948, when their overloaded C-46 crashed at Mexico City Airport on the way to Panama.

Sam Pomerance—The Velvetta Operations, to ferry non-stop flights of Spitfires from Czechoslovakia to Israel, were his idea. He developed the mechanics of how to install long-range fuel tanks that made the operation a reality. During Velvetta II, he died when his plane crashed during a winter storm in Yugoslavia on December 18, 1948

Stan Andrews and Bob Vickman—Two UCLA art students, killed when their IAF planes were shot down in separate incidents in July and October 1948. They were the ones that came up with the logo for the 101st Squadron, scribbling the Angel of Death on a cocktail napkin at a Tel Aviv bar in June 1948. Their design is still on Israeli F-16 jets today.

Harold Livingston—Worked for Trans World Airlines briefly after World War II before joining Al Schwimmer's operation. After the war, he wrote novels, episodes of TV series such as *Mannix* and *Mission: Impossible*, and wrote the screenplay for *Star Trek: The Motion Picture*.

Rudy Augarten—He did not see combat until October 16, 1948. What makes that remarkable is during the course of his time in the war, he would shoot down four Egyptian planes, a total matched only by one other pilot. Augarten, who had flown a P-47 Thunderbolt during World War II, made his four kills from a Me-109, a P-51 Mustang, and twice from a Spitfire. It was a remarkable display of flying skill.

In the 101st Squadron, Rudy Augarten and some other pilots remained in Israel to train the first class of Israeli fighter pilots to fill the void created by the departing volunteers. He returned to his studies at Harvard to complete his degree. He came back to Israel, where he served for two years as the commander of the air base at Ramat David. When he resigned from the air force, he did so with the rank of lieutenant colonel.

Sam Lewis and Leo Gardner—During World War II, when TWA became part of the U.S. Air Transport Command, Lewis gained experience flying multi-engine planes, including C-46s and Constellations loaded with troops and cargo. After the war, Al Schwimmer reached out to Lewis and another L.A. based pilot, Leo Gardner.

Lewis and Gardner, two experienced airline pilots, helped Schwimmer recruit U.S. pilots and trained many of them to fly the heavy aircraft they acquired in America. Lewis and Gardner both ferried the big planes to Panama and then to Czechoslovakia and Israel. Both men were among the founders of *El Al*, the new Israeli airline.

Lewis and Gardner were put on trial for violating the Neutrality Act. Lewis got off, as one of the jurors was said to have reasoned, he was involved only as a pilot. Gardner also went on trial. He was found guilty and fined $10,000.

After the war, Lewis was hired as one of *El Al* airline's first pilots. He moved to Israel in 1950. After retiring from the airline following a distinguished 30-year career, he continued to fly, working for the Schwimmer-run Israel Aerospace Industries. In 1980, he moved back to L.A. He died the following year. Gardner worked for a time as a captain for *El Al*, flying cargo between Israel and Europe.

Lastly, to **Charlie Winters**, a man who was technically not a *Machalnik* because he never fought, but deserves to be among those listed. Winters, a non-Jew, ironically was the only person to receive a prison sentence (18 months) for his part in violating the arms embargo, for providing B-17 bombers to Israel. Winters died in Florida in 1984. Some of his ashes were scattered over Mount Tabor, which according to Christian tradition, is the location of the Transfiguration of Jesus. The remainder of his ashes are buried in The Alliance Church International Cemetery, Jerusalem. He received a full pardon, awarded posthumously, by President George W. Bush, December, 2008.

Acknowledgements

I AM GRATEFUL to my colleagues at the *Inkbloods* for their merciless critiques. Their sharp eyes pointed out the many mistakes in my first draft and have helped drive me to be a better writer.

I'd like to single out and thank Pat Crumpler for her amazing one-on-one critique and spot-on suggestions.

Finally, but by no means last, to my wife Doreen. Like a fine wine, she truly gets better with age. I am lucky to have found her my second time around and have her in my life. At times, it's been a bumpy ride, but we've held it together.

About the Author

RICHARD (DICK) BERMAN was born in Boston, Massachusetts. He and his wife Doreen lived in New Jersey for thirty years before moving to South Florida.

Father of three, grandfather of four, Dick enjoys retirement, playing golf, traveling, reading, and writing. He is working on his next book, an adventure story featuring Eric Burns, the Israeli Mossad agent from his hit novel *The Collector*.

For information about special discounts available for bulk purchases, sales promotions, fundraising, and educational needs for *The Machalniks*, contact: sales@dickberman.com

You can visit the author's website at: DickBerman.Com
He can be contacted by e-mail at: Dick@DickBerman.com